Plate 1
The Sierra Madre Puma
(*Felis concolor azteca*)

The Puma
Mysterious American Cat

PART I
History, Life Habits, Economic Status, and Control
By
STANLEY P. YOUNG

PART II
Classification of the Races of the Puma
By
EDWARD A. GOLDMAN

Senior Biologists, Section of Biological Surveys, Division of Wildlife Research, Fish and Wildlife Service, U. S. Department of the Interior.

∾Ↄ|ⵛↄ∾

Dover Publications, Inc.
New York, New York

This Dover edition, first published in 1964, is an
unabridged and unaltered republication of the work
first published in 1946 by the American Wildlife
Institute. The frontispiece, which appeared in color
in the original edition, is reproduced in black and
white in this edition.

Library of Congress Catalog Card Number: 64-15509

Manufactured in the United States of America

Dover Publications, Inc.
180 Varick Street
New York 14, N.Y.

FOREWORD

WE HAVE attempted to bring together in orderly sequence the widely scattered literature concerning the puma throughout its vast range in North and South America. This has entailed the review of hundreds of published records covering the period from the first mention of the puma in European literature by Columbus on his fourth voyage to America in 1502, and from its recognition in Inca and Aztec cultures, to the present day. The book also outlines the general results of field studies of this animal carried on under government auspices during more than a quarter of a century.

Early stages in the work on classification were undertaken in collaboration with Edward W. Nelson, under whose direction as Chief of the Biological Survey (now the Fish and Wildlife Service) the control of puma depredations was organized in 1915. Collaboration with Nelson was, unfortunately, interrupted by his death in May 1934.

In common with many other American mammals of wide dispersal the puma has received many names, bestowed on animals supposed to represent distinct species. A number of these are pure synonyms, or are differentially applicable only to subspecies. A comprehensive account of the numerous subspecies is here presented for the first time. Despite the number of subspecies, the animal, whether found in North or South America, appears to vary little, if any, in habits. It is hoped that this volume will afford a better understanding of a distinctly American species, which with its mysterious and inscrutable ways is of surpassing interest and under a suitable measure of control deserves a permanent place as a wilderness animal.

STANLEY P. YOUNG
EDWARD A. GOLDMAN

Washington, D. C.
January 1, 1946

v

ACKNOWLEDGMENTS

HEARTY cooperation has been received by the authors in the preparation of this volume from a large number of individuals, to whom our sincere thanks are extended. Among those most helpful were Remington Kellogg and Frank M. Setzler, of the U. S. National Museum; Einar Lönnberg, of the Naturhistoriska Riksmuseum, Stockholm, Sweden; Seth Gordon, of the Pennsylvania Fish and Game Commission; Robert F. Hale, Malone, New York, and Frank H. Poley, John W. Crook, Everett Mercer, and Scott Zimmerman, of the Fish and Wildlife Service.

In addition to the collections in the U. S. National Museum, which formed the basis for the classification study, 199 specimens from other American museums and private collections were examined. Some of these, especially those from South America, were of critical importance in determining the status of the species in particular regions. For the loan of specimens and other courtesies we are indebted to Harold E. Anthony, George G. Goodwin, and George H. H. Tate, of the American Museum of Natural History; the late Thomas Barbour and Glover M. Allen, of the Museum of Comparative Zoology of Harvard University; Alfred M. Bailey, of the Colorado Museum of Natural History; Wilfred H. Osgood, of the Chicago Natural History Museum; J. Kenneth Doutt, of the Carnegie Mueum; the late Joseph Grinnell, and E. Raymond Hall, of the Museum of Vertebrate Zoology, University of California; Charles D. Bunker, of the Museum of Natural History, University of Kansas; Clinton G. Abbott and Laurence M. Huey, of the San Diego Society of Natural History; Rudolph M. Anderson, of the National Museum of Canada; Charles C. Adams, formerly of the New York State Museum; J. D. Magoon, of the University of Colorado Museum; and the late Donald R. Dickey, of Pasadena, California.

The distribution maps were drawn by Katheryne C. Tabb. The illustrations of skulls are by Gurney I. Hightower, photographer, under direction of A. J. Olmstead, of the U. S. National Museum. W. L. McAtee, of the Fish and Wildlife Service, edited the manuscript.

THE PUMA, MYSTERIOUS AMERICAN CAT
PART I
Its History, Life Habits, Economic Status, and Control
by
Stanley P. Young

CONTENTS

PART II

Classification of the Races of the Puma
by
Edward A. Goldman

CONTENTS

ILLUSTRATIONS

Plates

Text Figures

Tables

THE PUMA, MYSTERIOUS AMERICAN CAT

Part I

Its History, Life Habits, Economic Status, and Control

by

Stanley P. Young

I

INTRODUCTION

Early Records

THE PUMA, which occurs only in the Western Hemisphere, and is often called cougar, mountain lion, or panther, is one of the largest predatory animals of the Americas. It is generally grouped in the United States with the wolf, coyote, bobcat, and the occasional stock-killing bear by stockmen and game managers as a legitimate object of predator control. In its entire range, which at one time covered extensive areas of both the North and South American continents, the puma is exceeded in size among cats of the New World only by the jaguar (Plates 2, 3).

That the early American aborigines knew the puma we are informed by some of the rock inscriptions and shrines left by these people, particularly in the southwestern United States. It was also prominent in the lore of the Indian tribes of South America that were conquered by the Incas. Although known to prehistoric man, it apparently was not brought to the notice of Europeans before the account of Christopher Columbus, who during his fourth voyage in the year 1502, while exploring the coast of Honduras and Nica-

1

ragua, wrote: "I saw some very large fowls (the feathers of which resemble wool), lions [leones], stags, fallow deer, and birds." (Major, R. H., Esq., 1847: 193.) Later travelers and explorers between 1540 and 1587 who mentioned the animal in their narratives included Laudonniere, Hariot, Coronado, and Hawkins. Thus the puma has been known to the white man for more than 400 years, and during that period, particularly in the early settlement of the United States, numerous hair-raising tales have been woven around the puma, particularly as to its attacks on human beings.

Names of the Puma

This animal probably exceeds all other American carnivores in the number of names by which it is known. In addition to the term puma, here adopted as standard, it is also known by the following appellations: cougar, deer tiger, Mexican lion, panther, painter (corcuption of panther), and catamount.

The corrupted word "painter" was colloquially used throughout most of the middle and eastern United States. James Whitcomb Riley (1913: 172) fixed this name in American literature when he wrote:

> "Yes—and painters, prowlin' 'bout,
> Allus darkest nights. Lay out
> Clost yer cattle.—Great, big red
> Eyes a-blazin' in their head,
> Glitter'n' 'long the timber-line—
> Shine out some, and then unshine,
> And shine back—Then steady! Whizz!
> 'N' there yer Mr. Painter is
> With a hole bored spang between
> Them - air eyes! . . . ."

In Lower California, Mexico, the puma is referred to as "chim blea"; among the Apache Indians as "Yutin"; often by the Mexicans as "Mitzli," a name derived from the Aztecs; as "Pagi" in Chile; by some earlier Spanish authors as "red tiger"; and "Mischipichin" by the Ojibway Indians. Other names, as "Ingronga" of the Osages; "Ingonga-Sinda" of the Omahas; "Schunta-Haschla" of the Mandans; and "Ig-mu-tank-a" of the Sioux, were applied to the creature by the Plains Indians. Spanish-Americans refer to it as "Leon," a term often heard by Young in northern Coahuila, Chihuahua, and Sonora, while studying the animal there between the

Plate 2. The puma. Of all the wild cats in the Western Hemisphere is exceeded in size only by the jaguar. (Photo courtesy Phila. Zool. Gardens)

Plate 3. The jaguar. Largest of the wild cats of the Western Hemisphere. Now occurs rarely in southwestern United States, but is common in Central and South America. (Photo courtesy Ernest P. Walker, National Zoological Park, Washington, D. C.)

years 1916 and 1936. It is also known in Mexico as "leopardo."
Mountain lion is the name commonly used in the Rocky Mountain
area of the United States, while "cougar" is more often heard in the
Pacific Northwest. Catamount and panther (painter) were the
names most commonly employed in the states east of the Mississippi
River. In earlier colonial times the name "tiger" was applied to the
animal in present New York State, then known as New Netherlands.

According to Spears (1895: 190-196) the "plainsmen of all Argentina call the panther by a name that means 'the friend of man'
and that too in spite of the havoc it makes among their sheep." The
legend surrounding the adoption of the name "arose from an incident well authenticated in the history of Buenos Ayres," whereby
it appears that "In 1536 the people of Buenos Ayres, then a town of
2,000 inhabitants, were reduced to the point of starvation because of
a war with the Indians. One writer, Del Barco Centenera, asserts
that 1,800 of the 2,000 died of hunger. The dead were buried only
just beyond the palisades, because of the danger from Indians, and
in consequence many beasts of prey came to feed on the thinly covered bodies, a circumstance that added greatly to the terror and distress of the people. Nevertheless hunger increased so much that
many ventured out into the woods along the river seeking edible
roots, and with some success. Among these was a young woman
named Maldonada, who, getting lost, was found and carried away
by the Indians. Some months later, peace having been restored, Don
Rui Diaz, the Captain of the soldiers, learned that Senorita Maldonada was alive, and thereupon he persuaded the Indians to restore
her. He did this, not to relieve her from her slavery, but that he
might punish her for what he believed to be her treachery. He
thought she had deserted to the Indians, and so he condemned her
to be tied to a tree three miles from town and left there to be eaten
by wild beasts. . . . After two nights and a day soldiers were sent to
bring in her bones for burial, but to their great astonishment she was
found unhurt. She said a panther had remained with her and had
driven off the jaguars and other beasts of prey that came to destroy
her." Spears further states that in an old history of the town he
found the following sentence which translated reads:

"In this manner she that was offered to the wild beasts remained
free; the which woman I knew, and they called her Maldonada (ill
bestowed), whom they could better have called Biendonada (well

bestowed), since from this happening it was seen that she had not merited the punishment she had received."

The name "Miztli" of the Mexicans, according to Rafinesque (1832: 52), was coined from that of the fierce tribe named "Miztecus," who were subdued by the Spaniards between 1572 and 1580, and who regarded the puma as the emblem or progenitor of their nation. To be noted later is similar reverence for this carnivore shown by some of the tribes of the Inca civilization.

Cabrera and Yepes (1940: 168) recognize a single species, the *puma*, or *Leon americano*, the latter name given to it by the Spaniards owing to its resemblance to the lion of Africa, and it has been customary to apply this name in all of the American countries in which Spanish is spoken. Quoting these authors further:

"The name *puma*, also very much used, and which has been adopted in scientific language to designate the genus, is Quichua; in Araucana the same animal is called *paghi* or *trapial*; in Puelche, *haina*; in Guarani, *guasuara* or *yagua-pihta*; and in Tupi, *sussuarana*. The Brazilians denominate the animal, in Portuguese, as *onca vermelha*, or also, *leao*. The name *cuguar*, which appears in some natural history works, is not a word in any American language, but is a book term coined by Buffon, who was very fond of disfiguring the names of animals which he found difficult. He thus transformed the term *cuguacuarana*, a capricious transformation in turn from *sussuarana*, copied from the early traveler Marcgrave."

We favor the use of the name puma, which has already been widely accepted, and to which there seems to be the least objection. Historically this name is derived from usage by the Incas, whose Kingdom at its height extended some 2,800 miles along the South American coast and included the greater part of present-day Ecuador, Peru, and Chile. This name, as given to the animal by the ancient Peruvians, was also bestowed upon some of the early leading families of South America. According to Stevenson (1829: I: 111-114; II: 80-81) they were known at the time of his writings as "Caciques." Accordingly "two orders of distinction" were among them, "bearing the titles of the particular attributes of the puma . . . ." "Of these families the unfortunate Puma-cagua, or lord of the brave lion was a cacique; Colqui-puma, lord of the silver lion is another . . . ."

The Puma in Indian Lore

Of all the carnivorous animals the puma seems outstanding with respect to the reverence once shown it by the early inhabitants of Lower California. It was reported as distributed over a large part of that country by the early Jesuits at the time they established their missions there. The respect for the animal, which appears to have involved also the buzzard, continued for a long period following the beginning of these religious establishments. It appears that, because of this strong feeling among the people, the puma played a prominent part in the economic life of the Jesuit padres and the early Christianized natives. The animal's uneaten prey, whenever discovered, had for centuries formed a part of the annual subsistence of the Lower California Indians. A. Schott, with Clavigero as the source of his information, summarized this remarkable aboriginal trait as follows: ". . . the puma exercised so severe a rule over that unhappy peninsula that the work of civilization commenced by missionary Jesuits never could rise above a certain elementary state. The missions and presidios established there after years and years of labor could never succeed in raising their own supply of domestic animals, but had to depend for that on the states of Sinaloa, Sonora, and other parts of the Mexican empire.

"The prodigious spreading of the 'puma' over the peninsula of California seems to have been caused by a superstitious belief on the part of the natives, who did not dare to kill or disturb the animal in any way. It became one of the missionary labors to gradually overcome and remove this singular notion. Indeed the state of civilization among the California Indians had been so low that they in some respects depended on the success of the sporting puma. . . . the hungry Indians used to watch the gathering of the buzzards, and searched the ground carefully whenever they observed a number of these scavenger birds" spotting . . . "some carcass" which was "deposited upon or under ground. By these means these miserable savages were able to discover the remains of a puma feast, which such a lordly beast, after the fashion of all the 'Felidae or Canidae' had hidden away here, and slightly covered with soil." (Baird, S. F. 1859: 6.)

Directly opposed to the reverence shown the animal by the Lower California Indians was its use as game by the Inca rulers and their Indian subjects during the heyday of that civilization in ancient Peru.

It appears that in the spectacular hunting excursions in which the Inca kings indulged after the breeding season of the guanacos and vicunas as many as 30,000 hunters would take part in the drives, split up into "two parties, one going to the right, the other to the left, and forming a great circle of 20 or 30 leagues in circumference." This scheme the reader will recall is in reality the so-called "circular ring hunt" long in vogue centuries later in colonial America, and still practiced in the western United States with slight modifications in the driving of jack rabbits and coyotes to slaughter. As the human ring gradually closed in around the animals thus rounded up, as many as 40,000 head might be taken, including "lions, bears, many foxes, and wild cats. . . ." When the hunters sorted out the guanacos and vicuñas they wanted for their wool these were then shorn and later liberated. Others were killed for their flesh. Also a sufficient number of males and females were released, selected from the best and the finest, so that the species would be perpetuated. Each area chosen for the circular ring hunt was hunted every three years, and this rotation maintained a goodly supply of game. All the predators, including the puma, were killed, however, as "creatures [that] did harm to the game," and it was the wish of the Inca rulers and their Indian subjects "to rid the country of such vermin." We are further informed that the hunters "recorded the number of animals that had been killed, as well the vermin and the game, to know the number of head that had been killed and that remained alive; so as to be able to tell whether the game had increased at the next hunt." (Garcilasso De La Vega, 1869: 116-117.)

This historic account, probably the oldest authentic record of any game management plan in the Western Hemisphere, included control of the puma. It is of interest to note that the game management of these Indians included principles that are recognized as essential in the care of wildlife today.

Another incident of historical interest involving the puma concerns Pizano's arrival at Tumbez by ship. According to this account "there was some hesitation as to landing among a hostile people, and a Greek named Pedro de Candia volunteered to go first. Putting on a coat of mail reaching to the knees with a sword by his side and a cross in his hand, he walked toward the town with an air

as if he had been lord of the whole province. The Indians to find
out what manner of man he was let loose a lion [puma] and a tiger
[jaguar] upon him, but the animals crouched at his feet. Pedro de
Candia gave the Indians to understand that the virtue of the cross he
held in his hand had been the cause of this miracle. He returned to
his ship, which sailed back to Panama." (Ibid: 436.)

Thus the puma was involved in one of the first attempts at the
conversion of the South American Indians to Christianity.

As an aid to warding off human death, pricking on the breast
with a "sharpened bone" of a "white lion" [believed to be a light-
colored, possibly albino, puma] was prescribed by the early Aztec
physicians according to the Badianus Manuscript. This is believed
to be the first recording of any use of a part of the puma as of me-
dicinal value in North America. (Badianus Manuscript, 1940: 324.)

Some of the southwestern Indian tribes, as the Apaches and
Hualpais of Arizona, held the puma in especial awe, particularly its
wailing, which was associated with death. Some Indians of the far
west dried the paws for use in driving the evilness out of a sick
Indian by dangling them over his or her head.

Puma gall also was administered in extreme illness as it was believed to increase the power of the ailing individual to resist the
disease. It was thought that the doctored victim in a short time
would assume the fierceness of the puma.

The ancestors of the Cochite (Co-che-tee) Indians of Sandoval
County, northern New Mexico, had their "sacred lions," which
were carved side by side from the native rock. Present day descen-
dants state that these stone images were used as a shrine where long
ago tribal ceremonies were held, leading to the impression that these
sculptured pumas were of symbolic significance to some particular
clan or cult (Barnes, W. C., 1921: 570) long before the advent of
the Spaniards in the country now termed New Mexico. This prehistoric puma shrine is the only one of its kind known in the United
States.

An old legend with regard to the lynx which may also be applicable to all members of the cat family, including the puma, is as
follows:

According to Isidore of Seville: "They say the urine [of the
lynx] is changed to the hardness of a precious stone, which is called
'lincurius,' and by the following proof it is shown that the lynxes

are conscious of this, for when they have urinated they cover the urine with sand as well as they can, from a sort of meanness of nature, lest such a product be turned to the advantage of man." (Brehaut, Ernest, 1912: 225.)

Undoubtedly this belief came down through the ages to Isidore's time during the 7th Century (600-636, when he was Bishop of Seville, Spain) as he compiled most of his Etymologies from already century-old writings.

A slight modification of this legend, only to the extent that the excreta of the puma contributed to the formation of a precious stone, was narrated to me by a none too enlightened Mexican peon, near the Arizona border in 1916. This led me to believe that the legend may have been brought to Mexico centuries before by the Spanish invaders, and had from that time down to the present passed from one generation to another and became modified as related to me.

While engaged on an expedition during the fall of 1937 in the Carmen Mountains of northern Coahuila, Mexico, in which we successfully induced the puma to take its own picture in its natural habitat, several of our Mexican guides proved to entertain various amusing beliefs regarding this creature. Most interesting among these was that held by Pancho, our chief packer. Impatient, because of our early lack of success in luring the puma into the field of a set camera, he one day told me we didn't "savvy" the animal's habits. Noting that I displayed deep interest in learning what he had in mind, he finally in broken English told me that because of the pine smoke of our camp-fires all the "Leones" had moved to a secret rendezvous located in Juarez Canyon, some 2,000 feet lower than our base camp. The reason assigned for this was the desire of the "Leones" to avoid an infestation of lice which came to any animal, including man, whenever pine smoke penetrated the bodily hairs. If we desisted from burning pine wood and would use oak instead, all the "Leones" would soon return to the higher mountains again and begin to travel near our set cameras.

II

DISTRIBUTION OF THE PUMA IN THE AMERICAS — PAST AND PRESENT

THE PUMA ranges from near sea level to the higher mountain slopes. In California the animal practically reaches sea level along the coast northward from San Luis Obispo, but in this region it has been recorded at an elevation of 11,000 feet in the vicinity of Mount Whitney. In Pacific County, Washington, near the mouth of the Cedar River, a puma was seen above a tideland hay meadow but a few feet in elevation, where a deep coniferous forest surrounded this flat country in 1903. In this State likewise the animal ranges to the higher elevations of the Olympic and Cascade Mountains. In Oregon also the puma occurs from near sea level to the higher elevations of the Cascades and the Coast Range. In contrast is its remarkable occurrence in the valley of the Colorado River, where it has been recorded south of the hot desert area of Yuma, Arizona, where it frequents the dense growths along the river bottoms.

In South America the puma has been recorded at elevations of over 13,000 feet and also near sea level. Tate (1931: 254) reports that the animal is "by no means restricted to the mountains, but is captured from time to time in tropical forest, hundreds of miles from the highlands." One specimen, taken by him during his "last trip to Mount Duida," led to the conclusion that it had made "its home

LIBRARY
LOS ANGELES COUNTY MUSEUM
EXPOSITION PARK

Figure 1. Distribution of subspecies of *Felis concolor* in North and Middle America

1. *Felis concolor couguar*
2. *F. c. missoulensis*
3. *F. c. hippolestes*
4. *F. c. oregonensis*
5. *F. c. vancouverensis*
6. *F. c. olympus*
7. *F. c. californica*
8. *F. c. kaibabensis*
9. *F. c. browni*
10. *F. c. improcera*
11. *F. c. azteca*
12. *F. c. stanleyana*
13. *F. c. coryi*
14. *F. c. mayensis*
15. *F. c. costaricensis*

not in the highlands but in forests only a few hundred feet above sea level."

The present range of the puma extends from Patagonia in South America, through Middle and North America to the Peace River and Cassiar Districts of northern British Columbia, Canada, a total of approximately 100° of latitude. Its original distribution being also practically transcontinental, the animal was adapted to endure not only extreme cold of the high mountains but likewise the humid heat of tropical swamps and canebrakes. It doubtless has had the greatest natural distribution of any American mammal.

Cabrera (1940: 168-172) comments that, "Of all the American carnivores the puma is the one that has the most extensive distribution. It is found in fact from 50° N. Lat. to the Straits of Magellan and from the Atlantic Coast to the Pacific Coast. Between these limits where it does not exist it is because it has recently been exterminated, or because it has retired before the advance of civilization. This curtailment in range nevertheless has not been as rapid as in other cats. In the province of Buenos Aires for example pumas still remain in the mountains of the southern part and, at the same time are still abundant in the provinces of the interior of Argentina and Patagonia. Considering the fact that cities and their neighborhoods are not counted in the distribution of wild animals in general terms it may be said that in South America the puma is found everywhere."

In certain agricultural parts of South America the animal appears to be diminishing in numbers, and in one republic, Uruguay, we find "the small area of the country, completely exploited and given over almost entirely to private ownership practically since colonial days, did not offer peaceful asylum to large predatory animals, which, in a territory entirely devoted to the raising of cattle, soon became public enemies and were hunted and pursued everywhere. Thus, years ago, the big felines: the jaguars, pumas, and 'onzas,' etc., disappeared." (Anon. 1940: 128.)

NORTH AMERICA

United States.—The range of the puma in the United States at the present time includes southern Florida, where it occurs in very sparse numbers; possibly northern Louisiana; and wilderness areas west of the 100th Meridian. The heaviest concentration of the animal is in the Rocky Mountain States, and southward in the desert ranges of Arizona, Texas, and New Mexico. Farther west pumas are much less numerous, except in the coastal ranges of California, Oregon, and Washington, where they are rather abundant. The species is now regarded as extinct east of the Mississippi River, except in Florida. However, according to Cahalane, the National Park Service has received "persistent reports . . . from Shenandoah National Park that mountain lions are seen from time to time. The latest observation was made during last August [1944] in the northern part of the Park. The statement carefully specifies that the two animals seen were 'long-tailed cats.' " (Cahalane, Victor H. 1944. Letter to Dr. Remington Kellogg, U. S. National Museum, Washington, D. C., October 9, from National Park Service, Chicago.)

In some areas pumas are persistently hunted for bounty payments, and in others they are controlled in the interest of livestock and wild game. There are many areas where normal hunting and the vicissitudes of the wild probably will keep their numbers down. There are also, however, great stretches of wilderness that probably will never be touched by puma-control campaigns, and that are not profitable for hunting the animal for the bounty. Hence we conclude that the species will long continue to exist in the Americas.

Estimates by the Forest Service over a 14-year period (1928-1941) show this predator to be apparently holding its own in 8 national forest regions. See Table 1.

As of December 31, 1942, a grand total of 5,800 pumas were estimated on the National Forests of the United States.

These animals are so destructive to man's interests that they can not be tolerated except in the wildest areas. They have been exterminated in practically all of their former range in the United States east of the Mississippi Valley and are fast being eradicated from many parts of the West. In certain areas near and south of our southwestern border that are remote from human habitations, however, they will persist far into the future.

Alabama.—Hallock (1880: 2-3) listed the animal during 1880 in Choctaw and DeKalb counties.

Howell (1921: 41-42) says of the animal in this state: "The cougar, or 'panther,' as this animal is usually called, doubtless in early times occupied the greater part of the State; it is now [1921] nearly, if not quite, exterminated." . . . "Recent reports, although

Table 1. Estimate of number of pumas on national forests, 1928-1941

Region	1928	1929	1930	1931	1932	1933	1934	1935	1936	1937	1938	1939	1940	1941
1	484	515	489	493	466	465	489	462	482	380	414	450	450	480
2	440	361	389	417	464	402	364	351	374	311	299	300	310	310
3	542	766	780	1,020	982	1,024	1,107	960	935	865	875	902	860	830
4	561	751	942	1,195	1,335	1,158	1,518	1,012	1,134	1,400	1,300	1,300	1,400	1,400
5	2,075	2,023	1,818	1,656	1,623	1,525	1,511	1,562	1,500	1,230	1,434	1,200	1,100	1,200
6	1,653	1,146	1,100	1,008	977	883	896	920	1,005	1,050	1,257	1,367	1,350	1,500
8	----	----	----	----	2	2	4	4	6	8	8	10	10	10*
Totals	5,755	5,562	5,518	5,789	5,849	5,459	5,870	5,271	5,436	2,244	5,587	5,529	5,500	5,730

*Estimated for Ocala National Forest, Florida.
Note: With the exception of Region 8 all of the others are west of 100th Meridian.

rather indefinite, indicate that a very few still remain in the big swamps of the southern counties."

Arkansas.—Nuttall (1821: 118), one of the earliest to record the existence of the puma in this State, found it occurring in the vicinity of the Arkansas River, northwest of Little Rock, during the winter of 1819.

The animal in early times appears to have been fairly well distributed over Arkansas, particularly along and in the lower brakes of the Mississippi and Arkansas Rivers. Near the Louisiana border in Chicot County, southeastern Arkansas, Waddell (1887: 323) records the taking of three pumas in one day in the Crooked Bayou section during the spring of 1887.

Hallock in 1880 (8-10) listed the puma as still to be found in Cross, Greene, Jackson, Prairie, Phillips, Pulaski, and St. Francis counties.

A report of a single animal occurring in the Radding neighborhood of Franklin County was investigated by field men of the Biological Survey on September 25, 1920. From the information secured it was apparent that a small puma ranged in this area at that time, living on rabbits and other small mammals.

Arizona.—The animal is found throughout the State with the exception of the open, treeless valleys and bare mesas, though at times it crosses these in going from one mountain range to another. It is most prevalent in the eastern half of Arizona from the Mexican boundary northward to the Little Colorado River. Numerous observations have been made of pumas entering in, and departing from, the State across the international boundary near Nogales, Washington Camp, and Parker Canyon, all in Santa Cruz County.

This State contains probably one of the greatest numerical representations of this animal to be found at present in the West. In part this may be attributed to steady influx of pumas from Mexico.

Another probable factor is the superabundance of deer in most of the State. With but little, if any, winter kill, or lack of feed, a goodly population of deer has long been recorded in many parts of Arizona. Like other carnivores, the puma tends to increase and maintain its numbers in direct proportion to the available food supply.

To date [1942] more pumas have been taken in Arizona in the

predator control work of the State-Federal forces than in any other. For the period July 1, 1915, to June 30, 1941, a total of 2,146 were killed. In this removal scarcely a third of the puma's range in the State has been consistently hunted. Over an area of 3,600 square miles in western Yavapai County 47 pumas were killed during the fiscal year 1942, an average of approximately 1 puma to each 75 square miles. Twenty-six of these animals were taken in an area of about 1,200 square miles—a heavy concentration. The late "Jimmy" Owens, a private puma hunter, is reported to have killed more than 600 pumas on the Kaibab Plateau between 1907 and 1919.

Continuation of the policy by Federal-State hunters of not hunting where its depredations are not an economic factor, in addition to infiltration from Mexico, where little puma control is practiced, and a dependable food supply, assures the occurrence of the puma in Arizona for a very long period in the future.

Arizona is unusual in the distribution of the puma, three geographic races occurring within its borders, viz., *Felis concolor kaibabensis*, *F. c. azteca*, and *F. c. browni*. An extremely old male puma (*F. c. browni*), weighing 125 lbs., was taken on February 17, 1944, 50 miles northeast of Yuma in the vicinity of Squaw Creek, which is located in the Kofa Mountains (Plate 7, p. 68).

California.—In this State there are two geographic races of the puma. *Felis concolor californica* formerly occurred over almost the entire State, with the exception of the southeastern deserts, while *F. c. browni* is found in the wooded river lowlands of southeastern California and westward along the boundary of Mexico to near Calexico, in the Imperial Valley. While this race is mainly a dweller in heavy growths along the river courses, all under 1,500 feet in elevation, old puma hunters speak of its occurrence at times within the lower desert mountain ranges.

Beechey (1831: 79) was one of the first to record the puma's occurrence in California when, in writing of the country between Monterey and San Francisco during December, 1826, he said: "The lion and the tiger [probably the jaguar] are natives of these woods, but we never saw them; the inhabitants say they are small, and that the lion is less than the tiger, but more powerful."

California has paid a bounty on the puma for the past 36 years and during that time a total of 9,039 scalps have been turned in for bounty payments, totaling $215,370. In addition to this amount "thousands of dollars have been paid out in salaries and maintenance of State lion hunters." According to the State Division of Fish and Game (Anon. 1943: 1), "Lions are most abundant in the northwestern part of the State. More than half the total lion kill has been made in these counties—Humbolt County accounting for 10% alone." According to J. S. Hunter (1945: 1), Chief, Bureau of Game Conservation, "The [lion] kill in the various counties gives a good idea as to the part of the State in which the lion population is heaviest. . . . Since 1907, when the lion bounty payment became effective, sixty-two per cent of the lions killed, or 5,856, were from ten counties. These counties represent twenty-three per cent of the area of the State, and thirty-six per cent of the deer country. The ten counties where the lion kill is heaviest are: Humbolt, with 1,004 lions reported killed; Trinity, 836; Shasta, 636; Mendocino, 633; Monterey, 538; Siskiyou, 499, Lake, 470; Tulare, 429; Santa Barbara, 418; and Tehama, 393.

"In the four counties of Humboldt, Trinity, Mendocino, and Lake, the kill was thirty-one per cent of the total. These counties represent seven per cent of the area of the State, and thirteen per cent of the deer country. Lions are apparently more abundant in the northwestern part of the State than elsewhere. They are particularly scarce in the extreme eastern section. Only five lions have been reported killed in Modoc County in the past thirty-eight years; three from Alpine, and Inyo County has accounted for 22.

"Of the 177 lions killed in 1944, State lion hunters took 41."

Colorado.—In early times the puma was common from the crest of the Rockies westward to the Utah line. It occurred occasionally eastward from the Rocky Mountains well out onto the plains, particularly where brushy water courses afforded ample cover. The late M. J. McMillan, of Lamar, long a stockman-farmer in Prowers County, mentioned the occurrence of the puma along the banks and lower bottoms of the Arkansas River nearly to the Kansas State line, as not being uncommon during the late 90's and the early years of the present century. One of the first records of the puma in this section, so familiar to McMillan, was that made by Lieutenant J. W. Abert (U. S. Government, 1848: 405). While on a journey from Fort Leavenworth to San Diego, California, during the years 1846-1847, he lists the "panther" as being observed in the vicinity of Bent's Fort, on the Arkansas River in southeastern Colorado.

Allen (1874: 52) found it "not uncommon" in Park County during the early 1870's.

Early in this century Rio Blanco and Routt counties in northwestern Colorado were recognized as containing the greatest abundance of the animal, many noted puma hunts being held in this area, particularly by Theodore Roosevelt.

Of its occurrence on the plains of this State, Coues says: "It is only rarely seen on the prairie." (Dortt, Mary. 1879: 218.)

Connecticut.—Linsley (1842: 348), one of the earlier authorities as to the puma's occurrence in Connecticut, states: . . . "I saw a fine specimen, said to have been killed in the northern part of the State, exhibited in Mix's Museum some years since. Dr. Emmons says they are still found in St. Lawrence County, New York, where one man killed five with his dog and gun not many years since."

Goodwin (1935: 84-86) records the animal as formerly "not uncommon in the mountainous country of Litchfield County."

Delaware.—Records of the puma in Delaware are almost entirely wanting, though in colonial times this cat undoubtedly occurred in the State. Considering that adjacent areas in Maryland, Pennsylvania, and New Jersey supported the puma in greater or lesser abundance, it no doubt also ranged in Delaware. Plenty of puma food was available, particularly in the large numbers of white-tailed deer.

Warden (1819: 124) states: "All the wild animals common to Maryland and Pennsylvania are seen in the most unfrequented places of this State"—a comment made in the early part of the 19th century.

District of Columbia.—When first visited by the early explorers the area later set apart as the District of Columbia no doubt had the puma as part of its fauna. Philip (1861: 22) lists it as one of the mammals which formerly roamed "over its surface."

Florida.—During the course of field studies made in the winter of 1868-1869, J. A. Allen (1871: 161, 168) found the puma "not very unfrequent in the more unsettled parts of the State." He saw "several skins of it at Jacksonville said to have been taken up the river."

Near the close of the last century Cory (1896: 109) wrote that the panther was "not uncommon in the unsettled portions of the State.

"The Florida panther is apparently separable, at least subspecifically, from its northern congener, which it resembles in general marking, but differs in being more rufous or reddish brown in color, and in having the legs relatively longer and the feet decidedly smaller.

"A most noticeable character in the Florida animal is the small size of the foot. Several northern examples which I have examined have the foot at least four inches broad, while those of a Florida specimen of equal size would not exceed three inches.

"A female which I killed in April 1895 measured about seven feet from nose to tip of tail, and her forefoot measured two and seven-eighths inches in width. In a Colorado specimen of about the same length the foot measured four and one-eighth inches at the widest part, and another specimen three and seven-eighths inches.

"It is rare that a Florida panther exceeds nine feet in length, although it is claimed that they occasionally grow larger."

At about the same time Bangs (1898: 234-235) found it to occur in the more thinly settled parts of the State, but said that it was extinct in all of the region directly northeast of Florida, and in northern Florida as well. Of six specimens in his possession the largest stood 3 ft., 4 in. at the withers, and 3 ft., 6 in. at the rump.

Hamilton (1941: 688-689), discussing the recent status of the animal in Florida, writes: "The panther still occurs in the wilder parts of Lee, Collier, and Henchy counties." He records the finding of puma sign by Mr. Dyers "in the hammocks about 17 miles east of Fort Myers . . . ." Further, one was killed on October 19, 1939, near Bonita Springs, another near Estero on November 20 of that year, and one near Immokalee on April 3, 1941.

Rand and Host (1942: 6) record it near Sebring and Lake Placid in Highlands County during 1941.

Georgia.—It is apparent that the puma at one time occurred throughout all of the rougher sections of western Georgia.

In the late spring of 1773, while traveling north and west of Augusta, Bartram (1928: 63) in commenting on the cougar remarked: "Bears, tygers, wolves, and wild cats (*Felis cauda truncata*) are numerous enough . . . . This creature is called in Pennsylvania and the northern States 'panther,' but in Carolina, and the southern States, is called 'Tyger'; it is very strong, much larger than any dog, of a yellowish brown, or clay colour, having a very long tail; it is a mischievous animal, and preys on calves, young colts, etc."

Bartram's Travels was first published in Philadelphia in 1791, and in London in 1792. Coleridge read it in 1794, who later in his life called it "the last book written in the spirit of the old travellers." Wordsworth is believed to have taken Bartram's book with him to Germany in 1798. He was much inspired by it. Carlyle also praised it highly.

Bachman in 1849 (p. 3) listed the animal as occurring in Glynn and Wayne counties of extreme southeastern Georgia.

At about this same time also Lanman (1856: 352) mentioned the puma as occurring in north-central Georgia, northwest of Dahlonega, county seat of Lumpkin County.

Hallock, in 1880 (37, 40), reported it in Grady County, in the far southwestern portion of the State, and in the northern and western extremes with reference to Bartow County and the Hill Country where "the scream of the panther is not infrequently heard."

Harper (1920: 29; 1927: 317-320) discusses the occurrence of the animal in the Okefinokee Swamp region of southeast Georgia, where its presence was known from the middle 1860's to as late as the 1920's.

Idaho.—Townsend (1839: 149) was one of the first to mention the puma's existence in this State, when, in the early 1830's, he commented upon the animal's voice as heard while encamped in country included in present-day Idaho, when en route to the lower Columbia River.

The animal has remained more or less common in the mountainous sections of Idaho, and though control measures, seeking reduction of its numbers on cattle and sheep ranges, and to some extent on the game ranges within the National Forests, are in progress yearly, it nevertheless will long continue to exist in the State, because of the ruggedness of most of its habitat.

Between the fiscal years 1915 and 1941 a total of 251 pumas were killed in Idaho by hunters employed cooperatively by the State, livestock associations, and the Federal Government.

Whitlow (1933: 250) recorded two pumas taken within a short distance of Pocatello in 1927.

Illinois.—Cory (1912: 153), in his "Mammals of Illinois and Wisconsin," states: "The panther, or cougar, was formerly not uncommon throughout the wooded sections of Illinois and Wisconsin. The fact that it was considered rare by some of the early writers has little weight inasmuch as its habits were such that, in a country where the character of the soil and vegetation were such that its tracks could not be seen, its presence would be very likely overlooked; but as the country became settled they were driven out or killed, and it is extremely doubtful if any exist within our limits at the present time."

In the early 1850's Kennicott (1855: 578) recorded that but "a single individual has been known in the county [Cook]."

Indiana.—An early mention of the puma's pelt is in the invoices of Francis Vigo at Vincennes, who in the late 18th century was a fur shipper of an apparently large number of furs to London, via Montreal (Anon. 1943: 3, 15).

This large cat is believed to have never been common in the State. Some authorities state it was gone from Indiana by 1832-1833. It is supposed to have been most prevalent in the Dune region in the northern portion of the State. (Lyon, Marcus Ward, Jr. 1936: 160).

Evermann and Butler (1893: 138-139) state that it was formerly found in Franklin County in southeastern Indiana. They further say it "never was common. But few have been seen since 1835. Two young were taken east of Brookville [the county seat] in 1838. None have been reported for thirty years or more." Butler (1895: 37), speaking of the last of the elk in Indiana as the year 1830, says: "The panther followed soon after."

In Hahn's (1909: 540-542) resume of the distribution of the animal it appears that by the early 1830's it was exceedingly rare in its occurrence, and by the 1850's it had practically disappeared from the entire State.

Iowa.—In this State there is no evidence which would lead one to the conclusion that the animal was ever common. Allen (1869: 5-6), quoting Dr. C. A. White, at the time Director, Geological Survey of Iowa, relates that "The panther [in Iowa] has been known within our limits but very rarely."

Other authorities aver that it was "formerly common over the State, now extinct." (Van Hyning, T., and Frank C. Pellett. 1910: 218), but it is impossible to determine upon what basis this statement was made.

Kansas.—"American Panther. A specimen taken about nine years ago at Valley Falls, by Mr. Whitman, and identified by him. Probably only a transient visitor. Now and then known as crossing different parts of the State." (Knox, M. V. B. 1875: 18).

Cragin (1885: 42) wrote of the animal, "The panther or cougar, generally known in Kansas by the name of 'mountain lion,' seems to be more abundant in the southern part of the State this winter than usual. Seven specimens are known by the writer to have been observed (three of them killed, and a fourth, a cub, captured alive) in Harper, Barbour, and Comanche counties during the prolonged cold spell of December, and three of these have come under his personal observation. Others will doubtless be reported 'ere long from the same and other, especially western, counties. They have entered the settlements and approached the towns with more than wonted boldness, impelled apparently by cold and scarcity of food."

Mead (1899: 281) recorded: "*Felis concolor* were rarely met," but he stated, this animal "was occasionally found in central Kansas in its first settlement, was common along the southern line of the State, gets more common in the Indian Territory, now known as Oklahoma. Its habitat was along the timbered streams and the prairies and hills adjacent."

He further remarked that in the fall of 1859 the Sac and Fox Indians, with the aid of dogs, killed one of immense size in a heavily timbered bend of the Solomon River, a few miles above its mouth. This was probably in what is now the extreme northeast portion of Saline County. He also recalled seeing "one on the White Water in Butler County, close to Mean's ranch, where Towanda now stands" in 1865. Further that in the winter of 1864 he "rode almost onto a very large male lion lying at length upon the prairie some three miles south of the junction of the Medicine Lodge and Salt Fork Rivers, near the great salt plain. His color harmonized so completely with the dead, brown, buffa-grass that he was not observed until I was almost onto him. He was not disposed to move from his position, and not having my rifle with me, I rode around him at a distance of fifty feet, and talked to him, but could not induce him to move, except his eyes and head, which followed my every movement. A bunch of wild horses nearby in a ravine may have been his quest. I rode away, leaving him to his meditations."

According to Allen (1871: 5), the panther was "rare on the

prairies." This he attributed to the lack of "forest shelter." When the puma was found in the prairie country it generally made its abode along the heavier-timbered water courses and brakes, ranging at times to hunt upon the level grassy country in search of food.

Hibbard (1943: 61-68, 71), in his recent check-list of Kansas mammals, states that two races of puma occurred in the State. *Felis concolor couguar* was common in eastern Kansas "at the time of early settlement, but now extinct in the State," while *F. c. hippolestes* occurred "in western Kansas." William Applebaugh and J. H. Spratt are credited with killing the last Kansas puma on August 15, 1904, in Ellis County.

Kentucky—Early accounts indicate a fairly wide distribution of the puma in Kentucky. True (1889: 596-597), in his summary, mentions one killed south of Louisville in 1784, one in Allen County in 1815, and one believed to be the last of the species in the State, which was killed in 1863 a short distance from Lexington.

Imlay (1793: 299) recorded it among the Kentucky mammals near the close of the 18th century.

Warden (1819) mentioned it as part of the fauna of the State about 1819.

Funkhouser (1925: 40), quoting Garman in a statement made in 1894, is to the effect that "this species existed in the State within the past fifty years."

Bailey (1933: 47), in his "Cave Life of Kentucky," recorded its occurrence in Kentucky in association with the first early pioneers the latter part of the 18th century.

Louisiana.—Warden (1819: 524) mentioned it among the fauna of the State in 1819.

Louisiana still possesses ideal habitat conditions for the puma, at one time numerous within its borders. The animals have, however, gradually disappeared until now the species is believed to be extinct or of very rare occurrence.

Kopman, in 1921 (29), stated: "The few cougars remaining in the State appear to be pretty well concentrated in the bottoms, especially canebrakes along the Black, Tensas, and Ouachita Rivers. . . . Its prey is chiefly the larger kinds of game, especially deer, turkeys, and rabbits. In remote settlements it sometimes attacks the pigs, sheep, and calves."

Hollister (1911: 175-178) found it fairly common in the cane-brake region during February, 1904.

The Conservation Commission of Louisiana, in its report from April 1, 1914, to April 1, 1916 (1916: 42), stated of the puma that "while not exactly plentiful the 'lion' is far from being extinct in Louisiana, and skins, when they have not been too badly shot up, find their way into the fur market with regularity.

By 1936 Lowery (11-39) believed the animal to be "virtually extinct in the State, apparently occurring only in limited numbers along the Tensas and possibly the Atchafalaya River. One or two of the animals are killed every year or so in Madison or Richland parishes."

At present (1943) Lowery (234-235) believes the animal is re-stricted to the swamps of northeastern and eastern Louisiana, and the lower Atchafalaya River bottoms. Two pumas were recently reported feeding, however, on a freshly killed pig on the highway between Robeline and Spanish Lake, in Natchitoches Parish, western Louisiana.

Maine.—The puma was probably of rare occurrence throughout Maine, and Arthur H. Norton (1930: 402-403) states: "Rare, and probably never more than a straggler."

In his early compilation with reference to the zoology of Maine, Ezekiel Holmes listed the puma as occurring in the State, but made no comment as to its general distribution. (Maine, State of. 1861: 123.) Hitchcock (1862: 65) also recorded it among the mammalia of the State.

Cram (1901: 123) cites one killed about the year 1845 in the town of Sebago, located in Cumberland County, about 35 miles northwest of Portland.

Moorehead (1922: 57) recorded the finding of various mammal teeth, among them one of the puma, taken from shell heaps exca-vated in Hancock County.

Goodwin (1936: 50) reports one killed in 1891 near Andover.

Maryland.—In Maryland this animal was commonly referred to as the panther. Scott (1807: 28) mentioned it as occurring in the State, but at what points cannot be ascertained from his reference.

Audubon and Bachman (1851: 312) include it among the mam-mals of Maryland.

Meshach Browning (1928), a noted, early-day trapper in Maryland, gives a number of records of the puma's occurrence in Garrett County, northwestern Maryland, between 1791 and 1830, as follows:

Buffalo Gap, Deep Creek. The country abounds in panthers. (1791: 20.)

Blooming Rose. Directly within ten steps of me up rose the head and shoulders of the largest panther that I ever saw. He measured eleven feet, three inches, from the end of his nose to the tip of his tail. (1797: 78.)

Bear Creek Glades (near head of Bear Creek). Gunner presently came to a great crack in the rocks . . . to my astonishment a panther bounded out . . . September. (1803: 123.)

Big Gap of Meadow Mountain. Instead of a wolf we found a panther upon a tree. January (1819: 208).

Negro or Meadow Mountain. I took care to keep at a safe distance, and taking good aim I sent a ball whizzing through his brains, which put an end to a wild and furious monster. (1820: 213.)

Meadow Mountain, southern end, east slope, near Savage River. I had killed three out of four of the family. (1830: 275.)

Meadow Mountain, southern end. One taken. He measured nine feet, ten inches, from the end of his nose to the tip of his tail. (1830: 282.) (Browning, Meshach. 1928.)

Massachusetts.—During the early colonization period the puma was known to range the greater portion of this State. It was early outlawed, however, and persistent warfare on the part of everyone who carried a musket, dug pits, or set traps, gradually brought about its complete extinction, so that by the middle of the 19th century it was doubtful that a single individual remained. It was commonly referred to as the catamount. An early account of its occurrence in Massachusetts states: "Fifty years later (1738) the Boston Gazette reported the presence of a catamount in town, a creature well calculated to put the physiologies into the realm of the fabulous and impossible. Said the Gazette: 'To be seen at the Greay Hound Tavern in Roxbury, a wild creature, which was caught in the woods about 80 miles to the westward of this Town, called a Cattamount, it has a Tail like a Lyon, its Leggs are like a Bears, its Claws like an Eagle, its eyes like a Tyger, its countenance is a mixture of every Thing that is Fierce and Savage, he is exceedingly ravenous and devours all sorts of Creatures that he can come near; its Agility is surprising, it will Leap 30 Foot at one jump notwithstanding it is but Three months old. Whoever inclines to see this Creature may come to the Place aforesaid, paying a Shilling each, shall be welcome for their Money.' " (Greenlie, Sydney. 1929: 208.)

Allen in 1869 (153) wrote that the "(Panther) has probably been for some time extinct in Massachusetts, though undoubtedly once occurring here."

Emmons (1840: 36) had noted, however, nearly 30 years previous [1840] that "The Puma is not found at present in this State. It has, however, been seen in the western portion long since its settlement."

Crane (1931: 270) cites an occurrence of the puma as late as January 18, 1926.

Michigan.—Michigan probably had the animal throughout the State. In Washtenaw County, near the extreme southeastern border, Wood (1922: 13-14) recounts its occurrence from 1835 to 1870, the latter date being for the last puma seen in that area.

Wood (1914: 8) also gives records of the puma's former distribution in Jackson, Ontonagon, Oceana, Mason, Ingham, Montcalm, Allegan, Calhoun, Kalamazoo, and Eaton counties, but the animal has long been extinct in the State.

Minnesota.—Roberts in his interesting resume of vanished Minnesota mammals states that "The cougar was apparently never common," and Surber (1932: 12) says there is "scanty reference to it in the writings of the early explorers . . . ."

According to Herrick (1892: 68), "The most recent occurrence of the puma in Minnesota was in 1875, when a single individual was killed in Sunrise, Chisago County."

Mississippi.—DuPratz (1758: 91-92) was probably one of the first individuals to comment on the occurrence of the animal in this State, indicating it was not very abundant even at that early date, as he wrote [1758]: "I have seen two at different times about my habitation" [near Natchez].

Many parts of this State, however, contained areas suitable to the puma's existence, and Audubon, in 1851 (308) remarked on its occurrence in the low swampy sections.

A few years following Audubon's observations, Wailes (1854: 315) wrote: "The Panther is now rarely met with, except in dense and extensive swamps and canebrakes."

Hallock, in 1880 (92), reported that puma hunting was possible in Tunica County of this State, and also farther south along the Mississippi River in Washington County.

Missouri.—Watkins (1802: 70), writing from St. Louis, lists *Felis concolor* among the animals occurring in that vicinity at the beginning of the 19th century.

On May 20, 1834, Maximilian (1841: 357) report that along the Missouri River below Liberty, the animal was only occasionally seen.

That the puma continued to exist in Missouri well toward the close of the 19th century is indicated by an account mentioning one being driven into a tree on a bend of the Current River of south-central Missouri, where it was shot, in the fall of 1887. The animal's length is given as 7 ft., 9¾ in. (Anon. 1888: 493.)

Montana.—The puma occurs throughout most of the mountain ranges in the western part of the State. Sparing mention of it is found in early journals and narratives of the 19th century. At times it followed down the water courses and out onto the more open prairie country of the eastern part of the State, as noted also for Nebraska and Kansas, and southeastern Colorado.

Vernon Bailey found it at the Tilyou Ranch in Dawson County, eastern Montana, in 1887. (United States Government. 1888: 431.)

George Bird Grinnell recorded one seen in 1875 on the Yellowstone River "near the mouth of Alum Creek." (Ludlow, William. 1876: 63.)

Huntington (1904: 304) found it "out on a large plain at the base of the Rosebud Mountains [southeastern Montana] while riding about on an Indian pony and shooting sage grouse from the saddle . . . ."

For the period July 1, 1915, to June 30, 1941, a total of 268 pumas were taken in cooperative predator control work in the State. These, in the majority of instances, were removed from the livestock and game ranges of the national forests. The State contains the type locality of *Felis concolor hippolestes,* as well as of the more recently described *Felis concolor missoulensis.*

Nebraska.—Whether the puma occurred in Nebraska to the extent that it did in Kansas, as reported by Mead, is unknown. Aughey (1880: 119) wrote of having "only seen it a few times on the Niobrara and the Loup."

Nevada.—Up to the year 1889 very little was definitely known as to the animal's occurrence and distribution in Nevada. Later records tend to show, however, that the animal occurred in small numbers throughout most of the mountainous sections of the State.

Borell and Ellis (1934: 23) found evidence of its occurrence in 1927, in the Ruby Mountains of northeastern Nevada, which lie in Elko and White Pine counties.

Between the fiscal years 1915 and 1941 a total of 73 pumas were killed in the Federal-State puma control campaigns in the mountainous areas of eastern and central Nevada. The animal appears to have been absent from the Humbolt River valley and other desert sections of the western part of the State.

In the collection of the Museum of the University of Colorado at Boulder is a tanned puma skin (No. 3789) noted as having been trapped near Baker, White Pine County, Nevada, near the Snake Range close to the Utah border, during the winter of 1938 by H. Miller and D. Taylor.

New Hampshire.—Available records seem to indicate that the puma was not of great abundance in this State. Goodwin (1936: 50) states: "A few remained in northern Vermont and New Hampshire until about 1888."

Dearborn (1927: 311) relates of one being killed "on November 2nd, 1853 . . . in the township of Lee, Rockingham County." It is recorded as weighing "198 pounds and measured 8 ft., 4 in., from tip to tip." (Ibid: 312.) This is probably the same animal reported by Allen (1942: 236), now in the possession of the Woodman Institute, Dover.

Stone and Cram (1902: 290) put the disappearance of the puma in northeastern New Hampshire at about 1852. "But there are still rumors from time to time [1902] of them having been seen in the northern part of the State, especially since deer have become more common."

Jackson (1922: 13) says, however, that a pair "of cougars" existed in that State in the early 1920's, whose range extended "along the east side of the Androscoggin River in the town of Cambridge to the southern shores of Lake Umbagog."

New Jersey.—At the time Smith (1765: 502) compiled his history of New Jersey 13 counties were then in existence. Of these he states that the puma was common in all of them.

Warden (1819: 38) lists the "cougouar" along with the "bear and wolf" as mammals which had nearly disappeared from New Jersey by the early part of the 19th century.

Rhoads (1903: 128) states it was "originally found in every part of both states [Pennsylvania and New Jersey], but always more abundant in the Alleghany Mountains. In New Jersey it became extinct in the early part of the 19th century, the last probably occurring in Sussex or Warren counties as strays from northeastern Pennsylvania."

Rhoads (1903: 130-132) traced records of the puma's occurrence in the New Jersey counties of Burlington, Camden, Cape May, and Mercer. Undoubtedly it was in earlier times fairly well distributed throughout the entire commonwealth as the boundaries are known today.

Goodwin (1936: 50) states "the last cougars were destroyed between 1830 and 1840."

New Mexico.—The puma is widely distributed throughout the State but of late years, due to intensified hunting, is not as common as it was at the beginning of the present century. The animals may now be said to be confined mainly to the rougher mountainous sections west of the Rio Grande.

New York.—Formerly abundant throughout most of New York, and particularly in the forested regions of the Adirondacks, the animal was so reduced in numbers by the variety of attacks upon it that by the close of the last century it was nearly extinct.

A bounty of $20 was placed on it by the State in 1871, and between that date and 1882 a total of 46 were killed for bounty. These were taken in Essex, Franklin, Hamilton, Herkimer, Lewis, and St. Lawrence counties. The bounty was $10 less than that set for the wolf at the time, and continued in effect for approximately a quarter of a century.

Of the last of these animals in New York, the late Dr. E. W. Nelson made the following observations:

"Cornelius DuBois, Manager of Litchfield Park near Tupper Lake in the winter of 1899, when patrolling saw where a mountain lion had made an unsuccessful dash at deer, its several leaps being recorded in snow—the tail mark showing also.

"H. Pell Jones ran a small hunter's hotel at Elk Lake, Port Hudson, Essex County. He told Burnham [John B.] that a lion was killed by following its hunting circuit through a group of mountains surrounding Elk Lake in the winter of 1908. . . . Previous to the instance noted above he had seen no sign of lions for 15 or 20 years."

An early account of it by Pierce in 1823 (93) states: "Panthers . . . are occasionally seen in the southern section of the Catskill Mountains, but are not so numerous as in the middle region. A panther measuring in length about 9 feet was recently killed in the southern range; this animal is rarely seen; but from its strength, size, and ferocity it is regarded with terror, and considered the most formidable beast of the forest; their color is grey, the head small in proportion, the general form indicating agility; they have been known in ascending a ledge or tree to rise at a leap twenty feet from the ground."

Newhouse (1869: 58-59) wrote in his "Trappers Guide": "Full grown Panthers killed in northern New York have been known to measure over eleven feet from the nose to the tip of the tail, being about twenty-eight inches high, and weighing near two hundred pounds. Their color is a reddish brown above, shading into a lighter color underneath." Newhouse probably took his statement on the great size of the New York puma from that made by James DeKay in his "Zoology of New York," Part 1, Mammals, 1842: 48. It is no doubt an extreme exaggeration.

In the collection of the late J. H. Fleming is a specimen of *Felis concolor couguar* killed about 1847 on Croil Island, St. Lawrence County. This location is about 10 miles east of Morrisburg, Dundas County, Ontario, Canada.

North Carolina.—Lawson (1718: 117), an early recorder of North Carolina mammals, conveys the impression that the puma was quite common in this State at the beginning of the 18th century. He wrote: "This Beast is the greatest Enemy to the Planter, of any Vermine in Carolina."

Schoepf (1911: 107-108) included it among the mammals found in the thinly-settled woods of the State, 1783-1784.

In common with others of the larger predators along the Atlantic seaboard it gradually disappeared with human occupation of its old habitat, coupled with unrelenting hunting. It is now apparently extinct. Specimens have been recorded as having been killed near

Highlands and in Craven County about 1886. (Brimley, C. S. 1939: 2.)

Oberholser (1905: 7) in commenting on this occurrence states also that "the skin of one said to have been killed by a Mr. Drew, near Highlands, about 1886, was recently seen there by Mr. R. G. Murdock."

By the middle of the past century Audubon (1851: 311) reported that the cougar "has been nearly exterminated in all our Atlantic states."

North Dakota.—The records indicate that the puma ranged over all the prairie states, though not in abundance.

In North Dakota this animal appears to have been rare east of the Missouri River valley, its greatest abundance being confined to the western and rougher areas. It appears to have become extinct at the beginning of the present century. Bailey, Bell and Brannon, in 1914 (16) stated that "It is doubtful if the mountain lion still occurs in North Dakota, but specimens were secured not many years ago along the Missouri River Valley." No later record has been found than that by Vernon Bailey (1926: 146) of one killed by Clarence H. Parker, on "November 20th, 1902, about 25 miles down the Missouri River from Williston on the south side of the river."

While the puma is presumed to be extinct in North Dakota, strong evidence of its existence is related by Bach (1943: 14-15). About 8 miles south of Tagus, Mountrail County, North Dakota, and 1 mile west of Carpenter Lake, a puma was reported the evening of June 16, 1943. A cast of this animal's track seen on October 28, 1943, leaves little doubt but what it was a puma.

Ohio.—Explorations of certain mounds and village sites in Ohio have yielded leg bones, teeth, and lower jaws. These give evidence of use as ornaments and implements by the Mound Builders, in that the teeth, especially the premolars and the lower molars, were perforated for stringing and wearing on the body. With later observations of the animal's occurrence in the State a fair conjecture is that these puma remains in these prehistoric mounds were of animals taken within the confines of present day Ohio. (Mills, William C. 1907-1926: 28, 65.)

A few mounds have yielded exceptionally fine effigy pipes of the puma carved from ferruginous stone. (Ibid. 1917: 149-151.)

Trautman (1939: 136) states with reference to early records of mammals occurring in the vicinity of Buckeye Lake that *"Felis concolor couguar* was in the general vicinity of the area in 1805, and was probably in the Great and Bloody Run Swamps for several years thereafter." Smucker (1876: 45) related that in the autumn of 1805 Jacob Wilson, who was then living within a mile of Newark, treed with his dog and then killed a 'huge panther' that had previously raided his pig pen and carried away a pig. Brayton (1882: 8) considered this animal to have been *Felis concolor.*"

Kirtland in 1838 (176) recorded it as the "mountain cat" and "mountain tiger," saying, "The pioneer hunters blended both these species under the comman name of catamount, and seemed not to know that they were distinct. They both formerly inhabited this State, but have now disappeared. Mr. Dorfeuille has in his museum at Cincinnati well prepared specimens of each species that were taken in Ohio."

Oklahoma.—Mead (1899: 278) states this animal "was occasionally found in central Kansas in its first settlement, was common along the southern line of the State, yet more common in the Indian Territory, now known as Oklahoma. Its habitat was along the timbered streams and the prairies and hills adjacent."

Woodhouse (1853: 47) recorded that "he never found this animal very abundant," while engaged as naturalist with the Sitgreaves exploring expeditions. Speaking further of the cougar, he says, "It was observed in the Indian Territory in the neighborhood of a swamp; in Texas, in the open prairie; and in New Mexico, in the mountains."

Some distance southwest of the present town of Eufaula, located in McIntosh County, Gregg while on a circuitous route from Independence, Missouri, to Santa Fe, New Mexico, in the spring of 1839, mentions a supposed encounter between one of his men, who had been lost over night, and a puma. Calling the animal "panther," Gregg apparently questioned the man's reported encounter, recording humorously that "from a peculiar odor" which the individual's gun emitted on his safe arrival at base camp, the encounter had apparently been between the man and a "polecat." It is significant that throughout his discourse concerning the wildlife noted in his classic "Commerce of the Prairies," Gregg fails to mention the puma. Possibly, like Woodhouse, he too failed to find the animal in any large numbers upon the plains. (Thwaites, Reuben Gold. 1905: 106.)

Marcy (1853: 11, 50-55) records the killing of a puma on one of "the branches of Cache Creek" near its mouth, while camped in this vicinity in southwestern Oklahoma, on May 17, 1852, stating, "He was a fine specimen of the North American cougar (*Felis concolor*), measuring eight and a half feet from his nose to the extremity of the tail." Also, while on the headwaters of the Red River, called "Keche-ah-qui-ho-no," or Prairie Dog Town River of the Comanches, June 28, 1852, Marcy records the killing of another puma measuring 8 feet. This animal was killed by him as it was bounding towards Marcy, who at the time was decoying a herd of antelope by the use of a deer-bleat made to imitate the cry of a young deer that had been made by one of his Delaware Indian guides. Concealed as he was in using the "deer-bleat," apparently the puma was attracted to within "twenty steps" of Marcy, coming in bounds, when at this distance it was shot. Later Captain George B. McClellan, his companion, aided in the final killing of this puma.

Again (Ibid: 59), on July 4, 1852, while coming down the main Red River in extreme southwestern Oklahoma, he records killing another puma as it was leaving a water-hole.

At a point between 20 and 30 miles east of Antelope Buttes, northwestern Oklahoma (in the present Roger Mills County), Lieutenant J. W. Abert (1845-1846: 57), in his explorations during the fall of 1845, noted, "Whilst we were riding along on the edge of a deep ravine, peeping into it in search of water, a loud shouting burst from the party behind us, and on looking around we saw a large panther had started from his lair in the jungle nearby, and was bounding away over the hills. Such an unusual sight produced quite an excitement; but we were so wearied by our long march that we did not attempt to take him."

Oregon.—Lewis and Clark were probably the first to mention the puma's occurrence in the Pacific coastal area, stating, "The panther is found indifferently, either on the great plains of the Columbia, the western side of the Rocky Mountains, or the coast of the Pacific. He is the same animal that is so well known on the Atlantic Coast . . . on the frontiers or unsettled parts of our country. (Coues, Elliott. 1893: 864-865.)

They also record the purchase of a panther skin at Fort Clatsop from the Clatsop Indians, near sea level at the mouth of the Columbia River, on December 23, 1805, which was "seven feet long including the tail." (Ibid: 737.)

The early records are noted by Ross Cox. (1831: 131.)

The animal has been most abundant throughout the coastal and Cascade ranges. In the dry interior belt of central Oregon it has not been commonly known, but is again met with as one approaches the mountains of the eastern part of the State. Its frequency in these areas, however, is not comparable with the period of early settlement of the State around the turn of the 19th century. There has been a bounty on the puma almost continously from the early 1840's, when it figured prominently in discussions at the Oregon wolf meetings, to the present time, because of its livestock-killing tendencies. Aside from the large number (thousands) killed for bounties, a total of 229 pumas have been removed from the stock and game ranges of the State between the periods of July 1, 1915 and June 30, 1941, in federal-state cooperative predator control work. These have been taken mainly in the Cascade Mountains.

Pennsylvania.—The puma originally occurred in all parts of Pennsylvania. However, it appears to have concentrated more heavily in the Alleghany Mountains, whence came many printed accounts of its habits, prey, and depredations during colonial times.

William Penn was one of the first to record its existence in this State, namely, in August of 1683. He listed it as one of the "creatures for profit only, by skin or fur, and which are natural to these parts . . . " (Wildman, Edward Embree. 1933: 14.)

Accounts of its occurrence are given by Rhoads (1903: 130-132) in Berks, Bradford, Cambria, Cameron, Centre, Clearfield, Crawford, Elk, Forest, Lancaster, Luzerne, Lycoming, McKean, Mifflin, Monroe, Pike, Northhampton, Potter, Sullivan, Susquehanna, Tioga, Wyoming, and York counties. These records give the animal a wide distribution in Pennsylvania. He states that none has "been killed, so far as I can substantiate the accounts which have been published, since 1871, though one statement would imply that two had been killed in Clinton or Clearfield counties in 1891."

Rhode Island.—Similar to Delaware, records of the occurrence of the puma in this State are exceedingly rare, but Rhode Island undoubtedly harbored the species during early colonial days.

Mearns (1900: 3) lists it as one of the "wild mammals known to have inhabited" the State "during the historic period."

Allen (1942: 235) mentions a puma killed in "1847 or 1848 in West Greenwich, which for many years was preserved in the Museum of the Providence Franklin Society, and then was secured by the Boston Society of Natural History, in whose museum it still is."

South Carolina.—Schoepf (1911: 107-108), an early observer, mentions it among the indigenous mammals occurring in South Carolina.

Audubon and Bachman (1851: 256-257) record the occurrence of the puma in this State as made known to them by "an old resident of South Carolina," who had seen one during a large flood of the Santee River. Speaking of the animal as the cougar, they state that the old resident had seen "two or three deer on a small mound not twenty feet in diameter surrounded by a wide sea of waters, with a cougar seated in the midst of them; both parties having seemingly entered into a truce at a time when their lives seemed equally in jeopardy were apparently disposed peaceably to await the falling of the waters that surrounded them."

Warden says of it in 1819 (411), "From the eastern side of the mountains the buffalo, elk, and catamount have disappeared."

South Dakota.—Hoffman (1877: 95) stated, "Occasional specimens are captured in the oak groves on Oak Creek." This observation was made in the late 1870's, from the military post then located on the Grand River where it joins the Missouri River in present day Carson County.

Hallock (1880: 26) mentions the puma as numerous in the Black Hills during 1880.

Prior to Hallock's comment Ludlow (1875: 79), six years before, believed the animal "to be quite numerous in this locality (Black Hills)." Only one was observed, however, by members of his expedition.

In 1893 (342) Theodore Roosevelt wrote, "Though the cougar prefers woodland it is not necessarily a beast of dense forests only, for it is found in all the plains country, living in the scanty timber belts which fringe the streams, or among the patches of brush in the Bad Lands."

Louis Knowles, long familiar with the mammals of SouthDakota, reported one, a female, killed in early December, 1931, five miles south of the Hardy Ranger Station, in western Pennington

County, near the Wyoming border. This puma had been known in this locality for the two previous years, and was believed to have had a litter of kittens during this time. For the previous quarter of a century no other puma had been reported from the Black Hills section, according to Knowles. (Fish and Wildlife Service files.)

Tennessee.—Williams (1930: 180) records the animal as formerly occurring in Lauderdale County, in west-central Tennessee, and preying on pigs, young calves, and fawns.

According to information given Rhoads (1896: 201) a few were presumed to exist in the so-called "impassable brakes and harricanes" of the bottoms of Lauderdale County.

During the early settlement of Tennessee the puma was found on the Tellico River drainage in Monroe County. It was also recorded near Nashville, and at the beginning of the 19th century was not uncommon in the western portions of the State. Warden (1819: 351) mentions its occurrence at that time.

Hallock, in 1880 (153), notes it as occurring in the cane bottoms below Memphis.

Although now believed to be extinct Kellogg (1939: 268) records the presence of "a panther" that "was seen on May 30, 1937, by local residents on North Fork River near Crossville, Cumberland County."

While investigating coyote depredations in the vicinty of Ducktown in eastern Tennessee near Columbia, during 1932, I was informed by old-time residents that their forbears had often mentioned the presence of pumas in this area, and particularly their depredations on young livestock, such as colts. The animal had not been known to occur there, however, for "many, many years."

Texas.—According to information reported to Allen (1894: 198) by Attwater the animal was common in Aransas County in the late 60's. One is recorded as having been seen by "Captain Bailey" who rode "right onto one in the long prairie grass on Capano Bay about 1857. It was in the act of devouring a deer which it had killed."

Cope reported in 1880 (9) that this big cat was "common all over Texas."

Jones and Jackson (1941: 5-6), in their summary of game

animals in Young County, record its existence in small numbers from the 1880's to the present time [1941].

Attwater, in the early 90's also reported it in the "country west of San Antonio, but they are fast becoming killed out." (Allen, J. A. 1896: 80.)

A. Schott, in the observations made while on the Mexican Boundary Survey, found it along most of the international boundary "from the coast to the Rio Grande" and also "at El Paso del Norte." At that time he found that "the fertile valleys and tablelands of the lower Rio Bravo, Nueces, and other Texas rivers, form a rich support for a vast number of pumas and jaguars." ". . . Numerous herds of wild cattle, mustangs, mules, and horses, besides plentiful game" furnished the food supply for the animals at that time. (Baird, S. F. 1859: 5-6).

Bailey (1905: 162) found it to occur "in the rough and sparsely settled western part of the State . . . where" it laid heavy tribute "on colts, calves, and sheep."

Between the years 1915 to 1941 a total of 359 pumas have been killed on the livestock ranges of Texas by federal-state predatory animal hunters. Of this number nearly 50 percent, or a total of 158, were taken in Webb County, in the south-central part of the State, from 1929 to 1941. (Fish and Wildlife Service files).

Borell and Bryant (1942: 18-19) found this predator "fairly numerous in the higher part of the Chisos Mountains" during the late 1930's. They reported the killing of 55 pumas by one rancher in the area between 1929 and 1937.

The animal will long continue as a part of the interesting fauna of Texas, if for no other reason than that pumas will undoubtedly come into the State from Mexico, where they are very numerous. That country will continue indefinitely to be a reservoir from which pumas will invade Texas.

Utah.—A take of 322 pumas over approximately a 5-year period, 1936 to 1940, in 23 counties of the State, indicated that the animal is distributed throughout the central, mountainous portions of the State. It is scarce or entirely absent in the western desert region adjacent to the Nevada border. Of the aforementioned number 48 were taken in Wayne, 27 in Sevier, 26 in Garfield, and 22 in Emery counties, in south-central Utah.

Siler (1880: 673-674) mentions its occurrence on the Pauns-a-gunt Plateau of southern Utah.

In Zion and Bryce Canyon national parks, 15 and 4 pumas were the numbers listed, respectively, by the National Park Service as occurring in 1939 within the boundaries of these two scenic areas. (U. S. Goverment. 1939: 31).

Vermont.—Warden (1819: 430) includes the animal among the 36 quadrupeds occurring in this State in the early 19th century.

Commenting on the puma's occurrence in Vermont by 1853, Thompson (1853: 37) says: "They were formerly much more common in Vermont than at the present day, and have at times done much injury by destroying sheep and young cattle."

Osgood (1938: 438) considered it extinct by the late 1930's, though "there have been repeated reports of panthers seen and heard in various parts of the State, but to date none has been captured to secure a reward of $100 offered by a local paper for a Vermont panther, dead or alive."

Under date of September 16, 1943, the Washington Daily News (noon edition) printed the following: *"Barnard, Vt., Sept. 16.*—The last panther killed in Vermont was shot here in 1881 and it now is on view at the State House in Montpelier."

Virginia.—Perhaps the earliest record of the puma's occurrence in early Virginia is the notation of Captain John Smith, about 1609-1616, referring to "Lions." (Smith, Captain John. 1608, 1631 (1884).

In the Blue Ridge and Alleghany Mountains in earlier times, with their large numbers of game, particularly deer, affording a plentiful food supply, and other conditions making for ideal habitat, the animal was found in good numbers at the time of the State's settlement.

Nevertheless the Dismal Swamp area appears to have been the section where the animal held out longest. Hallock, in 1880 (153) lists the puma as still plentiful in this vast morass. Several years earlier (1877: 167) he listed it also as one of the animals occurring in this part of Norfolk County.

Beverley, an early Virginia historian, lists it among the animals killed in the so-called "vermin hunts" conducted by the hard-riding young Virginia aristocrats during the latter part of the 17th and the early 18th centuries.

It is now extinct in the State, but when it finally disappeared is difficult to determine.

Washington.—Cooper (1855: 90), an early observer, reported mountain lions "tolerably abundant, a half dozen having been obtained in the neighborhood within a year." This was at Steilacoom.

Swan (1857: 256) found it among the fauna occurring in the Shoalwater Bay region of southwestern Washington during his three years' residence, 1852 to 1855.

Meeker (1907: 198-200) mentions it as occurring in the Puyallup Valley during the early 1850's.

George G. Cantwell, during April, 1920, reported on a puma caught in a trap during the winter of that year, near Copalis, in southwestern Grays Harbor County.

The puma occurs in most of the mountainous areas of Washington, probably in its greatest numbers in the Olympics.

Taylor and Shaw (1929: 13) give its occurrence as in the "timbered areas throughout the State, probably more common in the Olympic Mountains than elsewhere, but present also in the Cascades and Blue Mountains."

One of the largest pumas ever seen by the writer in Washington was that mounted and displayed in the Old Albee House, which at the time, 1904, was a leading hotel of South Bend. The animal had been killed near this city in Pacific County during 1893.

Stanley G. Jewett in the late summer of 1920 found the puma very scarce in the Skagit River country, and in the mountain region to the eastward. His only evidence of its occurrence was in the vicinity of the Ashnola River, where three were trapped by the Gordon brothers in the winter of 1919-1920.

Webster (1924: 12) records a puma attack on man near Forks in Clallam County on June 4, 1924.

Brooks (1930: 66) notes its occurrence in the Mount Baker region, where, at certain times, it is very destructive to deer.

Sampson (1906: 33) in the earlier days of Mount Rainier National Park reported the puma as present in considerable numbers.

Washington is one of the few States of the Union for which a fully verified account of an unprovoked attack upon a human being is on record. This occurred in Okanogan County in 1925 and is discussed farther on in the text.

West Virginia.—During the early settlement of this State the puma was reported as very common in the Alleghenies. The animals were taken in these mountains throughout the greater part of the past century, but especially in the 1850's. Although now believed to be extinct the tracks of the animal, nevertheless, are reported by Kellogg (1937: 456) as having been seen "in the snow on Black Mountain during the winter of 1935 and also 1936." Black Mountain is in the Monongahela National Forest. In June of 1936 Kellogg (Ibid) also records "panther tracks" seen on Kennison Mountain, Pocahontas County.

Ingersoll (1906: 95) mentions one as entering a logging camp near Davis in northeast Tucker County in the summer of 1893. This information was apparently obtained from Porter (1903: 270).

Brooks (1910: 22) commented that "this big cat once roamed through all the forests of West Virginia and fed on deer and smaller mammals." In 1910 it was believed a "few still exist in our more secluded forests".

Wisconsin.—Lapham (1853: 339) listed the animal as occurring in northern Wisconsin in 1853.

Benjamin Bones, of Racine, shot one on the headwaters of Black River, December, 1863. (Hollister, Ned. 1908: 141; see also Trans. Wisc. Acad. Sci., Arts, and Letters 5: 256, 1882.)

A statement in the Wisconsin Conservation Bulletin for October, 1939, is: "It may be that one of these animals still remains in the State, for quite recently Conservation Warden Louis Oshesky of Oneida County had four reports on one being seen in his territory". . . . "two" were "reported as being seen . . . in Marinette County on January 2, 1909." The most recent record of one being killed in the State is of one reported by Daniel Farnham, of Manly, Douglas County, to have been taken in that county in 1908. (Cory, Charles B. 1912: 280.) According to A. W. Schorger (1938: 252) the only preserved specimen of Wisconsin cougar is in Lawrence College Museum at Appleton. The animal was killed by Samuel P. Hart in December, 1857, near Appleton. Other records reported are for Clark, Vernon, Fond du Lac, Calumet, Waushara, and Monroe counties. (Scott, W. E. 1939: 25.)

Wyoming.—In Wyoming the puma's occurrence is confined mainly to the western portion, where the Rocky Mountains form ideal habitat—a continuation of its range from central-western

Colorado, and eastern Idaho. Nineteen of these predators have
been removed from the stock and game ranges of the State during
25 years of cooperative state-federal predator control campaigns.
Yellowstone National Park, where for years past it has been given
full protection, probably contains the largest concentration of puma
at the present time, but up to the year 1930 Bailey (129-131) reported the animal "few and far between" even there.

Canada. — Within historical times the puma occurred from
Quebec to British Columbia, including Vancouver Island, although
no authentic records for Manitoba have been found. It was chiefly
confined to the southern portions of the Canadian provinces, with
the exception of British Columbia and Alberta, where it ranged
throughout the Rocky Mountains. Here it reaches its most northerly habitat, as previously noted, in the Peace River and Cassiar
Districts of British Columbia. It is apparently extinct at the present
time in all of the territory eastward from the province of Saskatchewan. Records of its former distribution in Canada include the
following:

In 1921 Hewitt (195) gave the range of the Canadian puma
from the "Rocky Mountains and westward to Vancouver Island, on
which it appears to be most common." Also at the turn of the century Fountain (1902: 74) recorded that he had "found the remains
of pumas in superficial deposits within a few miles of the shores of
Hudson's Bay . . . ."

Ingersoll (1906: 90) mentions its northern range into Canada as
extending "near Hudson's Bay."

Alberta.—While on an expedition to the Mount Robson and
Yellowhead Pass areas during the summer of 1912, via Edmonton,
Alberta, pumas were recorded by me in the vicinity of Crows Nest
and northward along the Rocky Mountains to the region of Banff.

In the Banff National Park area numbers of the animals have
occurred for an indefinite period, the area providing ideal conditions.
A remarkable observation of its attack on mountain goats made there
in the summer of 1933 is mentioned later. Its presence farther
northward along the mountains into Jasper National Park was not
personally determined at the time mentioned.

Preble (1908: 209) mentions records of this carnivore "near the
junction of Bow and Cascade Rivers," and also "near the Kananaskio
River in the mountains southwest of Calgary."

According to the compilation of North American big game records it is from this province that a puma of the greatest length has to date been reported; viz., of a male, killed by William A. Schutte, in 1935, which measured 112 inches from the tip of the nose to the end of the tail. This exceeds the previous record for a puma taken by the late Theodore Roosevelt near Meeker, Colorado, during 1901, which measured 96 inches. (Boone & Crockett Club. 1939: 527).

British Columbia.—The animal is found from the southwestern coast eastward to the Rocky Mountains, and as far north as approximately the 58th Parallel, in the vicinity of the Big Muddy in the Cassiar District.

Perry (1890: 412) stated that anyone who was desirous of hunting the animal in earlier days could proceed to any of the mountain districts of British Columbia, and soon have his wishes fulfilled.

In the early 1880's Hughes (1883: 103) says: "Vancouver Island and the islands adjacent thereto fairly abound with panthers, so that in many places on them sheep farming is entirely impossible. One family of persons, consisting of father and four sons, all of hunting proclivities, living within fourteen miles of Victoria . . . claim to have killed nearly 300 panthers since their arrival in the country to take charge of the sheep interests of the Puget Sound Agriculture Company, an off-shoot of the Hudson's Bay Company." The animal continues in abundance there to this day and has long had a bounty on its head, at times as high as $50.00.

In 1910 the puma was reported as "extremely plentiful on Vancouver Island, and some parts of the mainland, notably so in the Okanagan and Boundary District." (British Columbia. 1910: 27.)

In 1943 Carl (1944: 39) reports the puma as "occasionally present in the Forbidden Plateau area, fresh tracks being reported on Mt. Elma on the trail below Paradise Meadows."

According to Cowan (1939: 76) it "rarely enters the [Peace River] district, but in March, 1937, Mr. Ted Strand of Little Prairie shot a large female. Seton (1926: 52) cites Provincial Constable A. Forfar of Hudson Hope as having a skin taken November, 1921, near the junction of Cypress Creek with the Halfway River. This seems to be the northernmost record for North America."

Writing in 1932 Sheldon (201) states, ". . . There are three records of mountain lions having been killed by Indians in the Graham River Valley, north of the Peace River, in the last decade; the authenticity of these reports was confirmed by all the natives. James Beattie, a trustworthy Englishman, who lives at the mouth of Aylard Creek on the Peace River, says that within the last few years he has found tracks of three lions in the snow of early spring on the bluffs above his ranch."

Hewitt (1921: 195) says of it, "that the decrease in deer and sheep in the Lillooet region of British Columbia, which formerly abounded in such game, has been largely due to the depredations of cougars, which are increasing in that region, although a steady decrease in cougars in British Columbia as a whole is reported."

It is believed, however, that the animal will long be part of the fauna of British Columbia.

Manitoba.—No records of the puma have been found for this province. However, it is not unlikely with the abundance of deer there, and the fact that the animal occurred in the State of North Dakota in earlier days, that this predator ranged in at least the southern parts of Manitoba. Seton (1929: 50) is of the opinion that Tiger Hills in the southern part of the province were named for this animal.

New Brunswick.—The only record we have been able to find of the puma in this part of Canada is that given by Adams. His information was derived from Dr. Robb, at the time professor of natural history in the Provincial Museum, who mentioned an attack by a puma on a man "near the capital of the province in 1841."

As the animal occurred in Maine, and as New Brunswick harbored an abundance of its favorite food—deer—the puma may have ranged into the province from the southward in earlier days.

Ontario.—Nash (1908: 96) records that the puma is "now extinct in this province, where it never was very abundant. There are many old records of its capture along our southern border in the early settlement days, but its range does not appear to have extended very far north of our southern boundary."

However, Doel had earlier (1894: 23) stated, "It would . . . appear that the Panther has been known by the early settlers as a pretty well known resident over a large portion of the Province."

Orr (1909: 840) says of the animals in early day Ontario that they ". . . were the most persistent and relentless foes against which the new settlers had to contend. A pig, or a sheep, and occasionally

a large animal, easily fell a prey to one of them." He likewise recounts a puma attack on a young ranch wife "a little south and east
of Fingal," in southwestern Ontario.

Orr likewise mentions (1908: 266) the occurrence of the puma
about 1848 in the vicinity of Lambeth. And again the animal is
reported by him (1909: 260) in the vicinity of Tillsonburg, in the
township of Middleton. Finally he records (1911: 1442-1444) the
puma in Ontario about the year 1831, in the Wentworth County
area, bordering the western end of Lake Ontario.

Quebec.—The panther was formerly common in parts of Quebec
south of the St. Lawrence River.

From a reprint of a newspaper account that was published
(Anon. 1931: 37) at Picton [Ontario] for April 15, 1836, it appears
that a puma was killed at that time about 25 miles southwest of
Montreal.

In 1887 Lett (127, 129) was of the opinion that the puma
"abounded at one time in the Valley of the Ottawa in considerable
numbers." Also, that about 1777, 'the panther was found in every
part of Ontario and Quebec."

The last Quebec records (Seton, Ernest Thompson. 1929: 46-
47) are of one killed near Sherbrooke about 1840, and another near
Sorel on October 3, 1863. Apparently the latter specimen is that
mentioned as killed "near St. Francis, on the St. Lawrence River,
October 3, 1863." (Dionne, C. E. 1902: 274-281.) A skin from
Quebec is recorded by A. Leith Adams (1873: 59).

Saskatchewan.—Distribution records for this province are extremely rare. The puma undoubtedly occurred in earlier times in
the western part of Saskatchewan, particularly along timbered water
courses, comparable to those found in the Dakotas, Nebraska, and
Kansas, where the animal was known to occur in fair numbers.

A recent report concerns a puma killed on August 18, 1939, in
the electoral district of Kindersley, in west-central Saskatchewan.
The animal was taken on a farm south of the small town of Kindersley, about 50 miles east of the Alberta border, and 170 miles
north of Montana. (Clarke, C. H. D. 1942: 45.) This locality is
somewhat east of the Cypress Hills in the electoral district of Maple
Creek, where, according to Anderson (1937: 42) the animal has
persisted "until comparatively recent times," but "does not stray far
from the shelter of the mountains."

MIDDLE AMERICA

Throughout all of the Middle American countries the animal is found in suitable habitat at elevations from 5,000 to 9,000 feet, as well as in tropical forests down to sea level.

Costa Rica.—According to Alfaro (1897: 17) it ranges everywhere from the lowlands on both coasts up to altitudes of 8,000 and 9,000 feet in the mountains.

Guatemala. — Guatemala harbors the smallest race of pumas (*Felis concolor mayensis*), the type locality for which is La Libertad, Department of Peten.

Murie (1935: 22) in 1925 reported the animal rather common in the area north of Lake Peten, in northern Guatemala.

Honduras and Nicaragua.—As previously noted, it was along the Honduras-Nicaragua coasts that the puma was first recorded, and throughout the four centuries that have elapsed since the writings of Columbus both of these Central American countries have this animal within their borders.

Nicholas (1901: 384), in the account of his experiences in tropical America, at the turn of the century, mentions an abundance of pumas in the Honduran jungle.

Similarly Moe (1904: 19), listing the puma among other carnivora, along with the jaguar, ocelot, and coyote, speaks of the animal as "not uncommon."

In British Honduras, Murie (1935: 22) records the purchasing of two skins at El Cayo.

Mexico.—The puma is found in favorable habitat everywhere in this republic from sea level to timberline. Consequently it occurs in all of the Mexican States in more or less abundance. It was very well known to the Aztecs and other Indian tribes. Unusual abundance of this mammal was noted by the writer and associates during the early fall of 1937 throughout the Carmen Mountains in northern Coahuila.

Observations made along the international boundary, particularly in Sonora and Chihuahua, over the past 25 years, show that the puma commonly crosses into and at times returns from much of the mountainous area of southern Arizona and New Mexico. This infiltration was likewise noted by the naturalists on the Mexican-United States boundary survey more than a half century ago.

The animal will long persist in all of Mexico; nowhere does it appear to be diminishing in any appreciable numbers.

Panama. — Hill (1860: 140), an early traveler across the Isthmus, mentions this predator's occurrence along the banks of the Chagres River.

The Central American puma, known to the natives as "leon," was found by Goldman (1920: 169) to occur "here and there throughout Panama, but is rarely seen. On the stock ranges of the savanna region near the Pacific coast horses and calves are said to be attacked and killed by pumas, but such incidents are apparently of rare occurrence."

Carpenter (1935: 171) mentions it as occurring along the La Vaca River in the dense forests toward the foothills. It was in this region in the "sparsely settled Coto Region, which lies on the border of Panama and Costa Rica," that Carpenter found evidence of its occurrence.

Aldrich and Bole (1937: 160) report the puma as scarce on the Azuero Peninsula, and when found "was most apt to be seen in the wake of peccary droves."

Salvador.—Of this Central American republic, the least in area of all the American republics, Standley (1922: 326) wrote, "In a country so thickly settled most of the larger mammals have long since disappeared, and in Salvador there is no danger from the savage beasts that one popularly supposed to infest tropical lands. Jaguars and pumas, I believe, still are found in remote regions."

South America

The puma ranged practically the entire continent, though at the turn of the century it was apparent that it was becoming exceedingly scarce in some areas. As in North America the puma is being eliminated in areas devoted to the grazing of livestock.

With little or no protection ever afforded it, hunted, trapped, and killed at every available opportunity, and much disliked by the stock interests because of its depredations, the puma nevertheless will continue to hold its own indefinitely in the vast unbroken tropical forests of the larger river valleys, and along the slopes of the Andes.

Amazon River.—Bates (1875: 91-92), from observations made in the course of his long stay in the Amazon River country, concludes that "The puma is not a common animal in the Amazon forests. I did not see altogether more than a dozen skins in the possession of the natives."

Argentina and Patagonia.—Near the close of the last century the puma occurred in Patagonia in large numbers. Allen (1905: 173), quoting Prichard, says, "The distribution of this animal extends over the entire country. It is to be found in the Cordillera as on the pampas. . . . The number of pumas in Patagonia is very great, more so than any zoologist has yet given an idea of. During one winter two pioneers killed seventy-three near Lake Argentino. Near San Julian immense numbers are yearly destroyed, but lately, owing to the advent of settlers, they are becoming less numerous. At Bahia Camerones, on the farm of Mr. Green Shields, fourteen pumas were killed during the winter of 1900."

Prichard (1902: 251) recounts the presence of the animal throughout the entire distance he covered in the course of his long and memorable expedition through Patagonia.

Cunningham (1871: 106) records it in the Magellan Straits area, where, among other mammal specimens obtained, was that of a complete puma skeleton on the beach near Direction Hills, in extreme southeastern Patagonia.

Today Patagonia probably contains more pumas than are to be found in any other part of South America.

Bolivia.—The puma is known throughout the Andes of this republic. The type locality of *Felis concolor osgoodi* is at Buena Vista, in the Department of Santa Cruz.

Hartwig (1873: 462-463) mentions its occurrence in the Andean section of Bolivia, where often "impelled by hunger the Puma, or American lion, ascends even to the borders of eternal snow in quest of the vicuña and the deer."

Brazil.—While in southern Brazil during part of the years 1925, 1926, and 1928, Miller (1930: 15) found the puma "fairly common." However, "judging from the number of skins brought in for sale at Descalvados they" did "not equal the jaguar by one to two. Their preference in habitat" seemed "to be for the more open and drier portions, particularly in the vicinity of the low, sandy, openly wooded ridges which are of frequent occurence in some parts."

In the course of his explorations up the Purus River in northwestern Brazil, Fountain (1902: 85) after ascending it "some hundred miles . . . came to an extensive savanna. . . . Without exaggeration the country swarmed with game. There were thousands of small deer appearing to be hornless, and not assembled in close herds . . . . Jaguars and pumas were very abundant . . . ."

British Guiana.—Im Thurn (1883: 111), an early traveler and explorer in the British Crown Colony, found the cats, including the puma, more or less common throughout this territory, though seldom seen by man. He noted, "It is hardly possible to find an Indian house in which there are not teeth or portions of the skin of one of these species; . . . ."

Chile.—The puma has long been known to occur in this Pacific coast republic, where Molina (1782: 295-300) was one of the first to record it. Known locally as "pagi" from its earliest occurrence, it has been noted for its depredations on domestic animals, especially horses.

During the early 1820's Schmidtmeyer (1824: 82-84) mentions the necessity of keeping hunters and dogs on large estates in the Chilean Andes, where puma depredations on livestock were severe during the summer grazing period. As livestock was moved from one grazing pasture to another the hunters and their dogs went with the livestock, having as abodes small huts from which they hunted the puma as a curb to its depredations. He records also that puma meat was held in high estimation as a food by the hunters and herdsmen. In the winter season, when the herds returned to lower elevations, he was of the opinion that pumas crossed the Andes again between Chile and Peru, retiring into the midland forests.

Gay, a Chilean (1827: 65-68), writing during the same period as Schmidtmeyer, makes similar comment about the animal, stating, "On account of [its] destructiveness on estates the owners have been obliged to carry on regular campaigns for [its] destruction, placing a price on [its head]; also the cowboys persistently follow up any that have been discovered in the vicinity."

Darwin in 1833 (269) reported it as not uncommon, and stated that in central Chile he had noted its "footsteps in the Cordillera" . . . "at an elevation of 10,000 feet."

Colombia.—Bangs (1900: 99) records a female from Santa Marta, and a male from Dibulla, collected in the late 1890's.

Ecuador.—As in Peru, the puma is of olden record. Among the early Indian tribes conquered by the Inca rulers the puma was among the animals that were worshiped. (Garcilasso, De La Vega. 1869. II: 350.)

Lönnberg (1913: 4) mentions its occurrence on the "northwestern slope of Pichincha (the mountain on which Quito is situated)," where it occurs up to a height of 12,000 feet. Here too it is known to kill pigs, mules, and donkeys. He likewise records (1921: 9-11) a specimen collected near Gualea, northwest of Quito, at an elevation of 4,500 feet on the lower slope of the Andes.

Paraguay.—Apparently the puma is now extinct in this South American republic. Azara (1802: I: 120), at the beginning of the 19th century, reported the animal as then exceedingly rare, being much easier to kill than the jaguar and "for that reason the Paraguayans had almost exterminated it in that country."

Peru.—Historical records indicate that the puma has long been a well-known part of the Peruvian fauna. As depicted on ancient Peruvian pottery, or, by carvings on stone, and, as imaged in gold or silver offerings to the Sun, the puma was prominent. This was noted by the Chroniclers, who have given us so much information on the customs, economics, and governmental aspects of early Peru. These refer not only to the part played by the puma during the Incaic rule in this republic, but also during the civilizations antedating by many centuries that of the Inca domination.

The word "puma," as noted previously, comes from the early Peruvian Indians. Strong states, "Both the puma and jaguar figure predominantly in the ancient Peruvian arts of all known periods. The puma is clearly depicted in Inca times, and is also characteristic of the earliest known cultures of the Peruvian highland and coast. Decorated pots from the ancient shell heaps of Ancon, and carved stone designs from the ruins at Chavin de Huantar clearly depict the puma. The earliest of these cultures goes back at least to the time of Christ. The puma was evidently the animal counterpart of the great cat-god of the Andes. This god was worshiped in one form or another from Central America all the way down to Chile, and the manifestations of this deity are particularly common in Peru during all periods." (Strong, William Duncan, Director, Ethnogeographic Board, to Stanley P. Young, September 15, 1942. Letter in files of U. S. Fish and Wildlife Service.)

It was one of the animals maintained in the dungeons of some of the Inca rulers for use in the punishment of treason and disobedience among the Inca people.   These dungeons were in many respects not unlike the amphitheaters of the Romans, where the lion was used to dispose of early Christian converts.   One of these dungeons, as described by Means (1931: 348), which existed near the Inca capital of Cuzco, formerly held besides the puma, the jaguar and the bear. It contained blind doors and passages, the latter floored with sharp flint points, where there were released toads, vipers, and vermin. Into such a hades the human victim was forced, there to stay until dead.

We are informed by Garcilasso (1869: II: 429) of the reverence shown the puma and the jaguar in idol worship by the Indian tribes which were conquered and brought under the domination of Incaic civilization.

One of the 12 wards making up the Inca capital of Cuzco was named "Puma curcu." Literally the word means "lion beam," for it was here that pumas, which were presented to the Incas from time to time, were tied to beams and apparently kept until tamed.   Another ward was known as "Puma chupa," or "lion's tail." Some authorities have attributed this name to the fact that the ward tapered off like a tail of the puma between two water courses.

Tschudi (1849: 294), while traveling in Peru between 1838 and 1842, says of the animal in this republic, "it roams through the upper regions of the forest where he has almost undisputed hunting ground." He found it a severe depredator on domestic stock.   Mentioning it among the fauna inhabiting the warmer valleys, he adds (221) "When driven by hunger this animal ventures into the loftiest Puna regions, even to the boundary of eternal snow."

Thomas (1928: 259) lists a female puma of very red color taken in extreme western Peru near Cerro Azul.

Osgood (1914: 175), in the course of mammal field work during 1912, was informed that this creature, "in the mountains of western Peru . . . was fairly common and, as elsewhere, strongly addicted to the habit of preying on livestock."

Thus the history of the puma is long in Peru.   During the height of the Inca Empire, which extended from northern Ecuador south to the Maule River in Chile and eastward into the valleys of the Andes, but not to the Amazon country proper, we accordingly find the animal once distributed over a vast area of western South America, and furthermore its association with the Inca people shows that it must have been very abundant. From this area, therefore, we probably have the earliest American record of its contact with man.

Uruguay.—During the early 1890's Aplin (1894: 298) reports the puma "extinct in many parts of the country, but in the Monte, along the Uruguay River, it is still found." He adds, "An estancio living at Cordova in Argentina [told him] he [had] seen both pumas and jaguars coming down the big rivers on tree trunks."

Figueira (1894: 207-208) recorded in the 1890's that the puma was limited to the Departments of the north and east, and was disappearing from Uruguay.

Venezuela.—Robinson and Lyon (1901: 162), in the course of a six-week collecting trip in the vicinity of La Guaira, in northern Venezuela, at the turn of the century, found the creature "not rare," and add that "many hides were seen in the market at Caracas," of which La Guaira is the seaport town. They also report it as very "destructive to goats, calves, and pigs."

André (1904: 271) found the puma on the upper reaches of the Caura River, where he records a savage attack by one on the dogs of his exploring party—an attack that drove the dogs back to one of the boats and in the course of which it came close enough to be hit over the head with a paddle in the hands of one of the natives.

Osgood (1912: 60) says of the animal in western Venezuela, "cougars are not uncommon in certain districts near Maracaibo." Here, while collecting in the winter of 1911, he learned that the animal was known by the name of "Leon" or "Leon bayo," and "one hunter living on the shore of the lake and almost directly opposite Maracaibo is reputed to have killed twenty to thirty during the last fifteen years."

Throughout Venezuela, where the animal occurs, it is hunted mainly by dogs, as in the other parts of its American range.

III

HABITS AND CHARACTERISTICS

THE PUMA personifies grace in its movements and is exceedingly clean. Like the common house cat, it licks its hair, producing a sleek sheen. Viewing a fully developed puma, particularly the male, one readily understands its strength and endurance. Its ability to strike a powerful blow with its fore paws comes from the strong muscular development of the shoulders. The large paws have long, retractile claws with terrific ripping power. Study of its cranial structure reveals a well-set and heavy-boned jaw formed so that it does not have any backward or forward motion. This naturally enables the puma to absorb all necessary shock involved in its attacks. By striking, slashing, and biting this animal is able to kill prey even larger than itself. While the puma can not catch swift prey by running, its fine muscular coordination, cushioned feet, and ability to conceal itself enable it to make a stealthy approach. Then comes the pounce or spring and the striking in of the claws which are so constructed that the harder the victim tries to disengage itself the more firmly they hold. At times the puma, like the house cat, will manicure and sharpen its claws by standing on its hind feet and rapidly dragging the claws of the front feet with a downward motion against a stationary object, as a boulder, tree-trunk, or stump. This act may also bring satisfaction from stretching.

The puma is rarely seen by man. Even where it occurs in goodly numbers it is so elusive that the student must have good luck to observe it. Realizing this, more than a century ago, Lewis and Clark stated, the puma "is very seldom found, and when found, so wary it is difficult to reach him with a musket." (Allen, Paul. 1814: 178.)

E. W. Nelson and E. A. Goldman, in the course of their thousands of miles of travel through Mexico, often camped in the main habitat of the animal but seldom saw it. Thomas Belt (1928) fails to mention it in the account of his extensive wanderings in the wilds of Nicaragua, where he came into contact with practically all of the other felines inhabiting that country.

Of all the American cats the puma is exceeded in weight only by the jaguar. Although second in size to that animal, it is similar in strength. As a result of his experience in hunting these two big cats with dogs the writer holds that the jaguar is more fleet of foot, does not become easily winded, has greater endurance in a sustained run; hence it does not tree so readily as does the puma when closely pressed.

Size and Weight

Fourteen pumas killed by Theodore Roosevelt (1901: 435) and party during a hunting excursion in the Rio Blanco County section of northwestern Colorado, in January and February, 1901, were of the following measurements and weights:

Table 2. Size and weight of 14 pumas killed by Theodore Roosevelt in Colorado in 1901

Sex	Length	Weight (lbs.)
Female (yg.)	4 ft., 11 in.	47
,, ,,	4 ,, , 11½ in.	51
,,	6 ,, , 0 in.	80
,,	6 ,, , 4 ,,	102
,,	6 ,, , 5 ,,	105
,,	6 ,, , 5 ,,	107
,,	6 ,, , 9 ,,	108
,,	6 ,, , 7 ,,	118
,,	6 ,, , 7 ,,	120
,,	6 ,, , 9 ,,	124
,,	7 ,, , 0 ,,	133
Male	7 ,, , 6 ,,	160
,,	7 ,, , 8 ,,	164
,,	8 ,, , 0 ,,	227*

*Plate 6.

Musgrave (1926: 285) states, "The heaviest lion taken in this State [Arizona] weighed 276 pounds." This maximum published weight for a puma (*Felis concolor azteca*) is nearly 50 pounds greater than for *Felis concolor hippolestes*, as weighed by Theodore Roosevelt. This Arizona puma was killed near Hillside, Arizona, in March, 1917, by the late government predatory animal hunter, J. R. Patterson. The 276 pounds given as the weight of this creature was ascertained "after the intestines had been removed . . . . He measured 8 ft., 7¾ in., from the tip of his nose to the tip of his tail . . . ." (Seton, Ernest Thompson. 1929: 39.)

Three female pumas killed during December, 1941, in the Bloody Basin, Arizona, measured:

1. Length, 67 inches; tail, 26 inches; shoulder height, 25½ inches; age, 2 years.

2. Length, 73½ inches; tail, 26 inches; shoulder height, 25½ inches; age, 3½ years.

3. Length, 64 inches; tail, 24 inches; shoulder height, 24½ inches; age, 20 months.

Data for other Arizona pumas trapped during 1941 and 1942 are listed in Table 3.

Of 22 pumas killed by Frank Mayse, of Colorado Springs, Colorado, between 1926 and 1929, on the east side of the Pike National Forest, the largest, a male, weighed 164 pounds dressed. This weight was taken 4 days after death. It was an old and well-matured animal. A female killed during this period and believed to be well advanced in years weighed 80 pounds.

Bryon Denton of La Veta, Colorado, who has hunted pumas from La Veta to Monument Lake in the Sangre de Cristo Mountains, taking 24 between the years 1934 and 1941, states that the largest, a male, weighed 200 pounds. It was killed southwest of Monument Lake on Abbit Creek in Las Animas County, 35 miles north of the New Mexican boundary. He found that the animals in this section weighed on an average of between 150 and 175 pounds, the males being the heaviest.

A male puma (Plate 8) killed by John W. Crook, of Monte Vista, Colorado, who has long been in the employ of the Fish and Wildlife Service, but recently retired, weighed 217 pounds after the offal had been removed, and three days after death. It was taken from the San Isabel National Forest on Rio Alto Creek on January

15, 1927, and is the largest puma on record for the State, so far as the Fish and Wildlife Service records go.

Comparable was a male (Plate 9) killed by the late George M. Trickel, of the Fish and Wildlife Service, in the Horsefly section, west of Montrose, Colorado, on May 19, 1921, which weighed 207 pounds and measured 7 ft., 9 in.

A large male puma killed in the Meeker section of Colorado at the turn of the century by A. G. Wallihan (1901: 55-56) and party gave the following measurements: Length, 7 ft., 5 in.; shoulder height, 31 in.; girth back of forelegs, 33 in.; girth at center of body, 36 in., and at the flanks 25 inches. The forehead measured 6 inches between the ears; the girth of the neck was 18 inches; the fore leg, 18 inches around; and the tail formed 1/3 of the total length.

Table 3. Size and weight of pumas trapped in Arizona during 1941 and 1942

Sex	Age (years)	Weight (lbs.)	Total length (inches)	Tail length (inches)	Shoulder height (inches)
Male	4	140	84	30	27½
"	3	122	84	29	27
Female	2	73	78	29	24½
Male	5	143	85	34	27
"	5	125	83	38	28
Female	10	70	67½	26	26
Male	10	116	76	36	31
Female	4	76	72	27	23
Male	5	103	76	29	27
"	4	106	73	29	27
"	8/12	46	50	24	22
"	10/12	65	60	22	21
"	5	145	80	27	28
"	2	81	73	28	28
Female	4	76	72	27	23
Male	5	103	76	29	27
Female	4	77	73	29	30
Male	5	145	80	27	28
Female	2	69	72	27	26
"	2	70	74	28	28
"*	3	70	73	25	24
Male	2	80	76	28½	29
"	2	80	76	28	----
"	1	75	67	27	22

*Gave evidence of rearing young sometime during 1941; killed on November 5, 1941.

Other Colorado weights, and in some instances lengths, are:

Male: Length, 8 ft., 1 in.; weight, 150 lbs.; estimated age, 5 years; near La Veta, Colorado.

Male: Length, 8 ft., weight, 150 lbs.; near Fruita, Colorado.

Female: Length, 7 ft.; 15½ miles northwest of Gardner, Colorado.

Male: Length, 7 ft.; weight, 175 lbs.; Rifle Creek, west of New Castle, Colorado; December 27, 1937.

Male: Length, 8 ft., 8 in.; Dolores River Canyon, San Miguel County, southwestern Colorado; January 27, 1938.

Male: Length, 8 ft.; weight, 165 lbs.; Jug Gulch, 12 miles northwest of Loveland, Colorado; February 16, 1938.

Male: Length, 7 ft., 1 in.; weight, 135 lbs.; Texas Creek, Fremont County, central Colorado.

Male: Length, 9 ft., 6 in.; near Atchee, Garfield County, Colorado; April 12, 1938.

Male: Length, 7 ft.; weight, 160 lbs.; south of Basalt, Colorado; February 27, 1937.

Male: Length, 8 ft., 10 in.; near Redvale, Colorado; January 24, 1925.

Hamilton (1941: 689) records the weight of a puma killed near Bonita Springs, in Lee County, Florida, on October 10, 1939, as "145 pounds after considerable loss of blood," but does not give its sex. Another killed near Estero, in this State, on November 20, 1939, sex not given, "weighed just slightly less than 200 pounds."

C. R. Landon, of the Fish and Wildlife Service, reported under date of November 24, 1941, the killing of two pumas in the Eagle Mountains, Hudspeth County, Texas. A female, 2 years old, weighing 80 pounds, measured in total length 5 ft., 10 in.; tail length, 27½ in.; hind foot, 3½ in.; ear, 3 in.; height at shoulder, 24 in.; and a male, 3 years old, weighed 110 pounds and measured in total length, 7 ft.; tail length, 34½ in.; hind foot, 5 in.; ear, 4¼ in.; and height at shoulder, 28 inches.

R. Scott Zimmerman, of the Fish and Wildlife Service, reported on the killing of two of these animals in Utah. One of these, a male, killed near Kanosh, 3 years old, weighed 204 pounds. The other, a female, killed on the Minidoka Forest, 4 years old, weighed 175 pounds. No measurements are available but these two pumas are the largest in weight of any taken in this State.

An early record for Vermont is given by Thompson (1853: 38), who stated, "One of the largest taken in this State to my knowledge was killed in Rosbury, in December, 1821. It measured 7 feet from the nose to the extremity of the tail, and weighed 118 pounds."

According to Taylor and Shaw (1927: 58), James McCullough, of Ashford, Washington, "killed a cougar on Tum Tum Mountain in March 1895. It was a male, estimated to weigh 175 pounds, and measuring 9 feet from nose to end of tail."

Despite its size and weight the puma sometimes squeezes through surprisingly small openings. An adult female puma driven by dogs into a small cave near the summit of the Patagonia Mountains of southern Arizona had an apparent body diameter of nearly 14 inches. Yet she passed through an opening measuring nearly 6 inches less than her girth.

Coloration

There is a wide range of coloration among the various races of *Felis concolor*. Probably "red" or "brown" are the most common colors. The ears and tip of the tail are generally dark, while the belly as well as the rump extending to the first hind leg joints are white.

When the young are born they have rows of small irregular black spots which disappear entirely as they mature. Darwin inferred (1874: 528) that if young pumas are marked with "feeble stripes or rows of spots" . . . "the progenitor . . . was a striped animal," . . . "the young have retained vestiges of the stripes like the kittens of black cats, which are not in the least striped when grown up."

The 14 pumas killed in northwestern Colorado by Theodore Roosevelt (1901: 435) and party, measurements of which have been given, "showed the widest variation, not only in size but in color . . . . Some were as slaty gray as deer when in the so-called 'blue,' others rufous, almost as bright as deer in the 'red' . . . . The color phase evidently has nothing to do with age, sex, season, or locality."

Two of the largest of the pumas taken on the hunt by the Roosevelt party, a male and a female, which were mates "were not of the same color, the female being reddish, while the male was slate-colored." (Ibid.: 554.) The so-called "blue" color has been observed also in adult male pumas killed in southern Santa Cruz County, Arizona, on the watershed divide between Lyle and Parker Canyons of the Huachuca Mountains-Canelo Hills locality.

Felis concolor pearsoni, the South American puma with the most southerly range, varies as much in color as the animals mentioned by Roosevelt. Allen (1905: 177), quoting Hatcher, says, "frequently" Mr. Hatcher "saw and examined sets of from six to a dozen skins of these animals killed on the same farm and observed that in each instance there was every shade of color represented from very light brown or gray to dark tawny. This was true alike of individuals taken on the plains or along the mountains." Hatcher was of the opinion that "the color of the pelage" is "due very largely to the season, while at the same time depending somewhat on the age and sex of the individual."

In certain areas its color seems to vary with the seasons. As an example in the southwestern United States, particularly southern Arizona, during the summer months its color is not unlike that assumed by the Virginia white-tailed deer in the "red." This reddish cast becomes somewhat lighter during the late fall and winter months, when it tends more toward brown. It is supposed that the close similarity in color between the puma and the deer is a distinct aid to this predator in approaching the deer, its favorite prey.

Of his observations of the puma in Oregon and California, Newberry (1859: 36) says, "specimens [he] saw varied considerably in color, but otherwise there seemed to be no difference." One that he "attempted to shoot, on Pit River [California] was of a bright yellowish red, much like that of the summer coat of the Virginia deer; while a large and beautiful one, kept caged in San Francisco, was of a light mouse-color, scarcely tinged with red."

In some areas one color may predominate over another, as has been noted for Vancouver Island, B. C., where, according to John Fannin, brown is the common color, while the reddish coat is more rare. On the mainland of British Columbia the color prevalences appear to be the reverse of those on Vancouver Island.

Schomburgk said of those noted in British Guiana that "they are reddish-brown which lightens on the outside limbs, and assumes a white colour on the belly. Of a similar colour is the breast, and the reddish-brown, which is the prevailing colour of the body, is of a lighter tint at the muzzle and chin . . . the tail . . . is black on the tips." (Schomburgk, Sir Robert H., 1840: 325.)

Allen (1905: 173), quoting Brown, records the counting of "six lions one day while riding in the foothills of the Andes, in February, all of a decided ferruginous buff color. The gray species resembles our northern *Felis concolor* in pelage, and is most often met along the coast." In quoting Prichard, Allen also says of the young of *Felis concolor pearsoni* that this subspecies "is the silver-gray variety of puma most commonly met with in Patagonia."

The difficulty experienced by anyone attempting to determine from which locality a puma may have come when judging solely by the coloration of its skin is aptly put by Fountain (1902: 77), who says: "An American hunter whom I knew professed to distinguish a difference between North and South [American] specimens, but when put to the test he utterly failed to show the difference. Required to pick out the skin of a puma killed in Patagonia he selected one shot in New York . . . ; asked to point out a North American example he chose a skin from La Plata."

According to Cabrera and Yepes (1940: 169), as in other South American cats, specimens of the puma were found from time to time that are black or nearly black, and also more rarely still, cases of albinism are known.

Thomson (1896: 75-76) records the killing of a black puma in Brazil while hunting during 1843 in the Carandahy River section. "The whole head, back, and sides, and even the tail, were glossy black, while the throat, belly, and inner surfaces of the legs, were shaded off to a stone gray."

It is noteworthy that in North America these extreme white and black colorations apparently do not occur. There is no change in color due to moult as the loss of hair by pumas is so gradual as to be hardly noticeable. There seems to be no definite moulting period as in most of the other American carnivores.

Longevity

Other than records for individuals in confinement there is no definite information of the longevity of the puma. There is reason to believe, however, that the greatest age attained by this carnivore parallels that of wolves. Pumas known from the peculiarities of their tracks, such as missing toes or injured foot pads, have traveled certain ranges for known periods. These observations lead to the conclusion that an age of at least 18 years may be attained. A male puma dubbed by the stockmen of Santa Cruz County, Arizona, as "Old Cross Toes" was observed to use a travelway periodically for 10 years. When killed it was believed to have been at least 15 years old.

A female puma, killed during February 1942 in Granite Basin west of Prescott, Arizona, was estimated to be between 10 and 12 years old. The canine teeth were badly worn, and together with all of the other teeth, instead of having the usual lustrous, white color, were very yellow. As the animal weighed but 70 pounds, and had a total length of 67½ inches, the light weight had doubtless come about because of lessened predatory capacity due to its teeth.

Either the male or female puma will eventually wear down their teeth, which with advancing age may become very short. In this state they are often stained like a long-smoked meerschaum pipe. Teeth so worn make it difficult for the animal to kill its prey. In these respects they resemble an old "gummer wolf."

Grey (1908: 776) records a male puma, known for 12 years in its habitat within the Buckskin Mountains in the Grand Canyon area of northern Arizona; hunters familiar with its track, among them the late Buffalo Jones, had dubbed this animal "Old Tom."

C. Emerson Brown (1925: 265) lists a puma of the Philadelphia Zoological Garden as living 15 years after its arrival there.

The authorities in the National Zoological Park, Washington, D. C., have furnished the data[1] in Table 4, with regard to longevity of pumas in confinement at that place.

This shows an average life span in confinement of approximately 7½ years for the 12 pumas listed. Two of these, however, died prematurely, the place of confinement being too draughty. Most zoological park officials believe that the puma stands confinement remarkably well, provided it is furnished a den that is sunny and free from draughts. Pumas make docile animals, and often tame to the point where their keepers pet them at will.

---

[1]Records omitted of specimens that were returned to owners, young born that died at an early age, or others that were in the Zoo only a short time.

Table 4. Longevity records of 12 pumas kept in captivity at National Zoological Park, Washington, D. C.

Born	Acquired			Died			Period of confinement	
							Years	Months
Spring of 1888	April	18,	1888	June	23,	1894	6	2
Year 1892	November	2,	1893	January	19,	1900	6	3
------------	January	28,	1896	July	5,	1904	8	5
------------	"	",	"	March	16,	1901	5	2
Year 1902	October	",	1902	October	9,	1908	5	11
" 1903	December	26,	1904	"	11,	1910	5	9
------------	June	19,	1905	August	23,	1909	4	2
About 1906	August	11,	1908	December	7,	1914	6	4
May 23, 1914	November	24,	1914	June	12,	1920	5	7
Year 1916	February	16,	1917	December	2,	"	3	10
One-third grown	May	12,	"	"	21,	1930	13	7
About 6 weeks old	April	21,	1921	"	27,	1938	17	8

Strength

According to Zadock Thompson (1853: 37), if "the victim be a large animal like a calf, sheep, or deer, they swing it upon their back, and dash off with great ease and celerity, into some retired place, where it is devoured at leisure. Some years ago one of these animals took a large calf out of a pen in Bennington [Vermont], where the fence was 4 feet high, and carried it off on his back. With this load he ascended a ledge of rocks, where one of the leaps was 15 feet in height."

Apparently a common resort also for the puma in moving its kill is to turn the victim over on its back. Then grabbing it by the brisket it drags it along the ground with its feet in the air.

Belknap (1902: 486) records a female puma taken near Valley, Washington, which ". . . lifted" a "quarter of beef clear of snow and carried it about 200 yards, though she sank to her belly in the snow at every step."

Evans (1922: 344-345) records the instance of a puma in the Davis Mountains area of Texas dragging a dead 600-pound heifer out of a narrow spring-water hole and some distance up the side of a mountain, where the animal could more safely feed on the carcass. Evans states that his father who "was over six feet, and was 175 pounds of muscle . . . could not move this heifer, but went on back to the house to get a team of horses, as he did not think he could pull her up out of the hole by the saddle horn with one horse." It was when he returned with the team, 24 hours later, that he discovered the removal of the heifer by the puma, which he later trailed with dogs and killed.

Frank Mayse, of Colorado Springs, states that a 45-pound colt was carried 3½ miles by a female puma to her young, in a den. This observation was made in 1928 on the Pike National Forest, 18 miles northwest of Colorado Springs, Colorado.

Perry (1890: 407-408) recounts an incident of a puma, after "killing a good-sized Indian pony and its colt," dragged them across a meadow and over a high fence into the adjoining woods. Stating "this seems almost incredible"; still "instances are on record, attested by indisputable evidence showing equally great feats of their strength."

Schomburgk relates that in British Guiana a puma killed a mule and then "dragged it across a trench to the opposite side, although the trench was not quite full of water and the puma had to drag it a few feet up hill, after it landed with its prey on the other side." (Schomburgk, Sir Robert H. 1840: 325.)

Gay (1827: 65-68), writing of early days in Chile, states, "Large horses that have been disemboweled have been found hidden . . . at great distances after having been dragged over a trail so steep and difficult as to seem impossible if it were not for unmistakable evidence presented; cattle as heavy have been found under similar circumstances, and at times dogs have been stretched out almost without a movement as the result of a single blow."

Stamina

Here may be appended a note on the vitality of the puma which suggests that at times it may be likened to that of the proverbial house cat with its so-called "nine lives." Baird (1859: 6), quoting Kennerly, gives an earlier day observation of the puma's stamina, when he records: "Near Los Nogales [S. W. Arizona] in the month of June, we pursued a female panther which we succeeded in wounding very severely, the bullet having shattered the hind leg several inches above the ankle. It uttered a kind of howling cry, and fled [as] rapidly as it could and disappeared. Six days afterwards we came very suddenly and unexpectedly upon this same animal lying partly concealed in a fissure among the rocks. Although we were within 10 feet of it when we saw it, with its mouth opened showing its teeth in a very threatening manner and uttering at the same time a deep growl, it did not offer to spring. As soon as it was killed we observed the old wound. The weather had been warm, and worms were busy in the place where the leg was broken, and the animal had become so emaciated as to lead us to believe it had remained in the spot during the entire six days, certainly without food, and perhaps without water."

Other evidence seems to indicate that the puma is rather easily killed. Thus, Allen (1905: 172-173), quoting Prichard, says of the puma in Patagonia, that it "can easily be galloped down, as it rarely runs more than 300 yards or a quarter of a mile when pursued on horseback. It invariably stands at bay with its back to a bush or a rock." Quoting Barnum Brown, it is also recorded that in this region, "The natives do not hesitate to ride onto a lion and kill it with a stirrup iron if a gun is not handy." Mr. Brown experienced this manner of killing a puma on a hunt in this part of South America, stating, however, I "preferred . . . to shoot mine."

Patience

The puma, when trapped, does not fight the trap to the extent that do the other larger predators, such as the wolf, coyote, or stock-killing bear. It remains, after capture, fairly quiet, thrashing around but little with a trap on its paw. Consequently such size traps as the ordinary coyote trap will often hold a puma indefinitely.

The patient attitude of this animal when in a trap was shown by the actions of a female captured in Lyle Canyon on the west side of the Huachuca Mountains in Arizona, during January, 1918. Trapped in a No. 4½ steel trap, which had been set at a cow carcass, this puma took trap, chain, and drag-hook to the base of a sycamore tree about 60 yards away from the cow carcass. At this point it had attempted to spring into the tree, but on its first jump the trap chain swung around the base of the tree, and then hooked itself over the drag-hook, securely fastening the animal. Here it remained overnight until near noon of the following day. The hunter in visiting the scene of this trap set rode horseback within 10 yards of the trapped puma without seeing it. As he approached the point where the trap had disappeared the marks of the drag-hook on the sandy soil caused him to back-track, whence he very shortly and unexpectedly rode to where the puma was lying prone on the ground with its head resting on the jaws of the trap near its trapped paw watching the hunter. At the moment the hunter spied it the puma reared on its hind legs, attempted to jump up the trunk of the tree, but was hindered by the shortness of the coiled trap chain and drag-hook at its base. None of the terrain had been previously torn up by any thrashing around of the animal. It had lain there for the time mentioned, apparently resigned to its fate, and making during the interim no attempt to dislodge, gnaw, or break the large trap, its chain, or the drag-hook, which had so securely held it to the base of the tree.

Swimming Ability

While the puma appears to have a natural aversion to water, numerous instances of its ability to swim are known. If necessary it swims and does exceptionally well. When crowded by a pack of hounds it has been known to swim good-sized streams or small lakes in attempting to elude its pursuers. In chasing its prey the puma also sometimes enters water, but generally speaking, as an animal with a coat that does not resist moisture, its tendency is always to keep dry.

Cooper (1855: 74) observed, "The old idea that no feline animal will voluntarily take to water, though now contradicted by many proofs, is still prevalent. In this animal we have an instance to the contrary. A steamboat descending the Columbia River met with one swimming across where the river was at least a mile and a half wide, and without difficulty the men succeeded in capturing it, by means of a noose thrown over it."

Hughes (1883: 103) mentions his knowledge of "two instances of panthers being killed while swimming the Fraser River [British Columbia] at a point where the same is nearly a mile wide." In discussing the animal's occurrence and depredations in this province, and particularly on Vancouver Island, he says, "panthers do not appear to be deterred from traveling from island to island when game gets scarce . . . ."

Holt (1932: 73) reports seeing a puma swimming in midstream in the neighborhood of the Paraguaza Hills, Brazil, in late February, 1930. At this point he states the Orinoco River "is at least a mile wide"; the animal "was swimming east to west, and when inter-

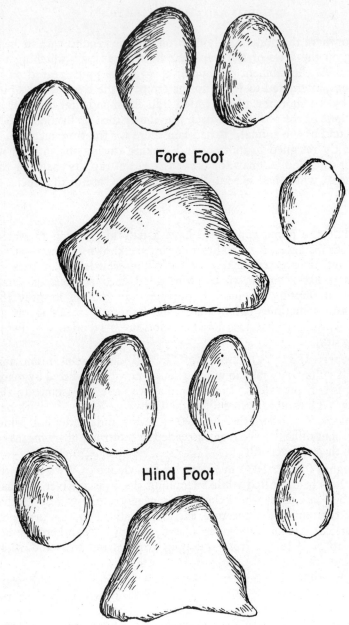

Figure 2. Diagram of average size puma track showing front and hind foot

Plate 4. Characteristic poses and facial expressions of the puma

By
M.A. JACOBSON © 1915

Plate 4. Characteristic poses and facial expressions of the puma (*Continued*)

Plate 4. Characteristic poses and facial expressions of the puma (*Concluded*)

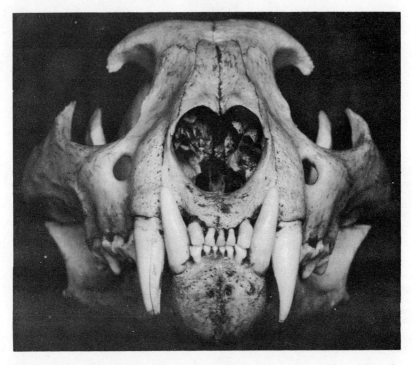

Plate 5. Frontal view of puma skull showing tooth arrangement which enables the animal to slash and tear its prey.

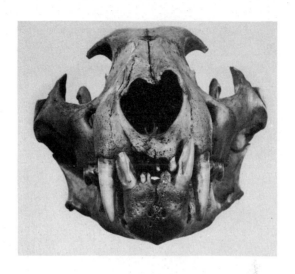

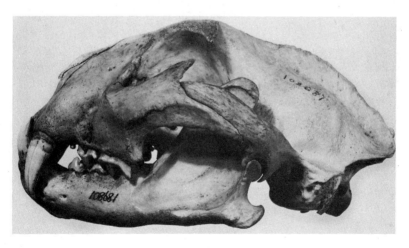

Plate 6. Skull of largest male puma (*Felis concolor hippolestes*) taken to date in the Americas. Killed by Theodore Roosevelt, February 14, 1901, near Meeker, Rio Blanco County, Colorado. Length, 9-5/6"; width, 6⅜"; length of entire animal (tip to tip), 96"; weight, 227 pounds.

67

Plate 7. A rare puma specimen (*F. c. browni*) killed in the Kofa Mountains, Yuma County, Arizona, 1944, by Government Hunter William Casto.

Plate 8. Puma that weighed 217 lbs., 3 days after death with offal removed. Killed on Rio Alto Creek, Eastern Saguache County, Colorado, January 15, 1927. Largest taken by any government hunter in Colorado. Its front foot track was 6¾" in width

Plate 9. 207-lb. puma taken May 19, 1921, Horsefly section, west of Montrose, Colorado. It measured 7 ft., 9 in. in length

Plate 10. Puma taken a number of years ago by Ramsey Patterson, who was then a government hunter. M. E. Musgrave, formerly of the Biological Survey, says this was one of the heaviest ever taken in Arizona. (See text, p. 53)

Plate 11. Poses of puma young constantly remind one of the family tabby. Note dark spots on pelt, which disappear as animal matures

Plate 12. Tracks of the puma in mud

71

Plate 13. "Scratch" of the puma made by it when covering its dung or urine. Carmen Mountains, Coahuila, Mexico

Plate 14. A. Typical travelway of puma in lower Rio Grande country, Texas. Scene in Webb County

Plate 14. B. Puma habitat—Sangre de Cristo Mts., Colorado, near foot of trail leading eastward to Mosca Pass, which General Fremont crossed on his ill-fated fourth expedition, 1849

Plate 15. Puma habitat looking east from San Luis Valley, Colorado, Mt. Blanca, Sangre de Cristo range, hidden in clouds

73

Plate 16. When forced to it the puma is a good climber. Scene shown here photographed as dogs were treeing an animal near Pagosa Springs, Colorado

74

Plate 17. The "stance" from which this puma jumped 13 feet following the boom of a flash-powder on a set-camera, using oil of catnip lure. Carmen Mountains, Coahuila, Mexico. (Young-Gregory Camera Expedition, September-October 1937— see text, pp. 94, 105, 169-170)

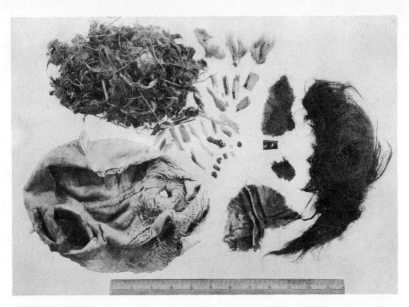

Plate 18. Stomach and contents of a puma containing human remains killed January 20, 1925, near Brewster, southwestern Okanogan County, Washington. At bottom is a scale indicating dimensions; at lower left the puma's stomach opened, showing size of pylorus; upper left, hair and bones of a colt or burro. At right are human remains, including compact mass of hair of the head; 2 pieces of blue denim; 1 piece of pocket material, showing seam; a discharged .38-caliber Smith & Wesson revolver cartridge bearing puma tooth marks (pocket-piece). The cloth, intimately tangled with human hair, and the cartridge shell were firmly imbedded in mass of human hair when the stomach was opened. (See text, p. 100)

Plate 19. The grave and tombstone of Philip Tanner, with crude engraving of a "panther." Tanner was killed by a puma a short distance from where burial took place. One of the earliest records in colonial America

Plate 20. Puma (*Felis concolor stanleyana*), Carmen Mountains, Coahuila, northeastern Mexico, October 1937. These pictures are the first ever to be taken by the puma itself, when it entered a camera-set area at night, lured by oil of catnip—the first time this bait has been used for this purpose. (Stanley P. Young—Tappan Gregory Camera Expedition, Coahuila, Mexico, September-October 1937)

Plate 21. Occasionally pumas captured young and held in captivity for a year or more make interesting pets

Plate 22. Young grow to maturity, remaining docile, and showing affection for their masters

Plate 23. When fully matured many pumas, though tamed and affectionate, may at times become so untrustworthy, fractious, and sullen as to cause their masters either to kill them or give them to some zoo.

Plate 24. Puma kittens relish and thrive on milk formulas fed to human babies. They immediately learn to take liquid food from a bottle nipple

cepted by the launch it became confused and tried to climb aboard . . . ."

From field observations made on the Purus River in Brazil, Fountain (1914: 190) noticed that "both jaguars and pumas take readily to water; . . . ."

Tracks

The tracks made by the padded feet of the adult puma consist of a well-defined wide and somewhat rounded and lobate triangular heel imprint with a somewhat pearlike outline to the right and left of the apex of which appear separately two oval toe impressions, and in front two more elongated impressions of the front toes. The four toes, which are lightly covered with hair, make a single confused imprint under certain ground conditions. A fifth toe on the inside of the leg, somewhat above the foot proper, never takes part in the track (Fig. 2; Plate 12).

Thus there are four well-defined impressions at the front, roughly in a semicircle, representing the digits, but no claw prints are in evidence unless the animal slips and extends them in regaining its balance. The front claws, though an inch in length, are encased in a sheath and seldom show in the track. When walking the hind foot is often placed in the imprint made by the fore paw, a trait which, with these padded feet, is conducive to silence in treading—a great advantage when stalking prey. Most of the front-foot tracks of adult pumas I have measured averaged 4 inches in length and 4½ inches in width. The large 217-pound male puma killed by Crook of the Fish and Wildlife Service in the Sangre de Cristo Mountains of Colorado made a front-foot track 6¾ inches wide. The full track of a puma often reminds one of the crown of some medieval king. The track of the hind foot is similar to that of the forefoot, but more narrow, and the heel-pad imprint is not so pronounced. The stride of the puma is fairly long (Plate 8).

Travel

The puma is a great traveler and generally has well-defined crossing points on its trails, where it passes from one watershed to another in its search for food. Many of these are in low saddles of watershed divides. At such crossings it is not uncommon to find "scratch hills" heaped up by the puma in covering its dung or urine.

(Plate 13.) As many as a dozen such hills have been noted in an area of 8 square feet. Sometimes old or fresh feces may also be noticed near them. The scratch hills may be from 3 to 6 inches in diameter and from 3 to 5 inches high.

The "travelway" may cross itself at irregular intervals, or it may be circular in shape. It covers many miles, and its permanency depends on the food supply. When this becomes scant the animal will adopt a new travelway. This may be a long distance away from former trails, to which, however, the animal may return, though this may not be for some time.

The length of time required for a puma to make the round of a travelway varies considerably. To illustrate, a trap set near a fresh scratch hill, May 5, 1942, on one Arizona range, trapped a puma on July 10, the first time it came directly over this part of the trail after the setting of the trap. Again, a trap set on May 4, 1942, took a puma on June 14, and another on July 10. These results, together with observations, indicated a circuit of the travelway every 15 to 18 days.

While primarily a dweller in rough mountainous terrain there are times when the North American puma, in shifting from one habitat to another, crosses wide expanses of plain and valley to reach new hilly and rocky terrain. In doing this it usually follows a water course, taking advantage of plant cover along the banks. (Plate 14 A.)

Illustrative of its open country travel is an item which appeared in The Survey for June 1940 (155), reading as follows: "A mountain lion was seen on the refuge [Sacramento Refuge, California] on May 27. It evidently was passing through on its way west to the mountains."

That the puma, though largely preferring high, rough terrain (Plate 14 B - 15), is not hindered by open and flat country in its travels from one section to another is recorded also by Woodhouse (1853: 47), who found the animal "in Texas, in the open prairie."

Price adds to the testimony in commenting on the puma's occurrence in Arizona, "The Mountain Lion is restricted to the brushy and timbered mountains of the entire region. Occasionally this beast travels across the valleys from one range to another. One was seen on the San Pedro River above the town of Fairbank [Cochise County] in February. It killed a colt in a pasture, and was tracked by dogs a dozen miles eastward into the Mule Mountains." (Allen, J. A. 1895: 253-254.)

It is these crossings of open country that give us the opportunity of learning that a puma may travel 25 miles or more in a single night. In southern Arizona the animal is known to cross level desert plains more than 50 miles broad, from one island-like mountain range to another. One such puma wanderer was found, where daylight had overtaken it, asleep in the shade of a palo verde tree growing in the midst of the plain.

The following instance gives evidence of distance traveled by the puma. Charles H. Vaughan, who at times has been a Federal puma hunter, and when not so employed, conducts puma-hunting expeditions, relates the following incident while employed as a hunter-guide by Clark Gable in February 1937:

"In the vicinity of Cave Springs on the east side of the Kaibab Forest a young puma about 4 months old was captured alive with the aid of dogs. Clark Gable desired to keep this young animal as a pet. He accordingly put a dog-collar on the animal with a name plate on it designated as 'Rowdy.' The young puma was held by a chain attached to the collar, and staked out near the hunting camp. During the first night after the capture it broke the snap on the collar and escaped. An attempt was made, after this discovery the following morning, to get the dogs to trail it, but to no avail—the dogs apparently refused to become interested because of having once captured it, a trait common in some puma-hunting dogs.

"A year later, almost to the day, Vaughan captured this puma with the collar still intact on its neck, in the vicinity of Indian Hollow. This area is approximately 75 miles distant around a mountain from the spot where this young puma had made good its escape. It, on its second capture, was found to have grown to a good size, and had killed a 5-point buck deer a short time before the final capturing of it."

Voice

Few, if any of the mammals lack the ability to make at least one sound, and some can make several, that denote, as with human beings, a particular mental reaction. These sounds are most frequently described by the terms: bark, chirp, grunt, howl, scream, screech, snort, whine, and whistle.

As to the ability of our large tawny American cat to scream, its

main utterance being usually so denoted, contrary opinions have been
held for many years. Some emphatically claim that the puma does
not scream; others that it does. From early colonial days the puma
and its voice have long held the interest of outdoors men. Some of
the cries attributed to the puma are manifestly beyond the ability of
any cat to emit. Thus it is averred that with the coming of the first
steamboats to the West their loud alarms were sometimes deemed
to be the cries of pumas. One instance (Crawford, 1944: 10) as told
by Walter B. Stevens—a tradition of the Osage, one of the branches
of the Missouri River—runs as follows:

"One day in early summer, Matthew Arbuckle rode into Papins-
ville. His horse was panting and flecked with foam. Matt told the
group which gathered about him that, while plowing on his claim
about a mile from the Osage, he had heard a terrible noise. He said
it was something like the scream of a 'painter,' only ten times as
long and loud.

"Uncle John Whitley, who had 'fit with Jackson' at New Orleans, and who was the acknowledged leader in that pioneer community, was sent for. He listened to Arbuckle and said the only
thing to do was to get the hounds together, take the guns, and go
after the varmint, which he reckoned must have wandered down
from the Rocky Range, as they called the Rocky Mountains in those
days. Uncle Jimmie Breckinridge seconded Captain Whitley, and
the settlers got ready. As the posse was about to start for the trail
a faint repetition of what Arbuckle had reported was heard. It was
sure enough a new and terrifying sound. Uncle John at once re-
membered that his pretty daughter, Mattie, had gone on her pony
to the river that morning.

" 'Ride, men!' he shouted. 'Ride! Mat went down to the river,
and I expect she's dead by this time.'

"There was mounting in hot haste, but before the start was fairly
under way here came Mattie with her hair flying. She had heard
the monster. Uncle John bade her get to the house and tell all of
the women-folk to keep within doors.

"Darkness and storm came on together. Captain John Whitley
led his party to Rock House, a cave forming a room twenty feet
high, thirty feet wide, and forty feet deep. There was no disturbance in the night, but at daybreak that nerve-racking sound brought
every man to his feet and set the hounds howling. The noise seemed

to show that the monster was coming up the river and was near.

"Uncle John posted his men for the encounter, every one behind a big tree. Four were told off with orders to have their knives ready and to wade in if the lead failed to stop the beast. Near Rock House was one of the sharpest of the scores of curves and bends of the Osage. Around the point and into view of the amazed settlers came slowly the 'Flora Jones,' the first steamboat to ascend the Upper Osage."

Similarly, with the very first approach of a steam locomotive on the completion of the Northern Railroad in New York State, the Frontier Palladium, of Malone, New York (Anon. 1850), states editorially on August 1, 1850: "Some of our gray-haired fathers, who had heard the scream of the panther when the site of our village was a wilderness wild, came out to see whether that animal was coming to regain his dominions."

Passing to less historical accounts of puma cries, we note that in the early 1830's, John K. Townsend (1839: 149) in the account of his journey across the Rocky Mountains to the Columbia River, wrote when encamped in the vicinity of the present Idaho-Oregon boundary en route to the Blue Mountains of Oregon, "Last evening as we were about retiring to our beds we heard distinctly as we thought a loud halloo, several times repeated, and in a tone like that of a man in great distress. Supposing it to be a person who had lost his way in the darkness and was searching for us we fired several guns at regular intervals, but as they elicited no reply, after waiting a considerable time we built a large fire as a guide, and lay down to sleep. Early this morning a large panther was seen prowling around our camp and the hallooing of last night was explained. It was the dismal distressing yell by which this animal entices its prey until pity or curiosity induces it to approach to its destruction."

Perry (1890: 411), regarding the puma's voice in the Pacific Northwest, says it is "a cry so unearthly and so weird that even the man of stoutest heart will start in affright; a cry that can only be likened to a scream of demoniac laughter. This is the cry of the male Cougar. If it is answered by the female the response will be similar to the wail of a child in terrible pain."

Audubon (1851: II: 311-312) thought that such reports "must be received with much caution, and may in many of their exaggerations be set down as vulgar errors." Nevertheless he believed "All the males, however, of the cat kind, at the season when the sexes seek each other, emit remarkable and startling cries, as is evidenced by the common cat, in what is denominated caterwauling. * * * * It is not impossible, therefore, that the male Cougar may at the rutting season have some peculiar and startling notes."

Commenting on the mountain lion in the early days of Vermont, Thompson (1853: 37) wrote: "During the day the Catamount usually lies concealed, but in the night prowls for his prey, and in early times his peculiar cry has often sent a thrill of horror through a whole neighborhood."

Woodhouse (1853: 37), while engaged as surgeon and naturalist of the Sitgreaves Expedition of 1851 down the Zuni, Little Colorado, and Big Colorado Rivers, and while in the vicinity of the San Francisco Mountain, Arizona, stated: "The cry of the panther * * * was occasionally to be heard."

Suckley (1860: 108) related of the puma in Washington Territory: "They are said to utter shrill screams, and at times loud whistling sounds, at night. Perhaps these, when much heard, proceed from the amatory conflicts and spiteful sanguinary courtships which, it is fair to suppose, exist as much among them as with their cousins, our domestic dependents."

Discoursing upon the puma as found in Florida, Maynard (1872: 3) says: "It is very inquisitive when its dominions are invaded during the day, and will often follow the intruder for some distance, uttering a low moaning cry, but is always careful to keep concealed.

"Besides this peculiar low note, it emits a variety of harsh sounds, some of which are only given during the night, and are quite terrifying when first heard, especially one in particular which resembles the scream of a woman in extreme agony. This cry is more frequently given in March, when the males are in pursuit of the females."

Allen (1874: 53), while studying mammals in Park County, Colorado, and when camped for one week near Montgomery, stated "Its cry was once heard near our camp at Montgomery."

Batty (1874: 51) stated: "When the cougar is hungry he will hang around the hunter's camp during the night, seldom coming nearer than one hundred yards, and occasionally giving his dismal howl, which is fearfully distinct to the ear of the hunter. He generally gives the prolonged howls, the first being the loudest, and the last one gradually dying out and sounding as if he was at your side.

His howls sound like O-O-O-Oh! O-O-O, repeated three times in succession. In fact the howl of the panther at night makes one more nervous than seeing the animal by day."

Again with regard to the animal in Florida, Elliot (1883: 72) in recounting his personal experience, commented: "At times the Cougar utters a peculiarly shrill cry or shriek; and I once heard this in the dead of night, when encamped on the St. John's River in Florida. The animal seemed to be directly over my tent; and the unearthly yell made my flesh creep, and brought me out to the fire, that was burning brightly before the tent, in a moment."

On this topic the testimony of so experienced an outdoorsman as Theodore Roosevelt (1893: 343) is of value. In an early account he wrote: "I am not sure that I ever heard one; but one night, while camped in a heavily timbered coulie near Kildeer Mountains, where, as footprints showed, the beasts were plentiful, I twice heard a loud, wailing scream ringing through the impenetrable gloom which surrounded the hills around us. My companion, an old plainsman, said that this was the cry of the cougar prowling for its prey. Certainly no man could well listen to a stranger and wilder sound."

Eight years later, when recording his experiences in puma hunting in northwestern Colorado, Roosevelt (1901: 434) further related: "Although a silent beast, yet at times, especially during the breeding season, the males utter a wild scream, and the females also cry or call. I once heard one cry while prowling for game. On an evening in the summer of 1897 Dr. Merriam had a rather singular experience with a cougar. His party was camped in the forest by Tannum Lake, on the east slope of the Cascades, near the headwaters of a branch of the Yakima. The horses were feeding nearby and shortly after dark a cougar cried loudly in the gloom and the frightened horses whinnied and stampeded. The cougar cried a number of times afterward, but the horses did not again answer. None of them were killed, however; and the next morning after some labor, all were again gathered together."

Again Roosevelt (Ibid: 556) tells of the Mathes brothers, stockmen ranching near Meeker, Colorado, one of whom had observed a crying puma. In this instance the puma "remained in the same place for many minutes, repeating its cry continually."

Whitney (1895: 253-254) wrote: "Their cry is as terror-striking as it is varied. I have heard them wail so you would swear an infant had been left out in the cold by its mamma; I have heard them screech like a woman in distress; and again, growl after the conventional manner attributed to the monarch of the forest. The average camp dog runs to cover when a cougar is awakening the echoes of the mountain. I should call it lucky, for those who hunt with dogs, that the lion does not pierce the atmosphere by his screeches when being hunted; for, if he did, I fear it would be a difficult matter to keep dogs on his trail. There seems to be something about his screeching that particularly terrorizes dogs."

Cory (1896: 109) recorded that "The cry of the cub resembles the screech of a Parrot, but it often utters a soft whistle. The cry of the old Panther somewhat resembles the screech of a Parrot, but is much louder."

Mead (1899: 279) states that the "unearthly scream of a panther close at hand will almost freeze the blood in one's veins, and for an instant paralyze almost any form of man or beast. My horses and mules tied to the wagon usually paid no attention to wild animals; but on this occasion they trembled like a leaf. Some Indian women and children were sitting around their camp-fires. They screamed and ran into their lodges." In this connection Mead was recounting an experience during January of 1868 while in camp near the mouth of Turkey Creek on the Cimarron River in what is now Woods County in northwestern Oklahoma. He further felt that "A panther's scream heard in the wilderness on a still night is an experience never to be forgotten. The memory of it will stay with one to the end * * * *" and that according to Mr. William Matthews, his former partner, the puma has "other tones of voice to suit the occasion, as other cats have * * * *."

Stone and Cram (1902: 291) state: "Though usually silent, they at times utter a loud penetrating scream."

Agreeing with Seton's statement that "it has just as many sounds as the common cat," Rhoads (1903: 134) makes the following comment as a result of observing the puma in the Philadelphia Zoological Garden: "[It] is capable of most of the gradations and tones of the domestic cat, and has a great similarity thereto in purring, mewing, caterwauling, and spitting notes. Multiply cat-calls by ten and you get the kind of noises that have done more than anything else to give the 'American Lion' its reputation for qualities which it does not possess."

Hollister, while in the field in Louisiana (1911: 175-178), says "Feb. 23 [1904] Heard panthers crying about nine o'clock last night. There were probably two of them as the calls were sounded at short intervals, sometimes only about a minute apart, and one seemed a little farther away. The animals were evidently moving along to the north. The cry is a long drawn out, shrill trill, weird and startling. It commences low on the scale, gradually ascends, increasing in volume, and then lowers at the end. * * * * Heard panthers again in evening * * * * Feb. 26. Heard panthers tonight on both sides of Bear Lake. * * * * Feb. 28. Heard panthers trilling wail across the lake tonight. * * * *

"I believe the pumas call more in the early spring than at any other season, and we were probably very fortunate in the time of our visit to the cane, as the experience was one of very great interest."

E. W. Nelson (1916: 412) says: "It has a wild screaming cry which is thrillingly impressive when the shades of evening are throwing a mysterious gloom over the forests. In the mountains of Arizona one summer a mountain lion repeatedly passed along a series of ledges high above my cabin at dusk, uttering this loud weird cry, popularly supposed to resemble the scream of a terrified woman."

After discussing the pros and cons on the scream of the puma Seton (1929: I (1) 72-78) says: "The cougar is sometimes a very silent animal, especially when hunting or hunted. But at other times, especially when signalling to its mate, when defying a rival, when making love, or when indulging in the song that is a mere expression of vigour, it has just as many sounds as the common cat; they are of the same types as those of the cat, but they are magnified and intensified to a scale fitted to the superior bulk of the Cougar, that is, about 20 times.

"Finally, the individual variation is so great in these animals that any general rule is sure to fail at times."

Enos Mills (1932: 200), who during most of his life was a keen observer of wild life, says: "Of the dozen or more times I have heard the screech of the lion, on three occasions there was a definite cause for the cry,—on one a mother frantically sought her young, which had been carried off by a trapper; and twice the cry was a wail, in each instance given by the lion calling for its mate, recently slain by a hunter."

Hornaday (1922: 37) says that pumas scream during mating,

and states the note is a "loud, piercing, prolonged" one "and has the agonized voice qualities of a boy or a woman screaming from the pain of a surgical operation. To one who does not know the source or the cause it is nerve-racking. . . . and it easily carries a quarter of a mile."

Bailey (1936: 263) comments on the voice of the puma to the effect, "That much discussed subject, the 'scream' of the mountain lion, is a delicate one because of some confusion in the interpretation of the scream. Generally the animals are silent, but they are by no means without vocal powers. When treed or cornered they have a repelling growl and snarl and hiss, and at times when they are free and alone they utter a loud call or cry that suggests a fair compromise between the caterwaul of a tomcat and the roar of a lion. It is heavy and prolonged, slightly rising and falling and fairly well indicated by the letters O-O-W-O-U-H-U-U. On two occasions, in the woods, on dark nights, the writer has heard this cry repeated several times at frequent intervals, and once from a cage in a zoological park. There was no mistaking its catlike quality in any of these cases, but it could hardly be called a scream. Still, if the animals have the vocal range of some other felines it is not improbable that they make sounds that could be called screams. The most common mistake in regard to mountain lions is in attributing to them the shrill 'woman-in-agony scream' of the full-grown young of the great horned owl, which is often heard, and when close on a dark night is fully as terrifying as any sound a real mountain lion could possibly produce."

Goldman stated (1939: 412) that the puma "* * * has a wild, weird scream-like cry not calculated to soothe the nerves of a night wayfarer on a lonely forest trail. This is uttered so infrequently, however, that some old hunters assert they have never heard the cry and are even skeptical that it is ever given."

Bryon Denton of La Veta, Colorado, who has had long experience in puma hunting throughout the Sangre de Cristo Mountains, says that the animal utters a scream, among several other vocal sounds; this he thinks is given during periods of heat.

A. B. Colgate, of Victor, Colorado, in relating some of his woodsman experiences, writes: "A good many years ago night overtook me while fishing about 5 miles down the canyon from where we now live. It was over 3 miles to camp. Mountain lions were plentiful then as now, as there was very little livestock, many deer, and most of the country was almost inaccessible. I was not afraid of them, being convinced they would never attack a human being on foot. * * * *

"As I started down toward camp a queer, half-human cry came from quite a ways behind me. I stopped, but being sure no one else could be up there, hastened on. In a few moments it came again, very much closer, and I realized what it was. The cat [puma] followed along near me for over 2 miles and yelled at least 6 times. I saw it twice; once as it jumped the creek behind me and went into the trees, and again as it leaped out onto a high ledge of rock up ahead. Daylight was almost gone, and it took all the nerve I could muster to slip down past the place where I had seen it. Just as I got by it let a final, drawn out, wailing shriek, not more than 50 yards away." * * *

"Not many years ago, on the upper Rio Grande [in Colorado] I returned to camp and found the wife and kids worried about a 'horrible screaming cry' up on the hill, that sounded like some woman in trouble. I ran up to the place they directed, and found what was expected,—fresh tracks of a medium-sized cougar, and the fresh tracks of a deer, running fast.

"Another time, in the same locality, my son and I were sleeping in a pup tent. Along in the night he dug an elbow into my ribs and whispered, 'What's that noise?' I awoke with the impression of some sort of noise, but was not long in doubt. Almost immediately the wild shriek of a cougar echoed through the valley. We found his tracks near camp when daylight came." (Colgate, A. B. 1941: Letter in files of Fish and Wildlife Service.)

In one of the Central American republics, Costa Rica, according to Alston (1879-1882: 62-63), the puma is found "at an elevation of from 5,000 to 6,000 feet, where the hideous sound of its howling is almost continuously heard in the breeding season."

Of its voice in South America, Darwin (1839: 329) stated, "It is a very silent animal, uttering no cry even when wounded, and only rarely during the breeding season."

Molina (1808: 208) says the Chilean puma ". . . in the season of its loves [its voice] becomes changed into a shrill whistle, or rather a frightful hiss, like that of a serpent."

Fountain (1902: 85) appears to give the best description, based on his experiences and observations, particularly while on the Purus

River of northwestern Brazil. He writes, "The cries and calls of all cats appear to me to be very much alike. They differ only in intensity of sound. For days together we did not hear either jaguars or pumas in the forests; then the whole night through they would be heard calling to each other. The noise they sometimes make is terrific, or appears to be so in these great solitudes, where there is generally the silence of death." He also states (1914: 64), "We could hear them crying and screaming at night, and they often came so close to our camp that we could hear them purring, for all three sounds are uttered by both jaguars and pumas. The screaming sound, much like that of a domestic cat when it is quarreling with others, indicated that these larger animals were also settling their disputes with tooth and claw."

Referring to the voice, also at times as a squall, Fountain says it was more apt to be heard at the time of mating. In view of there being no particular rutting season for the puma, its call, therefore, may be heard during any month of the year.

The foregoing notes relating to widely separated geographic regions in the United States—Florida, Louisiana, Vermont, the Great Plains, Rocky Mountains, the Southwest, the Pacific Northwest, and also in Central and South America,—all verify the "scream" as one of the voices, and doubtless the loudest utterance of this animal.

From observations on the animal in captivity the following concludes our record on this controversial subject:

While studying an adult male and female puma at the time of feeding in the late afternoon of January 10, 1921, in the Zoological Park of Denver, Colorado, the author was fortunate to hear the male give voice to a scream similar to that sound recorded by Beebe (1943: 115) as being heard in the Bronx Zoo of New York City. At midnight while standing in front of a caged puma, Beebe says, "It gave utterance to a loud, long drawn out quavering cry which seemed as if it would never stop, and epitomized the essence of wild nature. To imagine it multiply the most awesome yowl of a back-fence tommy by several times its amount of ominous, menacing, portentous, terrifying, appalling character, and you will realize what must now and then have frightened little Dutch babies fairly out of their cradles as they lay shivering in their fathers' log cabins in the wilds of Westchester many, many years ago."

Robert Bean, of the Chicago Zoological Park, states, "We have never yet had a female mountain lion which did not scream, and in various collections would probably have had 20 to 25 females. I have never heard a male puma scream, however, but they frequently whistle. Their voice is much like a man whistling on his fingers, and it is not coincident with the mating season as is the cat-calling of the female." (Bean, Robert. 1944: letter to Frank Dufresne in files of Fish and Wildlife Service, dated August 30.)

In comparing the vocal difference between the lion, the jaguar, and the puma, Martin (1833: 120-121), an early investigator, found the distance between the base of the tongue and the larynx in the lion [African] to be slightly greater than in the jaguar; ". . . but in the Puma; an animal equal or nearly so, in size to the Jaguar, the distance is reduced to an inconsiderable space, 1 inch or 1½ inches, according as the tongue is more or less protruded. * * * the circumference of the larynx of the Puma is also very inconsiderable. * * * In the jaguar we find a larynx indicating from its general magnitude considerable depth in the intonations of the voice, whereas in the Puma, if we take either its diameter or its distance from the termination of the palate and base of the tongue, we are led to expect neither the roar of the Lion nor the growl of the Jaguar, but the shrill tones of an animal, ferocious indeed, but of all others of the genus perhaps the most stealthy and insidious."

The puma with its scream might be dubbed the "lyric soprano" of the wild felines.

Sounds other than the scream made by the puma are very similar to those of the ordinary house cat, differing in proportion to the respective sizes of the two. These consist of low growls, a cat-like mew, a hiss, a spit, and caterwauling. Two-month old young emit a shrill whistle-like call when suddenly startled. While hardly in the category of a voice utterance, the animal's ability to purr differs not at all from that of the house cat. Generally louder, it seems to denote contentment or pleasure, particularly in the young at those times when they are lightly stroked down the back, or scratched under the chin, or on the rump near the base of the tail.

Stalking and Pouncing

The puma relies upon its senses of smell and sight in its foraging. Its smell is keener than that of the bobcat, though less so than in either the wolf or the coyote. It can see its prey for a long distance, but unquestionably it does much of its silent, cautious stalking by the sense of smell alone, taking advantage of every cover until within striking distance of its victim. Its sense of hearing also is acute.

Contrary to the common belief that the puma lies in wait in some tree or upon some rocky promontory ready to pounce upon unsuspecting prey, it does its main hunting for food in a manner comparable to that of the domestic cat, stealthily stalking its prey upon the ground, and, when near enough springing on its victim, and bringing it to the ground. It does not always succeed, however, and may lose intended prey which may escape with no more harm than some lacerating claw marks.

Hornaday (1922: 278-279) records the evidence of escape of a large buck mule-deer that had been severely attacked in the Hell Creek area of Montana. "In its struggle for its life the buck either leaped or fell off the edge of a perpendicular 'cut bank' and landed upon its back with the puma underneath." This action so injured the puma that it was unable to continue its assault. When shot later this deer had a wound on top of the neck from claws and teeth, both hind legs badly clawed, and the main beam of the right antler, still in the velvet, was broken half way up. The puma itself may not emerge unhurt from a bungled attack as the antlers and sharp-edged hooves of deer are effective weapons. The shock of the charge also apparently results in injuries which cause malformation of the bones of the skull. Nelson and Goldman (1933: 221-222) found that "the canines are rarely broken, but nasal and frontal contusions exhibited by a considerable number [of skulls] are evidently the result of mishap in bringing down their prey."

In a successful attack the puma maintains a vice-like clutch, to which its structure is well adapted. The Felidae in general have the clavicle or collarbone better developed than in most of the other carnivores, such as the dogs and wolves, and are thus more proficient both in striking and grasping with the fore limbs. The hind legs furnish most of the impulse for the spring and the results are phenomenal. The writer, in one instance, knew a puma to jump 13 feet on a slight downhill slope from a normal stance when it was startled by the sudden flash and report of a camera flash-powder. (Plate 17.) This was in northern Coahuila, Mexico, near the north-western terminus of the Carmen Mountains in October, 1937.

When treed by dogs a puma does not ordinarily climb the tree. Rather it leaps, traversing on its first jump a distance of from 10 to 18 feet. Also when jumping out of a tree, the animal hits the ground with its feet ready and bounds 15 to 20 feet at the first jump.

Merriam (1884: 31) was of the opinion that "a single spring of 20 feet is by no means uncommon," and cites an instance of a "measured leap over snow of nearly 40 feet." In another instance a leap of 60 feet was measured "but here the panther jumped from a ledge of rocks about 20 feet above the level . . ."

Cabrera and Yepes (1940: 169) say that one of these creatures has been known, in order to reach a deer, to make a jump of 12 metres [some 47 feet].

Illustrating the force of such a pounce is an observation related by the late Dr. E. W. Nelson. He came upon a recently killed deer lying in a small shallow basin. Marks in the soft earth showed where the puma had crept up within striking distance behind the trunk of an oak tree and then had leaped upon the grazing animal with such force that it had fallen and slid about 15 feet, apparently having been instantly killed.

Fortunately we have a few accounts of eye-witnesses to the killing of prey by a puma. Round (1938: 72) relates, "On July 4, 1935, Professor J. H. Allen, noted geologist of the University of Alberta, was motoring with his wife. About 6 miles west of Banff, in an area where once hundreds of bighorn sheep could be seen, he suddenly stopped his car and excitedly pointed at one of the strangest sights he had ever seen. Four Rocky Mountain goats were leisurely and in single file ascending a game trail leading toward a small ridge, and a short distance to one side a cougar paralleled their course. All were not more than 400 yards from the road when Professor Allen stopped his car.

"Suddenly the lead goat became aware of the cougar and bolted on the opposite side of the trail. A few moments later the next goat did likewise, yet the remaining two continued on their course. The cougar, changing his tactics, swung away on a semicircular course that brought it to the top of the small ridge ahead of the goats. The trail swung around the foot of the ridge.

"Strangely the cougar allowed the first goat to pass. Then, with what Professor Allen described as the most beautiful leap he had ever seen, it curved through the air and landed squarely on the other goat's back. The victim gave one cry and the two animals rolled from sight.

"Hurrying to Banff, Professor Allen informed local authorities of what he had seen and then guided the park superintendent and a warden to the spot. They discovered where the two animals had rolled behind some low bushes, noted that only the cougar's tracks led away from the scene, and deduced that the killer had carried its victim to a more secluded place. After following the cougar tracks for a short distance they came upon the remains of the goat, and a little later caught a glimpse of the killer."

Singer (1914:250-254) describes a puma's actions when stalking its prey. While puma hunting in Sonora, Mexico, with a guide, and "mounted one day on jennets" they neared "the top of a small saddle" . . . When he and his guide "suddenly stopped without word or sign, for our eyes had simultaneously met the object of our search. . . . The unexpected scene that lay before me surpassed anything I had ever witnessed in all my experience with wildlife. There sloped before us a pretty grassy glade where three deer, two does and a fawn, were leisurely feeding along. The grass, growing to the height of some 12 or 15 inches, and having been touched by the recent frosts, had taken on a red-brown color. Not 20 feet behind the nearest doe, and scarcely discernible, so perfectly did its color harmonize with the frost-nipped grass, was the long, lithe, tawny form of a cougar in the very act of stalking its prey with all the stealth and cunning known to its genus. So light, silent and cautious was his every move that he might be said to drift light as a wisp of smoke toward his prey before making the death-dealing spring. Now crouching with fierce aspect, forepaws extended, head laid between them, while his lithe tail oscillated at its extreme tip with a gentle waving motion, his pale gooseberry eyes glared malevolently upon his unsuspecting victim." At this point Singer fired and killed the animal, which was in a way regrettable, for if he had bided his time a little longer the observation of the puma's actual leap at its prey would have fully concluded a most interesting and rare observation.

An early observation in New Jersey agrees with Singer's account so far as it goes. Smith, the New Jersey historian (1765: 502-503), mentions that one day "an Indian hunting near Crosswicks, 1748, discovered a large buck feeding. Creeping up to shoot he heard something among the bushes, and presently saw a panther with his eyes so intent on the buck that he did not perceive him; the Indian watching his motions observed that while the buck had his head down to feed the panther crept, but when he held it up lay snug; he at last got unperceived within about 20 feet, and then making a desperate leap, fixed his talons on the buck's neck; after he had nearly killed him he would cease for a minute, give a watchful look around, and fall to shaking again; having done his work, and about to draw the carcass to a heap of leaves for future service, the Indian shot and got both."

The literature is scanty with respect to the relationship between the puma and the buffalo in early times, and indeed it is probable that the puma seldom tackled so formidable an animal as an adult buffalo. Flint (1856: 74) records an interesting observation related by Daniel Boone in Kentucky while returning home in company with his brother after his first exploration to that section in 1770. On the second day's travel toward their home "they heard the approach of a drove of buffaloes. The brothers remarked that from the noise there must be an immense number, or some uncommon confusion among them. As the buffaloes came in view the woodsmen saw the explanation of the unusual uproar in a moment. The herd was in a perfect fury, stamping the ground and tearing it up and rushing back and forward upon one another in all directions. A panther had seated himself upon the back of one of the largest buffaloes, and fastened his claws into the flesh of the animal wherever he could reach it until the blood ran down on all sides. The movements of a powerful animal, under such suffering, may be imagined. But plunging, rearing, and running were to no purpose. The panther retained its seat and continued its horrid work. The buffalo, in its agony, sought relief in the midst of its companions, but instead of obtaining it communicated its fury to the drove.

"The travelers did not dare to approach the buffalo too closely, but Boone, picking the flint of his rifle and looking carefully at the loading took aim at the panther, determined to displace the monster from its seat. It happened that the buffalo continued a moment in position to allow the discharge to take effect. The panther released its hold and came to the ground."

Unlike those noted buffalo-hunters, the plains wolves, pumas rarely joined forces or used teamwork in the bringing down of prey. However, Barnes (127: 68) records one such incident observed by "Thomas Abbott, a Utah pioneer [who] told me that in early days in Utah he once saw three mountain lions chasing a deer, one running at each side and the other at the rear," and adds, "Others inform me that they have seen them thus chasing deer up a canyon."

Following Man

The puma seems at times to approach man out of curiosity and with no intent to attack. In fact Cornish (1907: 199-200) avers that the animal sometimes "seeks the society of man," and then describes an observation in British Guiana, of a puma actually spending the night under a hammock. The noise that emanated from beneath the hammock, which its human occupant had blamed on croaking frogs, in reality was "probably the purring of the puma, pleased at occupying the 'next berth' below a man," according to the Indian guides.

E. A. Preble, formerly of the Biological Survey, now retired, whose writing ability and knowledge of American mammals and birds are hardly exceeded by that of any present-day naturalist, gives an account of a puma's possible interest in man. While camped at Paulina Lake, Oregon, enroute from the Deschutes River to Klamath Basin, on the night of August 5, 1896, he states, "A panther came through our camp, passing within a few feet of our beds, where we found his tracks in the morning. Our man (Thomas) heard something stirring about in the night just below the tent and got up to investigate, but did not locate the cause of the disturbance."

Goldman (1939: 413) says, "While hunting mountain sheep along the crest of the Charleston Mountains in Nevada it was impressive to find that I was being trailed in the daytime by a mountain lion, which was not seen, and it was only when my route was re-crossed that I discovered the fresh track of the animal persistently following each bend in my course." Goldman believed that the puma was doubtless prompted merely by curiosity and that he had been in no danger of attack.

A somewhat similar occurrence is that recorded by Dr. N. C. Fancher, a Kansas pioneer, though in this instance the puma was seen. In the spring of 1871 he was circled by a puma while over-looking a proposed land claim on the head of Fall Creek in Sumner County, south-central Kansas. When he saw that the puma was circling him he used several buffalo bones as a frightening device. He placed a buffalo horn on each of his feet and held a femur buffalo bone in each hand. Then yelling and jumping he clicked the bones together. However, the puma crouched "down like a cat and started crawling toward me, . . . [but upon] bellowing "desperately" and whacking "the bones savagely together," the animal "stopped, raised its head and looked away from me for the first time. It then turned and started to trot away, just as a cat would trot. I watched it until it passed over the divide three quarters of a mile away." (Roenigk, A. 1933: 24-25.)

In such cases it is difficult to decide whether the animal was stalking the man as prey, but the man is likely to think so.

Barnes (1927: 68) writes of "a trapper in Idaho by the name of Frank Peet, who habitually shot grizzlies, yet had been followed by a cougar in such an uncanny manner on several occasions that he feared this animal more than any other in the woods."

Attacking Man

From field observations and recorded incidents in the literature there is no doubt but what the puma sometimes makes unprovoked attacks upon human beings. This trait is neither general nor common. Roosevelt (1901: 432-433) summed up the situation well when he said, "The cougar is as large, as powerful, and as formidably armed as the [Old World] Indian panther, and quite as well able to attack man; yet the instances of its having done so are exceedingly rare. But it is foolish to deny that such attacks on human beings never occur . . . it cannot be too often repeated that we must never lose sight of the individual variation in character and conduct among wild beasts."

The almost universal fear of the puma is based mainly on its mysterious ways, size and power to do harm, not on its aggressiveness, for as a rule it is notoriously timid in relation to man, even permitting one to climb the tree where it has taken refuge from dogs and place a rope about its neck. However, many incidents have been related of attacks upon men, among which it is difficult to segregate facts from fiction.

An uncontrovertible modern instance occured in 1924 in the vicinity of Malott, Okanogan County, Washington. On December 17, at 11:30 a. m., a boy 13 years old was sent on an errand to a neighboring ranch. He took a short-cut along a trail through a coulee, and when he failed to return a search revealed his remains. Tracks of the boy and of a puma in the light snow told the story. It was apparent that the cat had been following the boy, keeping to one side of the trail in the brush. When the boy saw the animal he had become frightened and ran to the base of a small tree with the apparent intent of climbing it to avoid the animal. However at this point he was struck down and partly devoured. The opinion formed by those inspecting the scene of the attack was that the puma had leaped at least 10 feet in its attack on the boy. A general hunt followed but without success, owing to the obliteration of the tracks and other signs by the large number of persons who took up the pursuit, seeking the liberal bounty that was offered. About a month later a grown female puma about 3 years old was taken in a coyote trap by a local rancher, some 4½ miles from the point where the boy was killed. Its stomach (Plate 18) contained a small undigested mass, which upon examination in the Food Habits Research laboratory of the Biological Survey proved to consist of hair from the boy's head, two bits of blue jeans, and a part of a pocket from his overalls, containing an empty brass cartridge shell which he was known to have carried as a pocket-piece. It is probable that if the boy had not run no attack would have been made, as these animals have often been known to follow people, as previously mentioned, apparently out of curiosity.

One of the earliest, if not the earliest, records of a puma attack, though still somewhat obscure, concerns that upon Philip Tanner. His tombstone, in an old cemetery at Lewisville, Chester County, Pennsylvania, near the Pennsylvania-Maryland border, reads, "Here lye the body of Philip Tanner who departed this life May 6, 1751—age 58 years." From what can be learned from the historical record, Philip Tanner was killed by a "panther" at the edge of woods at a spot called Bettys Patch, near Lewisville, about one-half mile from the cemetery. A crude image of a puma is cut on the tombstone. (Plate 19.)

Apparently in those early colonial days the stone engravers at times attempted to depict on the tombstone the incident causing the death of an individual. In the same cemetery there exists a tombstone inscribed along with a hand reaching for the four or five of diamonds—leading one to believe a card game was in progress, or a gambling card game resulted in the demise of this latter individual.

Another early account is that recorded by Cuvier and Griffith (1827: 438-439) for New York. . . "Two hunters went out in quest of game on the Katskill Mountains, in the province of New York, on the road from New York to Albany, each armed with a gun, and accompanied by his dog. It was agreed between them that they should go in contrary directions round the base of a hill, which formed one of the points in these mountains; and that, if either discharged his piece the other should cross the hill as expeditiously as possible, to join his companion in pursuit of the game shot at. Shortly after separating one heard the other fire, and, agreeably to their compact, hastened to his comrade. After searching for him for some time without effect he found his Dog dead and dreadfully torn. Apprised by this discovery that the animal shot at was large and ferocious, he became anxious for the fate of his friend, and assiduously continued the search for him; when his eyes were suddenly directed, by the deep growl of a Puma, to the large branch of a tree, where he saw the animal crouching on the body of the Man, and directing his eyes toward him, apparently hesitating whether to descend and make a fresh attack on the survivor, or to relinquish its prey and take to flight. Conscious that much depended on celerity the hunter discharged his piece, and wounded the animal mortally, when it and the body of the Man fell together from the tree. The surviving Dog then flew at the prostrate beast, but a single blow from its paw laid the Dog dead by its side. In this state of things, finding that his comrade was dead, and that there was still danger in approaching the wounded animal, the Man prudently retired, and with all haste brought several persons to the spot, where the unfortunate hunter, the Couguar, and both the Dogs, were all lying dead together." (Footnote: "This incident was related to Major Smith by Mr. Scudder, the proprietor of the Museum at New York, where the animal was preserved after death as a memorial of the story.")

Roosevelt (1885: 32-33) believed that, "When the continent

was first settled, and for long afterward the cougar was quite as dangerous an antagonist as the African or Indian leopard, and would even attack men unprovoked. An instance of this occurred in the annals of my father's family. Early in the present century one of my ancestral relatives, a Georgian, moved down to the wild and almost unknown country bordering on Florida. His plantation was surrounded by jungles in which all kinds of beasts swarmed. One of his negroes had a sweetheart on another plantation, and in visiting her, instead of going by the road he took a short cut through the swamps, heedless of the wild beasts, and armed only with a long knife, for he was a man of colossal strength, and of fierce determined temper. One night he started to return late, expecting to reach the plantation in time for his daily task on the morrow. But he never reached home, and it was thought he had run away. However, when search was made for him his body was found in the path through the swamp, all gashed and torn, and but a few steps from him the body of a cougar, stabbed and cut in many places."

An account of a puma attack in the Cascade Mountains of Oregon near Mount Hood, states that the puma "jumped at a man as he lay in his blankets, but as soon as the man partly arose and shouted for assistance, the animal bounded into the brush and disappeared. In talking it over we all came to the conclusion that the panther had seen the man move under his blankets and had mistaken him for some less formidable antagonist, and that when the deception was revealed to him he threw up the job at once." (Anon. 1884: 1161.)

The Oregon Sportsman (1916: IV: 61) credits an attack on a little girl, to whose aid the mother had come in Curry County, Oregon.

John R. Leach, a practicing pharmacist of Portland, Oregon, states regarding an experience with a puma in eastern Oregon, "When I was a youngster a cougar fooled around me all one night. . . . I was sleeping in a saddle blanket and no doubt had a mingled horse and human smell. When I would remain quiet it would come up within ten feet of me and did that two or three times, but would run when I moved." (Leach, J. R. 1941: letter to Stanley P. Young, in files of Fish and Wildlife Service.)

Perry (1890: 413-420) records six unprovoked attacks from

pumas as occurring in western Washington and southern British Columbia, during the period of early settlement and development.

Bourke (1892: 39) gives a rather melodramatic story of a puma attack in the area between Florence and Tuscon, Arizona, shortly before General Crook took charge of the Apache Indian campaign in the late 1870's. Here a wounded survivor of the Gatchell-Curtis train "had wandered aimlessly in different directions, and soon began to stagger from bresh to bresh; his strength was nearly gone, and with frequency he had taken seat on the hard gravel under such shade as the mesquites afforded.

"After a while other tracks came in on the trail alongside of those of the man—they were the tracks of an enormous mountain lion! The beast had run up and down the trail for a short distance, and then bounded on in the direction taken by the wanderer. The last few bounds measured twenty-two feet, and then there were signs of a struggle, and of *something* having been dragged off through the chapparal and over the rocks, and that was all." Searchers found footprints of this human victim which were easily followed in the sandy, gravelly formation that led to a waterhole where he had, before being attacked by the puma, quenched his thirst, washed his wounds, used a small piece of his clothing for a bandage, and then scribbled his name on a "rock in his own blood."

The testimony as to puma attacks upon man is mixed for South, as well as for North America, but in review the conclusion is the same, such attacks while rare, do occur.

Brown (1876: 334) records an unexpected face-to-face meeting with the animal in British Guiana near Wonobolo Falls of the Coremtyne River. Being unarmed and facing the predator which was "half crouched, and its head erect" . . . "as long as I did not move the puma remained motionless also, and thus we stood, some fifteen yards apart, eyeing one another curiously. I heard that the human voice is potent in scaring beasts, and feeling that time had arrived to do something desperate I waved my arms in the air and shouted loudly. The effect on the tiger was electrical; it turned quickly on one side; and in two bounds was lost in the forest."

In discussing the animal in Chile, Gay (1847: 66), in comparing it with the African lion, says that unlike the lion it lacks courage and does not run in pursuit of its prey. Far from being offensive to man it, on the other hand, is cowed and flees from him to hide in the rougher parts of its habitat. He recounts, however, one incident in the vicinity of Chuapa, where a girl and her father were simultaneously attacked by a puma, being moved more to do so by hunger.

In the story of his South American voyage, Darwin (1839: 328) said of the puma, " . . . except in most rare cases, as a female having young, is never dangerous to man," but in Chili he heard "of two men and a woman who had been killed by them."

Osgood (1920: 240-241) gives a vivid account of an experience he had with a puma in Venezuela during February 1920. From his description there is little doubt that the animal meant to attack when, as Osgood says, after meeting it almost head-on, "it started from behind some low bushes at my left and fifty feet, or at the most sixty feet, in front of me. . . . It started toward me immediately, growling savagely, its eyes blazing, tail lashing, and if there was any indication that it did not intend to make away with me I failed to recognize it. It did not come on the run, however, and whether it would have done so or not I cannot say, for its long feline strides were so full of determination I did not care to await developments, but promptly fired a load of buckshot full into its face. . . . At any rate there is at least one person who is sufficiently convinced that some cougars under some circumstances may be far from cowardly."

Allen (1905: 171), quoting Hatcher, records an account of an unprovoked attack from a puma experienced by Theodore Arneberg, in the autumn of 1898, while engaged in field work as Chief Engineer of the Southern Division of the Argentine Boundary Commission. This attack occurred near Lake Viedma, where "the animal [Arneberg came upon unexpectedly] not only made no attempt to escape, but instantly and without warning attacked the intruder in the most savage manner. Springing upon him with its full force it hurled him to the ground, although Mr. Arneberg is a large powerful man, and the lion seizing him by the lower jaw succeeded in breaking out several teeth and otherwise mutilating its then comparatively helpless victim, before one of his companions could rush up and despatch the thoroughly angered brute, which, after it had been killed, was found to be a very old male."

Roosevelt (1926: 24-27) records an attack by a female puma

on Dr. F. P. Morena, at the same locality. With nothing more for bodily defense than a prismatic compass in a leather case, Dr. Morena was knocked to the ground by the spring of the animal from behind. This female lacerated his mouth and back, but in the tussle on the ground he succeeded in getting free. By the use of his poncho as a shield and by severe rapping of its head with the compass he succeeded in holding off the creature until he got within calling distance of his camp. An Indian helper dispatched this puma finally with the aid of his bolas. This episode took place in the late 1870's. Twenty-one years later, in April 1898, a similar attack occurred in the same area. Dr. Morena held to the opinion that apparently in this particular area pumas ran entirely counter to those of other regions in their fear of humans. Here it was found that the "Indians, who elsewhere paid no attention whatever to the puma, never let their women go after wood for fuel unless two or three were together. This was because on several occasions women who had gone out alone were killed by pumas."

This phase of our book may well be summed up by quoting from Audubon (1851: 309). After recounting in detail instances of puma attacks on a human brought to his attention, he says, "We have given these relations of others to show that at long intervals and under peculiar circumstances, when perhaps pinched by hunger, or in defense of its young the cougar sometimes attacks man. These instances, however, are very rare, and the relations of an affrightened traveller must be received with some caution, making due allowance for a natural disposition in man to indulge in the marvellous."

From modern experience it should be added that rabid pumas will and have attacked humans, but in Audubon's time the rabies factor was not understood.

Attracted by Catnip

As is well known catnip is very attractive to the domestic cat; it is also favored by wild felines, including the puma. Experiments have indicated that it has a soothing effect on the nervous system, similar to that of opiates in the human. In some of the larger circuses catnip has been used for years in gentling animals of the cat family. The use of catnip oil to lure both pumas and bobcats into traps, as well as to cause them to take self-photographs in their undisturbed habitats has been remarkably effective. (Plate 20.) (Gregory, T. 1938.)

Most puma hunters hold that the animal is not easily attracted by artificial scents. However, in a series of trapping experiments conducted in Arizona it was observed that, with one exception, this carnivore was attracted to whatever type of fresh scent was used. Those tested included various animal scents, and synthetic fetid scents, descriptions of which are given later under trapping technique.

Playfulness

That our big cat is at times playful in the wild is the opinion of various observers. Indicative is an observation near the mouth of the Columbia River in Oregon, recorded as follows: "In a small glade in the forest, where from the sign it was evident that two or more of them had been gamboling, and like two kittens scurrying around in the grass, and then bounding against the trunk of a tree at a point at least ten feet from the ground, they had ascended apparently on the run, tearing off great pieces of bark, and leaving claw marks a foot long on each side." (Anon. 1884: 1162.)

Similar evidence was observed near Cherry Creek Pass in the Canelo Hills of southern Arizona, located in Santa Cruz County, during March, 1918. It seemed in this case, from study of the ground, that the cavorting that had taken place was related to the amorous desires of one of the pumas. Numerous traces of fresh urine and dung scratches were noted about 12 feet from the base of the pine tree which the cats had been jumping against.

William Casto, a noted puma hunter of Arizona, observed a two-year old puma playing with a large grasshopper as the house cat toys with a mouse, the observation being made in a small grassy flat some 5 miles east of Blue Post-office, in northeast Greenlee County.

In Captivity

Occasionally pumas when captured young and held in captivity (Plates 21, 22, 23, 24) make interesting pets. Some remain perfectly docile and show much fondness for their master, even following him about much like a dog. Others, after reaching maturity, become so untrustworthy that they must be disposed of; these often reach some zoological park.

That successful attempts were made in early Peru to tame the puma is apparent from a study made in the ancient Inca capital of Cuzco. As previously mentioned (Distribution—Peru), of the 12 wards making up this Inca metropolis, one was named "Puma Curcu." This term means "lion beam," and it was in this ward that pumas apparently were tied to beams until tamed.

Its use as an animal of torture also may be mentioned here. The terrific mutilation that the puma is capable of inflicting was apparently a main reason for its use in the dungeons of the Inca rulers for the repression of treason and disobedience. See also p. 48-49.

Azara (1802: 123) also recorded its domestication, mentioning a priest in Paraguay who kept a castrated puma kitten for a year, which was allowed to run loose without any mischief being noted, except in attacking chickens of the neighborhood. At the end of a year the priest presented it to Azara, who kept it on a leash for four months and found it an interesting pet. It played with all and took special pleasure in licking the skin of the negro servants, particularly if they had been perspiring. Its antics, such as playing with an orange and eating, were similar to those of the house cat. It apparently knew its home, for one day on being turned loose it returned of its own free will, jumping a fence to do so.

Allen (1905: 172) credits Prichard with the following remarks on the South American animal, *Felis concolor pearsoni:* "Puma cubs . . . in captivity become very tame. One settler [In South America] whom I met had two cubs about a year old. They were attached to their new home and though they would follow a horse for two hundred yards or so they invariably returned after a short distance to the shanty of their owner. Another puma cub . . . was wont to fight battles royal with the hounds, but in the cold of winter would lie among them for warmth. . . . So long as they were well fed they were docile, but when hungry their fierce nature reasserted itself."

Spears' (1895: 196) observations, made on the plains of Patagonia, are to the effect that while great killers in the wild pumas may make charming house pets, but none of them were ever kept longer than three years. They were never killed because of bodily harm to the attendants of the households, but because of the instinctive dislike for dogs and their appetite for colts and lambs. It was these failings that sooner or later got a puma into trouble on the ranch, and then even the wife and children plead in vain for its life.

The captive recorded by Cooper (1860: 74); which was taken when swimming the Columbia River in the early 1850's, ". . . was sent to California, where [he] . . . saw it exhibited in December 1855. It was then full grown, very fat, and with beautiful glossy fur of a rich brown color. * * * It was restless and playful, but with that treachery characteristic of the race in every movement. Its keeper ruled it with a rod of iron, to which it always showed strong objections by growling, spitting, and obstinately refusing to obey commands as long as it dared to resist."

In 1925 a female puma more than a year old held in captivity in Manhattan, near Bozeman, Montana, was trained to draw a small sulky, and on occasions was driven, so hitched, down the main street of this western village.

Enemies and Enemy Evasion

Other than man, with his guns and traps, the puma, at least when full grown, has few enemies against which it cannot defend itself when required. Its superior agility, great strength, tough skin, and sharp claws and teeth, make it a formidable adversary.

The great strength and endurance of the wolverine have often been recorded, but considering the relative sizes of the puma and the wolverine, the ability of the latter to defend itself, even to the extent of defeating a puma is remarkable.

Grinnell (1926: 31) records the maiming of a puma by a wolverine, which, however, was so helpless that it was found by a hunter who despatched it. It had been "chewed and scratched in a terrible manner and one leg broken. There was some snow on the ground showing the track of a wolverine." Presumably this occurrence noted by Grinnell was on the headwaters of the Green River in Wyoming.

Whenever observations have been made in habitats where the jaguar and puma both occur, it is apparent that these two cats have no liking for each other. On meeting a combat is sure to follow. Hudson (1895: 48) writes of the warfare between them, and his, as well as other South American accounts record the puma as being the victor in the majority of these feline bouts.

On the other hand the grizzly bear is credited with being master of the puma. Accounts of puma-grizzly bear clashes, observed during the heyday of the western "mountain men," and particularly during that decade of the early 19th century when the fur exploitation held sway, tend to show that the puma gave the grizzly of the Rockies a wide berth.

The South American peccary, considered the main prey of the jaguar, is also killed by the puma at times. However, these fast-moving creatures when in herds are credited with putting a puma to flight.

When pressed by dogs the puma sometimes displays fox-like traits in attempting to get away. Sometimes it will take a circuitous route, bringing it back to its track, and begin another circular line of travel within the first one. This practice has been observed in the open boulder country of central Arizona, where the animal can dash from one boulder pile to another. It has been known also to make several sharp turns, apparently to throw the dogs off the track. When it succeeds in doing this a puma has been known to lie down and rest until again discovered by its trailers, when it bounds off to the next boulder cover. Hunting the puma in such a habitat generally results in an exhausted pack of dogs with badly cut-up feet at the end of the chase. At times, too, the puma succeeds in eluding the dogs, the contest ending in its favor. (Musgrave, M. E. 1923: Fish and Wildlife Service files.)

Darwin (1882: 270) says that in certain parts of South America "when pursued [by dogs] it often returns on its former track, and then suddenly making a spring on one side, waits till the dogs have passed by."

Sex Ratio

As among mammals in general the sex ratio of the puma appears to hold reasonably close to the proportion of 50 : 50. Of 490 pumas killed on the livestock and game ranges of Arizona, 1930-1941, 240 were females and 250 males. Segregating by years the numbers making up this total, the following results are obtained:

Table 5. Sex ratio of Arizona pumas

Year	Females	Males	Total
1931	20	26	46
1932	13	24	37
1933	23	18	41
1934	22	16	38
1935	39	40	79
1936	34	34	68
1937	19	23	42
1938	22	12	34
1339	13	20	33
1940	21	23	44
1941	14	14	28
Totals	240	250	490

Data for the same period are tabulated below for three other States:

Table 6. Sex ratio of Utah pumas

Year	Females	Males	Total
1931	14	10	24
1932	34	24	58
1933	27	28	55
1934	12	10	22
1935	30	26	56
1936	31	28	59
1937	33	24	57
1938	41	43	84
1939	42	27	69
1940	34	22	56
1941	28	36	64
Totals	326	278	604

Table 7. Sex ratio of New Mexico pumas

Year	Females	Males	Total
1931	45	25	70
1932	12	13	25
1933	18	13	31
1934	5	12	17
1935	12	7	19
1936	13	12	25
1937	10	4	14
1938	4	9	13
1939	11	15	26
1940	12	10	22
1941	2	6	8
Totals	144	126	270

Table 8. Sex ratio of Texas pumas

Year	Females	Males	Total
1931	5	4	9
1932	17	16	33
1933	26	23	49
1934	9	13	22
1935	16	18	34
1936	21	26	47
1937	19	13	32
1938	22	15	37
1939	13	9	22
1940	8	10	18
1941	14	10	24
Totals	170	157	327

In addition there were 13 pumas killed in Colorado, including 6 females and 7 males. Thus in the five States enumerated there was a grand total of 1,704 pumas taken, of which there were 68 more females than males.

According to statistics of the California Fish and Game Department, on pumas offered for bounty during the four years, 1930-1933, 54 percent were females. In the six-month period, January 1 to June 30, 1942, a total of 92 puma skins were turned in, of which 48 were females and 44 males. (Outdoor Calif. 1942: III.) Of the total kill of 162 pumas made in 1942 under the California bounty law, 85 were females and 77 were males. (Anon. 1943: 1.)

These statistics seem to show a tendency for a slight excess of females over males in the sex ratio of pumas of the southwestern United States.

Breeding Habits

Mating.—Aside from the regular menstrual periods the female comes into heat almost immediately after the young are born; the period of heat approximates 9 days. As many as four or five males will follow the female, fighting over her until the victor obtains the first breeding privilege. This first breeding may be followed by union with other males. The animals are at least 2, and probably 3, years old when they begin breeding.

Denning.—The den or lair where the young are born often is located in some rocky cavern on a mountainside, under an uprooted tree, or in some other nook proctected from the elements. On the other hand, where the topography is not rough but has heavy underbrush, the lair is in a dense thicket. As with the wolf and coyote, no bedding is prepared.

Bruce (1918: 152-153) describes a puma den located near Wawona, California, and occupied by a female puma and three kittens approximately 10 days old; it was on a rocky bluff and measured 6 feet long and 2 feet wide. "The nest was bedded with pine needles, probably carried in the den by wood rats for their nests," sometime before occupancy by this mother puma. "There was also a small opening, perhaps 8 inches in diameter, through which the sun would shine on the kittens in the nest."

Use of thickets as den sites is admirably reported by Everett M. Mercer, of the Fish and Wildlife Service, from observations in central Arizona. Accompanied by Giles Goswick, a government puma hunter, on November 13, 14, and 15, 1943, pumas were hunted in a locality known as Pine Mountain, about 37 miles southeast of Mayer, Arizona.

"On November 13, Mr. Goswick's hounds treed an unusually large tom lion just below the rim southwest from the peak known as Pine Mountain. The lion was killed. The following day, November 14, the hounds struck the track of a female lion on the first bench below the rim northeast from the peak and perhaps three miles from where the tom lion was jumped. The District Agent and Mr. Stewart, a local cow man, found a grandstand seat from which to watch the chase at a point on the rim, and about the middle of the day a white-tail doe and a live fawn were observed browsing on a hillside about 300 yards to the left and below where we were sitting. Little did we suppose at the time that the lion the dogs were trailing would be jumped within fifty yards of where the deer and her fawn were browsing. The dogs were on a two-day-old track and it was hours before they finally worked up to the point where the lioness was jumped. She was finally treed and killed after dark about two miles west of this point in a canyon leading off to a different watershed. It was found that she was suckling young, and on the following morning, November 15, we returned to the rim for the purpose of trying to locate the young lions. Mr. Goswick knew the approximate point where the lioness was jumped and concluded that her kittens might be in that vicinity. I also observed two dogs working on a rock slide less than 30 yards from where the kittens were found, and it was noted that they could smell where the lioness had walked many times back and forth across the rock slide. Mr. Goswick back-tracked the dogs to a point where the lioness was jumped the day before and shortly thereafter he located the kittens.

"The point where the kittens was located was covered with an unusually thick growth of mountain mahogany. This shrub was so thick and the ground so rough and rocky that it was difficult to approach the point on foot. The lioness had several beds and the kittens had been playing over an area about 30 or 40 feet across. There is little doubt but that they were born at this point, as considerable hair coming from the belly of the lioness was found in one particular bed. The hunter approached the point from one side and I from the other, and as we approached the point we jumped a white-tail buck and doe. The fawn observed the previous day was not seen on this occasion, but was doubtless nearby in the brush. Deer tracks and deer beds and other fresh sign of deer was observed throughout the thicket. In fact, several dozen white-tail deer were ranging within a few hundred yards of the point where this lioness had raised her kittens.

"The abundance of deer in this locality would indicate that they have little fear of the mountain lion. Certainly they do not change their range just because of the presence of mountain lions.

This lioness had wandered aimlessly all over the country for a mile each direction, in fact it was difficult for the dogs to follow her, as they could smell lion scent just about any place they went.

"Mr. Goswick has located a goodly number of lion cubs during his experience as a hunter with the Service, and he advised the writer on this occasion that real young mountain lions were invariably found in a habitat duplicating the locality where this litter had been found. During August of this year he took three mountain lion kittens on a brushy point between two canyons leading off the rim of Walnut Creek northwest of Prescott. They had been born and raised at that point and their main cover was the brush and a large pine log. Another litter found a few years ago was less than 10 days old, as the kittens' eyes were not yet open, and they were located in an oak thicket on a hillside in the Mazatzal Mountains northeast from Phoenix, Arizona."

All evidence to date indicates that the female puma seeks complete isolation from her kind at the time she gives birth to her young.

Frequency and size of litters.—The puma seems to breed once every two to three years, having from one to six kittens, which may be born at any time or month of the year.

One of the largest litters of the puma on record in the files of the Fish and Wildlife Service was that observed by Hunter Robert L. Hoggatt, of Price, Utah, on July 18, 1940, in Avintaquin Canyon, Uinta National Forest, Duchesne County, Utah, approximately 24 miles north of Price. This litter included six kittens—one male and five females. These were born while the mother was in the trap.

Puma litters, in the experience of government hunters in Utah, usually number from one to three, with an average of two.

A pregnant female puma, killed February 20, 1942, near Parowan, Irion County, Utah, was found on examination after death about to give birth to young. A caesarian operation was performed and three kittens removed which were fully developed. By the use of artificial respiration they were revived and taken by horseback to a car five miles away, and then driven the remaining distance to Parowan. They readily took cow's milk, but died within a few days. Their weight was 14 ounces each at the time they were removed from the mother. The mother weighed 109 pounds.

Among 24 pumas killed by Bryon Denton between 1934 and

1941 in the La Veta, Colorado, area, three females were found to contain three embryos each.

Gestation.—Fuller (1832: 62) records a female in captivity which "admitted the male on December 28, and brought forth on the night of April 2 two young." This represents a period of 96 days from copulation until birth of the young.

Attwater records a pair of pumas kept in captivity in Texas which produced "two litters of kittens of four each—the first, April 4, 1891, the second, June 4, 1892." (Allen, J. A. 1896: 80.) In this instance also the period of gestation was found to be 96 days.

Young.—When between a week and 10 days old the eyes of the young are partially open, and by the end of the second week after birth they are fully open. Normally they are suckled for 4 or 5 weeks, but if not prevented will continue nursing until nearly half-grown.

When about 6 weeks old the young readily partake of fresh meat. Two of this age when fed raw liver greedily consumed a quarter of a pound each in a very short time.

At birth puma young vary in length from 8 to 12 inches, and in weight from 8 to 16 ounces. It has been observed that among the newly born of *Felis concolor hippolestes*, the largest race, the length is 12 inches, and weight 16 ounces. They grow rather slowly at first. When approximately 8 weeks old they weigh about 10 pounds. At the age of 6 months weights have been recorded from 30 to 45 pounds. From this time on the animal appears to develop more rapidly. As a yearling it has been found to have nearly doubled its weight.

The young are densely spotted and the tail is ringed. These markings gradually disappear as the adult stage is reached; occasionally a few faded spots will be found on half-grown individuals.

The young pumas are tender along the back and so continue until about a year old. A sharp blow with a small club will easily deform the animal. It may be this vulnerability to back injury when young that occasionally produces a sway-backed puma; such individuals have been seen by the author on several occasions among pumas in zoos.

The young of a litter get along without serious conflict but strangers may fight desperately.

Three pumas, between 3 and 4 months old, and of different mothers, including a brother male and sister female and a lone male, when allowed to associate with one another for the first time indulged in a fierce fight. The two males so scarred each other that they soon died, and the female later died from mutilations experienced while participating in the same fight.

In the Rocky Mountains observations have been made showing that the female puma after killing a deer has returned to her lair and taken the young with her to feed on the prey. After feeding the young were then returned to the den. It has been further observed that in most instances but one feeding takes place, and the prey is never visited again. However, it may also be visited repeatedly until the entire carcass is consumed. Some puma hunters hold to the opinion that when repeated visits are made to the prey with the young, it is by an old female with worn teeth, and if there is but a single feeding it is the work of a much younger female, who, providing sufficient food is available, will kill a fresh victim for each feeding. Some hunters also believe this is the general rule, even when young are not involved.

Young pumas are able to kill their own prey long before they are fully matured. Animals from a third to half grown have left telltale evidences in their habitat of having killed not only small prey, as ground squirrels and rabbits, but also young fawns.

The female puma is inclined to defend her young but apparently not against man. Instances are on record of females with young sufficiently grown to travel that have refused to tree or run any distance when pressed by dogs. Instead such a female will refuse to run, comes to bay, and fights the dogs. On the approach of humans, however, the animal will abandon the young and make for the first convenient tree. If further unmolested the family would no doubt reassemble.

Family Ties

After the young have fully matured it is questionable as to how long they remain with the mother.

Numerous young of the puma approximately two years old, and weighing in the neighborhood of 80 pounds, have been found in the company of the mother.

IV

PARASITES AND DISEASES

GENERALLY speaking the puma appears to be exceptionally free from ecto-parasites. One reason for this, particularly in relation to fleas, is that the puma uses no one den for any great length of time, nor does the den usually have litter that would provide habitat for fleas.

Generally barren, and shorn of any particular litter of forest debris in most instances, its den or sleeping point is more apt to be composed of solid rock, upon which it seeks repose. When not in a den, and on cross-country travel, throughout its travel route resting points are too infrequently made on the same spot to permit of flea incubation.

I am indebted to Dr. R. R. Parker, Director, Rocky Mountain Laboratory, U. S. Public Health Service, Hamilton, Montana, for the following information on flea occurrence in the puma:

". . . . Mr. G. P. Holland, Agricultural Scientist of Kamloops, B. C., Canada, has determined the fleas taken from a mountain lion to be *Arctopsylla setosa* (Roths.) 1906. Mr. Holland further states: 'This species occurs on a number of carnivores—we have specimens from black and grizzly bears, coyotes, lynx, wolverine and now from

117

mountain lion. The species was described from females only, and in 1936 Wagner supplied the description of a male which he referred to this species. Jellison and Good (1942, p. 23) agreed that Wagner was correct in associating his specimen with Rothschild's *setosa*. My own series also confirms this, and compare well with your material.' "

The following ticks have been recorded as infesting the puma: *Amblyomma cajennense*,[1] *Boophilus microplus*,[1] *Dermacentor cyaniventris*,[1] *Dermacentor variabilis*,[2] *Ixodes ricinus*,[2] and *Ixodes cookei*.[2]

Being a woods-loving creature, it is not surprising that the animal is host to these ticks. The most frequent spots for attachment of such parasites, according to the author's observation, are the ears or the areas behind them, where probably they are most sheltered from the puma's grooming operations.

Of the louse family, only one, *Trichodectes felis*, has come to the attention of the author, it being reported as occurring on the puma in Brazil.

Comparatively little is known concerning the internal parasites of this large cat. The following have been recorded, all from Brazil:

Roundworms: Filaroides striatum (Mol.) 1858.

Tapeworms: Taenia (Echinoccus) *digarthrus* (Diesing) 1813.

Two species of adult cestodes are recorded from the puma by Hall (1920), namely *Taenia taeniaeformis* and *Echinococcus granulosus*, both of which were found in *Felis concolor*. Later Skinker (1935) described a new adult cestode from North American carnivores and named it *Taenia lyncis*. Specimens were recorded from *Lynx rufus* and also from *Felis concolor azteca*, *Felis concolor hippolestes*, and *Felis concolor oregonensis*. The immature stages of this tapeworm are bladder-like cysts attached to the mesenteries of deer of the genus *Odocoileus* and complete their development only when eaten by the larger carnivores. Deer in turn are infected by fecal contamination which contains eggs from the adult cestodes living in the intestines of the carnivore.

Natural death in the wild appears to come from such causes as starvation brought on by badly worn or broken teeth, injuries sustained from defensive reactions of prey, as severe cutting by hoofs or

---

[1]Recorded from South America.
[2]Recorded from North America.

laceration from horns, or in contact with other pumas. Advanced age slows the animal's ability to kill until finally it succumbs from starvation. Old male pumas have been killed that were mere shadows of their former selves.

The only disease so far known seriously to affect pumas in the wild is rabies. To what extent this occurred among the animals in earlier times is unknown. Rabies was prevalent among wolves and coyotes in the period of early settlement of the western United States and it is not unreasonable to assume that the puma also was infected.

Instances of unprovoked attacks on humans by pumas may have been the acts of rabid animals. Storer (1923: 1-4) verifies this in his account of an attack that took place during the present century near Morgan Hill, California. A female puma set upon two boys, and a young lady, who came to their rescue, only to be badly mutilated. Seven weeks later rabies manifested itself in two of the victims, who soon died.

Old-time stockmen voice the opinion that whenever livestock survives attacks from this predator the animals died anyway from tetanus resulting from the deep scratches or claw punctures. As the early symptoms of rabies and tetanus (lockjaw) are similar, probably some of the deaths of mutilated livestock may have come from unrecognized rabies. It is well substantiated that all livestock, other domestic animals, and many of the mammals in the wild, particularly cats, wolves and coyotes, fall victims to the disease of rabies.

Pumas, when held in captivity for any length of time, and particularly in association with other animals, may become afflicted with various diseases. Tumors have been known to develop in confined pumas. A large male kept in the zoo at Albuquerque, New Mexico, from the time it was 3 months old, developed a large tumor on its side and was finally killed when approximately 13 years old to end its sufferings.

V

ECONOMIC STATUS

THE ECONOMIC status of the puma depends upon how much men can utilize the animal and to what extent it preys upon domestic and wild animals of value to man.

The Puma as Food

Hariot (1587: 333) records that in early Virginia "the inhabitants sometimes kill the Lion and eat him."

Catesby (1743: Appen. xxv), in discoursing on the puma, noted that "their flesh is white, well tafted, and is much esteemed by the Indians and white people."

Chittenden (1935: 820) says, "The American panther (*Felis concolor*), the 'painter' of the trappers, is of very little importance in fur trade history. Its flesh, however, was accounted the choicest which the wilderness afforded, not excepting even the tail of the beaver or the more delicate morsels from the buffalo. 'Painter meat' was the synonym of anything which was particularly excellent."

The following is a quotation from the Philadelphia Record for June 18, 1939: "*Ely, Nev., June 17 (UP).*—Mountain lions as food are highly recommended by Mr. and Mrs. Otto Neilson and

Mr. and Mrs. Ralph Kauffman, who tried out a couple of young ones. The lion tenderloin, they reported, tasted a little like pork and quite a bit like chicken. In addition they collected the State bounty for killing them."

Bryon Denton of La Veta, Colorado, has utilized every puma killed by him, a total of 24, for food. He has found the meat to be very tender, resembling veal. Further, he declares, the front shoulders and ribs make excellent and very palatable roasts. "Jerky" or salted and sun-dried puma meat sent in to Washington by some of the field men of the Fish and Wildlife Service was relished by all who tried it.

Experience in South America as to the palatability of puma flesh is corroborative.

Azara (1802: 128) records that in Paraguay he had seen his peones choose the meat of the puma in preference to beef at times.

Darwin (1839: 135) in the account of his part in the voyage of the Beagle along the coasts of South America wrote of puma meat: "At supper, from something which was said, I was suddenly struck with horror at thinking that I was eating one of the favorite dishes of the country, namely, a half-formed calf, long before its proper time of birth. It turned out to be Puma; the meat is very white, and remarkably like veal in taste. Dr. Shaw was laughed at for stating that 'the flesh of the [African] lion is in great esteem, having no small affinity with veal, both in colour, taste, and flavour.' Such certainly is the case with the Puma. The Gauchos differ in their opinion, whether the Jaguar is good eating, but are unanimous in saying that cat [puma] is excellent."

Use of the Skin and Other Parts

It is popularly believed that skins of animals of the cat tribe are thin and easily torn or penetrated, and that if it were not for the protective covering of hair the felines would suffer untold hardships. Nevertheless the puma has an outstandingly tough skin. Seldom, if ever, do we recall that any dog has succeeded in lacerating the puma's skin when fighting an animal at bay. Nor have we ever observed that a puma in falling out of a tree when wounded or killed has had its hide penetrated by the points of dead limbs or other sharp obstacles against which it catapulted to the ground. Old scars occasionally found upon the puma skin are the result in nearly all instances from the clawing received in fighting with its own kind, or from the penetration by a hoof or antler of deer or their allies, used in protecting themselves from this enemy.

Some of the uses to which the skin has been put also indicate its toughness and good wearing qualities. For instance it was employed in making quivers, as reported by Hoffman (1877: 95) while serving as a medical officer in the U. S. Army at a military post on the Grand River, Dakota Territory. He noticed that puma ". . . skins are seldom brought to the trader's store to exchange, as they are valued by the Indians in the manufacture of quivers." Because of its various shades, such as reddish brown, these quivers were often attractive, beautiful in their design, as well as very serviceable.

Catlin also noted the use of puma skin for a quiver while painting a picture of the Chief, Mah-to-toh-pa, during his sojourn among the Mandan Indians in the 1830's. (Donaldson, T. 1887: 401.)

The claws of the puma were used by early day western Indians in ornamentation, as were occasionally also some of the teeth.

Lewis and Clark found the skin of the animal worn by men of the tribes of the lower Columbia River, as a small robe, reaching to the "middle of the thigh, tied by a string across the breast, with its corners hanging loosely over their arms." (Coues, E. 1893: 776.)

Occasionally in the earlier days the puma skin was used for carriage robes, as well as for (Plate 25) rugs and saddle cloths, and saddles by some Plains Indians. The tip of the tail was at times employed for ornamenting horse bridles near the ear-strap, and for covering the iron rings of the saddle cinch. Some of the early trapper-hunters made trousers from tanned puma skins, and many pioneer settlers in the more remote sections of North America used the entire skins for couch or bed coverings.

The value varied considerably. In early times, according to Ludlow (1876: 63) in the northern plains area, "the skins of the Cougar were formerly imported in large quantities from the east and from California for purposes of trade with the Indians. A few years since a good skin was sometimes sold for seven or eight buffalo robes; but at present [1875] they have little or no commercial value."

According to Periolat (1885: 391), "skins of the panther, mountain lion, Mexican lion, California lion, etc., are all known to the trade as panther skins, and are worth only fifty cents to two dollars and fifty cents. They come mainly from Montana and the Rocky

Mountain region." The use they were put to was mainly that of floor mats.

Anderson (1934: 4060) records that of the Canadian furs taken during the season of 1930-31, 491 puma skins averaged in value $2.00 each.

As to use of puma skins in South America, Edward Chace writes, "Their ordinary boleradora strings they spiraled from guanaco necks, or cut from marehide where it was thickest, but they used lion skin for balling to kill. That stretches and ties itself in such tight knots that the animal stands no chance of kicking free. It cuts in so badly that it would ruin a horse." (Barrett, R. and K. 1931: 81.)

Miller (1930: 16), in the late 1920's, while in the southern Matto Grosso area of Brazil, found the "skin of the puma . . . of little value commercially, bringing only two or three dollars (15 or 20 milreis)." He reports its use in the making of sandal soles and as being sufficiently strong and durable for that purpose.

Molina (1808: 211) had observed in the latter part of the 18th century while in Chile that "the skin serves for various uses; good leather for boots or shoes is manufactured from it, and the fat is considered as a specific in the sciatica."

As mentioned previously, the Peruvian Incas made a ceremonial use of the puma skin, and at times of its skull. At one of the principal feasts held in November at Cuzco, puma skins with the skulls were first prepared with gold ear-pieces for the ears, the teeth likewise replaced with gold, as well as the claws. The pelts, so decorated, were then so encased over the persons who were to wear this ceremonial dress that the head as well as the neck was covered, the remainder of the pelt hanging from the shoulders. (Markham, C. R. 1873: 45.)

Food Habits

Distance traveled in hunting.—Pumas find most of their prey near the rougher and more inaccessible canyons, where they may live and breed with a minimum of disturbance. One of the most striking things about these animals is the distance to which they will go for food. They have often been known to travel 25 miles or more in a night apparently without resting for any appreciable length of time.

Hiding food.—Stalking and killing have been dicussed on pages

93-98. After taking one meal from a victim the puma will often, but not always, cover the remaining portion with debris, as sticks, stones, dry leaves, and small limbs and twigs.

In the burial of its prey after the first meal is taken the puma sometimes will completely cover the carcass, with none of its parts showing. Occasionally, however, the head, feet, or tail may protrude after the burial. The debris is generally heaped up and over the carcass by the use of the front feet, and will be left in the final shape of a low mound. Where sunken ground is taken advantage of the burial may be so complete as to make it rather difficult to locate unless one actually stumbles upon the loose soil and other debris covering the prey.

After a lapse of from two to three days it will return to the carcass for additional feeding. This may go on over a period of a week or more, up to 10 days, if the meat keeps well, for the puma does not seem to relish tainted or putrid meat. If the meat keeps palatable the visits to the carcass may continue until all the edible portions are entirely consumed.

Generally the prey is dragged to a secluded spot. A full-grown goat, killed by a puma in the Carmen Mountains of Coahuila, was dragged along a canyon floor and then up a very steep mountainside for more than 400 yards and covered, after the first meal, under an oak thicket. A six-month old thoroughbred colt was killed in a field by a puma in Turkey Creek Canyon of the Canelo Hills, 70 miles south and east of Tucson, Arizona. Its body was then dragged more than 100 yards to the side of the field under a barbed-wire fence, and then on up into a small side canyon several hundred yards, where it was covered. Nearly a week later the puma was captured in a steel trap at this point. One remarkable thing was that, although this puma several nights previously had succeeded in making its escape from steel traps set at the carcass, this had not deterred it from returning to feed once again from the carcass, at which time it was finally caught.

Communal feeding.—Frequently more than one puma may feed on a single carcass. Near a cow carcass, exposed during January, 1918, in Lyle Canyon, Santa Cruz County, Arizona, I trapped one at a time six pumas of various sizes. Evidently they were the parents and two litters of offspring. They fed from the carcass in an ever-dwindling group for a period of approximately three weeks.

The trapping of each animal at the carcass was no deterrent to the return of the remaining animals. Unlike the wolf, the pumas in this instance were returning to the carcass not to seek the missing member of the family group, but to satisfy their appetites. In this instance the cow carcass had remained fresh for many weeks owing to freezing weather.

A puma hunter, while scouting the country northwest of Del Norte, Colorado, on December 18, 1924, found a freshly killed five-point buck on the divide between La Garita and Old Woman Creeks. He noted puma tracks and became convinced that this deer was very recent prey. With the aid of good tracking snow he immediately set out on horseback, following the puma tracks as they led away from the deer carcass. Within a quarter of a mile he jumped four pumas and succeeded in killing all with a rifle. They included an old female and three half-grown young.

Frequency of meals.—Some hunters in the western United States have observed that the puma, following a heavy meal from its freshly killed prey, has laid up from three to four days before eating again. In seeking seclusion for the period the animal chooses a rough and rocky area, generally inaccessible to man or dogs, or other enemy, apparently with the purpose of insuring freedom from disturbance. This trait of the puma resembles that of the wolf after heavy gorging.

While tracking a female puma with the aid of dogs for 11 consecutive days, on the west side of the Sangre de Cristo Mountains, in Colorado, south of Mosca Pass, on north Zapata Creek, all within the San Isabel National Forest, Colorado, John W. Crook observed that during this period two full-grown rams of the Rocky Mountain sheep, and a 5-point buck, had been killed by the puma. When finally treed by the dogs and then killed by Crook it dressed 160 pounds. He found that the sheep had been almost entirely consumed, and that the puma had laid up a day or two following the killing of each ram. A foot of snow assisted him in picking up the animal's trail from each sheep carcass, but new falling snow caused him eventually to lose the track. It was not until the carcass of the buck deer was found and the snow ceased that he was able to kill the creature. From this observation Crook decided that this puma had killed prey and eaten heavily every third day.

In another instance Crook trailed a male puma for three days,

December 11-13, 1926, before the dogs treed it in the vicinity of the middle fork of Carnero Creek, southern Colorado. Despite the baying of the trailing hounds the animal had apparently not heard them because a freshly killed deer was found which showed that the puma took prey while the dogs were on its track.

J. Stokley Ligon also records an instance of depredations by a large male puma while being followed in the Zuni Mountains of New Mexico. For almost a week the hunter was continuously on the trail of this puma behind his dogs. During this period a large deer, a colt, and a yearling were found that the puma had killed. When a puma is followed day after day not all kills can be located due to the devious route the animal takes, especially while hunting prey. Even the trailing dogs will not follow all the crooks, turns, and circles, but invariably switch to a fresher trail where it touches the older, although the puma perhaps has covered much ground and made a kill before crossing its former trail. In summer small deer are often entirely eaten up, leaving little or no evidence of a kill.

Behavior when eating.—Untamed adult pumas kept in captivity have been observed to be exceedingly ferocious while eating, growling, hissing, and spitting at intruders, human or otherwise. Griffith (1827: 439) quotes Major C. H. Smith as to the "abstracted ferocity" of the animal when engaged with its food. "A puma which had been taken and was confined was ordered to be shot, which was done immediately after the animal had received its food. The first ball went through his body, and the only notice he took of it was by a shrill growl, doubling his efforts to devour his food, which he actually continued to swallow with quantities of his own blood till he fell."

Baby pumas held in confinement exhibit intense ferocity when fed meat such as raw liver, and become exceedingly difficult to handle. This may be the result of the unloosening of a pent-up nervousness which becomes apparent in the bodily movements. These characteristics are speedily manifested, coupled at all times with evidences of anger, intolerance, and fierce hatred, not only by each to its brothers and sisters, but also to the person who but a short time previous to feeding may have fondled them and received affection in return. If one places the hand on an infant puma's back when it is eating raw meat the back becomes rigid, and this tendency to "freeze" is accompanied by low growls and snarls. Once the raw meat is entirely consumed, however, be it ever so small or large portion, these savage demonstrations subside as quickly as they arose, and the customary docility on the part of each kitten is quickly resumed toward its mates, as well as toward their human benefactor.

Fondness for blood.—At times a puma seems to satisfy its hunger from blood alone to the exclusion of other parts of its prey. The opinion is held that this generally occurs after the animal has but a short time previously gorged on meat, which it is then inclined to shun in preference to the blood of the newly-killed prey. Both in the wild and in captivity pumas are exceedingly fond of fresh bloody liver.

Abstinence from water.—When water is scarce the puma apparently is capable of existing for long periods without it. This seems particularly evident in some of the dry semi-desert areas of southwestern Utah.

Stomach contents.—To illustrate the choice of food by the puma we have available the results of both field and laboratory examinations of stomach contents. The data in the first table below were assembled from the reports of all the Fish and Wildlife Service hunters throughout the western United States over a period of five years, 1918 to 1922. They show the frequency with which several food items were found month by month. A certain stomach might have contained 2 or more different kinds of food, as for instance,

Table 9. Stomach contents of pumas as shown by field examination, 1918-1922.

Food	Jan.	Feb.	Mar.	Apr.	May	June	July	Aug.	Sept.	Oct.	Nov.	Dec.	Total
Deer	24	32	18	13	14	5	17	9	3	7	27	19	188
Beef	15	28	12	22	4	9	15	10	8	6	7	8	144
Horse	3	4	----	2	----	1	1	3	----	2	----	4	20
Sheep or goat	1	----	4	2	----	4	4	----	1	----	----	----	16
Elk	5	1	4	2	----	----	----	----	----	----	----	----	12
Bait	----	----	1	2	1	----	----	----	----	----	----	----	4
Grass, sticks, or berries	----	1	1	----	----	1	1	----	----	----	----	----	4
Pork	----	----	----	----	----	----	----	----	----	----	----	2	2
Antelope	----	----	----	----	----	----	1	----	----	----	----	----	1
Rabbit	----	----	----	----	----	----	----	1	----	----	----	----	1
Ground squirrel	----	----	----	----	1	----	----	----	----	----	----	----	1
Carrion	----	----	1	----	----	----	----	----	----	----	----	----	1
Total	48	66	41	43	20	20	39	23	12	15	34	33	394

Table 10. Stomach contents of pumas as shown by laboratory examination

Season	Number stomachs	Percentage	Deer	Porcupine	Sheep Goat	Horse Cow	Other* Mammals	Birds	Carrion	Grass	Total percent
Spring March-Apr.-May 16 - 13 - 2	31	volume	56.0	14.7	6.4	9.7	10.0	trace	3.2	---	100
	31	occurrence	58	19	6	10	13	3	3	---	---
Summer June-July-Aug. 7 - 3 - 6	16	volume	56.3	25.0	---	6.2	12.5	---	---	---	100
	16	occurrence	56	25	---	6	13	---	---	---	---
Autumn Sept.-Oct.-Nov. 4 - 6 - 10	20	volume	42.5	30.0	7.5	10.0	5.0	---	5.0	trace	100
	20	occurrence	45	35	10	10	5	---	5	5	---
Winter Dec.-Jan.-Feb. 9 - 14 - 23	46	volume	72.6	16.4	5.4	2.2	0.1	---	1.1	2.2	100
	46	occurrence	74	17	9	2	4	---	2	2	---
Annual	113	volume	60.4	19.5	5.3	6.2	5.5	trace	2.2	0.9	100
Annual	113	occurrence	62	22	7	6	8	1	3	2	---
Percentages by volume of annual food of puma collected in states listed											
Arizona	25	volume	55.0	10.4	10.0	20.0	2.6	---	2.0	---	100
Colorado	2	"	100	---	---	---	---	---	---	---	100
Idaho	1	"	100	---	---	---	---	---	---	---	100
Montana	16	"	75.0	25.0	---	---	---	---	---	---	100
New Mexico	37	"	40.5	36.4	2.8	8.1	6.8	---	2.7	2.7	100
Oregon	1	"	100	---	---	---	---	---	---	---	100
Texas	11	"	68.2	---	4.5	---	27.3	trace	---	---	100
Utah	12	"	66.7	16.7	8.3	---	---	---	8.3	---	100
Washington	8	"	100	---	---	---	---	---	---	---	100

*Miscellaneous occurrences of mammals found in stomachs of pumas included a single record each for the armadillo, badger, cotton rat, pocket gopher, rock squirrel, and skunk, and four of rabbits.

Plate 25. Pumas when pelted for sale or making into trophies such as rugs, are skinned, stretched and dried "flat"

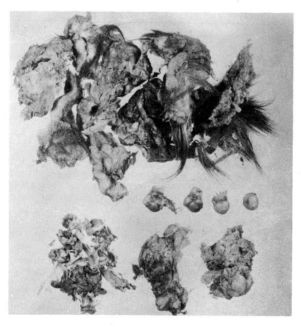

Plate 26. Stomach contents of a female puma examined May 1935, consisting nearly 100% of porcupine remains. Note scarcity of quills despite the volume of flesh consumed

Plate 27. A puma "scat" consisting of approximately 80% porcupine quills. Thus at times large quantities of porcupine quills pass through the entire digestive tract of the animal. How the puma continues to live following such a meal is a question

130

both beef and deer remains, in which case it was tabulated as one stomach containing beef and one stomach containing deer. This explanation is necessary in order to make clear that the totals in the table do not represent the exact number of stomachs examined, but rather the number of times that the given items were found in the stomachs.

The laboratory findings summarized in the next table (10) show the percentages of the different food items by volume, as well as by frequency of occurrence. The analyses of 113 puma stomachs collected in 9 western states were made by Charles C. Sperry, of the Fish and Wildlife Service.

Dixon (1925: 40-41), in his examination of 43 California puma stomachs, found that "2 stomachs out of the 43, less than 5%, contained domestic stock, while 34 out of the 43, or 80%, contained deer," the animal's favorite food. He lists the largest meal of the puma that came under his observation in the analyses as weighing 3,624 grams, or approximately 8 pounds.

In a report on the management of the Roosevelt elk in 1943, John E. Schwartz presented the following statement of food remains found in 28 droppings of pumas collected in the Olympic Peninsula, Washington.

Table 11. Food items of Washington pumas as shown by dropping analyses

Food item	Occurrence	
	Number	Percent
Washington varying hare (*Lepus washingtoni*)	11	32.25
Deer (*Odocoileus columbianus*)	8	23.55
Elk (*Cervus canadensis roosevelti*)	3	8.82
Pine squirrel (*Sciurus douglasii*)	2	5.88
Mountain beaver (*Aplodontia rufa*)	2	5.88
White-footed mouse (*Peromyscus* sp.)	2	5.88
Wood rat (*Neotoma* sp.)	2	5.88
Meadow mouse (*Microtus* sp.)	1	2.94
Flying squirrel (*Glaucomys s. sabrinus*)	1	2.94
Bones	1	2.94
Hair	1	2.94
Total	34	100.00

NORTH AMERICA

Under this heading are grouped the accounts of predation upon wildlife and upon domestic animals in North America, the latter causing the principal demands for control of the numbers of pumas.

Wildlife

These forms are considered in two categories, the plant eaters and the meat eaters, and the former group is subdivided into big game and other herbivores. In addition a few creatures of less easily described food habits are mentioned last.

Deer.—The puma requires for proper sustenance large quantities of food. This need, coupled with abundant power to kill, leads to its preference for large game. Some authorities believe that one mule deer, or equivalent, per week is a normal requirement of the animal. Of smaller deer, as the white-tail, consumption would be even greater.

The killing of 50 or more deer for food per year by the puma makes it an important deer slayer. In aggregate kill it is surpassed now only by the coyote, which while of lesser killing capacity is much more numerous.

The number of deer killed by pumas varies according to the abundance and species of deer, as well as to the age, and to some extent, the sex of the puma. Mature males generally kill the greatest number of deer because they spend much of the time on their extensive travelways and make many kills, from each of which they may eat but little, killing again when hunger urges them, or when opportunity tempts them, even though not hungry.

A female puma, though she may at times make as frequent kills as a male, is then killing for two or three kittens, and the victims are usually devoured to the bone. She generally cares for her young until practically grown, at which time the family is apt to account for a deer about every third day. By the time the kittens are grown the parent may have another set of kittens, when she will restrict her killing until the kittens are old enough to eat meat freely.

Young pumas, as yet unskilled in killing, and adults handicapped by age, kill but few deer. Such animals often resort to smaller prey or even carrion.

Observations in the mountainous areas of the southwestern

United States tend to show that while-tailed deer are the easiest victims of pumas, though by far the most difficult for man to stalk and kill. The reason is that the range of the mule deer includes open park types of country, valleys, and sparsely wooded foothills, where pumas rarely venture. White-tailed deer, on the other hand, constantly range in the brushy and more rugged country which is not only the favorite abode of pumas but the cover which gives them an advantage in killing their prey.

Before intensive Federal-State control of the puma in New Mexico, according to Ligon (1927: 50-52), this predator exacted a tremendous toll of deer, particularly in the Upper Gila River drainage, which he considered the "best deer and turkey range" in that State. He states that the puma killed from 2,500 to 3,000 deer annually in the Gila Basin. Because of State, Federal, and cooperating hunters using intensified control measures this drain was practically eliminated. With decrease in the number of pumas, Ligon found that there was an influx of coyotes. Despite this animal's depredations and intensive hunting by man, deer increased.

The puma's foundness for venison makes it essential that this large cat be given full consideration in any management plans for areas where it occurs on deer range, and particularly so in tracts little grazed by livestock. Here pumas undoubtedly serve as a check on undue increases of deer, which increases in certain portions of the western United States during the past quarter of a century have resulted in overpopulations, far beyond the available food supply. Under such circumstances a moderate puma population may well be encouraged. If over-abundance of pumas threatens the welfare of the deer herds, the balance can easily be restored by hunting them sport or through the speed with which regular puma control may be applied.

Elk.—Of the predators affecting the elk in the Olympic Mountains area of Washington, Schwartz's studies (1943: 54) showed that the puma is the leader. Apparently this animal can kill elk without difficulty, as he cites an example of one weighing 76 pounds that had killed an elk in healthy condition which weighed nearly 9 times as much as itself.

Moose.—Preble (1908: 208-209) was informed by Indians in the vicinity of Fort Laird, southwestern Mackenzie, Canada, that the puma "has been known to kill moose."

Mountain sheep.—As an enemy of mountain sheep Grinnell (1904: 289-293) wrote, "While, of course," it "cannot overtake sheep in a fair chase," the puma lies "in wait for them among the rocks, killing many, because the sheep range is on ground suitable for the lions to stalk them on; that is to say, among the rocks on steep mountain sides or the edge of cañons." According to Mr. Hofer, pumas appear to choose favorite lurking spots on mountainsides, where they lie ready to pounce on a passing sheep. At such points as many as 18 sheep skulls had been found.

Beaver.—Warren (1927: 146-149) lists the puma as an enemy of the beaver, and states that in depredating on this fur-bearer carnivores apparently succeed "by surprising them when on land, or perhaps occasionally when in very shallow water." Also, "they may steal upon a victim when it is at work cutting down a tree, or trimming one after it has been felled, or traveling across country from one water to another. Mills gives several instances where a number of beavers were thus killed by cougars and coyotes."

A male puma taken in Monitor Canyon, near Delta, Colorado, was noted to have killed a beaver shortly before it was caught, December 25, 1938. It was a large puma, measuring 8 ft., 10 in. in length.

Allen (G. M., 1942: 250), quoting Major Allan Brooks, says of the puma on Vancouver Island, British Columbia, in 1939: "Over the whole northern third of this island beaver have been decimated by cougars of late years, and they will take many years to recover if they ever do."

Mice.—Perry (1890: 407) notes, "One day, while shooting ducks on a marsh near Sumas Lake [Southern British Columbia], I saw a large animal going through some eccentric motions, and drawing near I saw it was a Cougar trying to catch something that was concealed beneath a cotton-wood log about ten feet long and three feet in diameter. He would stand erect behind the log a yard or more, and at the same time would spring over it and strike heavy blows, first with one paw and then with the other, at some object on the ground. I watched him roll the log over several times before he saw me, but when he did he beat a hasty retreat. Curious to know what he was trying to catch, I, by the aid of a pole that I found near, rolled the log over, and found two mice. It was a most ridiculous and awkward figure that the great brute made in trying to catch his diminutive prey."

Mountain Beaver.[1]—As recorded by Taylor and Shaw (1927: 57), C. A. Stoner, of Ashford, Washington, states that in some sections of the State pumas "are said to feed occasionally on mountain beaver," or the sewellel, as it is commonly called.

Brooks (1930: 66) also records this food habit near the Mount Baker region of northern Washington, where, after extirpation "of the deer by the Cougar the animal was reduced to living on the abundant Mountain Beaver."

Peccary.—The puma is probably not so habitual a killer of peccaries as is the jaguar, but during the spring of 1943 an Arizona rancher reported a puma as having killed one peccary and a wild domestic sow, and that both were covered in the same place.

Porcupine.—One of the favorite foods of the puma is the flesh of the porcupine (Plate 26). Occasionally the puma will swallow some of the quills intact, but large quantities seem to do no damage; they must be softened in the alimentary tract, as they are sometimes found in the excreta. Their stiffness there probably is due to drying after they are expelled (Plate 27). They are injurious, however, when they become profusely imbedded in the lips, tongue, or roof of the mouth. The puma in killing this animal apparently turns it over on its back, then proceeds to rip open the region of the abdomen and gains access to the edible portions with its powerful claws. The wolf and coyote kill it by grasping firmly in the mouth by the nose and shaking it until dead much as a cat does with a rat. No indications are apparent that the puma uses this method.

In the Adirondack region of New York State, before pumas became extinct, H. H. Bromley (1871: 692) quoting Putnam, recorded, "Dead ones have been found in the woods, having been killed by the spines of hedgehogs which they had attacked."

John Mayse, who has killed numerous pumas in the Pike's Peak region of Colorado, has observed sign in the Pike National Forest, indicating that female pumas had helped their young obtain the porcupine for food. In these instances it was apparent that the mother had knocked porcupines out of aspen trees, then descended to the ground and killed them for her offspring. The only places

---

[1]Not closely related to the common beaver.

in the puma's body where porcupine quills have been found by Mayse have been the shoulders, never the paws. He believes that those imbedded in the paws are pulled out by the puma with its teeth.

In the Rocky Mountain region of the United States most of the porcupines killed for the young were destroyed in the fall and early winter. With the exception of the skin and lower intestine most of the porcupine is consumed at a single feeding. Occasionally, however, the animal's quills are eaten with the skin, to be disposed of as indicated in the foregoing.

Coyote.—While tracking a puma on the Peavine Grazing Unit of the Eldorado National Forest in California, on June 7, 1928, with the aid of a dog, the trail led to a coyote den. Here evidence showed that two coyote pups, about one-third grown, had been killed and eaten by the puma. Still remaining in the den were three other puppies that had not been molested. Evidently the two which had been killed and devoured were killed outside the entrance of the den while the five puppies were at play.

In the course of trapping coyotes during August of 1938, 30 miles north of Ashfork, Arizona, George Carpenter reported, "While driving my car up into a 'U'-shaped clearing in the cedar facing Aubrey Cliffs, I noted a large lion track. Stopping my car I followed [it] . . . about 200 yards. At this point the tracks turned abruptly to the right, the lion traveling in great strides for about 150 yards, keeping just inside the cedar line. Slowing to a very short step, walk, or creep for a short distance, the lion then leaped about twenty-five feet through the limbs of a cedar tree, hitting a coyote I had trapped along or on the left side, for all the ribs of the coyote's left side were broken, besides a lot of skin and hair was gone. A short fight took place, for the ground was badly disturbed in a thirty-foot circle. In examining the coyote I noted a two-inch hole in its throat, and that the lion had lapped all of the blood it could get.

"Following this the lion tracks showed that the animal had walked about 20 feet, then pawed out a small space in the ground under a large cedar tree, and at this spot had rested for some time. From this point the lion was trailed for about 5 miles when a rain overtook us and blotted out the tracks." (Carpenter, G. 1942: letter in files of Fish and Wildlife Service.)

Some western hunters state this often happens. Not only will the puma kill a trapped coyote, but also other smaller mammals, as the bobcat and fox. In some instances apparently the puma plays with a trapped animal as a house cat does with a mouse, finally killing it more in sport than to satisfy hunger.

Marten.—Bryon Denton, of La Veta, Colorado, during 1937, observed two instances of pine martens being preyed upon by pumas. On of these martens was killed near Blue Lakes, 23 miles southwest of La Veta, on the San Isabel National Forest; the other on the same forest about 4 miles south of Cucharas Pass. These martens were pounced upon in open glades surrounded by timber. In each instance the marten had been ripped down the stomach and all of the animal with the exception of the skin, portions of the head, and lower intestines, was consumed.

Puma.—One of the rare observations of cannibalism among adult pumas is recorded from the Huachuca Mountains in Santa Cruz and Cochise counties, Arizona. While in the course of making an extensive collection of mammals in this state during 1894-95, W. W. Price, as recorded by Allen (1895: 253-254), was an eyewitness to this trait. It appears that in the late winter "at nightfall near the summit, two mountain lions came mewing about the door of a miner's cabin. The man shot through the door, killing one, a gaunt female. The next day he threw the skinned carcass a short distance from the house. During the night the other lion came and ate nearly the whole of it; on the following evening the animal again returned, uttering a peculiar cry. The miner wounded this one, but it escaped into the thick brush. In company with the man I trailed the beast some distance through the snow, but we finally lost the track. The man kindly gave me the skull of the female he had killed." The skull of this specimen is apparently the same one listed in Allen's account of the mammal specimens taken by Price and studied by Allen. This incident might also be described as carrion feeding.

Early in 1945, F. D. Perkins, located near Tucson, Arizona, trapped a puma which, while in the trap, was killed by another puma, following which the animal partook of a meal from it. A large hole was left in the side of the animal—apparently the feeding proceeded until the puma was gorged. The head of the trapped puma also was badly crushed as "if it had been shot with a shotgun." (Anon. Jan. 30, 1945.)

A male puma will devour its own young, as does sometimes the domestic tomcat where the female is not at hand to guard them. In February, 1925, a hunter was detailed to the Wetmore District of the San Isabel National Forest, about 30 miles west of Pueblo, Colorado, to control a puma infestation reported by Forest Service officials and stockmen. While hunting on the morning of February 10 the hunter succeeded in killing a female that was nursing young. From signs noted the hunter believed there was also a male and possibly several young ranging in the immediate vicinity. The following day the hunter returned to the place where he had killed the female, but did not find any fresh tracks or signs. Then on the 12th he went six miles north of this point. It was on this day that a stockman, while riding for cattle, tracked a puma which traveled near to the place where the hunter had killed the female. At this time there was good tracking snow on the ground. When the hunter was informed he immediately returned, and his dogs found what evidently had been the den of the female. There the hunter found the remains of two puma kittens, parts of which had been devoured. From all indications the puma that had been tracked by the stockman had returned to this den and killed the kittens. The size of the tracks led them to believe that the animal was a male.

The hunter continued his efforts to capture this puma. On March 11 he succeeded in getting a run for it with his dogs. From all indications the dogs bayed the puma on a large boulder in a small open park, a battle royal took place, and the lead dog was killed, the puma then making its escape. The hunter used all the hunting sense which his experience had taught him. He was fairly certain that some of the signs that he had found were made by the female that he had killed on February 10, but also that fresher signs were made by the male that killed the dog on March 11. These indicated that this puma was looking for its mate and had on several occasions visited the old den where the young had been killed and devoured. The hunter set traps close to these tracks, and put catnip scent on each puma scratching close to the den. Two of these scratchings were on a pine-covered slope a short distance above the den. The hunter dropped two small logs on each side of these scratchings parallel to each other and about 2½ feet apart. On the upper side of each scratch he placed two traps, carefully concealing them level with the ground and covering them with pine needles. The arrangement of these logs left only two ways that the puma might enter to sniff the scratchings and 10 days later, March 21, it was trapped.

Some puma hunters hold to the opinion that the female endeavors to keep her offspring away from any male until they grow large enough to evade the male.

Skunk.—McLean (1917: 39) reports the finding of a half-chewed skunk, "a striped one, judging from the black and white hairs found" in the stomach of a small puma killed near Coulterville, Mariposa County, California, November 8, 1916.

Skunk hair has been found in puma dung throughout most of the animal's range in the United States.

Turkey.—While collecting and exploring during the Wheeler Surveys, Coues and Yarrow (1875: 40) reported of the puma, "In certain localities in New Mexico and Arizona it wages a terrible warfare upon wild turkeys, destroying hundreds of them, and depopulating their former breeding places to such an extent that in a few years the race will have become almost extinct in this region if measures are not taken to prevent the wholesale slaughter." This prophecy of 70 years ago was rather overdrawn, as the wild turkey still survives on the ranges involved.

Fish.—Occasionally some puma trappers succeed in trapping the animal by using a lure the base of which is decomposed fish. The success of this lure corroborates reports by some of the hunters of the Far West of a puma's eating trout offal.

Snails.—Listing the more common foods partaken of by the animal in the Sumas Lake area of southern British Columbia, Perry (1890: 407) includes snails, but probably meant the large yellow slug (*Ariolimex columbianus*) found in the Pacific Northwest.

To what extent snails may form a portion of the puma's diet at certain times is not known. It is known that a house cat, which at times ate these slugs, became violently ill, but after severe vomiting would recover and would again, after several weeks, repeat the performance.

Livestock

Pigs.—Cory (1896: 110) states, "Panthers kill many small mammals, as well as deer, when they can get them. They are very fond of hogs and a good place to look for a panther is in the vicinity of some drove of semi-wild pigs. When once a panther becomes a 'pig eater' he prefers pig to any other kind of food."

Calves.—Lieutenant Emmons, of the Wilkes Exploring Expedition, found while in the Willamette Valley near Champoeg, Oregon, in 1841, enroute overland to Sacramento, California, that livestock was much harassed by pumas. On the pioneer Johnson's ranch near here he wrote: "These voracious animals are numerous and bold; the night before we arrived they had entered the pen and killed a calf regardless of the dogs; and an alarm was given on the night of our stay, when all the guns were in requisition, and noise enough was made in getting ready to scare away dozens of them." (Wilkes, C. 1845: IV: 372.)

Horses.—Merriam (1899: 104) quotes C. H. Townsend with regard to the Mount Shasta area of California during the middle 1880's, as follows: "It is practically impossible to raise colts in the Shasta County hills on account of these pests. They destroy many hogs and young cattle, but do not present so serious an impediment to the keeping of these animals as in the case of horses. Mr. J. B. Campbell, who trapped two panthers for me in 1883, told me that he had actually never seen more than two or three of the numerous colts born on his stock range, as they had been killed and devoured by panthers soon after birth."

During the period of early settlement in the La Veta, Colorado, area, Bryon Denton states that the raising of colts was impossible, particularly in the Cucharas section, because of the puma's fondness for horse flesh.

Bailey (1931: 290) recounts a case of extreme depredations of the puma on brood mares and saddle horses. Seventy brood mares and 40 saddle horses were placed during October of 1890 in a community pasture of 40,000 acres near the headwaters of the Gila River in New Mexico. "The following May they [the owners] found only 19 of the saddle horses, only a part of the mares and no colts. The mountain lions had taken the rest, including all the colts."

Between the years 1916 and 1919 observations then made showed puma depredations were so severe on colt-raising, in what is known as Corn Canyon, a spur off the west side of the Huachuca Mountains of Santa Cruz County, Arizona, as to make unprofitable the raising of young horses. In this instance likewise the tracing and following of puma tracks proved a migration from the higher Huachucas to their lower reaches, even far to the west into the main Canelo Hills, where also colts were destroyed.

J. Stokley Ligon believes that the puma's fondness for horse flesh will often cause the animal to abandon all caution, and that it is not unusual for pumas to kill grown horses. He records during the winter of 1912-13 9 saddle horses killed on one ranch in the Mogollon Mountains of western New Mexico.

The killing of a full-grown horse was reported by B. H. Beauchamp, a Federal hunter. During the early summer of 1920 he chased a puma with dogs on a stock range located on the west side of the Galiuro Mountains in Graham County, Arizona. The trail finally led into a rough section that became impassable on horseback. Dismounting from his horse, which he then tied to a tree, Beauchamp continued on foot. The manner in which the dogs were baying caused him to think that it would be but a short time before the puma would be treed and he could despatch it and return to his mount. However, the chase lasted much longer than he anticipated, for night came and he was forced to call off the dogs and abandon the hunt. As the darkness made it impracticable for him to climb back up the mountainside to his horse, which he felt would be safe until morning, Beauchamp spent the night in a prospector's cabin at the foot of the range. Early the next morning he went for his horse. On reaching the spot he found to his dismay that another puma had attacked and killed his horse, thus leaving him afoot and a long way from his base camp. Study at the scene showed that a terrific battle had taken place in spite of the horse being handicapped by the picket rope. Profuse claw marks and much biting on the neck and shoulders of the horse were in evidence, and it had been fed upon not long after succumbing to lacerations and a broken neck.

At this point, concluding the observations on the puma's fondness for horse meat it is apropos to state briefly that the flesh of the burro, or small donkey, is likewise relished. Many instances of the killing of burros by the puma are on record from the southwestern ranges of the United States, as well as in the northern states of Mexico, where burros are commonly used as pack animals.

Sheep and goats.—Barnes (1927: 69) states, "In a single night a cougar may ravage a stock farm, wreaking its desires particularly on colts, sheep, calves, and pigs. Phineas Bodily [of Kaysville, Utah] tells me that he saw one kill ten sheep in as many minutes; it bit each one in the back of the head and the whole performance was over before any sounds were made. He has known a cougar to jump a nine-foot fence, taking a grown sheep with it."

The animal is capable of an astonishing amount of killing in a short time. Near Glade Park, in western Colorado, during the early 1920's a single puma during one night entered a herd of bedding ewes and killed 192 of them.

During one February night in 1926 a puma attacked the sheep herd of Stewart Hoffman, which was being wintered in the west end of Montrose County, Colorado, and killed 32 of the sheep. Two of these were covered with snow by the puma, which later on two consecutive mornings returned to the scene of the killing. On the second morning tracks in the snow indicated that a coyote had visited one of the buried sheep simultaneously with the puma, only to be killed, its head having been crushed by a blow of the puma's paw.

A kill of 40 sheep and goats was made by a puma on the Pat Sullivan ranch located near the mouth of the Pecos River [Texas], August 10-11, 1924.

During the early part of 1944, District Agent Everett M. Mercer, of the Fish and Wildlife Service, in charge of predator and rodent control for the Arizona District, reported that a female puma with yearling cubs killed 18 sheep in one night on a ranch located in the Bloody Basin area of Arizona. This animal returned the following night and killed 27 sheep.

This characteristic of killing prey far above needed food requirements seems to hold true of the puma throughout its range. The losses to stockmen are sometimes large. District Agent Mercer reported from the Pine Mountain area, 37 miles southeast of Mayer, Arizona, that prior to a campaign against the pumas the sheepgrowers lost from three to five thousand dollars' worth of sheep each winter. Intensive mountain lion control for two years stopped the depredations.

While studying and photographing pumas on the southern reaches of the Carmen Mountains in northern Coahuila, Mexico, in the late summer of 1937, I heard complaints of puma losses from the goat ranchers. The herds numbering from 50 to 500 were generally attended; nevertheless there were certain canyons around 4,500 feet elevation where the ranchers never permitted a small herd to graze. To do so invariably meant losses from pumas which, for the small owner, might mean the wiping out of his principal property. There appeared to be a migration of the puma from the higher mountains to the low country, for no apparent reason than a possible change in foods, for the higher Carmen Mountains to the north supported an abundance of white-tailed deer (*Odocoileus virginianus carminis*), together with many rodents, other small mammals, in addition to one of the heaviest populations of puma personally noted in North America. The goats and burros of the lower country seemed to be the main incentive for the puma migration.

General.—Padre Francisco Javier Clavijero, of the Society of Jesus, writing of Lower California in the 17th century, stated, "Although the climate of California is not prejudicial to animals taken from New Spain, the scarcity of food and abundance of lions retard their increase. Pasturage being poor, horses, cows, sheep, and goats naturally scatter, seeking food in the out-of-the-way places where they find herbs or shrubbery of any kind. Consequently, being out of sight of their keepers, they fall easy prey to the lions, which kill their colts and calves, and even at times the mares and cows, and commit ravages on sheep and goats. For this reason it has been necessary every year to bring the stock [from New Spain to Mexico] required for the presidio [fort]. (Browne, J. R. 1887: 172.)

SOUTH AMERICA

Instances of similar depredations are on record for many parts of South America. Typical is that recorded by Prichard (1902: 252), who says, "The destruction wrought by pumas upon flocks of sheep is immense. One animal killed upwards of 100 head from among a single flock. One night alone its total amounted to fourteen."

Allen (1905: 172) quotes Barnum Brown, who while in Patagonia country "counted sixty little lambs lying dead on a side hill where, during the night, a lioness with two cubs had run through the bunch batting the lambs as a kitten plays with a ball."

From Prichard he also quotes (Ibid: 173), "In strong contradistinction to the habit of *Felis onca* (jaguar), *F. c. puma*, when hunting, kills a number of animals from a flock or herd. To one only of these kills, however, does it return, and it always makes some pretense of burying the victim singled out for its meal, throwing upon the body in many cases merely a small bunch of thorns. This custom of the puma is frequently taken advantage of by the shepherds, who poison the chosen carcass."

The type of *Felis concolor greeni,* obtained near Curraes Novas, State of Rio Grande Do Norte, Brazil, was taken because of its killing young goats. Pumas were reported also to have killed young horses and donkeys in the same region.

In the period of early colonization of British Guiana, according to Schomburgk (Sir R. H. 1840: 326), pumas were so destructive on cattle farms that dogs were customarily kept for hunting them.

According to Gay (1847: 66-67), the animal in its Chilean habitat lives on various animals, including the fox, guanaco, goat, and even skunks, in spite of their "insupportable odor." Of domestic stock he mentions the animal's particular foundness for horsemeat, and also at times beef, causing great damage to the producers of livestock. Haciendas located near the mountains are often visited by the puma in its hunt for food, and likewise on the more isolated ranges. Dogs are used for the control of puma depredations under such circumstances.

A number of other accounts dealing with wildlife preyed upon by South American pumas follow:

Brehm (1890: 487) states, "All smaller, weaker mammals serve him [the puma] as food. Coatis, Agoutis, Pacas, and the Brockets."

Like Brehm, Brown (1876: 334), referred to the Agouti as the accourie, mentions this rodent as one of the puma's foods in British Guiana.

For that country Schomburgk (Sir R. H. 1840: 326) records of pumas, "They follow in the woods the herds of Peccaries, and watch their motion in order to seize upon .the stragglers." On the same page he notes that the Indians of British Guiana call it by a name translated as "deer tiger."

Miller (1930: 15) charges "the pumas of the Matto Grosso area of Brazil with killing the pampas deer (*Blastocerus b. campestris*), the anteater (*Tamandua t. chapadensis*), the brocket (*Mazama simplicicornis*), and the rhea, sometimes referred to as the South American ostrich."

Darwin (1882: 269) mentions the ostrich [rhea] and the vizcacha, "and other small quadrupeds, as prey" in La Plata, Argentina.

According to Prichard (1902: 250), the huemul, one of the most beautiful deer of South America, also becomes prey at times of the puma.

Cunningham (1871: 109) listed the puma as one of the principal enemies of the guanaco in areas near the Straits of Magellan.

Spears (1895: 195-196) names the guanaco as "the panther's staple food . . . indeed, no living being of the desert, except man, escapes its appetite for murder, one may say, for it claws down the whirring partridge as she springs from her nest, which it afterwards robs of its eggs; it kills the ostrich [rhea] as he sets in his nest, and then after hiding his body it returns to the nest and eats the eggs with gusto; it snatches the duck or goose from its feeding place at the edge of a lagoon; it crushes the shell of the waddling armadillo; it digs the mouse from its nest in the grass; it stalks the desert prairie dog (*Vizcacha lagostomus trichodactylus*), and dodging with easy motion the fangs of the serpent it turns to claw and strip out its life before it can coil to strike again."

From all of the foregoing it becomes evident that although the puma takes a wide range of foods, both wild and domestic, nevertheless its favorite food, when available, is unquestionably the deer. Its extensive range attests to this fact, and in general it may be said the puma "goes with the deer."

VI

HUNTING AND CONTROL

FROM THE EARLIEST times man in the Americas has combated the puma. This has been mainly for the protection of his domestic animals, but sometimes has assumed the form of sport. The Incas always despatched it when taken in their spectacular ring hunts for the vicuñas and guanacos, believing it to be a detriment in a game country.

Indian hunting.—Coues (1867: VI: 285-286) records the earlier day Arizona Indians as pursuing the puma "successfully with only their bows and arrows," for he "found skins in their possession cut in various places with the sharp stone points of their arrow-heads."

Gadow (1908: 371-372) describes a very interesting manner in which the puma was killed by the Indians in southern Mexico. In this scheme, whereby the animal "is shot by lantern light, the hunter in ambush attracting the beast to the spot by the sound of a primitive instrument composed of a hollow piece of bamboo and a string, which, in the hands of a native, can be made to imitate the note of a hind or kid." Again, instead of bamboo being used, a three-inch piece of "stag's cannon bone, with a thin film pasted over one of the ends of the tube" is used. ". . . by sucking at the other end a squeak-

Figure 3. Patagonian bolas used in South America for capturing game, including the puma—1, 2, 4. Bolas used by Eskimos for capturing birds—3

Figure 4. Use of bola on horseback

Plate 28. The small wire-haired terrier dog is an exceptionally good type of puma dog. (See Catesby, 1743: II: xxv)

Plate 29. The late Ben Lilly, last of the mountain men, and unexcelled as a puma hunter. He served several years as a government hunter in New Mexico and Arizona

Plate 30. Lilly and hunting companions; some of the excellent puma dogs he used on the game and livestock ranges of New Mexico

Plate 31. Ben Lilly, on the start of a camp move. With his dogs and the simple equipment shown in this photograph Lilly passed long periods in the wildest sections of the mountains of the Southwest. He followed the trails of pumas and camped in their haunts until they succumbed to his tireless pursuit

Plate 32. Finis—puma dogs attempting to climb for final combat with a puma (not shown) that they have just "treed." (Photo courtesy of Richard T. Lewis, Spokane, Washington)

Plate 33. Pumas when crowded closely by dogs and man readily take to trees to escape their adversaries

Plate 33 (*Continued*)

Plate 34. Five pumas, a complete family trailed and killed in 3 days near Mount Rainier, Washington

Plate 35. Government puma hunter and his dogs in Colorado, March 1928

Plate 37. A rare occurrence of a puma "treed" in the giant cactus or Sahuaro, of the southwestern deserts of the United States

Plate 36. Female puma killed in Lake County, Oregon. Inset: one of the 4 young comprising the litter traveling with her, taken alive

Plate 38. Trap most suitable for pumas (No. 4½), showing double-pronged "drag hook" attached to 8-foot chain.

Plate 39. Puma trap pan covered with canvas. Note slot on far edge of canvas which fits about trigger. Canvas cover keeps the small pit clear beneath trap pan. Trap is now ready to be covered.

Plate 40. Trap-setting cloth used for retaining earth removed in process of sinking puma trap in selected spot. It holds all surplus earth not needed for burying trap, which can conveniently be tossed away from area of trap-set.

Plate 41. Deer—favorite prey of the puma. Buck killed by a puma in New Mexico. Contrary to its general habit, no attempt had been made by the puma to bury this deer. The carcass, found on its side as illustrated, furnished an excellent opportunity for making a set of 3 or more traps 15 to 20 inches away

Plate 42. Part of acre of catnip plants from which pure oil of catnip was extracted by the Bureau of Biological Survey for use as lure in trapping pumas. (See Young, Stanley P., 1940, Catniping our Big Cats; and Gregory, Tappan, 1939, Lion in the Carmens)

Plate 43. Preliminary for a 2-trap "blind" set for pumas. In the saddle of a divide the traps are placed in a narrow part of the trail. A small stick or other obstruction should be placed between the traps and one at either approach, to make the puma step into one of the traps rather than between or over them. Such a set captured the 207-lb. puma shown in Plate 9

160

Plate 44. Small stick placement on a puma trail, an aid to breaking puma's regular step when used for completed blind trap sets. Here traps are concealed in foreground between rocks and small sticks

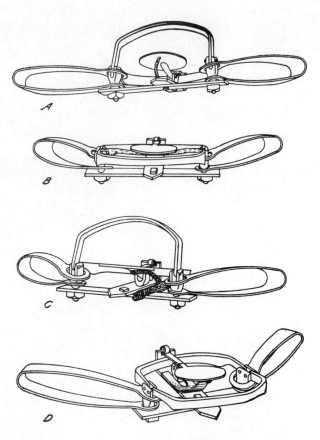

Figure 5. Devices to prevent capturing small animals and birds in traps set for pumas or other predators: *A*, Pan supported by twig (grass or a light coil spring may be used); *B*, splint support; *C*, forked-twig support; *D*, Biological Survey trap pan spring

Plate 45. The Biological Survey trap pan spring

ing note was produced.   The lantern, of course, is intended to enable
the sportsman to see the sight of his gun, and the reflected light in
the eyes of his prey. . . . Thus equipped, armed with a miserable gun
and a machete, these Indians go out night after night until one of
them is lucky enough to bring home the coveted 'lion' or tigre
[jaguar]."

Use of bolas.—Use of the bolas for hunting in South America
began many centuries ago.   Church (1912: 294) gives one of the
best descriptions of this device (see Fig. 3-4), stating, "It was, at
the time of the conquest [in Peru] used by all of the tribes which
occupied the open areas of the Plata Country, from its northern
frontier to the Straits of Magellan.   Later it was adopted by the Argentine 'cowboy,' the Gaucho, as a most efficacious arm for capturing
any quadruped.

"The bolas were also extensively used by the Indian tribes of
Uruguay and the southern part of Rio Grande do Sul, in Brazil, and
in these districts the grooved bola is occasionally found.   It is a
sphere or spheroid, generally of stone, with a groove cut around it,
and is often met with on the plains of central Patagonia, where, when
they find one, the Indians treasure it as the weapon used by their
ancestors.

"There were many forms and sizes of bolas, but, in general, they
may be reduced to three, and consisted of three thongs made of
hide, or of ostrich or guanaco sinews, plaited in four plaits, and about
seven or eight feet in length.   At one of the ends of each thong a
globular stone, about the size of a billiard ball, was suspended in a
hide bag, and the other ends were united.   This set of bolas was used
principally for hunting the guanaco, deer, puma, and any large game.
By holding one bola in the hand, the others were swung round the
head with great velocity, while running or on horseback, and, from
a short distance, launched at the animal it was sought to capture.   I
have seen a powerful Gaucho bring down a horse at a distance of
fifty yards or more.   The weapon, when it leaves the hand, revolves
in a circle, each thong 120° distant from the others, the circle thus
covering a diameter of from 14 to 16 feet.   Whenever one of the
balls is arrested by an obstacle the whole three wind so tightly
round it that it is frequently quite difficult to disentangle them.   A
wild bull or a horse having his legs thus ensnared drops helpless to
the ground."

Darwin (1882: 270) mentions the ease with which the puma was killed in the open country of South America. Here "it is first entangled with the bolas, then lazoed, and dragged along the ground till rendered insensible. At Tandeel (south of the Plata)," he was informed "within three months one hundred were thus destroyed."

Pit trapping.—The use of pits to capture animals traces back to pre-historic times. The pit was probably one of the earliest man-made traps. As constructed and put into use in various parts of Europe, and later in early North and South America, it was modified in its construction to meet local conditions. In general the pit consisted of a hole dug of varying depth along a game trail. In the center a dirt column was left. On this was put the bait, as a lure, in the form of a live sheep, preferably a bleating lamb, or a young dog. Often the bait animal was left in discomfort so that it would squeal intermittently. The predator would thus be attracted, and in making a jump for the bait would fall into the pit. This was generally fenced so as to make it impossible for the captured animal to jump again to freedom. Sometimes the pit was covered with brush and litter. When the animal trod upon this flimsy roofing in its attempt to reach the bait its weight would cause it to crash through to the bottom of the pit, from which it could not extricate itself on account of the depth. Often, too, stakes were set in the bottom of the pit with sharp points upward, upon which the falling animal would be transfixed. This generally caused a lingering death of the trapped creature.

Whether the use of the pit was brought to the Americas by primitive man, or whether this plan of capturing an animal was developed independently in the Americas is a question still unsolved. However, pits were found in wide usage throughout most of America at the first coming of the white man, and continued in use well into the 19th century, and, in some instances, even during the present century. All species of predators and big game were captured by it. The earlier accounts mention the capture of wolves, bears, deer, elk, pumas, and jaguars. Its earliest recorded use in North America that we have been able to find was near Albuquerque, New Mexico, near the close of the 16th century. (Lummis, C. F. 1920: 145-146.)

The latest record we have is by Prodgers (1922: 108-109), for Bolivia, where, during his visit to the lands of the Challana Indians in La Paz during the summer of 1903, he barely escaped falling into one. While on this journey, and nearing his destination known as Paroma, he came to a point in the trail where his pack mule refused to walk. Going "on a few yards to see what the ground was like," he "found a lot of brush cut down and lying across the path. Probing with a stick, he found it quite hollow underneath, and could not touch bottom." It turned out to be a pit trap. A study of this pit "showed it to be a hole with perpendicular sides, about twelve feet long, and then covered over lightly with branches and brush." While used mainly for the jaguar in this part of Bolivia, it was used for the puma as well.

Payment of bounties.—Prior to organized efforts for the control of any predator there generally is more or less lengthy trial of the bounty system. In relation to the puma this method had an early start indeed, as it was used by the Jesuit priests in Lower California in the latter part of the 16th century.

The inducement offered the natives was a reward of one bull for each puma killed. This "custom prevailed always after, during the time that they [the priests] had control of the missions." (Brown, J. R., and A. S. Taylor. 1887: 171-172.) This scheme was thus in effect for more than a century, and may be credited with being the earliest recorded bounty scheme to be put into effect on the Pacific slope for any predator.

Settlers on the Atlantic seaboard early began the payment of rewards for destruction of predators. Bounties for killing the puma came into effect some years after the wolf bounty acts of colonial America. When wolves began to disappear rewards for the killing of other depredating mammals, and later for some birds, were provided by legislation. More than a century elapsed before Pennsylvania began paying a puma bounty in 1807, though it had paid wolf bounty since 1683. A rather full digest of the early bounty acts is to be found in "The Wolves of North America." (Young, S. P., and E. A. Goldman. 1944: 337-368.)

Throughout the 19th century and up to and including the present time bounties have generally been in effect in States, provinces, or counties where puma depredations have been experienced. Paid from public or private funds or both, bounties through the years have amounted to a large sum. As in the case of the wolf, bounty acts for the control of the puma spread westward as new lands became populated and developed. They were patterned after the early colonial acts of Massachusetts, Virginia, New York, and Pennsylvania. New York was one of the last of the states on the Atlantic seaboard to pay puma bounty, this commonwealth continuing the plan until the close of the past century. Often the commonwealth bounty was supplemented by local rewards, either by a county or by stockmen as individuals or in association. These combined rewards ranged at times from $50 to $500 per animal, but more often from $15 to $25. Comparatively few puma bounties are now operative, due mainly to the extirpation of the animal from a large part of its range. A summary of the bounty laws in effect for the year 1937 shows 9 western states were then offering puma bounties ranging in sums from $50 per animal in Colorado to $2 in Nebraska.

Bounties are often fraudulently claimed and, for a variety of reasons, may fail to accomplish the desired results. In the way of more direct action hunting by dogs, trapping, and poisoning are resorted to.

Use of dogs.—The Kentucky fox hound, and a cross between the Walker hound and the bloodhound, have been found among the most satisfactory dogs for trailing pumas, though any good dog may tree one.

Catesby (1743: II. xxv), as far back as the middle of the 18th century, and one of the first to remark upon puma hunting with dogs, said, "The smallest one, in our company, with his master, will make him [the puma] take to a tree, which they will climb to the top of with the greatest agility. The hunter takes this opportunity to shoot him, though no small danger to himself, if not killed outright, for descending furiously from the tree, he attacks the first thing in his way, either man or dog, which seldom escapes alive."

The hunter must keep up with the pack, for a puma that fights at bay, instead of treeing, may kill all of the dogs. The hunting of the puma with trained dogs not only requires much endurance on the part of both man and dogs, but also patience, persistence, and a full understanding of the animal's habits. In several of the western States there were, and still are, a few individuals who have hunted this animal with trained dogs for many years. Their reputations as successful puma hunters makes them in demand by the sporting fraternity, and at times by some of the larger livestock raisers, who hire them by the month for puma control on their ranges. Foremost among such hunters was the late Ben V. Lilly, the last of the "mountain men," who, when not working for the Federal government, was employed by private stock interests. His last assignment of this kind was on the G.O.S. range near Silver City, New Mexico.

Darwin (1882: 270) says that in South America pumas "were likewise hunted with dogs" belonging "to a particular breed called 'Leoneros'; they are weak, slight animals, like long-legged terriers, but are born with a particular instinct for this sport." He made the interesting observation that the behavior of condors sometimes is an aid to those hunting the puma with dogs. If a group of "condors glide down [to a certain spot] and then suddenly all rise together the Chileno knows that it is the puma, which, watching the carcass, has sprung out to drive away the robbers." (Op. cit.: 183.) Sometimes dogs are brought to such spots and often they succeed in striking a fresh puma track.

Poisoning.—The use of poisons in puma control is not recommended by the Federal government, and it is unsafe to expose poisons on ranges where hunting dogs are being used.

The stock interests and others never attempted to poison the puma with strychnine to anything like the extent they used this drug for the killing of wolves and coyotes. This can be attributed in part to the relative inaccessibility of puma habitat. However, when good opportunity arose, strychnine was exposed where it might be taken by this animal.

Baird (1859: 5) quoted Kennerly as having found the inhabitants of Sonora, along the Mexican boundary in the late 1850's using strychnine for killing pumas. "They poison with this substance the carcasses of the animals that have been slain, and not only often succeed in thus killing the Leones [name used for the animal by the Mexicans] but a great number of wolves also."

Hallock (1877: 9), in discussing the puma's habit of returning to its kill, said, "This habit is sometimes taken advantage of by his human enemy, who, poisoning the hidden carcass with strychnine, often manages to secure the Panther when it comes back to eat again."

Another early statement relating to the southwestern United States reads, "Many pumas are poisoned by the sheep and cattle men of the southern counties, when their visits to the flocks and herds become too frequent. I have often seen their hides nailed to the walls of the lonely cabins of the stockmen there, and, upon inquiry, have found that they were poisoned in at least three cases out of four." (Anon. 1884: 1163.)

Prichard (1902: 252) states that the puma in Patagonia is at times prone to kill several animals at one time, but that it returns "to only one of these kills." . . . "It always makes some pretense of burying the victim singled out for its meal." . . . "This custom of the puma" is "taken advantage of by the shepherds who poison the chosen carcass."

Trapping.—Schomburgk (Richard. 1848: II: 68), during the 1840's viewed a trap designed for catching pumas and jaguars in British Guiana. This contraption consisted "of a large box the thick boarded covering and similar flooring of which is clamped on all four sides with strong iron bars, and has at the one end a drop-door which is held up by means of a trigger-board. Within (and at the other end of) the box is a compartment divided off from the main chamber by strong iron bars, in which a sheep or goat is enclosed, and the trap then set in a somewhat out-of-the-way part of the estate. When the jaguar or puma creeps through the drop-door into the box to secure the bait and treads on the trigger-board the door drops behind it, and the thief is caught." Twenty to thirty pumas and jaguars are reported to have been taken yearly in such traps.

In the United States trapping has been one of the principal means employed to take pumas under organized control procedure. Traps of sizes 14 and 4½ (Plate 38-39) have generally been used. Although some persons oppose the use of such traps as inhumane no better or more practical device is yet available.

In trapping the puma attention to simple details is essential. Though the puma trapper need not be so cautious about suppressing human scent as does the trapper of wolves or coyotes, it is well nevertheless when placing a trap for him to stand or kneel on a setting cloth (Plate 40). This may be about 3 feet square and made of canvas, oil-cloth material, or the skin of a sheep or calf. It is useful in preventing disturbance of the ground about the trap set, and is convenient in that excavated soil can be placed on it so that the residue, not needed in completing the set, can be easily removed. Further upon the completion of the job the trapping equipment can be rolled up in it and carried away.

Minor trapping details include removing rust from traps, boiling them in water to eliminate the conspicuous fresh odors noticed when they come from the manufacturer, carefully repairing traps with faulty springs, taking care that the trap pan moves freely on its pivot, and seeing that the jaws are adjusted to close snugly and quickly.

Either of the traps recommended may be set on a known travel-way of the puma, preferably at a point where the route narrows, as on the saddle of a divide. Scratch hills made ideal places for setting traps, but should be left in a natural condition. The puma may be trapped as it stops to visit a scratch hill, being attracted either by the odor from the hill itself or by a catnip or other lure placed thereon as described later.

When the carcass of a domestic animal, deer, or other prey found in a control area shows unmistakably that a puma did the killing, at least three traps should be set around it, each 15 to 20 inches away. When the carcass is found lying on its side (Plate 41), one trap should be set, as later described, between the fore and hind legs, another near the rump, and a third near the back parallel with the loin. These traps require no lure other than the carcass. Frequently it is well to set a fourth trap 6 to 8 feet away, if tracks show the exact route taken by the puma in approaching or leaving the carcass.

Trappers, especially when using the No. 4½ trap, should take every precaution to safeguard livestock and valuable or harmless wild animals, and, where necessary, should post signs to warn human beings.

Traps set along a trail and near an obstruction intended to divert the puma closer to a scratch hill are only partly successful. The trapper may, however, take advantage of the puma's keen sense of smell by putting a few drops of oil of catnip, or other scent, in the center of the undisturbed scratch hill as a lure. Pure catnip oil should be diluted with pure petrolatum, in the proportion of 40 drops of the catnip oil to 2 ounces of petrolatum.

A lasting lure devised by employees of the British Columbia Game Conservation Board, and tested by the writer in the United States, may be prepared as follows:

The petrolatum-diluted catnip oil is spread thinly over a piece of cotton batting about 8 inches square, and this is covered with another piece of the same size. The catnip-oil sandwich thus made is placed on a rusty or lacquered tin pie plate that will be inconspicuous against the bark of a tree, particularly any of the conifers. Two or three feet from the ground the tree is blazed to make the sap flow, the cut being made to fit the plate. The plate is spiked over this blaze, with the batting next to the tree so that the cotton will be kept moist by the sap. To prevent its being torn out by a bear the plate should fit snugly into the cut, the lower edge flush with the bark. The plate should be perforated with small holes so that the scent will escape slowly and also should be shaded from the sun as much as possible.

Such scent stations should be placed on trees along creeks where pumas are known to travel, particularly near deer trails that lead to water. They are probably best placed on trees in narrow canyons, where the chances of successful trapping are greater because of the narrowness of the path along which the puma must travel. The writer has known catnip pans to be visited by pumas as long as 6 months after placement, and in British Columbia the game authorities report a puma's visit to a station 10 months old. After the scent station is made traps should be set, as described later, near the base of the tree. The puma, attracted by the catnip odor in the plate, steps into the trap when approaching the lure.

As previously mentioned, catnip oil has been used successfully as a scent for luring pumas into the field of a set camera, so as to obtain a self-taken photograph of them in their undisturbed habitat. For the record it will be of interest to further add that this was done in the fall of 1937, and for the first time by anyone, in the Carmen Mountains, which are located in northern Coahuila, Mexico. These pioneer experiments in determining the effectiveness of catnip as a lure, as well as the great liking for catnip by our large wild cats, is clearly portrayed in the photographs that were obtained at the time mentioned. Gregory, T. 1938: I: (3): 70-81; (4): 110-120; Young, S. P. 1940: 4:(6): 4-8.

This animal is attracted also by a variety of animal scents. In March, 1940, a female was trapped by the use of rotted bobcat scent placed on a pile of oak leaves approximately 16 inches back of the trap which was set slightly to one side of a trail which this puma was known to travel. A slight sidestep made in sniffing this scent caused the animal to step squarely into the trap. Other lures that have been successfully used are skunk musk, fetid scents consisting of ground-up colon, anal gland, and urine of the puma, eel and sturgeon oils, and rotted salmon mixed with a small amount of zinc valerate. Generally the use of these scents as lures has been most successful when exposed near puma scratch hills.

The hole for the trap set should be dug about 15 to 20 inches from a carcass, a single undisturbed scratch hill, or a tree on which a scent station has been placed, or directly in a trail where it narrows naturally or is made to narrow by rocks, brush, or other obstructions placed at the sides (Plate 43, 44). The hole should be only slightly larger than the trap, and just deep enough to hold the set at a level slightly lower than the surrounding ground, with the drag and chain buried beneath it. The drag, which should preferably be of ½-inch wrought iron, should be attached to one end of the chain by a figure "8" swivel, and it should end in two well-curved prongs (Plate 38). Bedding the drag under the trap, of course, requires more excavation. The drag chain should be at least 8 feet long, and attached to the base of the trap or to one of the springs.

At scratch hills it is well to place a trap on either side, the springs at right angles to the known direction of approach. In a trail the traps should be in line, the springs at right angles to the direction of travel. Experiments have proved that most of the larger predators, and particularly the puma, tend to avoid stepping directly on any hard object in a path. Knowing this tendency, the trapper may place a stick or stone between the two traps and another at each approach. These will cause the animal to break its gait and step into one of the traps rather than over or between them. In approaching a scratch hill, a scent station, or a carcass where sets have been made, or in passing over a blind set in the trail, the predator is usually caught by one of the forefeet, though it may step into a bedded trap with a hind foot. No scent is used at carcass or blind sets.

After the trap has been firmly bedded near an undisturbed scratch hill, scent station, or carcass, or in a trail, it should be covered with earth and the surroundings left in a condition as nearly natural as possible. Dry horse or cow manure finely pulverized may be used to cover the inside of the trap jaws. Extreme care should be taken to keep all dirt from under the trap pan, and to see that the open space there is at least one-fourth of an inch deep. The trap pan should be covered by a pad made of canvas or old de-scented cloth and cut to fit snugly inside the jaws. The area should then be covered with finely pulverized earth, leaving it looking as nearly as possible as it did before the trap was buried. Finishing such a task properly and thus leaving the ground over the trap in a perfectly natural condition, so that it blends with the surrounding area, is an art that requires much practice.

When traps are set near carcasses additional care should be taken to underpin the trap pan so that it will not spring under the weight of a magpie, buzzard, or other carnivorous bird that may be attracted to the carcass.

In forested areas a puma hunter may find his traps sprung by small mammals, for squirrels and other rodents, and sometimes small birds, may dig or scratch around and between the jaws of the trap. Unless the trap pan is properly supported these animals are unnecessarily endangered, and in addition the trap is frequently sprung. This may be prevented by setting the trap pan so that it will carry a weight of several pounds.

One simple way of underpinning is to place a small twig perpendicularly from the base snugly up to the middle of the pan; some hunters use a fine, coiled steel spring. Such contrivances will permit the trap pan to carry the weight of the smaller mammals or birds without endangering them or releasing the trap jaws and thus spoiling a set well placed for a puma. Devices adjusted to puma traps to prevent their being sprung by small mammals and birds are illustrated in Figure 5. The Biological Survey pan spring (Plate 45), developed some years ago, patented and given to the public, can readily be attached to the No. 14 steel trap. A slightly larger spring is required for the No. 4½ trap.

Conclusion

The puma is distinctly an American predator, exceeded in size among such animals only by the jaguar. With its uncanny skill as a killer and its vast range, greatly exceeding that of the jaguar, it may be recognized as the leading predator of the New World.

Puma nature is admirably summed up by Tappan Gregory (1938: 71), when he writes, "A mountain dweller, ghost-like marauder, roaming the reaches of the night on silent pads; lithe, sinewy . . . death on game and domestic stock; legendary terrorist through the ages—yet inculpable withal, impelled by instinct to live in the exercise of the talents with which he is endowed by nature, conscious only that he must live by eating and that he must eat the only food he knows—fresh meat; unwittingly running counter to the edicts of civilization in seeking food where and when he can find it, taking it ruthlessly in inexorable pursuit; timorous, querulous, and puzzled in his contacts with man."

To which the writer would add: May it long survive in many of the wilder parts of the Western Hemisphere where there is little, if any, reason for adopting measures of control. There are many areas where normal hunting and the vicissitudes of the wild can be depended upon to keep pumas within reasonable limits, but there are also great stretches of wilderness areas that probably will never be touched by any puma-control campaigns. The animal's great fondness for venison has been previously mentioned. It is the author's opinion that this large cat should be given full consideration in any management plans for areas where it occurs on the same range with deer, and particularly on ranges little grazed by livestock. Here pumas may serve as a check on undue increases of deer that exist in numbers far in excess of the available food supply. Once again, therefore, it is reiterated that under such conditions a moderate puma population may well be encouraged, all of which will serve to perpetuate the puma as a part of the interesting fauna of the Americas.

THE PUMA, MYSTERIOUS AMERICAN CAT

Part II

Classification of the Races of the Puma

by

Edward A. Goldman

VII

INTRODUCTION

The Carnivorous animals with numerous appellations, including puma, mountain lion, panther, cougar, catamount, and others, are recent cats of the genus *Felis* (subgenus *Puma*), of the family Felidae.   Among American cats the pumas are exceeded in size only by the jaguars.   Deadly and successful in dealing with their natural prey, the pumas in relation to man are singularly shy, skulking, elusive creatures with a marvelous facility for keeping out of sight.   In the present revision all of the forms are treated as geographic races, assignable to a single species, *Felis concolor*. The puma has a vast range, extending from northern Cassiar (Big Muddy River) and the Peace River District in Canada, to the Straits of Magellan in South America; and formerly it was transcontinental in distribution from the northern United States or southern Canada southward.   It seems doubtful whether any other land mammal has a more extended range from north to south.   Complete intergradation between races is evident in some cases, and the relative value and combination of characters presented indicate such close relationships that intergradation can safely be assumed where lack of material for study leaves gaps in our knowledge.   Even the single known insular population on Vancouver Island, British Columbia, agrees so closely with that of the adjacent mainland in essential characters that subspecific treatment seems fully warranted.

In reviewing the puma group 30 recent subspecies are accorded recognition. The revision is based mainly on a study of the extensive material brought together especially in connection with the predatory animal control work conducted since 1915 by the Fish and Wildlife Service, of the U. S. Department of the Interior, formerly the Bureau of Biological Survey of the U. S. Department of Agriculture, and other collections in the United States National Museum, now numbering 565 specimens. Many of these are skulls without skins, and others skins without skulls. These specimens have been augmented by 199 from other American museums, making a total of 764 examined (see "Acknowledgments," p. vii). The assemblage has included the type or topotypes of nearly all of the described races. This unparalleled wealth of material has afforded a basis for accurate appraisal of the range of individual and geographic variation, and led to satisfactory assignment of most of the specimens.

VIII

HISTORY

THE HISTORY of the Felidae, or cat family, as shown by the fossil record, extends with many ramifications far back in geologic time. The family has been traced to common ancestry with the Miacid family of Creodonts or primitive carnivora of the Tertiary period.

Fossil representatives have been found in all the principal horizons of the Middle and Later Tertiary, according to Matthew (1910: 289). He traces in detail the evolution of two great phyla: One of these, the Machaerodonts, from *Hoplophoneus* of the Oligocene, through *Machaerodus* of the Miocene and Pliocene, reached extinction in *Smilodon*, the great sabre-tooth of the upper Pleistocene of the New World. The other phylum, comprising the true cats, he regards as derived from *Dinictis* of the Oligocene. From this genus structural succession led through *Nimravus* and *Pseudaelurus* of the Miocene, to *Felis* of the Pliocene and Pleistocene, and the numerous genera of the present time.

The Felidae have short, stout limbs, armed with powerful, retractile claws and short jaws adapted to seizing and holding prey. Along with this distinctive physical equipment came the development of habits of concealment, stealthy approach, climbing, and lying in wait to pounce on the victim with the chances favoring its being quickly overpowered and killed. The cat family thus presents a great contrast to the Canidae, or dog family, another carnivorous offshoot of Miacid ancestry. Unlike the cats, the dogs as a group

179

developed long slender limbs and non-retractile claws, adapted for speed on open ground, and acquired long jaws for snapping and slashing at prey. These hunting methods led to teamwork, association in groups, and higher development of social instincts and intelligence than in the cats. The cats, however, have been similarly successful in evolution as attested by the number and diversity of species, and their nearly worldwide distribution.

Felis concolor has no near living relatives. The remains of extinct species from New World deposits usually regarded as of Pleistocene age prove that puma-like animals existed in the comparatively recent past. *Felis daggetti* J. C. Merriam from the asphalt deposits of Rancho La Brea near Los Angeles, Calif., equalled or perhaps exceeded in size the largest pumas of the present time. It differed notably from the living regional race, *californica*, in larger size, more massive cranial proportions, and more decided backward curvature of the coronoid process of the mandible. Another species, *Felis bituminosa* Merriam and Stock is nearer the modern species in size, but differs markedly in cranial details. Compared with *californica* its interpterygoid fossa is broader, with the sides more divergent anteriorly. The auditory bullae are more flattened anteriorly, the anterior margin forming a more evenly transverse line; other points of divergence also are apparent. The question of whether or not these species were contemporaneous can probably not easily be answered, especially as the escape of gases tended to produce churning movements and the displacement of material held in the asphalt. The characters, however, suggest that *daggetti* may represent an earlier stage in a line of development that led through *bituminosa* to living *californica*, which is also represented in the asphalt deposits. Hibbard (1942: 263) records the finding of a lower carnassial of a cat slightly smaller than a puma, and resembling the same tooth in *Pseudaelurus*, from the lower Pleistocene deposits of Meade County, Kans. Various names have been applied to remains of cats from Pleistocene deposits in the East, some of which may have been allied to the existing puma. Most of them appear to have been larger, however, and their affinities are imperfectly known.

According to Major (1847: 193), the honor of being the first European to record the puma apparently must be given to Columbus. An observation made during his fourth voyage in the year 1502 while exploring along the coast of Honduras and Nicaragua is quoted as follows: "I saw some very large fowls [the feathers of which resemble wool], lions [leones], stags, fallow deer, and birds."

Perhaps the earliest reference to the puma in the United States is that of Captain John Smith (1608-1631, p. CVI). In describing the animals of Virginia about 1609-1610 he wrote: " . . . there be in this country Lions, Beares, woulues, foxes, muske catts, Hares fleinge squirells and other squirrels. . . ."

During the 17th century the puma also became known in South America, especially Brazil, through the published works of Marcgrave (1648: 235) and Ray (1693: 169). Knowledge of the species became more general, however, during the 18th century. Barrere (1741: 166) applied the pre-Linnaean binomial name, *Tigris fulvus*, to the form known as the "tigre rouge" in Cayenne, and as "le tigre rouge" it was treated by Brisson (1756: 272), who referred to its occurrence in Guiana and Brazil. The species was formally named *Felis concolor* by Linné (1771: 522).

Buffon (1776: 222), supplementing his account of "le couguar" (1761: 216), lists the "cougar de pensilvanie" of which a crude figure (Pl. CXIX) is given, based on a description sent him by Colinson. The animal was regarded as remarkable for the length and slenderness of body, shortness of limbs, and length of tail, the latter believed to be 3 or 4 inches longer than in the "cougar de Cayenne." The animal was assigned to a range in Carolina, Georgia, and Pennsylvania.

This description became the basis for *Felis couguar* Kerr, the first North American form to receive a name in 1792. Meanwhile a second South American name for a member of the group, *Felis puma*, from Chile, was proposed by Molina (1782: 295).

Few puma names were proposed during the 19th century. Rafinesque (1832: 62) attached the name *Felix* [sic] *oregonensis* to a species "found in the western wilds of the Oregon mountains or east or west of them." The validity of this name was discussed by Stone (1899: 34) and by Merriam (1901: 590), the latter opposing its acceptance. The animal described was clearly a puma, and although the habitat was so loosely fixed the name must be applied, in the absence of an earlier one, to some part of the vast region to which reference was made. The puma of Florida, which in 1899 was named *Felis coryi* Bangs, was described in 1896, and in 1897 *Felis hippolestes* and *Felis hippolestes olympus* were named by Merriam from the western United States.

In a first revision of the pumas in 1901, Merriam listed 11 forms of which 3 were treated as new, and the group was divided into 6 species. Evincing a continued interest in pumas, Merriam in 1903 added *Felis azteca browni* from the desert region of southwestern Arizona. *Felis improcera* was described from Baja California by Phillips in 1912, and *Felis concolor söderströmi* from Ecuador by Lönnberg in 1913. Cabrera (1929: 312) expressed the opinion that all forms of the puma, whether North or South American, are subspecies of *Felis concolor*. In the same year Nelson and Goldman (1929: 346) reduced 7 nominal species to one and recognized 19 subspecies, of which 3 were described as new. A few names have since appeared, including *Felis concolor cabrerae* Pocock (1940: 308) for pumas from northern Argentina, and *Felis concolor araucanus* Osgood (1943: 77) for those of south-central Chile.

Felis concolor was transferred to the genus *Puma* proposed by Jardine (1834: 266). Severtzow (1858: 385) in his classification of the cats, treated *Puma* as a subgenus under *Panthera*. Some later authors, including Allen (1916: 579) and Pocock (1917: 336), have accorded *Puma* full generic rank. In the present revision the name is treated as a subgenus of *Felis*.

Among cat names requiring consideration in connection with *Felis concolor* are *Felis fossor* and *Felis misax*, proposed by Rafinesque (1817: 437). Rafinesque based these names on the account of the traveler Le Raye. He quoted from p. 189 of Le Raye's journal, as follows: "We killed a wild cat (near the Yellow Stone river) which resembled the domestic cat, and was about the same size. It was of a sallow colour, and had a tail nearly the length of the body. This little animal is very fierce, and often kills Cabree [antelope] and sheep by jumping on their neck, and eating away the sinews and arteries and then sucks the blood." Commenting on this quotation Rafinesque says: "This short notice refers probably to a new species of cat, very similar to the cat seen by captain Lewis, but not killed (see Travels, p. 266), which I call *Felis fossor*, and likewise to the *Felis concolor*. This species I shall call *Felis misax*, and characterize thus: Tail nearly as long as body, which is entirely sallow and unspotted."

Reference to Lewis and Clark (266) shows that *Felis fossor* is based entirely on this passage: "In going through the low grounds on Medicine river [Sun River, Montana,] he met an animal which at a distance he thought was a wolf; but on coming within 60 paces, it proved to be some brownish-yellow animal standing near its burrow, which, when he came nigh, crouched and seemed as if about to spring on him. Captain Lewis fired, and the beast disappeared in its burrow. From the track and the general appearance of the animal he supposed it to be of the tiger kind." Coues (1893: 372) suggested that the animal was probably a wolverine, *Gulo luscus*. Certainly it cannot clearly be identified as a cat. *Felis misax* is also loosely based on a description and data that obviously cannot be applied with precision to any known cat. The name should, therefore, be treated as unidentifiable. Fifteen years later Rafinesque (1832: 63) apparently based the name *Felis macrura* on the same account by Le Raye, but the tail is said to be "as long as the body, which is from one to two feet long only."

The name "*Felis concolor niger* Cuv." was applied by Levy (1873:197) to "el Tigre Negro" of Nicaragua. Levy seems to have regarded the animal as a black jaguar, "very ferocious but rare," the puma being listed separately as *Felis concolor*.

IX

GENERAL CHARACTERS

The subspecies of *Felis concolor*, subgenus *Puma*, form a compact group readily distinguished from the other cats by the combination of large size, slender form, long cylindrical tail, short ears, and the plain color of adults. In the young widely-spaced black spots form a different pattern from that of the young in other cats examined (see subgeneric characters, p 195). The cranium is short and rounded. General observations indicate that the breeding season extends throughout the year. From one to six young are produced at a birth, the average being two, at least in the western part of the United States. The dental formula is I. 3-3; C. 1-1; P. 3-3; M. 1-1 = 30

$$\text{I. } \frac{3\text{-}3}{3\text{-}3} \quad \text{C. } \frac{1\text{-}1}{1\text{-}1} \quad \text{P. } \frac{3\text{-}3}{2\text{-}2} \quad \text{M. } \frac{1\text{-}1}{1\text{-}1} = 30$$

as in typical *Felis*.

The sexes are alike in color, but males are larger than females. The skulls of adult males are distinctly larger, more angular and massive, with more strongly developed sagittal and lambdoid crests than those of adult females. The skulls of the females, conversely, may be distinguished by their smaller size and more smoothly rounded brain case, with lesser development of sagittal and lambdoid crests. The dentition is heavier in the males, but not far out of line with the differences in cranial proportions. While size and angularity usually serve to separate male and female skulls some of the males of a smaller form may resemble the females of a larger race. For example some of the larger female skulls of *hippolestes* closely approach some

183

male skulls of *azteca* in size and angularity. In male skulls the temporal ridges unite to form a sagittal crest earlier in life than in those of females. The ridges unite first near the lambdoid crest, development proceeding forward to a broad V-shaped junction on the posterior part of the frontal region; but in some females of advanced age the crest may be limited to a short posterior section.

In the puma, the cranial sutures are all, or nearly all, clearly discernible at birth. The upper surfaces of the parietal and interparietal are smooth, with no trace of the sagittal or lambdoid crests. The interparietal, viewed externally, appears large and prominent. The bone homologized with the reptilian tabulare by Weber (1927, band 1, 67) and others, is a distinct element, partially overlapped anteriorly by the squamosal, extending all along the outer side of the exoccipital. The entotympanic portion of the auditory bulla, the name adopted by Van der Klaauw who made detailed studies (1931, 51), is small and appears quite distinct from the tympanic region, but rapid expansion of the entotympanic results in early fusion of the two. The postorbital processes of the frontals are only slightly indicated, but the postorbital processes of the jugal are already nearly as prominent as in an adult. At birth a short anterior projection from the parietal fits into and squamosely overlaps a corresponding recess in the posterior border of the frontal. Soon thereafter the parietal projection begins to lengthen and overlapping the frontal extends gradually forward and upward with age, as a narrow flattened process, reaching in adults to near the summit of the frontal ridges. This bone element may be known as the bregmatic process of the parietal. In advanced age it coössifies with the frontal. The first cheek teeth to appear are narrow, trenchant premolars that bear little or no resemblance to those of the permanent set. Among the first bones to fuse are the supraoccipital and the exoccipitals, soon followed by the basioccipital. Widely separated temporal ridges also appear on the parietals, ending abruptly at the fronto-parietal suture, and become united as the beginning of the sagittal crest on the median line of the interparietal, the latter narrowing partly through encroachment of the parietals. The sagittal crest is most prominent in males, but is developed in both sexes and normally extends forward in adults to the posterior part of the frontals. It is very short, however, in many fully adult and even old females and scarcely reaches forward beyond the interparietal, leaving the temporal ridges narrowly separated. In advanced age most of the bones of the skull are more or less completely coössified; but the nasal sutures and those between the overlapping parts of the jugal and zygomatic arm of squamosal remain open. The suture between the two halves of the lower jaw remains distinct, but owing to interdigitation the rami are firmly knit together. The height of the sagittal crest and the extent of closure of sutures in the skull are general indices of age.

In the races of *Felis concolor* superficial resemblances frequently mask the more essential features. Specimens of widely separated races may be practically indistinguishable in external appearance, especially when due allowance is made for the usual wide range of individual variation in color. Two fairly well-marked and in some regions strikingly different color phases are presented. These are a plain gray or brown phase and a red phase. These extremes, which may appear at the same locality, are, however, so completely bridged by intermediate tones that the use of the term "phase" seems open to some question. The term mentioned, while convenient in descriptive work, may imply more sharply differentiated grouping by color, than is warranted. There are large and small races, and size and cranial modifications are more dependable than color in tracing the relationships of subspecies. While the skulls agree closely in the more important characters, indicating that they are conspecific, all of the cranial elements are subject to modifications that in diversity of pattern or combination show subspecific or regional race relationships. Aside from the size and general form of the skull, some of the principal characters of taxonomic value are the following: Outlines of zygomata, the sides of which may gradually converge to the sides of the rostrum, or there may be distinct notches at the antorbital foramina, as viewed from above; posterior extension of jugal which may or may not reach plane of glenoid fossae; height of frontal region, and depth and width of rostrum; form of nasals; depth of frontal pit; width of interpterygoid fossa; direction taken by opening of lachrymal foramen. The dental characters are remarkable for their approach to uniformity in the races of *Felis concolor;* minor differences only in size and sculpture are presented.

The subspecies or geographic races of the puma, like those of other animals, are based on combinations of characters, including size, color, and details of cranial and dental structure that prevail in areas over which environmental conditions tend to be uniform. The areas, varying greatly in size, and representing the range of the species as a whole, embrace every kind of habitat from the lowlands at sea level in the tropical and temperate zones of North and South America to near timber line in both continents, reaching to such extreme altitudes as 13,000 feet in southern Mexico and along the higher Andes. Whymper (1892, 229) records the occurrence of the species at 14,762 feet northeast of Mount Pichincha in Ecuador. Response to climatic conditions is well shown by the long pelage of *incarum* from the high Andes of Peru in contrast with the extremely short pelage of *greeni* from the tropical lowlands of eastern Brazil. Characters regarded as subspecific may be maintained with a fair degree of constancy over areas of considerable extent; but evidence of intergradation is not lacking and the boundaries between subspecies are more or less arbitrarily drawn along lines representing the nearest approach to accuracy, as shown by specimens examined. These lines, especially in South America, are provisional as very extensive regions remain unrepresented by specimens. As all parts of the puma cranium are subject to modifications that may be regarded as of subspecific significance, differential details may not be shown by the standard measurements taken. Subspecies differing considerably in such details may, when allowance is made for individual variation, present about the same standard measurements. It follows, therefore, that the measurements have only a limited value in making determinations.

A number of cranial contusions, revealed in the examination of puma skulls, are apparently due to mishaps in bringing down prey. The injuries commonly resulted in the permanent distortion or malformation of the nasals or frontal bones. One skull bears a deep crease across the frontals, such as might have been made by the point of a deer antler. In marked contrast with the jaguar, the canines in the puma are rarely broken. This is probably due to differences in the method of attack, the puma being more subject to falls in making flying leaps and biting soft parts that do not particularly endanger the canines. The heavier jaguar, on the other hand, apparently brings its canines to bear with bone-crushing violence, and these teeth are more likely to be broken.

X

PELAGE AND MOLT

The pelage is longer and softer in the cooler climates that prevail in the northern and southern parts of the range of the species, and in the high mountains, including the Andean chain, across the Equatorial region. It is shorter and harsher in texture in the tropical lowlands of Central and South America. Changes in pelage are gradual, the new coat replacing the old almost imperceptibly. The spotted young lose their marking by slow degrees; some of the spots may be retained, especially on the lower parts of the flanks and the inner sides of forearms in certain individuals until they are about one-third grown. Pelages are usually longer in winter than in summer in the colder climates and in the high mountains of both North and South America, suggesting an annual molt; but there are notable exceptions and apparent irregularity in the changes as winter specimens in short pelages are sometimes seen. As breeding occurs throughout the year, some irregularity in pelages may be due to individuals arriving at maturity at all seasons. In the tropical regions no seasonal pelage alterations are clearly discernible.

XI

VARIATION

Variation in the puma is assignable to several categories, of which perhaps the most obvious and important are geographic and individual, more or less intimately associated.

A. Geographic Variation

The races of *Felis concolor* are all very similar in the more essential features and are believed to intergrade throughout the vast range of the species, which formerly included practically all of the South American mainland and still extends far north in North America. The component subspecies are the expression of geographic variation in size, weight, color, and minor details of structure in response to environmental and genetic influences. Owing to general external similarity in appearance the subspecies are based mainly on characteristic patterns of cranial structure, in which gross size is combined with general agreement in certain proportions, and details that prevail with a fair degree of constancy over a geographic unit or area. Such areas may be rather limited, but as a rule they are of large extent. All of the races are inhabitants of the mainland, except *vancouverensis*, which is restricted to Vancouver Island, British Columbia. Although there is at present no geographic connection between this insular race and those living on the adjacent mainland, the distinguishing characters are similar in comparative value to those that denote subspecies on the mainland. Among the larger subspecies *hippolestes*, *olympus*, and *missoulensis* occupy sections of the northern part of the range of the species. Similar large subspecies, as *pearsoni*, however, mark the far southern extension of the group. Between these extremes in latitude smaller pumas, including *mayensis* of Guatemala, *costaricensis* of Costa Rica, and *bangsi* of Colombia, are the rule.

Geographic variation in color is more or less closely associated with individual variation as examples varying from plain gray or brown to rich rufescent tones may occur at the same locality. Marked variation in color is exhibited throughout the range of the species. In Brazil, Liais (1872: 461) regarded two color phases as representing different species. To one of these, known to the Portuguese as "onça vermelha" (red ounce), he gave the name *Felis sucuacuara* to distinguish it from the "sucuarana de lombo preto" (black-backed ounce) which he recognized as *Felis concolor*. The red phase received the name "tigre rouge" by the French in Guiana. Rufescent tones appear to be most prevalent in tropical regions while in more northern and southern latitudes and along the Andes of South America plainer colors are usually exhibited. In the United States the pumas of the more humid northwest coast region and of Florida are darker than those of the interior and the arid Southwest. The most southern subspecies, *pearsoni*, has been reputed to be extremely variable in color. Prichard (1902: 251), however, mentions the "silver-gray variety" as most commonly met with in Patagonia.

Geographic variation in puma skulls is well shown in the combinations of cranial features that distinguish the subspecies. While the more essential cranial characters are maintained throughout the range of the species, progressive alteration in detail from north to south is clearly indicated. Some of the most obvious of these alterations are the following. In the northern races there is a distinct notch where the antorbital foramina open at the anterior ends of the zygomata, as viewed from above. In the southern races, by contrast, the zygomatic angle is reduced and the outer surfaces converge more gradually to the sides of the rostrum. In the northern races the jugal, underlapping the zygomatic arm of the squamosal, ends posteriorly well in front of the glenoid fossa. Its posterior extension is progressive through the chain of subspecies southward until in *pearsoni* it usually reaches to near the middle of the plane of the glenoid fossae. The fronto-nasal pit, conspicuous for its depth in *vancouverensis* and adjacent mainland forms, becomes gradually shallower through the races to the southward until in *pearsoni* hardly a trace is left.

B. *Individual Variation*

By individual variation is meant all of the degrees of divergence from a typical mean exhibited by large series of conspecific skins and skulls from any given locality. The range of this variation in the puma is extensive, and as in other cats should be given careful consideration in the identification of specimens. While subspecies with confluent ranges may differ considerably in size, an unusually large individual of a small form may be similar in size and, therefore, apt to be confused with an unusually small individual of a large form.

Individual variation in color of upper parts in some of the races of *Felis concolor*, may extend from plain grayish or brownish to rich "cinnamon" or "tawny" in specimens from the same locality. The extremes may be mentioned as gray or brown, and red phases, but they are linked by many intermediate stages.

The skulls of males, compared with those of females, are usually decidedly larger and more angular, with more prominent development of the sagittal and lambdoid crests. Individual variations involve all of the cranial characters, but these are usually within rather circumscribed limits. The size and form of the auditory bullae vary greatly and are, therefore, of limited value as diagnostic characters. The teeth present a moderate range of individual variation in size. Some races have larger teeth than others, but owing to close conformity in pattern of sculpture teeth are of limited value in making subspecific determinations.

XII

EXPLANATIONS

A. *Measurements*

All measurements of specimens are in millimeters. The weights given are in pounds. Owing to the limited number of specimens of which external measurements and weights were available, the relative size of the various subspecies is more accurately shown by the measurements of skulls. While consideration of cranial dimensions is very useful, race determinations must often be based on structural details that are not revealed by the standard measurements taken. The external measurements, unless otherwise stated, were taken in the flesh by the collector, as follows: *Total length,* nose to end of terminal vertebra; *ta'l vertebrae,* upper base of tail to end of terminal vertebra; *hind foot,* back of heel to end of longest claw. Adult males usually exceed females in size, and the measurements are, therefore, presented according to sex. In some cases, so few nearly typical examples are available that the measurements given may not represent the normal range of individual variation, and too broad generalizations should not be based on them. The cranial measurements are of typical adults, unless otherwise stated, and were taken with vernier calipers by the author. In measuring irregularly curved contours, the vernier reading is apt to be altered with each slight change in the application of the points, or even with the degree of pressure exerted. The calipers were, therefore, always held in as nearly the same position as possible; and whenever practicable, the vernier was read before the calipers were removed.

The cranial measurements are as follows:

Greatest length.—Length from anterior tips of premaxillae (gnathion) to posterior point (inion) in median line over foramen magnum.

Condylobasal length.—Length from anterior tips of premaxillae (gnathion) to posterior plane of occipital condyles.

Zygomatic breadth.—Greatest distance between outer borders of zygomata.

Height of cranium.—Vertical distance from lower border of palatines to summit of frontals, at posterior plane of postorbital processes. This measurement is difficult to obtain with accuracy, owing to sloping border of palatines.

Interorbital breadth.—Least distance between orbits.

Postorbital processes.—Distance between ends of postorbital processes.

Width of nasals.—Width of nasals between anterior ends of frontal processes.

Width of palate.—Distance at narrowest point between outer sides of interpterygoid fossa.

Maxillary tooth row.—Distance from front of canine to back of carnassial, at alveolar border.

Upper carnassial, crown length and crown width.—Antero-posterior diameter of crown at cingulum, and transverse diameter at widest point anteriorly.

Lower carnassial, crown length.—Antero-posterior diameter at cingulum.

Upper canine.—Antero-posterior diameter at alveolus.

B. *Colors*

The pelage of pumas, like that of many other mammals with banded hairs, presents blended colors difficult to segregate and describe. The names employed of colors in quotation marks are from "Ridgway's Color Standards and Nomenclature, 1912." They represent approximations to color tones and are supplemented by generally understood, modifying or comparative terms.

C. *Specimens Examined*

Specimens examined, unless otherwise indicated, are in the United States National Museum, including the Biological Surveys collection.

D. *Use of Distribution Maps*

No attempt has been made to present keys to the subspecies of the puma. The construction of satisfactory keys to closely intergrading subspecies is not very practical, and it is suggested that recourse to the distribution maps will afford more reliable clues to the identification of specimens.

XIII

LIST OF SUBSPECIES WITH TYPE LOCALITIES

193

XIV
GENUS FELIS Linné
Subgenus *Puma* Jardine

Felis Linné, Syst. Nat., ed. 10, vol. 1, 1758, p. 41. Type *Felis catus* Linné.
Puma Jardine, Natur. Lib., vol. 2, Mamm., Felidae, 1834, p. 266. Type
Felis concolor Linné.

Subgeneric characters.—Size large; form slender; tail usually slightly
less than two-thirds length of head and body, cylindrical; ears short, rounded.
Young with widely-spaced black spots arranged in three irregularly interrupted, longitudinal dorsal lines, three to five more or less clearly defined
longitudinal nape stripes, and irregular transverse rows extending from flanks
more or less completely across abdomen; elongated spots, tending to become
confluent, arranged in a semi-circle opening outward over shoulder; throat
and under side of neck blackish; adult plain colored. Cranium short, rounded; parietal with a narrow flattened bregmatic process extending diagonally
forward and upward over frontal, reaching in adults to near summit of
frontal ridge; mandible with symphysis short, abruptly upturned, the angle
between rami broadly rounded; canines short, exposed length of upper canines about equal to width of anterior nares as in typical *Felis*, but lateral
grooves absent or obsolescent.

Remarks.—The spotted young suggest that *F. concolor* may be descended from a handsome progenitor the adults of which were striped or spotted.
The arrangement of the color pattern in the young puma appears to be unlike that of any other existing species. Most of the black juvenal markings
gradually disappear early in life, but may persist longer in some individuals
than in others. In the skin of a half-grown young (No. 80769 U.S.N.M.)
from Glendale, Oreg., the black markings were just being lost. Oblique
stripes near the top of the shoulders, and spots over the upper parts in general
are still indicated by an admixture of blackish or dark tawny hairs; and on
the under parts, and inner sides of limbs irregular blackish spots or transverse
bars are present.

The plain color of the puma, often closely matching that of the deer of
the same region, must be of great assistance to this predator in stalking its
favorite prey. The deficient eyesight of deer, compared with the marvelous
vision of such animals as the mountain sheep, may permit the close approach
of a puma unobserved, or possibly may result in its being mistaken for another
deer, even in the open.

The skull of *F. concolor*, compared with those of other cats, especially
the larger existing species, exhibits many remarkably close resemblances and
some notable differences. The shortness and general rotundity of the cranium is a characteristic feature, in contrast with the more angular general
form in the other large cats. The upper outline is convex, much as in some

leopards (*Felis pardus*), without the sagittal concavity, present in the lion (*Felis leo*), the tiger (*Felis tigris*), and the jaguar (*Felis onca*). The symphysis of the mandible is shorter, more strongly upturned, and the angle between rami more rounded anteriorly than in any of the four species mentioned. In essential details of sculpture, the teeth in *F. concolor* agree closely with those of the typical members of the cat family, but the lateral, longitudinal grooves present in the canines in *Felis catus* and many other species, including *F. leo*, *F. tigris*, and *F. pardus*, are obsolescent or absent. In the slight development or absence of these grooves, *F. concolor* approaches *F. onca*, but departs rather widely in other important respects. The canine grooves vary considerably in development in the Felidae as a whole. In typical *Felis* the upper canines are normally scored on the outer side by two short, narrow, distinct grooves which extend vertically, parallel to one another, but do not reach either the apex or the cingulum. The anterior groove is usually longer and more clearly defined than the posterior one, which may be inconspicuous or even absent in some individuals. Single grooves, similar in character, are normally present in the outer sides of the lower canines. This general arrangement of canine grooves, with slight modifications, is common to a considerable number of the Felidae, including the ocelot and other New World forms. The lion, tiger, and leopard differ, however, in the possession of pairs of grooves on the inner, as well as the outer, sides of the upper canines.

The skull of the puma, in general form, resembles that of *Lynx caracal*, as pointed out by Pocock (1917: 337). Points of resemblance are the generally rounded outlines, short muzzle, ascending branches of maxillae broad and rounded above, and postorbital constriction deep and evenly rounded. It differs, however, in many important features, notably the much lesser anterior depression of the muzzle and correspondingly greater relative height of anterior nares, more evenly rounded orbit, and in the possession of a vestigial upper premolar (absent or early deciduous in *Lynx caracal*). The puma and caracal are widely different in external appearance, and the only reason for pointing out cranial resemblances is to convey some idea of the diversity and complexity of combinations of characters presented by members of the cat family. *Felis concolor* was transferred to the genus *Puma* proposed by Jardine (1834: 266). To the same genus he also assigned several distantly related species including *Felis pajeros* and *Felis yaguaroundi*, the latter one of the most divergent of New World cats. Severtzow (1858: 385) in his classification of the cats regarded *Puma* as a subgenus under the genus *Panthera*. Some later authors, including Allen (1916: 579) and Pocock (1917: 336) have accorded *Puma* full generic rank. In the tendency toward generic division, Allen (1919) in reviewing the "Small Spotted Cats of Tropical America," assumed what seems an extreme position, as his classification of these cats, like his treatment of *Puma*, approaches generic recognition for each

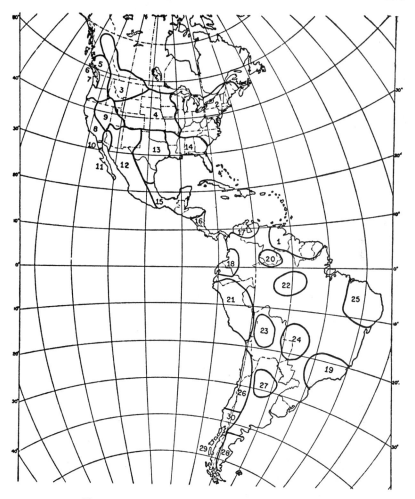

Figure 6. Distribution of subspecies of *Felis concolor*

1. *Felis concolor concolor*
2. *F. c. couguar*
3. *F. c. missoulensis*
4. *F. c. hippolestes*
5. *F. c. oregonensis*
6. *F. c. vancouverensis*
7. *F. c. olympus*
8. *F. c. californica*
9. *F. c. kaibabensis*
10. *F. c. browni*

11. *F. c. improcera*
12. *F. c. azteca*
13. *F. c. stanleyana*
14. *F. c. coryi*
15. *F. c. mayensis*
16. *F. c. costaricensis*
17. *F. c. bangsi*
18. *F. c. söderströmi*
19. *F. c. capricornensis*
20. *F. c. anthonyi*

21. *F. c. incarum*
22. *F. c. borbensis*
23. *F. c. osgoodi*
24. *F. c. acrocodia*
25. *F. c. greeni*
26. *F. c. puma*
27. *F. c. cabrerae*
28. *F. c. pearsoni*
29. *F. c. patagonica*
30. *F. c. araucanus*

specific type. Divergent branches of the cat family may properly be accorded generic distinction, but the difficulty in so large and varied an assortment of species is evidently to determine just where to draw separative lines. The generic characters commonly employed by many authors have obviously been superficial, and the comparative studies which would serve as a basis for an appropriate alignment of genera have apparently not yet been made. Meanwhile, many species, while differing in detail, agree closely in what seem to be the more essential characters, and to place nearly every one of these in a separate genus is to lose the significance that attaches to the genus as a classification unit, and serves no useful purpose.

Felis concolor is a wellmarked species of the family, with no near living relative. It possesses numerous differential features, but none of the fundamental or trenchant characters that I would associate with a full genus. On the contrary, it is linked with typical *Felis* in dentition and other important structural respects through species differing mainly in details. Compared with other cats, however, it stands somewhat alone in combination of characters, especially the color pattern and the cranial features pointed out. For convenience in classification, at least pending more comprehensive studies of the family as a whole, it is suggested that *Puma* should be treated as a subgenus of *Felis*.

XV
FELIS CONCOLOR AND SUBSPECIES
FELIS CONCOLOR Linné
[Important synonymy under subspecies]

Geographic distribution.—Formerly transcontinental from British Columbia and central Alberta to southern Quebec and the New England States and south throughout Middle America and the South American mainland. Still ranging north to Cassiar, but now extinct in eastern Canada and the central and eastern United States, except Florida. The species has also disappeared in the more densely settled parts of South America.

General characters.—Size large. Form slender. Tail long and rather long-haired, especially on distal two-thirds of upper side where the pelage is longer than on back. Ears small, short and rounded, without elongated, terminal tufts. Pelage of medium texture, short and rather bristly in tropical forms, longer and softer in those from the more northern and southern regions. Spotted when young, becoming plain-colored in adult.

Color.—Upper parts in adults ranging from plain grizzled gray without a trace of buff or tawny, as in the gray phase of some specimens of *pearsoni*, and dark brown as in some individuals of *oregonensis*, through numerous shades of buff, "cinnamon," and "tawny" in the red phase, to the rich "cinnamon-rufous" and "ferruginous" usual in tropical forms, the general tone darkest and most intense from top of head along median dorsal area to base of tail. Shoulders and flanks becoming rather abruptly lighter, ranging through light "tawny" or "cinnamon-buff" to "pinkish-buff" or gray, paling more gradually on outer sides of limbs and feet. Under parts in general usually dull whitish, more or less overlaid with buff across abdomen. Under surface of neck varying from pale gray, or "pinkish buff," to near "cinnamon-buff"; sides of muzzle at base of vibrissae usually black in sharp contrast with surrounding areas; upper lips, except where invaded by black muzzle patch, chin, and throat nearly pure white; ears black externally, with or without grayish median patches; tail above usually similar to back, somewhat lighter below, the tip black, the black usually extending forward from 2 to about 4 inches on upper side. *Young*: Color pattern widely-spaced black spots on a field of buffy tone (in several North American forms at least). Size and arrangement of markings variable, but dorsal area with a more or less distinct median row of narrow elongated spots, uniting in some specimens to form a narrow black line on rump, closely paralleled on either side by a row of larger black spots; nape with three to five more or less interrupted black longitudinal stripes, the outermost broader and more conspicuous than the others, curving inward toward median line near top of shoulder and thence outward and downward behind shoulder, continued in an irregular row of spots reaching under parts; shoulders bearing two distinct spots, one above the other; flanks with somewhat irregular vertical rows of spots continued downward across belly; a black stripe extending from corner of eye backward across cheek; limbs and tail irregularly mixed black and buff, the black predominating; ears black externally, whitish internally; sides of muzzle black; median portion of upper lip, adjoining lower part of rhinarium, lower lip, and chin pure white; throat and under side of neck extensively dusky; pectoral and inguinal regions whitish, more or less invaded by dusky spots.· These spots, well defined at birth, mainly disappear with the first molt, but traces of them may persist, especially on flanks, under parts, and inner sides of limbs until at least half-grown. A transverse black bar on inner side of forearm often remains for some time after the other spots have disappeared.

Skull.—General form short and rounded; sagittal crest convex in outline; postorbital constriction moderately deep and rounded; lambdoid crest with a deep lateral concavity; parietal with a narrow, usually tapering, flattened, spicule-like bregmatic process extending diagonally inward and upward over frontal, approaching or reaching temporal ridge, becoming blended with frontal in advanced age; symphysis of mandible very short, and abruptly upturned, the angle between rami rounded anteriorly; canines rather short, with subapical lateral grooves (prominent in some members of the family) normally absent or obsolescent. When present, the canine grooves are usually shallow and reduced to single inconspicuous lines on the outer surfaces of the teeth.

Remarks.—(For general discussion see under subgenus.)

FELIS CONCOLOR CONCOLOR Linné

Tigre Rouge; Cayenne Puma (Pls. 84, 90)

Cuguacuarana Brasiliensibus, Tigre Lusitanis, Marcgrave, Hist. Rerum. Natur. Brasiliae, 1648, p. 235. From Brazil (Part).

Tigris fulvus Barrere, Essai sur l'Hist. Nat. France Equinox, 1741, p. 166.

Felis concolor Linné, Regni Animalis, Appendix to Mantissa Plantarum, Part 2, 1771, p. 522.

Puma concolor Jardine, Natur. Lib. Vol. 2, Mamm. Felidae, 1834, p. 266 (Part).

Felis concolor var. *wawula* Lesson, Nouv. Tab. Regne Animal, 1842, p. 50. (Based on the *"wawula"* of Schomburgk 1840, p. 325.)

Felis concolor var. *soasoaranna* Lesson, Nouv. Tab. Regne Animal, 1842, p. 50. (Based on the "soasoaranna" of Schomburgk, 1840, p. 325.) From "open savannahs of the Orinoco."

Leopardus concolor Gray, Proc. Zool. Soc. London, March 14, 1867, p. 265 (Part).

Felis sucuacuara Liais, Climats Geol. Faune du Bresil, 1872, p. 461. Based on the *"sucuarana vraie"* or "l'Onca vermelha" of Brazil (Part).

Puma puma concolor Allen, Bull. Amer. Mus. Nat. Hist., Vol. 35, Art. 30, Aug. 9, 1916, p. 579.

Felis concolor wawula Nelson and Goldman, Journ. Mamm. 10 (4): 347, Nov. 11, 1929. From Demarara River, about 40 miles above mouth, British Guiana.

Type locality.—Here restricted to the Cayenne region, French Guiana.

Type specimen.—Not designated.

Distribution.—Eastern Venezuela, British Guiana, Surinam, French Guiana and parts of northern Brazil; limits of range unknown.

General characters.—Size medium; median dorsal area "cinnamon-rufous" or "ferruginous"—one of the most vividly colored members of the group; skull with rostrum strongly compressed laterally, between ascending branches of maxillae; auditory bullae large; dentition heavy. Somewhat similar to *bangsi*, of Colombia, but color richer, more rufescent and cranial characters distinctive. Near *anthonyi* of southern Venezuela in size, but color lighter in general tone than in the type of that form, and skull differing in details. Differing from *borbensis* of the valley of the Amazon River in apparently larger size and important cranial features.

Color.—Top of head, neck and median dorsal area to base of tail rich "cinnamon-rufous" or "ferruginous," the general tone nearer the latter color along posterior part of back and rump, becoming light "tawny" on sides of neck, shoulders, along flanks and on outer surfaces of limbs, paling gradually to near "light pinkish-cinnamon" or "cinnamon-buff" on feet; lips, except a downward extension of conspicuous blackish spots at base of vibrissae, chin and throat whitish; under surface of neck between "pinkish-buff" and "cinnamon-buff"; chest, inner sides of limbs and inguinal region dull whitish (purest white on inguinal region), belly more or less distinctly buffy, palest and tending to become whitish along median line; face in general buffy-brownish, the whitish supra-orbital spots moderately distinct; ears black externally, narrowly edged with gray, thinly clothed internally with whitish hairs; hairs around pads on feet brownish-black; tail above near "ochraceous-tawny" on proximal half and near buckthorn brown on distal portion, heavily mixed with black, becoming light ochraceous-buffy below to dark brownish or blackish tip (in an example from Paramaribo, Surinam the tip above and below is brownish; in one from Caura Valley, Venezuela the black extends forward about 4 inches on upper side).

Skull.—Size medium; zygomata rather narrow and tending to converge anteriorly; ascending branches of maxillae laterally compressed, giving them a pinched in appearance; nasals flattened anteriorly, the median groove of moderate depth, blunt or rather squarely truncate posteriorly; jugal reaching plane of anterior wall of glenoid fossa; auditory bullae large and fully inflated; dentition heavy, the upper sectorial with a prominent internal cusp —larger than usual in the group. Compared with that of *bangsi* the skull is larger, more elongated; zygomata comparatively less widely spreading, more convergent anteriorly; nasals flatter, somewhat depressed anteriorly, more receding from nares; auditory bullae larger, more inflated; dentition much heavier, the upper sectorial with a larger internal cusp. Similar in general to that of *anthonyi* of southern Venezuela, but skull narrower; frontal region much narrower; nasals less highly arched, more flattened anteriorly; ascending branches of premaxillae more compressed, or "pinched in "laterally; interpterygoid fossa much narrower; auditory bullae large, about as in *anthonyi;* dentition similar, but upper carnassial with internal cusp more prominent. Skull larger and heavier in structure than in *borbensis;* rostrum more compressed laterally between ascending branches of maxillae; nasals less highly arched, more depressed and V-shaped along median line posteriorly; interpterygoid fossa relatively broader; auditory bullae relatively larger; dentition much heavier; upper carnassial with internal cusp more prominent.

Measurements.—No external measurements are available. *Skull* (two adult females, one from the Caura Valley, Venezuela, and the other from Surinam, respectively): Greatest length, 175.8 mm.; condylobasal length, 165.3, ——; zygomatic breadth, 116.5, 113.7; height of cranium, 60.7, 63.5; interorbital constriction, 30.8, 31.2; postorbital processes, 65.5, 54.4; width of nasals (at anterior tips of frontals), 9.9, 13.6; width of palate (across interpterygoid fossa), 25.8, 26.4; maxillary tooth row (front of canine to back of carnassial), 56.6, 56.2; upper carnassial, crown length, 22.2, 22.7, width, 11.9, 10.6; lower carnassial, crown length, 17, 16; upper canine, alveolar diameter (antero-posterior), 12.8, 12.8.

Remarks.—In describing *F. concolor* Linné referred to Brisson, Marcgrave, Ray, and Buffon. The first reference is to Brisson, whose diagnosis was copied as follows: "Felis exflavo rufescens, mento et infimo ventre albicantibus." The animal was assigned to a habitat in "Brassilia." The description might apply to anyone of several regional races now known to inhabit the Guianas and Brazil. Merriam (1901: 593) gave the type region as probably southeastern Brazil, and he used a skull from Piracicaba, about 80 miles northwest of the city of Sao Paulo as a basis for comparison. Nelson and Goldman, regarding Merriam as the first reviser, accepted Merriam's conclusion and regarded the vicinity of Sao Paulo as the type region. Specimens from Piracicaba were assumed to be typical. This assignment to a type locality might be treated as final, but further consideration of the case has convinced me that it was based on an erroneous assumption. The principal Linnaean reference is to Brisson who in turn cited Barrere as his first and main authority, and described the animal under Barrere's name for the "tigre rouge" of Cayenne. Brisson gave the habitat as Guiana and Brazil. Other Linnaean references are to authors writing of Cayenne or northern Brazil. In view of the foregoing it seems obvious that the designation of the far southern Sao Paulo region as type locality for a species now known to subdivide into numerous geographic races was an error that should be corrected by restricting the name *concolor* to the puma inhabiting the Cayenne region, French Guiana.

The name *"Felis concolor var wavula"* as published by Lesson (1842: 50) was a nomen nudum, but he referred to "Sch." The reference is evidently to Schomburgk (1840: 325-327) and the account upon which Lesson's name was based regarded by Nelson and Goldman (1929: 347) as giving it validity is as follows:

"The Indian distinguishes two species of the Puma, the Wawula or Deer Tiger and the Soasoaranna. The latter appears to be more restricted to the open savannahs of the Orinoco, the former frequents as well the coast regions as the savannahs. I have recognized in the two specimens which the Museum of the Zoological Society possesses, the Puma of the Orinoco; and although they are generally not known in British Guiana, I have seen a skin of one which had been killed about 40 miles up the Demarara River. The head seemed to be small in proportion to its size, the body was long, and the fore feet very stout; its tail, as far as I can remember, more than half the length of the body, and ending in a tuft of black hair.

"I am enabled to give a more detailed account of the second species, the Wawula Arowa of the Arawaks, or Deer Tiger of the colonists. In colour they are of a reddish-brown which lightens on the outside of the limbs, and assumes a white colour on the belly. Of a similar colour is the breast, and the reddish-brown which is the prevailing colour of the body is of a lighter tint at the muzzle and chin. It is covered with thick fur, which relates likewise to the tail, which, as in the Puma of the Orinoco, is black on the tips. The eyes are of a brown colour. The head is small; higher in proportion than any of the spotted kinds, strongly built before and light behind. Its proportion will become apparent from the following measurement of a subject which was killed at the savannahs of the Rio Branco, and which is now in my possession. It stood behind 2 feet, and before 1 foot 10 inches; and its whole length from the nose to the tip of the tail was 6 feet 2 inches.

"It is very destructive to the cattle farms, and it is so powerful an animal, that I have been told by an eye witness, that it killed a mule and dragged it across a trench to the opposite side, although the trench was not quite full of water, and the Puma had to drag it a few feet up hill, after it landed with its prey on the other side. My informant, who had watched its proceedings, had meanwhile sent for his gun, and shot him while attempting to pull the mule into the wood. They seem to be particularly partial to dogs, and a great number of those which are kept by the settlers for the purpose of hunting, are killed and eaten by them. They follow in the woods the herds of Peccaries, and watch their motion in order to seize upon the stragglers, being well aware that if they attacked the flock, they would be overpowered and torn to pieces. They hunt as well by day as in the night, and feed also on deer and the smaller domestic animals. They give birth to two young ones, seldom three, which have spots of a darker hue, more or less visible, according as the lights fall upon them, and which I have been told they lose after the first year.

"Cuvier doubts that the cats just described form two different species. I do not venture to combat his opinion, as I saw only a skin of the Puma of the Orinoco, which was similar to the specimens at the Museum of Zoological Society, and agrees with Mr. Bennett's description, while the second, and of which I possess a specimen, resembles Wilson's figure of the *Felis concolor.*"

Felis concolor var. *soasoaranna* Lesson appears to have been based on another local name of the same animal as the "wawula," the two being from the same general region. This opinion seems to have been first expressed by Cuvier, as shown by Schomburgk (l. c.).

The pre-Linnaean name *Tigris fulvus* Barrere (1741: 166), based on the "tigre rouge" of Cayenne, probably applied to an animal identical with or very similar to the "wawula." Buffon (1776; 223) quoted M. de la Borde, Royal Surgeon in Cayenne in reference to the three kinds of carnivorous animals in the country. These were first the jaguar, called "tigre," second the animal known as the "tigre rouge," and third a species called "tigre noir." The last mentioned was figured by Buffon (l. c.: 42) as "Le Cougar Noir." In the highly fanciful illustration the upper parts of the animal are black and the under parts and sides of head white, with a sharp line of demarcation. It may represent a black phase of the puma as authors, including Cabrera (1940: 169), state that black or nearly black individuals occur in South America. Two specimens, skins only, from Serra da Lua (Mountains of the Moon), Amazonas, Brazil are referred to the present form mainly for geographic reasons, as skins alone do not afford reliable diagnostic characters.

Specimens examined.—Total number, 6, as follows:
Brazil: Serra da Lua, Amazonas, 2 (skins only).[1]
Surinam: Paramaribo, 1 (skin only);[2] exact locality unknown, 2 (1 skin without skull; 1 skull without skin).
Venezuela: Caura Valley, 1.

FELIS CONCOLOR COUGUAR Kerr
Eastern Puma (Pls. 74, 80, 86)

Cougar de Pensilvanie Buffon, Hist. Nat., Suppl., vol. 3, p. 222, 1776.
Felis couguar Kerr, Animal Kingdom, p. 151, 1792. Name based on Buffon's description and plate illustration.
F[elis] pensylvanica Link, Beytr. zur Naturgesch. Zweytes Stuck, p. 90, 1795. Apparently intended to apply to the cougar, presumably of Pennsylvania.
Felis dorsalis Rafinesque, Atlantic Journ. and Friend of Knowl., vol. 1, no. 1, 1832, p. 19. Alleghany Mountains, Pa.
Felis concolor True, Proc. U. S. Nat. Mus., vol. 7 (1884), p. 610, 1885 (in part).
Felis couguar Merriam, Proc. Washington Acad. Sci., vol. 3, p. 582, Dec. 11, 1901.
Felis concolor couguar Nelson and Goldman, Journ. Mamm., 10(4): 347, Nov. 11, 1929.
Type locality.—Pennsylvania.
Distribution.—Extinct. Formerly eastern United States as far north as Maine and to southern Ontario and Quebec. Doubtless intergrading to the southward with *coryi*.
General characters.—A medium sized or rather large, dark subspecies. Similar to *coryi*, of Florida, but cranial characters, especially the anteriorly more convergent zygomata and narrower, flatter nasals, distinctive. Similar in general to *hippolestes*, of Wyoming, but smaller, and skull differing in detail.
Color.—"Body and legs of a uniform fulvous or tawny hue . . . Ears

---

[1]Chicago Nat. Hist. Mus.
[2]Mus. Comp. Zool.

light-colored within, blackish behind. Belly pale reddish or reddish white. Face sometimes with a uniform lighter tint than the general hue of the body."—De Kay (1842: 47.)

Skull.—Similar to that of *coryi*, but less elongated; nasals narrower and flatter; zygomata more widely spreading posteriorly, turning more abruptly inward and converging anteriorly; postorbital processes shorter; jugal less extended posteriorly; auditory bullae usually smaller, bulging less prominently below exoccipitals; dentition about as in *coryi*. Compared with that of *hippolestes*, the skull is somewhat smaller, less elongated; zygomata more strongly bowed outward posteriorly, more abruptly turned inward and converging anteriorly; nasals broader posteriorly, and narrower, less widely spreading anteriorly over nares; auditory bullae smaller, bulging less prominently below exoccipitals; dentition about the same.

Measurements.—Emmons (1840: 35) gives the "whole length" of one of the largest individuals, presumably male, from New York as 9 feet (=2,-743 mm.); tail of a male, 2 feet, 3 inches (= 686 mm.); tail of a female, 1 foot, 9 inches (= 534 mm.). *Skull.* (Two adults, sex unmarked but obviously females, from the Adirondack Mountain region, New York, respectively): Greatest length, 184, ——; condylobasal length, 168.7, 165; zygomatic breadth, 134.5, 127.8; height of cranium, 66.4, 62.5, interorbital breadth, 35.8, 35.9; postorbital processes, 73.2, 71; width of nasals (at anterior tips of frontals), 16.4, 14.5; width of palate (across interpterygoid fossa), 27.8, 295.8; maxillary tooth row, alveolar length (front of canine to back of carnassial), 55.8, 54.3; upper carnassial, crown length, 22.2, 20.3, width, 10.9, 10.7; lower carnassial, crown length, 16.7, 15.2; upper canine, alveolar diameter (antero-postero), 11.8, 10.9.

Remarks.—The puma formerly ranged throughout the Eastern States, but apparently became extinct many years ago. Surprisingly few specimens found their way into museum collections. Skulls from the State of New York are assumed to represent typical *couguar* which was described from Pennsylvania. The skulls indicate that it was a well-marked form, differing from *coryi* and *hippolestes* in cranial features such as commonly distinguish other subspecies. Unfortunately no skins that have not been exposed to light for a long period are known to be available for comparison, and the color is therefore imperfectly known.

A fragmentary skull from Capon Springs, W. Va., has wide spreading zygomata and in other characters appears to be near typical *couguar*. Among early specimen records, according to R. M. Anderson, a skin in the National Museum of Canada was taken at Three Rivers, Quebec, in 1828. A mounted specimen in the Museum of the Boston Society of Natural History was captured at Wardsboro, Vt., November 20, 1875.

Felis dorsalis Rafinesque (1832: 19) from Alleghany Mountains of

Pennsylvania was described as spotted on sides with a black band all along the middle of the back, the total length 10 feet, and "very different from *Felis pardalis*, by size four times larger."

Specimens examined.—Total number, 8, as follows:

New York: Adirondack Mountains, 1 (skull only;); Catskill Mountains, 1 (skull only);[1] Essex County, 2 (1 skin only; 1 skull only); "St. Lawrence County," 2 (skulls only).[1]

Pennsylvania: Elk County, 1 (skull only).

West Virginia: Capon Springs, 1 (skull only).

FELIS CONCOLOR MISSOULENSIS Goldman
Montana Puma (Pls. 46, 55, 64, 73, 79, 85)

Felis concolor missoulensis Goldman, Journ. Mammal. 24(2): 229, June 8, 1943.

Type locality.—Sleeman Creek, about 10 miles southwest of Missoula, Montana County, Montana.

Type specimen.—No. 262116, ♂ adult, skin and skull, U. S. National Museum (Biological Surveys collection); collected by Ronald and Carrol Thompson, December 30, 1936.

Distribution.—Northern Rocky Mountain region from Yellowstone National Park, Wyoming, north to Jasper Park, Alberta, northern Cassiar (Big Muddy River), and the Peace River District, British Columbia; east to southwestern Saskatchewan and northwestern North Dakota; west to the Wallowa Mountains, northeastern Oregon. Intergrades on the west with *oregonensis* and on the south with *hippolestes*.

General characters.—Size large; color rather pale; skull large and massive, but relatively short and rounded, with widely spreading zygomata. Differs from *hippolestes* of central western Wyoming in cranial details, especially general shortness, and wider spread of zygomata. Differs from *oregonensis*, of the Cascade Range, Washington, in paler color as well as in cranial details.

Color.—*Type:* Top of head, neck, and narrow median dorsal area near "tawny," slightly darkened by black-tipped hairs; over the same parts an admixture of white hairs is too sparse to materially affect the general tone; tawny of narrow median dorsal area giving way rather abruptly to light "cinnamon," paling gradually along sides and outer surfaces of limbs to near "pinkish-buff" on feet; upper lips, except blackish spots at base of vibrissae, chin, and throat pure white; under surface of neck pale buff, or between "pinkish-buff" and "pale pinkish-buff"; chest, inner sides of limbs and under parts dull white, the "drab-gray" under color showing through; middle of

---

[1]New York State Mus.

face a grayish-brown mixture; supraorbital spots white, as usual in the group; ears blackish externally, becoming grayish near edges, covered internally with longer white hairs; hairs around pads on soles of feet blackish; tail above similar to back, but less distinctly tawny, more mixed with black to near tip, which is black for about 2 inches, becoming brownish-buffy below. In a skin from 18 miles southeast of Hamilton, Mont., the median dorsal area is more vivid and near "orange-cinnamon" in tone. One from Jasper Park, Alberta, the farthest north of any examined is rather dark in color, but within the usual range of individual variation.

Skull.—Similar in general size to that of *hippolestes,* but shorter, broader, and somewhat flatter; zygomata more widely spreading; rostrum and palate distinctly shorter; vestigial upper premolars set in a narrower space behind canines; diastema behind lower canines shorter; dentition about the same. Compared with that of *oregonensis* the skull is similar in general size, but is shorter, broader and flatter; zygomata more widely spreading; frontal region less elevated; rostrum and palate usually shorter, but vestigial upper premolars set in a gap of similar extent; diastema in lower jaw shorter; dentition usually lighter.

Measurements.—No external measurements available. *Skull* (type and an adult male from 12 miles east of Hamilton, Mont., respectively): Greatest length, 221.8, 222.5 mm.; condylobasal length, 203.5, 200.3; zygomatic breadth, 164.3, 162.3; height of cranium, 81.5, 79.3; interorbital constriction, 45.4, 47.8; postorbital processes, 78.7, 85.2; width of nasals (at anterior tips of frontals), 18.5, 17.2; width of palate (across interpterygoid fossa), 28.6, 32.6; maxillary tooth row, alveolar length (front of canine to back of carnassial), 65.7, 65.3; upper carnassial, crown length, 22.7, 23, crown width, 12.5, 12; lower carnassial, crown length, 17.7, 19.2; upper canine, alveolar diameter (antero-posterior), 16.8, 15.4. Two adult females, one from Adair Ranch, Glacier National Park, Mont., and the other from Crow's Nest Pass, Kootenay District, British Columbia, respectively: Greatest length, 189.4, 190; condylobasal length, 169.6, 175; zygomatic breadth, 135.3, 139; height of cranium, 67.3, 70; interorbital constriction, 36, 41.6; postorbital processes, 67.4, 76.6; width of nasals (at anterior tips of frontals), 13.4, 15.9; width of palate (across interpterygoid fossa), 29.5, 31; maxillary tooth row, alveolar length (front of canine to back of carnassial), 57.2, 53.9; upper carnassial, crown length, 21.6, 20.7, crown width, 11, 10.7; lower carnassial, crown length, 16.3, 15.7; upper canine, alveolar diameter (antero-posterior), 12.8, 11.5.

Remarks.—The range of *missoulensis* along the Rocky Mountains, in Alberta and British Columbia, marks the northern limit of the disribution of the species. The most northern authentic record appears to be that of A. L. Rand (1944: 40), who states that one was taken by an Indian on the Big

Muddy River in northern Cassiar District, British Columbia, several years ago. He says: "The skin was hung in the Hudson Bay Company store for some time, and several trappers told of seeing it. . . . Its rarity here on the northern limit of its range is indicated by the fact that the Indian who caught it did not know its identity." Cowan (1939: 76) refers to the killing of a large female by Ted Strand of Little Prairie, south of Hudson Hope, British Columbia, in March 1937. Another northern record is that of Seton (1926: 52), who quotes Provincial Constable E. Forfar of Hudson Hope in regard to the killing of a mountain lion near the confluence of Cypress Creek and Halfway River, the Halfway River being one of the tributaries of the Peace River north of Hudson Hope. On the south, in northern Wyoming, *missoulensis* passes rather abruptly into *hippolestes*, which differs most obviously in the relatively narrower, more elongated skull. Between the Rocky Mountains and the Cascade Range *missoulensis* intergrades with *oregonensis*. Specimens from Dayville, Oregon, are somewhat intermediate in characters. A skull from Clearwater River, 50 miles northwest of Banff, Alberta, has an elevated frontal region resembling that of *oregonensis*, but in broad, rounded contour, and in broad interpterygoid fossa and other details agrees with missoulensis.

Specimens examined.—Total number, 53, as follows:

Alberta: Clearwater River (50 miles northwest of Banff), 1 (skull only); Jasper Park ("back of Interlaken towards Jacques Lake"), 1[1]; Waterton Lakes Park (near Kelly Oilwells), 1.[1]

British Columbia: Crow's Nest Pass (near Edgewood), 6 (skulls only).

Idaho: Clearwater, 2; Coolin, 1 (skull only); Elk City, 1; Little Salmon River, 2; Selway River, Bitter Root National Forest, 3 (1 skull only); Sheep Creek, Boise National Forest, 6 (5 skins without skulls).

Montana: Adair Ranch, Glacier National Park, 3 (skulls only); Fort Keogh, 1 (skull only); Gardiner River, 1; Hamilton (12 miles east), 1; Hamilton (18 miles southeast), 2 (1 skin only); Sleeman Creek (10 miles southeast of Missoula), 1 (type).

North Dakota: Fort Union, 1 (skull only).

Oregon: Upper Imnaha River, Wallowa County, 1.

Wyoming: Blacktail Creek, Yellowstone National Park, 4 (1 skin without skull); Buffalo River, about 20 miles southeast of Jackson Lake, 1 (skin only); Jackson Lake, 1 (skull only). Park County, 5 (skulls only); Wapiti River, 2 (skulls only); Yellowstone National Park, 5 (1 skull without skin).

---

[1]Nat. Mus. Canada.

FELIS CONCOLOR HIPPOLESTES Merriam
Rocky Mountain Puma (Pls. 47, 56, 65, 74, 80, 86, 91)

Felis hippolestes Merriam, Proc. Biol. Soc. Wash. 11: 219, July 15, 1897.
Felis oregonensis hippolestes Stone, Science (n.s.) 9: 35, Jan. 6 1899.
Felis concolor hippolestes Nelson and Goldman, Journ. Mamm. 10(4): 347, November 11, 1929.

Type locality.—Wind River Mountains (near head of Big Wind River), Wyo.

Type specimen.—No. 57936, skin and skull, ♂ old, U. S. National Museum (Biological Surveys collection); collected by John Burlingham, November 1892.

Distribution.—Rocky Mountain region from Wyoming, except northwestern part, south through southeastern Idaho, northeastern Utah, and Colorado to northern New Mexico. Formerly east in the prairie states to undetermined limits.

General characters.—Maximum size perhaps the largest of all the subspecies; general color rather pale; pelage long, full and soft; skull very large, elongated; dentition light. Similar in size and color to *missoulensis* of the northern Rocky Mountains but cranial proportions, especially the greater total length of skull and relatively narrower zygomata, distinctive. Similar also in size to *oregonensis* of the Cascade Range, but color paler; skull differing in detail, notably the lesser elevation of the frontal region. Closely resembling *azteca* of the Sierra Madre of Chihuahua and the Mogollon Mountain region of New Mexico and Arizona in color, but larger; pelage longer; dentition heavier. Compared with *kaibabensis* of northwestern Arizona the present subspecies is darker in general color, the dark median dorsal area more clearly defined; skull broader.

Color.—About as in *azteca*, including similar variation in color tones.

Skull.—Very large—maximum size equaling or exceeding that of any of the other subspecies. Similar in size to that of *oregonensis*, but frontal region more flattened, less bulging above anteriorly; frontal pits near posterior ends of nasals shallower; nasals less depressed or deeply sunken in frontal pit posteriorly; lambdoid crest, especially in older males, forming a narrower lateral shelf, but tending to project farther posteriorly over foramen magnum; interpterygoid fossa usually wider; small anterior upper premolar usually set in a longer interspace between canine and second upper premolar, leaving distinct gaps before and behind (small anterior upper premolar more nearly filling this space in *oregonensis*). In general about like that of *azteca*, but much larger; dentition usually heavier. Differing from that of *kaibabensis* mainly in greater width. Compared with that of *missoulensis* the skull is similar in general size, but more elongated, and relatively narrower, the zygomata less widely spreading; rostrum and palate longer; vestigial upper premolars set in a wider interval behind canines; diastema behind lower canines longer; dentition about the same.

Measurements.—Three adult males from the vicinity of Meeker, Colo., respectively: Total length, 2,438, 2,336, 2,286 mm.; weight, 227, 164, 160 pounds. Three adult females from the same vicinity, respectively: Total length, 2,134, 2,058, 2,006; weight, 133, 124, 120. *Skull* (type): Greatest length, 227.4 condylobasal length, 204.4; zygomatic breadth, 160; height of cranium, 81.8; interorbital breadth, 48.5; postorbital processes, 83.5; width of nasals (at anterior tips of frontals), 17.8; width of palate (across interpterygoid fossa), 33.3; maxillary tooth row, alveolar length, 66.5; upper carnassial, crown length, 23, width, 12.7; lower carnassial, crown length, 17.7; upper canine, alveolar diameter, 16.7. Two adult males from the vicinity of Meeker, Colo., respectively: Greatest length, 237, 213.2; condylobasal length, 210, 197.6; zygomatic breadth, 162.5, 147.9; height of cranium, 85, 79.5; interorbital breadth, 46.2, 45.5; postorbital processes, 83.2, 81; width of nasals (at anterior tips of frontals), 15.3, 19.5; width of palate (across interpterygoid fossa), 30.8, 30.3; maxillary tooth row, alveolar length, 66.9, 62.8; upper carnassial, crown length, 22.9, 23.9, width, 12.1, 12.9; lower carnassial, crown length, 17.5, 17.5; upper canine, alveolar diameter, 15.3, 14.9. Two adult females from the vicinity of Meeker, Colo.: Greatest length, 203, 199.2; condylobasal length, 184.4, 178.9; zygomatic breadth, 133.7, 131.4; height of cranium, 70.9, 68.5; interorbital breadth, 38, 37.7; postorbital processes, 69.3, 72.4; width of nasals (at anterior tips of frontals), 15.2, 16.7; width of palate (across interpterygoid fossa), 29.2, 27; maxillary tooth row, alveolar length, 57.6, 58.5; upper carnassial, crown length, 20.2, 21.6 width, 10.6, 11.4; lower carnassial, crown length, 15.3, 16; upper canine, alveolar diameter, 11.3, 12.3.

Remarks.—The body measurements and weights available of the larger pumas are too few to afford a very reliable index to comparative sizes. The skulls, however, and especially the greatest length dimension, suggest that *hippolestes* may slightly exceed any of the other races in maximum size attained. On the south in New Mexico this race passes gradually into *azteca* which it closely resembles in color but from which it differs in decidedly larger size. Typical skulls of *hippolestes* contrast rather strongly with those of *azteca* of comparable sex and age, but skulls of females of the former may resemble small males of the latter. The skulls of male and female pumas normally differ in size and angularity, and it is unusual to find such close resemblance between the sexes, even in different forms. The single skull of an animal labeled male, but apparently female, from Catherine, Ellis County, Kans., is near *hippolestes*, but is not typical. This specimen, killed August 15, 1904, is the only one available from that settled region where the species is now extinct. The skull is rather narrow, with broad nasals, and in this latter character suggests gradation toward *coryi*. An imperfect skull of a mature female, No. 34955, American Museum of Natural History, labeled Duluth, Minn., but bearing no more definite data is included with *hippolestes* to which it appears to be nearest. It differs from typical *hippolestes*, however, very appreciably in the narrowness of the zygomata, especially posteriorly where the reduced spread brings the sides of the zygomata into more nearly parallel lines than is usual in the subspecies. In addition the nasals are broader and the postorbital processes shorter than usual in *hippolestes*. The Duluth skull contrasts rather strongly with *couguar* from New York. It is more elongated, with zygomata considerably less widely spreading posteriorly, the nasals broader, postorbital processes shorter and auditory bullae larger. The incompleteness of the data for the Duluth specimen suggests possible error as to locality. If the skull really came from Duluth or vicinity, it may represent an extinct form closely allied to *hippolestes*, that inhabited much of the forested region east of the Rocky Mountains.

Specimens examined.—Total number, 46, as follows:

Colorado: Atchee, Garfield County, 1 (skull only;[3] Basalt (3 miles south), 1 (skull only);[3] Cañon City, 3 (skulls only);[4] Cotopaxi (7 miles southeast), 1 (skull only);[3] Dotsero, 1 skull only); Durango (18 miles north), 1 (skull only);[3] Drake, 1 (skull only);[3] Fort Collins, 1 (skull only);[3] Gateway, 1 (skull only);[3] Granby, 1 (skull only);[3] Greenhorn Mountain, Huerfano County, 1 (skull only); Greystone, 2 (skulls only);[3] La Veta, 1 (skull only);[3] Marvine, 1 (skull only); Maybell, 1 (skull only);[3] Meeker, 12 (skulls only); Newcastle (3 miles northwest), 2 (skulls only);[3] Texas Creek, 1 (skull only);[3] Paradox, 1 (skull

Utah: Provo, 1 (skin only).

Kansas: Catherine, Ellis County, 1 (skull only);[1] Sparks, Doniphan County, 1 (lower jaw).

Minnesota: Duluth, 1 (skull only).[2]

New Mexico: "Northern New Mexico," 1 (skull only).

Utah: Provo, 1 (skinn only).

Wyoming: Bear Lodge Mountains (head of Bear Creek), 1 (skull only); Cora, 1; Green Valley, 1 (skull only); Wind River Mountains, near Cora, 1 (type); Wolf, 2 (1 skin only).

---

[1] Kansas Univ. Mus. Nat. Hist.
[2] Amer. Mus. Nat. Hist.
[3] Mus. Univ. Colorado.
[4] Two in Mus. Univ. Colorado.

FELIS CONCOLOR OREGONENSIS Rafinesque

Cascade Mountain Puma (Pls. 47, 56, 65, 75, 81, 87)

Felix [sic] *oregonensis* Rafinesque, Atlantic Journ. 1: 62, June 20, 1832.
Felis oregonensis Stone, Science (n.s) 9: 35, Jan. 6, 1899.
[*Felis*] [*concolor*]? *oregonensis* Elliot, Syn. Mamm. North Amer., Field
  Columb. Mus. Publ. 2: 294, March 6, 1901.
[*Felis*] *concolor oregonensis* Elliot, Mamm. Middle Amer., Field Columb.
  Mus. Publ., Zool. Ser. 4, pt. 2, p. 454, 1904.
Felis concolor oregonensis Elliot, Cat. Mamm. Field Columb. Mus. Publ.,
  Zool. Ser. 8: 392, 1907.

Type locality.—Ohanapecosh River, Mount Rainier National Park,
Wash.

Type specimen.—Not designated.

Distribution.—Cascade Mountain region from the mainland of south-western British Columbia south through Washington and Oregon, except the upper part of the Rogue River Valley, to near the California boundary, inter-grading on the east with *missoulensis,* on the west in Washington with *olympus,* and on the south with *californica;* altitudinal range from sea level to near timberline on the higher mountains. Upper Sonoran to Canadian Zones.

General characters.—Size very large; color dark. Skull characterized by distinct, but not extreme inflation of the frontal region, and the depth of the median frontal pit. Closely resembling *californica* of California, but larger, coloration somewhat darker, the dark facial markings and black tip of tail usually more extensive and conspicuous; cranial features, especially the more expanded frontal region, distinctive. Similar in size and color to *olympus* of the Olympic Mountains, Wash., and to *vancouverensis* of Vancouver Island, British Columbia, but somewhat paler and brighter, more suffused with "cin-namon," less brownish than either, and cranial details different. About equal to *missoulensis* of Montana in size, but color darker, averaging richer "cinna-mon" or "tawny"; skull distinguished by the anterior inflation of the frontal region, a character further developed in *olympus* and *vancouverensis.*

Color.—Very similar to *olympus,* and presenting the same individual vari-ations, but usually paler and brighter, more suffused with "cinnamon," less brownish; median dorsal area in the more rufescent specimens, clearer "tawny," less extensively mixed with black. *Young* (about one-third grown): Dorsum less distinctly overlaid with black.

Skull.—Size very large; frontal region rather high and prominent; frontal pits near posterior ends of nasals rather deep. Similar in size and gen-eral form to that of *missoulensis,* but frontal region higher, more bulging, less flattened anteriorly; interpterygoid fossa usually narrower; frontal pit deeper;

vestigial upper premolar set in a shorter interspace behind canines; diastema behind lower canines distinctly longer; dentition heavier. Similar in size, and form of zygomata to those of *olympus* and *vancouverensis*, but frontal region less extreme in height and prominence; frontal pits less deeply excavated; dentition about the same. Compared with that of *californica* the skull is larger; frontal region more swollen anteriorly, less flattened above; dentition heavier.

Measurements.—No body measurements available. *Skull* (two adult males, one from Lake Chelan, and the other from Willard, Skamania County, Wash., respectively): Greatest length, 229.4, 207.5 mm.; condylobasal length, 209.3, 192.4; zygomatic breadth, 160.4, 147.8; height of cranium, 85.5, 77.2; interorbital breadth, 50.1, 46; postorbital processes, 82, 74.5; width of nasals (at anterior tips of frontals), 19.7, 17.5; width of palate (across interpterygoid fossa), 31.5, 29.1; maxillary tooth row, alveolar length, front of canine to back of carnassial, 66.5, 62.6; upper carnassial, crown length, 25.7, 23.8, width, 13.9, 12.3; lower carnassial, crown length, 18.2, 16.7; upper canine, alveolar diameter (antero-posterior), 17.1, 15.4. Two adult females, one from Mount Rainier National Park, Wash., and the other from near Estacada, Clackamas County, Oreg., respectively: Greatest length, 192.5, 190.0; condylobasal length, 180, 174.3; zygomatic breadth, 133.5, 132 2; height of cranium, 69.5, 67.8; interorbital breadth, 38.8, 39.4; postorbital processes, 72.1, 69.4; width of nasals (at anterior tips of frontals), 14.7, 13.8; width of palate, 29.7, 28 5; maxillary tooth row, alveolar length, front of canine to back of carnassial, 59.1, 58; upper carnassial, crown length, 23.1, 23.9; width, 11.2, 12.2; lower carnassial, crown length, 16.2, 17.2; upper canine, alveolar diameter (antero-posterior), 13.2, 13.3.

Remarks.—Nelson and Goldman (1932: 105) restricted the name *oregonensis*, which had been loosely applied to the pumas of the "Oregon Mountians," or the northwest coast region of the United States, by designating Mount Rainier National Park, Washington, as the type locality. Owing to faunal diversification within the park it seems desirable for still greater precision to fix the type locality as along the Ohanapecosh River, southeastern corner of Mount Rainier National Park. Specimens from that locality are, accordingly, regarded as typical.

The Cascade Mountains puma has an extensive range west of that of *missoulensis* of the northern Rocky Mountain region, extending in Oregon to the Pacific Coast. On the Olympic Peninsula in western Washington it gives way to the more extreme form *olympus*. Few specimens are available from east of the Cascade Mountains in Washington and Oregon, but these indicate gradation toward *missoulensis*. Specimens from Dayville, eastern Oregon, are rather pale, but in combined characters seem nearer to *oregonensis*, to which they are referred. In southwestern Oregon *oregonensis* partakes of the characters of the generally smaller subspecies *californica*, but little material is avail-

214   THE PUMA, MYSTERIOUS AMERICAN CAT

able for study, and the line separating them on the coast is drawn rather arbitrarily near the State boundary. Additional material is needed, especially from near the coast, as a basis for more definite conclusions.

An animal about half-grown, from Glendale, Oregon, was taken when just losing the juvenal dark spots. Oblique black markings near top of shoulders and spots over upper parts in general are still indicated by an admixture of blackish or dark tawny hairs; and on the under parts, especially the limbs, blackish spots or transverse bars are present.

Specimens examined.—Total number, 63, as follows:
British Columbia: Roche River, 2 (skulls only); Vernon, 1.[1]
Oregon: Agness (12 miles east), 4; Battle Creek, 1 (skull only); Cold Springs (near Estacada), 1 (skull only); Clackamas River (50 miles above Estacada), 1 (skull only); Dayville (Murderer Creek), 5; Drew (9 miles southeast), 2; Estacada, 5 (2 skulls without skins); Fort Umpqua (skull only); Glendale, 3 (1 skin without skull); Glide, 1; Goldbeach, 1; Illahe, 2; Marial, 1; Marmot, 1 (skull only); Marshfield, 1 (skull only); Oak Grove Butte (near Estacada), 3 (2 skulls without skins); Pistol River, Curry County, 5 (1 skull without skin); Polk County, 1 (skull only); Quartz Creek (near Tiller), 1; Reed, 1; Rock Creek, 14 miles northwest of Trail, Jackson County, 1.
Washington: Dollar Mountain (near Republic), Ferry County, 1 (skin only); Lake Chelan, 1; Lewis (10 miles east), Lewis County, 1; Loomis, Okanagan County, 2; Ohanapecosh River, Mount Rainier National Park, 5; Republic, Ferry County, 2; Skates Mountain District, Lewis County, 1; Trout Lake, Mount Adams, 1 (skull only); Vance (12 miles southeast), 4; Willard, 1.

FELIS CONCOLOR VANCOUVERENSIS Nelson and Goldman
Vancouver Island Puma (Pls. 48, 57, 66, 81, 87)

Felis concolor vancouverensis Nelson and Goldman, Proc. Biol. Soc. Washington 45: 105, July 15, 1932.

Type locality.—Campbell Lake, Vancouver Island, British Columbia.
Type specimen.—No. 211519, ♂ adult, skull only, U. S. National Museum (Biological Surveys collection); collected by W. R. Kent, September 13, 1915.
Distribution.—Known only from Vancouver Island.
General characters.—A very large dark form, closely allied to *olympus* and *oregonensis* of the adjacent mainland, but upper parts apparently darker rufous, and cranial characters, especially the more elevated frontal region, distinctive.

[1]Amer. Mus. Nat. Hist.

Color.—An adult from Vancouver Island (No. 194247, Mus. Vert. Zool.). Top of head, neck, and median dorsal area to base of tail near "cinnamon-rufous," moderately mixed with black on posterior part of back and rump; sides of body and outer surfaces of limbs cinnamon-buffy, paling gradually to "pinkish-buff" on feet; upper lips near sides of nose, lower part of cheeks, and chin nearly pure white; under side of neck suffused with "pale pinkish-buff"; chest, inner surfaces of limbs and median line of abdomen dull white; upper surface of muzzle dark brownish; areas at base of vibrissae on sides of muzzle deep black; light supraorbital markings distinct; ears blackish externally without distinct median spots, whitish internally and narrowly edged with gray; hairs around pads on soles of feet blackish; tail above about like posterior part of back, becoming pinkish-buffy below (tip missing).

Skull.—Size about as in *olympus* and *oregonensis* but frontals, high in those races, still more highly arched anteriorly, bulging prominently upward, or "humped," in front of postorbital processes; fronto-nasal pit (at posterior ends of nasals) deeper; nasals usually more convex in upper outline between anterior points of frontals, as viewed from side, owing to posterior depression in fronto-nasal pit, with a deeper median trough as viewed from rear; lambdoid crest usually less sinuate in outline, the lateral margins shelving more broadly and evenly outward from brain case; lower border of mandible usually straighter; dentition about the same.

Measurements.—No external measurements available. *Skull* (type and another adult male from Campbell River Valley, Vancouver Island): Greatest length, 215, 213.7 mm; condylobasal length, 197.8; 197.8; zygomatic breadth, 146.4, 145.9; height of cranium, 80, 78; interorbital breadth, 44.2, 44; postorbital processes, 79.4, 78.4; width of nasals (at anterior tips of frontals), 15.3, 16.4; width of palate (across interpterygoid fossa), 27.8, 27.3; maxillary tooth row, alveolar length (front of canine to back of carnassial), 62.8, 63.2; upper carnassial, crown length, 24.4, 24.2, width, 13.2, 12.7; lower carnassial, crown length, 18.4, 18; upper canine, alveolar diameter (antero-posterior), 15.2, 15.8. Two adult females from Vancouver Island, respectively: Greatest length, 194.5, 187; condylobasal length, 178.8, 172.8; zygomatic breadth, 136, 125.5; height of cranium, 72, 71.2; interorbital breadth, 41.8, 38.5; postorbital processes, 80, 72.5; width of nasals (at anterior tips of frontals), 16.9, 15; width of palate (across interpterygoid fossa), 27, 26.7; maxillary tooth row, alveolar length (front of canine to back of carnassial), 56.5, 55.7; upper carnassial, crown length, 21.8, 22.4, width, 11, 11.7; lower carnassial, crown length, 15.5, 16.4; upper canine, alveolar diameter (antero-posterior), 12.8, 13.5.

Remarks.—While the puma of Vancouver Island is closely related to the mainland races, comparable material now available shows that the differences pointed out are well marked, and in most individuals quite uniform and constant. While darker and more somber colors generally prevail, occasional examples approach some of the dark tropical forms in intensity of rufescent tone, as shown in No. 12449, Museum of Vertebrate Zoology, from Parksville, Vancouver Island. This specimen, an adult male, taken April 24, is near "cinnamon rufous" along the back. In the steeply arched frontal region and depth of the fronto-nasal pit *vancouverensis* presents an extreme in development in the group. The unusual median indentation of the fronto-nasal region, the convexity of the posterior part of the nasals, and the highly arched frontal region give that part of the skull a distinctly more sinuous upper outline than in other races. In *oregonensis* and in *olympus* the skulls are more variable, the frontal region is rather arched, the fronto-nasal pit rather deep and the lambdoid crest rather widespreading in some specimens, but a distinctly nearer approach in cranial characters to the paler forms, *missoulensis* and *hippolestes*, of the Rocky Mountain region, is exhibited. *F. c. vancouverensis* is the only insular form known.

Specimens examined—Total number, 19, all from Vancouver Island, as follows: Buttle Lake, 1 (skull only); Campbell Lake (type localtiy), 3 (skulls only); Campbell River Valley, 1 (skull only); Nanoose Bay, 2;[1] Nootka Sound, 4 (skulls only);[1] Parksville, 1;[1] Quatsino, 1 (skull only); Quinsome Valley, 1 (skull only); within 20 miles of Victoria, 4 (skulls only); without definite locality, 1 (skin only).

FELIS CONCOLOR OLYMPUS Merriam

Olympic Puma (Pl. 92)

Felis hippolestes olympus Merriam, Proc. Biol. Soc. Wash. 11: 220, July 15, 1897.

Type locality.—Lake Cushman, Olympic Mountains, Wash.

Type specimen.—No. 77973, [♀] adult, skin and skull, U. S. National Museum (Biological Surveys collection); collected by Thomas Hayes, April 18, 1896.

Distribution.—Olympic Peninsula region of western Washington, intergrading to the east with *oregonensis*.

General characters.—Size very large; color very dark; pelage long, full, and soft. Skull exhibiting marked inflation of the frontal region, and depth of median frontal pit. Similar in size and color to *oregonensis* of the Cascade Range, but general tone somewhat darker and duller, more brownish, less suffused with "cinnamon," and cranial details, especially the more elevated frontal region, different. Closely allied to *vancouverensis* of Vancouver Island, B. C., but upper parts less deeply rufescent, and cranial details distinctive.

Color.—Top of head, neck and usually broad median dorsal area to base of tail varying from dull, dark brown to dark, deep "tawny," rather heavily

---

[1]Mus. Vert. Zool.

mixed with black, becoming dull "clay color," the dark hairs thinning out on shoulders, sides and on outer surfaces of limbs, paling gradually to dark "pinkish-buff" on feet; upper lips near sides of nose, and chin nearly pure white; under surface of neck varying from grayish to pinkish-buffy; chest, inner sides of limbs, and median line of abdomen dull white, the darker basal color showing through; face in general grayish-brown, the dark markings prominent, but light supraorbital spots indistinct; black areas at base of vibrissae on sides of muzzle conspicuous, and smaller black spots at base of supraorbital vibrissae often present, especially in the younger animals; ears usually black externally, the median, grayish spots absent or indistinct, rather narrowly edged with gray, thinly clothed internally with whitish or light-buffy hairs; hairs around pads on soles of feet blackish; tail above usually about like back becoming dull "clay color" below to near tip, which is black, the black extending forward 3 or 4 inches on upper side. *Young* (about one-third grown): Ground color near "clay color," the back rather extensively overlaid with black.

Skull.—Size very large; frontal region high and prominent; frontal pits near posterior ends of nasals deep. Closely resembling that of *vancouverensis* but frontals and nasals less extreme in convexity. Similar in size to that of *oregonensis*, but frontal region rising higher in front of postorbital processes; frontal pits deeper.

Measurements.—No body measurements available. *Skull* (two adult males, one from Elwha River and the other from Soleduck River, Olympic Mountains, Wash., respectively): Greatest length, 228.2, 211.5 mm.; zygomatic breadth, 155.8, 151.9; height of cranium, 84, 77.6; interorbital constriction, 51.6, 45.2; postorbital processes, 82.5, 76.6; width of nasals (at anterior tips of frontals), 17.4, 16.1; width of palate (across interpterygoid fossa), 32.3, 29.7; maxillary tooth row, alveolar length (front of canine to back of carnassial), 66.4, 63.4; upper carnassial, crown length, 25.4, 24.2; width, 12.3, 12.4; lower carnassial, crown length, 17.7, 16.7; upper canine, alveolar diameter (antero-posterior), 15.3, 15. The type and another adult female from Queets River, Olympic Mountains, Wash., respectively: Greatest length, 188.8, 195.8; condylobasal length, 174.4, 180.7; zygomatic breadth, 126.7, 136.5; height of cranium, 68.5, 69.7; interorbital breadth, 38.8, 41.5; postorbital processes, 71, 72.6; width of nasals (at anterior tips of frontals), 16.8, 15.8; width of palate (across interpterygoid fossa), 27.3, 28.9; maxillary tooth row, alveolar length (front of canine to back of carnassial), 57.4, 58.8; upper carnassial, crown length, 22.4, 23.4, width, 11.7, 12; lower carnassial, crown length, 16.2, 16.2; upper canine, alveolar diameter (antero-posterior), 13.7, 13.2.

Remarks.—The dark general color of this race is shared with *vancouverensis*. The latter, however, on the basis of scanty material, appears to be somewhat more rufescent in tone. The dark colors of the two races are evidently associated with environmental conditions, their habitat being somewhat isolated sections of the great forest near the Pacific coast. The general region has an excessive rainfall, and is fog enshrouded during much of the year. The difference in color between *olympus* and *oregonensis* though relatively slight is quite appreciable, especially when skins in numbers are compared. In cranial details, *olympus* closely resembles *vancouverensis*, but the latter presents more extreme development of features pointed out.

Specimens examined.—Total number, 23, as follows:

Washington: Bogachiel River, Clallam County, 1; Clallam County, 1; Coal Creek, Jefferson County, 1; Elwha, 3; Elwha River, Clallam County, 4; Humptulips (Stevens Creek), Olympic Mountains, 2 (skulls only); Lake Cushman (type locality), 1; Larch Mountain, Thurston County, 1; Mattheny River, Jefferson County, 2; Olympic Mountains, 2; Puget Sound, 1 (skull only); Queets River, Jefferson County, 3; Tenino (15 miles east), 1.

FELIS CONCOLOR CALIFORNICA [May]

California Puma (Pls. 48, 57, 66, 91, 92)

Felis californica [May], California Game "marked down" (pamphlet issued by Southern Pacific R. R. Company, San Francisco), 1896, p. 22.

Felis hawveri Stock, Bull. Dept. Geol., Univ. California 10 (24): 482, figs. 4a-4b, Apr. 23, 1918. From Hawver Cave, near Auburn, Calif.

Felis oregonensis californica Grinnell and Dixon, Univ. Calif. Pub. Zool. 21 (11): 330, Apr. 7, 1923.

Felis concolor californica Nelson and Goldman, Journ. Mamm. 10 (4): 347, Nov. 11, 1929.

Type locality.—Kern County, California. Probably the Kern River basin in the Sierra Nevada.

Type specimen.—A mounted specimen probably destroyed in the San Francisco fire of 1906.

Distribution.—California, except desert region in southeastern part, north to closely adjoining portions of Oregon, except coast region, and south to include the Sierra Juarez and San Pedro Mártir mountain region of northwestern Baja California; altitudinal range from sea level to near timber line on high mountains. Lower Sonoran to Canadian Zones.

General characters.—A medium-sized, dark subspecies, closely resembling *oregonensis* but smaller, general tone of coloration somewhat paler, the dark facial markings and black tip of tail usually more restricted; cranial features, especially the more flattened frontal region, distinctive. Similar to *browni* of southwestern Arizona, but darker and cranial characters slightly different. Differing from *hippolestes* of central western Wyoming in smaller size and darker color, the tone of median dorsal area usually shading more gradually into that of sides (median dorsal area usually more clearly defined and contrasting with color of sides in *hippolestes*); cranial characters distinctive. Differing from *kaibabensis* of northern Arizona in smaller size, darker color, and relatively broader skull.

Color.—Top of head, neck and rather broad median dorsal area to base of tail varying from dark, buffy-brown to "tawny," more or less heavily mixed with black, becoming cinnamon-buffy or dull "clay color" on shoulders, sides and outer surfaces of limbs, paling gradually to near "cinnamon buff" or "pinkish-buff" on feet; upper lips near sides of nose and chin nearly pure white; under surface of neck varying from gray to "pinkish-buff"; chest, inner sides of limbs, median line of abdomen, and inguinal region dull white, the darker basal color showing through; face in general grayish-brown, the blackish areas at base of vibrissae prominent, and light supraorbital spots rather indistinct; ears usually black externally without distinct lighter median spots, edged with gray, thinly clothed internally with whitish hairs; hairs around pads on soles of feet blackish; tail usually about like back above, becoming cinnamon-buffy or dull "clay color" below to near tip which is black, the black extending forward about 3 inches on upper side.

Skull.—Size and structural details much as in *azteca*; frontal region usually slightly more elevated, less flattened, more depressed along median line; interpterygoid fossa narrower. Closely similar to that of *browni*, but frontal region rising higher anteriorly; zygomata usually more widely spreading; nasals less depressed anteriorly; dentition heavier. Differing from that of *improcera* in about the same characters as from that of *browni*. Contrasted with that of *oregonensis* the skull is smaller; frontal region sloping upward more gradually and evenly from rostrum, less bulging anteriorly, more flattened above; frontal pits near posterior ends of nasals shallower; dentition relatively lighter, the large molariform teeth decidedly shorter anteroposteriorly and canines slenderer. Smaller and more rounded than that of *kaibabensis*, with zygomata relatively more widely spreading.

Measurements.—An adult male from Pine Valley, headwaters of Carmel River, Monterey County, Calif.: Total length, 2,033 mm.; tail vertebrae, 750; hind foot, 280; weight, 148 pounds. Two adult males from Sequoia National Park, Calif., respectively: Total length, 1,952, 2,134; tail vertebrae, 784, 724; hind foot, 292, 260. Four adult females from localities in California, respectively, as follows: Dunlap (5 miles north), Fresno County: Total length, 1,879; tail vertebrae, 711; hind foot, 267; weight, 90 pounds. Kern River (25 miles above Kernville): Total length, 1,829; tail vertebrae, 686; hind foot, 254; weight, 80 pounds. Laguna Indian Reservation (2 miles southwest), San Diego County: Total length, 1,829; tail vertebrae, 711; hind foot, 267; weight, 100 pounds. Marble Fork Bridge, Sequoia National Park: Total length, 1,779; tail vertebrae, 711; hind foot, 254; weight, 80 pounds. *Skull:* Two adult males from Sequoia National Park, Calif., respectively: Greatest length, 213.3, 195.5; condylobasal length, 191.4, 180.3; zygomatic breadth, 153.5, 142.5; height of cranium, 79.7, 73.7; interorbital constriction, 43.1, 40; postorbital processes, 77.8, 76; width of nasals (at anterior tips of frontals), 19.4, 18; width of palate (across interpterygoid fossa), 29, 29.6; maxillary tooth row, alveolar length (front of canine to back of carnassial), 60, 57; upper carnassial, crown length, 24.5, 22.8, width, 12.8, 11.5; lower carnassial, crown length, 17.5, 16.5; upper canine, alveolar diameter (antero-posterior), 14.2, 14.3. Two adult females from localities in California, respectively, as follows: Dunlap (5 miles north), Fresno County and Wawona, Mariposa County: Greatest length, 183.5, 181.6; condylobasal length, 170, 164.4; zygomatic breadth, 129.6, 122.4; height of cranium, 70.5, 66.3; interorbital constriction, 40.2, 37.5; postorbital processes, 74.7, 69; width of nasals (at anterior tips of frontals), 17, 16.8; width of palate (across interpterygoid fossa), 27.3, 27.7; maxillary tooth row, crown length (front of canine to back of carnassial), 55, 54.9; upper carnassial, crown length, 22.2, 21, width, 10.7, 10.2; lower carnassial, 15.2, 15.4; upper canine, alveolar diameter (antero-posterior), 12.4, 11.9.

Remarks.—A careful investigation of the status of the name of this vaguely-described form has been made by Grinnell and Dixon (1923), and I agree with their general conclusions. *Felis hawveri* was based on a lower jaw, the character regarded as diagnostic being the peculiar shape of the angle. Examination of the type specimen shows malformation of the angular process, probably due to early injury. Merriam and Stock (1932: 7) recognized this abnormality and referred the specimen to the modern species, *Felis concolor.* It appears to be inseparable from *californica.* This regional race appears to occupy practically all of California except the desert, southeastern part inhabited by *browni,* and it ranges south through northwestern Baja California to the Sierra Juarez and Sierra San Pedro Mártir. The vicinity of San Quentín might be named as approximately its southern limit on the west coast of the peninsula. The race *californica* includes decidedly darker and longer-furred animals than do *browni* or *improcera.* The specimens from the Sierra Nevada and the mountains inland from Santa Barbara have the black tips of the long overlying hairs much longer than in *browni.* These dark tips add to the generally darker shade of this form. The top and sides of the head are similar in general color to the top of the back but are appreciably darker.

Two adult females in the Museum of Vertebrate Zoology from the coast range in San Diego County differ from more northern specimens in having shorter black tips of the long overlying hairs on the body, thus showing gradation toward *browni.* One of these specimens (No. 37424), taken in May, 2 miles southwest of the Laguna Indian Reservation, has a much darker, more rusty rufous color than *browni,* especially on the neck and shoulders. The other specimen has a generally more grayish shade with the rusty rufous of a duller tone and most marked on the crown and nape. The subspecies *cali-*

fornica belongs with *azteca* and the more northern geographic forms in having the rostrum relatively high and narrow with a high comparatively narrow and heart-shaped anterior nasal opening as compared with *improcera* and to a lesser degree with *browni*. The skulls and teeth are also somewhat larger. Instead of the uniformly high-arched profile of the cranium beginning at the occiput and ending at the anterior end of the nasals shown by *improcera*, and to a lesser degree by *browni*, these other forms have the outline of the skull most strongly arched over the temporal area.

The skull of *californica* is remarkably like that of the geographically removed form, *azteca*, in size and essential details. Some skulls are practically indistinguishable. The more elevated frontal region, with a slight median depression in *cal·fornica* (a character more developed in *oregonensis*), together with the narrower interpterygoid fossa are, however, usually distinctive. The two forms normally differ in color, *cal·fornica* being generally darker, with a broader dark median dorsal area, but the wide range of individual variation would leave some specimens difficult or impossible to allocate on the basis of color alone.

Typical *californica* averages paler and the dark markings, especially the black tip of the tail, are apt to be more restricted than in typical *oregonensis*, but many specimens of the two are practically indistinguishable in color, and as elsewhere in the group the skulls afford more trustworthy differential characters. In the region near the Pacific coast in northwestern California and southwestern Oregon *californica* passes gradually into *oregonensis*, and some specimens might with similar propriety be referred to either form. Those from Grants Pass and vicinity seem, in the sum of the characters presented, nearer to *cal·fornica*, but some individuals considered alone might be referred to *oregonensis*. Three skins of animals taken at Marble Fork Bridge, Sequoia National Park, January 26, 1924, are in full winter pelage. Two of these are grayish and one is of the more rufescent or tawny type, indicating that the color is not determined by the season.

Specimens examined.—Total number, 115, as follows:

Baja California: Rancho San Antonio, San Pedro Mártir Mountains, 1 (skull only).

California: Baird, 3 (2 skins only; 1 skull only); Big River (head), Mendocino County, 1;[1] Brush Creek (head), east side of Kern River, 25 miles above Kernville, 1;[2] Buckman Springs, San Diego County, 1 (skin only); Clough Cave, south fork of Kaweah River, Tulare County, 4 (skins only);[1] Coyote Creek, 2 miles east of Cold Flat, Santa Clara County, 1 (skull only);[1] Covelo, 1; Crockers, Tuolumne County, 2 (skulls only);[1]

---

[1] Mus. Vert. Zool.
[2] San Diego Soc. Nat. Hist.

Dunlap, 2;[1] Dorrington (5 miles east), Calaveras County, 1 (skin only);[1] Fremont Peak (4 miles south), 1 (skull only);[1] Gaxos Creek (head), 1 (skull only);[1] Genesee, 1 (skull only); Gilroy, 1 (skull only);[1] Helena, Trinity County, 1 (skull only);[1] Laguna Indian Reservation (2 miles southwest), San Diego County, 1;[1] Laguna Ranch, Gabilan Range, 1 (skull only); Lake County, 1 (skull only); Little Pine Canyon, Santa Barbara County, 1 (skull only); Long Valley (2 miles south of west end), Lake County, 1 (skull only);[1] Los Pinos Mountain, San Diego County, 1;[1] Lumberyard Ranger Station (2 miles south), Amador County, 1 (skull only);[1] Lynchburg, Placer County, 1;[1] Manikin Flat (near Kaweah), 1;[1] Marble Fork Bridge, Sequoia National Park, 3;[1] McCloud Station (12 miles east), Shasta County, 1 (skull only);[1] Merced (8 miles northeast), 1 (skull only);[1] Mesa Grande, San Diego County, 1;[2] Monterey, 1 (skull only); Mount Hamilton (16 miles southeast), 1;[1] Orestimba Creek (north fork), Stanislaus County, 2;[1] Pack Saddle Creek (head near Tulare-Kern County line), 1 (skull only);[1] Pine Mountain, Ventura County, 1;[1] Pine Valley, headwaters of Carmel River, Monterey County, 1 (skull only);[1] Salmon River, 1 (skin only); San Bernardino Mountains, 2 (skulls only);[1] San Diego County, 1 (skull only);[1] San Emigdio Canyon, Kern County, 1 (skull only); San Rafael, 1 (skull only); Santa Barbara (20 miles northeast), 1 (skull only);[3] Sespee River, Ventura County, 1 (skin only);[1] Shasta County, 6 (skulls only); Sierra National Forest, 2 (skulls only); Smith River, 2 (skulls only); Squaw Creek Ranger Station, Shasta Country, 1 (skull only);[1] Squaw Valley Creek (near McCloud Country Club), Shasta County, 1 (skull only);[1] Strawberry Creek, San Jacinto Mountains, 1;[1] Soquel Creek (1 mile south of head), Santa Cruz County, 1 (skull only);[1] Stage Station (3 miles north), Mariposa County, 1 (skull only);[1] Sugar Pine Ranger Station (2 miles south), Placer County, 1 (skull only);[1] Upper Mattole, 1; Wawona, 5 (4 skulls only)[1] Yosemite National Park, 2 (skulls only);[1] Zaca Lake (3 miles east), 1.[1]

Oregon: Bald Mountain (west of Selma), 3 (1 skull only); Florence Creek (30 miles northwest of Selma), 1; Grants Pass, 3; Grants Pass (10 miles south), 1; Grants Pass (15 miles west), 1; Grants Pass (63 miles northeast), 2; Grants Pass (43 miles northeast), 9 (6 skins only); Holcomb Peak (25 miles south of Grants Pass), 1; Horse Mountain (10 miles northwest of Selma), 1; Kirby Peak (10 miles southeast of Selma), 2; Marble Mountain (10 miles south of Grants Pass), 1; Monger Peak (15 miles south of Grants Pass), 2; Peavine Mountain (25 miles west of Grants Pass), 2; Pine Creek (29 miles northwest of Selma), 1; Rock

[3]Donald R. Dickey collection.

Creek, Jackson County, 1; Selma (15 miles southeast), 2; Selma (35 miles west), 1; Soldier Creek (15 miles west of Selma), 1; Waldo (15 miles west), 1; Williams, 1.

FELIS CONCOLOR KAIBABENSIS Nelson and Goldman

Kaibab Puma

Felis concolor kaibabensis Nelson and Goldman, Journ. Wash. Acad. Sci. 21 (10): 209, May 19, 1931.

Type locality.—Powell Plateau, Grand Canyon National Park, Ariz. (altitude 8,700 feet).

Type specimen.—No. 171186, ♂ adult, U. S. National Museum (Biological Surveys collection); collected by J. T. Owens, April 15, 1911.

Distribution.—Kaibab plateau north of the Grand Canyon of the Colorado River in northwestern Arizona, Nevada, and Utah, excepting northern and northeastern parts.

General characters.—A large, long-haired, pallid subspecies, with dark median dorsal area comparatively ill defined, the general tone, merging with less contrast than usual into that of sides of back, owing in part to a reduction in the overlying black wash present in most forms of the group; skull large, narrow, and elongated. Most closely allied to *hippolestes* of central western Wyoming, but generally paler, the dark median dorsal area less clearly defined; skull narrower. Larger than *azteca* of Chihuahua, and differing otherwise in about the same characters as from *hippolestes*. Differing from *californica* of California, in larger size, paler color, and relatively narrower skull. Closely resembling *browni*, of southwestern Arizona, in color, but larger and cranial characters distinctive.

Color.—*Type:* Top of head, neck, and rather poorly defined median dorsal area to base of tail light tawny, very thinly and inconspicuously overlaid with black, the tawny element deepest along lower part of back and rump, paling gradually through "cinnamon-buff" on sides of neck, shoulders, along flanks and on outer surfaces of limbs to pale "pinkish-buff" on feet; lips, lower part of cheeks, chin, throat, chest, and inguinal region white; under surface of neck suffused with "pinkish buff"; belly overlaid on sides with "pale pinkish-buff," becoming whitish along median line; inner sides of limbs dull white, the drab basal color showing through; face in general buffy gray, with large, whitish, supraorbital spots; blackish areas at base of vibrissae on sides of muzzle rather inconspicuous; ears blackish externally, broadly edged with gray, which extends also in a band across middle, thinly clad internally with white hairs; hairs around pads on feet brownish-black; tail above light tawny, becoming dull pinkish-buffy below to tip which is black, the black extending forward about 3 inches on upper side.

Skull.—Very similar to that of *hippolestes*, but still narrower and relatively more elongated, less rounded in general outline as viewed from above; zygomata less widely spreading; interpterygoid fossa narrower; dentition lighter. Similar in general to that of *azteca*, but larger and differing otherwise in about the same proportions as from *hippolestes*. Larger and more elongated than that of *californica*, with flatter frontal region and relatively less widely spreading zygomata. Approaching that of *browni* in narrowness, but decidedly larger, with heavier dentition.

Measurements.—No external measurements available. A female about ready to bear young, from Parowan, Utah: Weight, 109 pounds. *Skull* (type and another adult male from the vicinity of the type locality, respectively): Greatest length, 216.8, 217.3 mm.; condylobasal length, 195.8, 199.7; zygomatic breadth, 141.6, 142 6; height of cranium, 75.2, 76.8; interorbital breadth, 43.4, 43.2; postorbital processes, 75.5, 79; width of nasals (at anterior tips of frontals), 19.4, 22.1; width of palate (across interpterygoid fossa), 29, 27.9; maxillary tooth row, alveolar length (front of canine to back of carnassial), 62.4, 61.5; upper carnassial, crown length, 22.5, 23.1, width, 11.8, 11.7; lower carnassial, crown length, 17.3, 16 8; upper canine, alveolar diameter (antero-posterior), 14.9, 14. An adult female from Kaibab National Forest, Ariz., and one from Pine Valley Mountains, Utah, respectively: Greatest length, 189.6, 186.5; condylobasal length, 171.7 171; zygomatic breadth, 127.5, 128.8; height of cranium, 68.2, 65; interorbital breadth, 41.3, 37.6; postorbital processes, 75, 75.2; width of nasals (at anterior tips of frontals), 16.2, 15.9; width of palate (across interpterygoid fossa), 27.2, 27.4; maxillary tooth row (front of canine to back of carnassial), 58.5, 55.4; upper carnassial, crown length, 21.5, 22, width, 11, 11; lower carnassial, crown length, 15.8, 16.4; upper canine, alveolar diameter (antero-posterior), 12.5, 12.7.

Remarks.—The puma ranging throughout the greater part of Utah and Nevada is closely allied to *hippolestes* of the Rocky Mountain region to the east. In the desert basin of western Nevada pumas have apparently not been numerous in recent time and near relationship to *californica*, representing a population center in California, is not so evident. Specimens from Richfield and Thousand Lake Mountain, in south-central Utah, have the light tawny coloration usual in *kaibabensis*, but the rather broad skulls indicate gradation toward *hippolestes*.

Specimens examined.—Total number, 43, as follows:

Arizona: Bright Angel, Grand Canyon National Park, 1 (skull only); Fredonia (Rock Canyon), 3 (2 skins only; 1 skull only); Kaibab National Forest, 1; Powell Plateau, Grand Canyon National Park, 1 (type); South Canyon, Kaibab National Forest, 2.

Nevada: Currie, 2 (skulls only); Egan Range, 25 miles southwest of Cherry Creek, 2 (skulls only); Fish Creek (near Eureka), 1 (skin only); Hot Creek, near Keystone, Nye County, 1 (skull only); Pot Hole Summit, near Keystone, 1 (skull only); Potts, 1 (skull only);[1] Potts (Monitor Mountain), 2 (skins only); Shoshone, 1 (skin only); Spruce Mountain, Elko County, 1 (skin only); Sunnyside (15 miles west), 2 (1 skull only); Ward Mountain, White Pine County, 1 (skull only).

Utah: Antelope (near Manti), 1 (skull only); Bull Valley Mountain, 4 (3 skulls only);[2] Circleville (southeast of), 1; Kanab, 1 (skin only); Kanarraville (8 miles east), Iron County, 1;[2] Marysvale (southeast of), 1; Modena, 2 (1 skull without skin);[2] Monroe Canyon, Sevier County, 1; Parowan, 1; Pine Valley Mountains, 2 (skulls only); Steamboat Mountain, Pine Valley Mountains, 1; Richfield, 2; Thousand Lake Mountain, Wayne County, 1; Willow Creek (near Richfield), 1 (skull only).

FELIS CONCOLOR BROWNI Merriam

Colorado Desert Puma

Felis aztecus browni Merriam, Proc. Biol. Soc. Wash. 16: 73, May 29, 1903.
Felis azteca browni Miller, North Amer. Recent Mamm., 1923, Bull. 128, U. S. Natl. Mus., p. 157, 1924.
Felis concolor browni Nelson and Goldman, Journ. Mamm. 10 (4): 347, Nov. 11, 1929.

Type locality.—Colorado River, 12 miles below Yuma, Ariz.

Type specimen.—No. 125719, skull only, ♂ adult, U. S. National Museum (Biological Surveys collection); collected by Herbert Brown, February 1903.

Distribution.—Desert plains and low mountains of the Colorado River valley in southwestern Arizona, southeastern California, northeastern Baja California and northwestern Sonora; mainly Lower Sonoran Zone.

General characters.—A medium-sized, pallid, desert subspecies, very similar to *cal'fornica* of California, but paler and cranial characters slightly different. Closely allied to *azteca* of the Sierra Madre of Sonora and Chihuahua, but paler, the general tone of median dorsal area passing gradually into that of sides (darker median dorsal area more sharply defined and contrasting with color of sides in *azteca*); skull differing in slight details.

Color.—Top of head, neck, and rather broad median dorsal area to base of tail, varying from light "tawny" to dark "cinnamon-buff," thinly overlaid with black, the general tone deepest on rump, paling gradually to buffy grayish or "cinnamon-buff" on sides of neck, shoulders, along flanks and on outer surfaces of limbs, becoming "pinkish-buff" on feet; lips, lower part of cheeks, chin and throat pure white; under surface of neck pale "pinkish-buff"; chest, inner sides of limbs and inguinal region dull whitish, the dusky basal color

---

[1]Mus. Vert. Zool.
[2]Amer. Mus. Nat. Hist.

showing through; belly pinkish-buffy along sides, becoming dull white along median line; face in general brownish or buffy-grayish, the blackish areas at base of vibrissae on sides of muzzle and whitish supraorbital spots rather inconspicuous; ears blackish externally, edged with gray, thinly clothed internally with white hairs; hairs around pads on feet brownish black, tinged with gray; tail along median line above near "cinnamon-buff," with a more or less distinct dusky median line becoming pinkish-buffy along sides and grayish below to brownish-black tip, the brownish-black extending forward 1 to 3 inches on upper side where in one specimen it becomes continuous with the dusky median line.

Skull.—Closely resembling that of *californica*, but rather narrow, the zygomata less widely spreading; nasals slightly flatter, more depressed anteriorly; dentition somewhat lighter. Also closely similar to that of *improcera*, but upper outline from anterior ends of nasals to occiput a less uniform curve, the sagittal crest descending less steeply; lambdoid crest less depressed, the margin more upturned, somewhat less projecting posteriorly over foramen magnum; nasals less flattened anteriorly, the median groove deeper at anterior margin (than in the type); dentition about as in *improcera*. Differing from that of *azteca* in about the same characters as from that of *californica*.

Measurements.—*Type* (in flesh): "Tip of nose to tip of tail 7 ft. 4 in. [= 2,235 mm.]; tail 28½ in. [= 724 mm.]. Weight 170 pounds." An adult male from Colorado River, 20 miles north of Picacho, Calif.: Total length, 1,981. *Skull* (type): Greatest length, 205; condylobasal length, 183.2; zygomatic breadth, 139.3; height of cranium, 74; interorbital breadth, 43.5; width of nasals (at anterior tips of frontals), 16.5; maxillary tooth row, alveolar length (front of canine to back of carnassial), 57; upper carnassial, crown length, 20.4, width, 11.2; lower carnassial, crown length, 15.2; upper canine, alveolar diameter (antero-posterior), 14. An adult female from 18 miles south of Tres Posos, northeastern Baja California: Greatest length, 173.4; condylobasal length, 159; zygomatic breadth, 124; interorbital breadth, 37.3; postorbital processes, 67; width of nasals (at anterior tips of frontals), 15.1 maxillary tooth row, alveolar length (front of canine to back of carnassial), 55.9; upper canine, alveolar diameter (antero-posterior), 12 8.

Remarks.—*F. c. browni* appears to be a recognizable geographic race that has developed in the intensely dry and hot desert region outlined in the paragraph on distribution. It is closely allied to *californica* with which it intergrades along the mountain barrier west of the desert area in upper and lower California. A specimen from the Hualpai Mountains in central western Arizona, referred to this form, shows gradation toward *azteca*. Specimens are lacking from much of the intermediate desert country between the type localities of *browni* and *improcera* but the similarity of these subspecies indicates their close relationship. The pelage of *browni* is shorter and thinner than in either *californica* or *azteca,* as might be expected from the hotter climate of its habitat. The black tips of the long overlying hairs on the back, which noticeably darken the general color of *californica,* are so reduced in *browni* that they are difficult to see and have little effect on the general tone. The top and sides of the head are paler and grayer than the body, thus contrasting with *californica* in which these parts are darker and more dusky-grayish than the back.

Specimens examined.—Total number, 9, as follows:

Arizona: Colorado River (12 miles south of Yuma), 1 (type; skull only); Colorado River ("Arizona side," 20 miles north of Picacho), 1;[1] Hualpai Mountains, 3 (1 skull without skin; 2 skins without skulls).

Baja California: Cataviña (6 miles northwest), 1 (skin and skull);[1] Colorado River (15 miles south of U. S. boundary), 1 (skin only); Tres Pozos (18 miles south, near delta of Colorado River), 1 (skull only).

California: Colorado River ("California side," 20 miles north of Picacho), 1.[1]

FELIS CONCOLOR IMPROCERA Phillips
Baja California Puma

Felis improcera Phillips, Proc. Biol. Soc. Wash. 25: 85, May 4, 1912.

Felis concolor improcera Nelson and Goldman, Journ. Mamm. 10 (4): 347, No. 11, 1929.

Type locality.—Calmallí, Baja California, Mexico.

Type specimen.—No. 12704 (♀) adult, skin and skull, Museum of Comparative Zoology, collected by E. W. Funcke, September 1911.

Distribution.—Vizcaino Desert region and south to the mountains of the Cape region, Baja California; doubtless intergrading to the north with *browni* along the Gulf of California and with *californica* near the Pacific coast.

General characters.—A medium-sized, short-furred, pallid, desert subspecies closely resembling *browni* of the lower Colorado Valley; color about the same, but slight cranial characters distinctive. Also closely allied to both *californica* of California, and *azteca* of the Sierra Madre of Chihuahua, but paler than either and skull slightly different.

Color.—About as in *browni.*

Skull.—Closely resembling that of *browni,* but upper outline from anterior ends of nasals to occiput a more nearly uniform curve, the highest point near posterior plane of postorbital processes, and the sagittal crest sloping more steeply; lambdoid crest more depressed, the margin less upturned, and tending to project farther posteriorly over foramen magnum; nasals (in the type specimen) more flattened anteriorly, the median groove shallower at anterior margin; anterior nares more nearly circular (decidedly broader than high in the type specimen, and less distinctly inverted heart-shaped than usual in the

---

[1]Mus. Vert. Zool.

group); dentition about as in *browni*. Differing from those of *californica* and *azteca* in about the same characters as from that of *browni*, but to a somewhat more marked degree.

Measurements.—No body measurements are available. *Skull* (type, sex unmarked but obviously female): Greatest length, 183 mm.; condylobasal length, 166; zygomatic breadth, 123.6; interorbital breadth, 37.5; postorbital processes, 68.4; width of palate (across interpterygoid fossa), 27.5; maxillary tooth row, alveolar length (front of canine to back of carnassial), 59.3; upper carnassial, crown length, 20.3. An adult female from 10 miles west of Miraflores, Sierra de la Victoria, southern Baja California: Zygomatic breadth, 126.2; interorbital breadth, 39.4; postorbital processes, 70.7; width of nasals (at anterior tips of frontals), 17.3; maxillary tooth row, alveolar length (front of canine to back of carnassial), 54.8; upper carnassial, crown length, 20.6, width, 10.6; lower carnassial, crown length, 15.5; upper canine, alveolar diameter (antero-posterior), 11.4.

Remarks.—The status of this form is somewhat uncertain owing to lack of suitable material for study. It was regarded by its describer as a distinct species of small size owing to the erroneous assumption that the type, and at the time the only known specimen, was an adult male. The type, marked male by the collector, is unquestionably an adult female, as determined by careful comparisons with large series of skulls of similar age representing both sexes of closely allied subspecies. The nasals, in this specimen, appear to be abnormally flattened anteriorly. The skull is abnormal in the number of upper incisors which is reduced to five, the inner one on the right side being the missing tooth, as shown by the median suture between the premaxillae. The five teeth are evenly spaced, the first incisor on the left side having become centered and opposed to the first incisors on both sides in the lower jaw. The outer upper incisors are directed slightly forward in a manner unusual in the group. The general condition of the anterior part of the skull suggests deformity such as might result from an early injury. In fact, deformities of the anterior part of the skull are not very uncommon in pumas, and are probably the result of falls or contusions received in attacking their prey. If the form of the nasals in the type should prove to be abnormal there would remain little to differentitate this form from *browni;* and in any case distinction cannot be great as flatness of the nasals, less extreme in degree, seems to be a character of the latter subspecies compared with its close relatives, *californica* and *azteca.* In the specimen referred to *improcera*, from Miraflores, in extreme southern Baja California the nasals have, unfortunately, been broken out and their character cannot be determined. In the two skulls available, however, the upper outline is remarkably even, the frontal region high behind the postorbital processes, the sagittal crest taking a more sharply descending curve than is usually exhibited by related subspecies, and other slight differences have been pointed out. The Miraflores specimen (March) is in very short pelage, somewhat shorter than those of *browni* examined. It seems best to retain the name, at least until more material is available for comparison. In color *improcera* seems to be within the normal range of variation presented in *browni*.

Specimens examined.—Two, as follows:

Baja California: Calmallí, 1 (type);[1] Miraflores (10 miles west), 1.[2]

FELIS CONCOLOR AZTECA Merriam

Sierra Madre Puma (Pls. 49, 58, 67, 76, 82, 88, 82)

Felis hippolestes aztecus Merriam, Proc. Wash. Acad. Sci. 3: 592, Dec. 11, 1901.

[*Felis*] *aztecus* Merriam, Proc. Biol. Soc. Wash. 16: 73, May 29, 1903.

Felis azteca azteca Miller, North Amer. Recent Mamm., 1923, U. S. Nat. Mus. Bull. No. 128: 157, 1924.

Felis concolor azteca Nelson and Goldman, Journ. Mamm. 10 (4): 347, Nov. 11, 1929.

Type locality.—Colonia Garcia (about 60 miles southwest of Casas Grandes), Chihuahua, Mexico (altitude 6,700 feet).

Type specimen.—No. 99658, skin and skull, ♂ adult, U. S. National Museum (Biological Surveys collection); collected by H. A. Cluff, October 17, 1899.

Distribution.—New Mexico, Arizona south of the Colorado River, except southwestern portion, and south over the mainland of Mexico at least to Jalisco; altitudinal range from sea level to timber line on high mountains.

General characters.—A medium-sized, rather pale subspecies, about like *hippolestes* of Wyoming in color, but pelage shorter; size decidedly smaller; dentition lighter. Not very unlike *browni* of the lower Colorado River Valley, but darker, the darker tone of median dorsal area forming a narrow zone contrasting strongly with sides (general tone of dorsum more diffused in *browni*); skull differing in slight details. Usually smaller than *stanleyana* of Texas; upper parts darker, more distinctly tawny, and black on tip of tail less restricted; cranial details, especially the lighter dentition, distinctive.

Color.—Top of head, neck, and rather narrow, well-defined median dorsal area varying from buffy-gray and "ochraceous-tawny" to light "cinnamon-rufous," more or less obscured by black-tipped hairs, giving way rather abruptly to grayish or cinnamon-buffy tones on sides of neck, shoulders, and flanks, and extending down over outer surfaces of limbs, paling to gray or "pinkish-buff" on feet; upper lips, except usual blackish area at base of vibrissae, chin, and throat nearly pure white; under surface of neck varying from pale gray to "pinkish-buff"; chest, inner sides of limbs, median line of

---

[1]Mus. Comp. Zool.
[2]Mus. Vert. Zool.

abdomen and inguinal region dull white, the darker basal color showing through; face in general brownish-gray, the whitish supraorbital spots usually distinct; ears black externally, with more or less distinct grayish median spots, edged with gray, thinly clothed internally with whitish or light buffy hairs; hairs around pads on soles of feet blackish; tail about like back above, becoming grayish or pale buffy below to near black tip, the black usually extending forward 2 or 3 inches on upper side. *Young* (in first pelage): Ground color near light "pinkish-buff."

Skull.—In general form about like that of *hippolestes,* but decidedly smaller; dentition usually lighter. Closely resembling that of *californica;* frontal region usually slightly flatter, less depressed along median line; interpterygoid fossa broader. Very similar to that of *browni,* but somewhat broader, the zygomata more widely spreading; nasals less depressed anteriorly; dentition heavier. Compared with that of *stanleyana,* the skull is smaller, less massive; zygomata relatively more widely spreading; dentition lighter, the difference in size most obvious in the canines and carnassials.

abruptly to grayish or cinnamon-buffy tones on sides of neck, shoulders, and

Measurements.—An adult male and female from Cloverdale, N. Mex., respectively: Total length, 1,830, 1,727 mm.; tail vertebrae, 737, 711; hind foot, 261, 241. An adult male from Animas Mountains, N. Mex.: 2,085; 762; 280. Two adult females from San Andres National Wildlife Refuge, Dona Ana County, N. Mex., respectively: Total length, 1,600, 1,625; tail vertebrae, 736, 712; hind foot, 254, 254; ear from notch, 89, 102. *Skull* (type and an adult male topotype, respectively): Greatest length, 202.9, 214.3; condylobasal length, 184.5, 199.6; zygomatic breadth, 146.9, 146.3; height of cranium, 72.4, 76.5; interorbital breadth, 40.7, 43.8; postorbital processes, 73.9, 76.7; width of nasals (at anterior tips of frontals), 18.3, 23.3; width of palate (across interpterygoid fossa), 30.8, 31; maxillary tooth row, alveolar length (front of canine to back of carnassial), 60, 64; upper carnassial, crown length, 21.6, 23.2, width, 12.2, 11.4; lower carnassial, crown length, 15.6, 16.8; upper canine, alveolar diameter (antero-posterior), 15, 14.3. Two adult female topotypes, respectively: Greatest length, 175.7, 176.3; condylobasal length, 165.7, 165; zygomatic breadth, 127.2, 119.4; height of cranium, 63.9, 60.5; interorbital breadth, 36.9, 34; postorbital processes, 71.8, 66.8; width of nasals (at anterior tips of frontals), 15.4, 16.3; width of palate (across interpterygoid fossa), 28.8, 28; maxillary tooth row, alveolar length (front of canine to back of carnassial), 54.4, 56; upper carnassial, crown length, 20.3, 22, width, 10.2, 10.2; lower carnassial, crown length, 15.7, 15.5; upper canine, alveolar diameter (antero-posterior), 10.7, 10.8.

Remarks.—The range of this subspecies in the Sierra Madre and northeastern Mexico extends north and becomes merged with that of *hippolestes* in western and northern New Mexico and eastern Arizona. *F. c. azteca* is very similar to *hippolestes* in color and cranial characters, but is decidedly smaller, with shorter pelage. Some of the topotypes taken even in winter are in short, rusty, worn coats. Individual variation in color is extraordinary, occasional specimens from Arizona approaching tropical forms in rich rufescent tones. Most specimens from the Gila National Forest and adjoining territory in western New Mexico agree closely with typical *azteca*, but the skulls of some are indistinguishable from some of the smaller crania of typical *hippolestes*. The skull of *azteca* is remarkably like that of *californica* in size and essential details, in spite of rather wide geographic separation. The flatter frontal region and broader interpterygoid fossa are, however, usually distinctive; and *azteca* is normally paler with the dark, median dorsal area more restricted.

Specimens examined.—Total number, 228, as follows:

Arizona: Apache, Peloncillo Mountains, 1; Baboquivari Mountains, 1 (skin only); Beaver Creek, Yavapai County, 3 (2 skulls without skins);[1] Blue, 15 (13 skulls without skins); Blue Mountains (head of Eagle Creek), 1; Blue Range, 1; Blue River, White Mountains, 1 (skull only); Burro Creek, Mohave County, 1; Camp Verde (18 miles northeast), 1; Cibecue (upper Salt Creek), 2 (1 skin without skull; 1 skull without skin); Clifton, 8 (1 skin without skull); Clifton (84 miles north), 1 (skull only); Clifton (65 miles north), 1 (skin only); Clifton (50 miles north), 2 (1 skin without skull); Clifton (57 miles north), 1; Clifton (Roasin Canyon, 45 miles north), 1; Cloverdale, 1; Fish Creek, Tonto National Forest, 3 (skulls only); Flagstaff, 1 (skull only);[1] Fort Bowie, 1; Fort Grant (5 miles west), 1 (skull only);[2] Fort Verde, 4 (2 skins without skulls; 2 skulls without skins);[1] Galiuro Mountains, 3; Graham Mountains, 6 (1 skull without skin); Mogollon Mountains, 3 (skulls only);[1] Perkinsville (9 miles northeast), 1; Pinal Mountains, 1; Pine, 2 (6 and 12 miles northeast, respectively); Portal, Chiricahua Mountains, 1 (skull only); Prescott, 1; Prescott (55 miles southeast), 5 (skins only); Prescott (20 miles northeast), 1 (skull only); Rousenrock Canyon (40-45 miles north of Clifton), 2;[3] Safford (12 miles southwest), 1 (skull only); Seneca Springs (25 miles south of Seligman), 1 (skull only); Sonoita, 2; Tucson (near), 2; Verde River, 4 (skulls only);[1] Wagoner, 2; Yavapai County (without exact locality), 1 (skull only).[1]

Chihuahua: Chuechupa, 1 (skull only);[2] Colonia Garcia (type locality), 18 (5 skulls without skins);[2] Gallego, 1; Pacheco, 1 (skull only); Pacheco River, 2; Rio Alamos, Sierra Madre, 2;[1] exact locality unknown, 1 (skull only).[1]

Jalisco: Bolaños, 1 (skull only); Los Masos, 1 (skin only);[1] Mineral San Sebastian, 1 (skull only).[1]

New Mexico: A. L. Mountain (25 miles southwest of Magdalena), 1; Alma, 3; Animas Mountains, Hidalgo County, 5 (1 skin without skull); Black Range, 2; Bluewater, 3; Brannon Park (30 miles north of Fierro), 1; Chloride, 5; Cloverdale, 2 (1 skin without skull); "Coppermines," 1 (skull only); Cuba (12 miles east), 1; Datil Mountains, 3 (1 skull without skin); Elk Mountains, 1 (skull only); Fairview, 2; Gila (12 miles northwest), 1; Gila National Forest, 24 (skulls only); Hachita (40 miles southwest), 1; Hermosa, 1; Jemez Mountains (head of Santa Clara Creek), 1 (skull only); Las Vegas Mountains (Harvey's Ranch), 1 (skull only);[4] Luna, 2; Magdalena (80 miles southwest), 3 (1 skull only); Mimbres, 1 (skull only); Monticello (20 miles north), 3; Mountain Air, Cibola National Forest, 2; Noonday Canyon, Gila National Forest, 2; Pinos Altos (25 miles northwest), 1; Potter Ranch (near Tularosa), 1 (skin without skull); Pratt, 1 (skull only); Queen, 1; Reserve, 7 (4 skins without skulls 2 skulls without skins); Rio Arriba County, 1 (skull only); Sacramento Mountains, 1;[1] San Andres National Wildlife Refuge, Dona Ana County, 2; San Luis Mountains, 1 (skull only); San Mateo Mountains (35 miles northeast of Fairview), 1; San Mateo Mountains, 2; Santa Rita, 1 (skull only);[4] Silver City (mountains northeast), 2; Socorro, 3; Spring Canyon, Hidalgo County, 1; Strawberry Canyon (near Pine), 1 (skull only); Tularosa, 1; Tusas (10 miles west), 1.

Sinaloa: Escuinapa, 3 (2 skins without skulls; 1 skull only);[1] Los Pieles, 1 (skin only).[1]

Sonora: Exact locality unknown, 1.[2]

Zacatecas: Chichimaquillas (20 miles east of Fresnillo), 1; Colorada (40 miles north of Fresnillo), 1.

FELIS CONCOLOR STANLEYANA Goldman

Texas Puma (Pls. 49, 58, 67, 76, 82, 88, 93)

Felis concolor youngi Goldman, Proc. Biol. Soc. Wash. 49: 137, Aug. 22, 1936

Felis concolor stanleyana Goldman, Proc. Biol. Soc. Wash. 51: 63, Mar. 18, 1938. Substitute name for *Felis concolor youngi,* preoccupied by *Felis youngi* Pei (Paleontologica Sinica, ser. C., vol. 8, fasc. 1, p. 133, May 1934), for a fossil species from the Lower Pleistocene of China.

Type locality.—Bruni Ranch, near Bruni, southeastern Webb County, Tex.

Type specimen.—No. 251419, ♂ adult, skin and skull, U. S. National Museum (Biological Surveys collection): collected by Ira Wood, October 6, 1934.

---

[1]Amer. Mus. Nat. Hist.
[2]Mus. Comp. Zool.
[3]Donald R. Dickey collection.
[4]Kansas. Univ. Mus. Nat. Hist.

Distribution.—Texas and northeastern Mexico, intergrading on the west with *azteca* and on the east with *coryi*.

General characters.—Closely allied to *azteca* of the Sierra Madre of Chihuahua, but larger, and upper parts lighter, more suffused with gray, less distinctly tawny; black on tip of tail usually more restricted; cranial details, especially heavier dentition, distinctive. Similar in general to *coryi* of Florida, but much paler, and skull differing notably in form of nasals. Distinguished from *hippolestes* of the Rocky Mountains in Wyoming by somewhat smaller size, paler color, and cranial features.

Color.—Top of head, neck, and median dorsal area usually between "tawny" and "ochraceous-tawny," suffused with buffy-gray, slightly darkened by black-tipped hairs along posterior part of back; sides of neck, shoulders, and flanks near "cinnamon-buff," paling to "pinkish-buff" on feet; upper lips, except usual blackish areas at base of vibrissae, chin, and throat nearly pure white; under surface of neck "pinkish-buff"; chest, inner sides of limbs, and median line of abdomen dull white, the darker basal color showing through; inguinal region nearly pure white; face in general brownish-gray, the whitish supraorbital spots distinct; ears blackish externally, with grayish median spots, thinly clothed with white hairs internally; tail similar to posterior part of back above, becoming grayish below to near black tip, the black nearly pure extending forward about 1 inch on upper side.

Skull—Closely resembling that of *azteca*, but larger and heavier; zygomata relatively less widely spreading; detention heavier, the size difference most apparent in the canines and carnassials. Similar in size to *coryi*, but nasals much more depressed, usually narrower; dentition similarly heavy. Compared with that of *hippolestes* the skull is similar in length, but is narrower, less massive; zygomata and frontals distinctly narrower; dentition similar.

Measurements.—*Type:* Total length, 2,134 mm. Two adult females from 22 miles south of Sierra Blanca, Hudspeth County, Tex., respectively: Total length, 2,108, 2,083; tail vertebrae, 787, 762; weight, 85, 95 pounds. An adult female from 18 miles south of Allamore, Hudspeth County, Tex. *Skull* (type and an adult male from 30 miles southeast of Cotulla, Tex., respectively): Greatest length, 218.7, 213.3; condylobasal length, 198.5, 194.4; zygomatic breadth, 141.9, 144.8; height of cranium, 77, 78.8; interorbital breadth, 42.5, 40.9; postorbital processes, 74.8, 73.4; width of nasals (at anterior tips of frontals), 17.1, 16.2; width of palate (across interpterygoid fossa), 29.2, 31.3; maxillary tooth row, alveolar length (front of canine to back of carnassial), 68.4, 64.8; upper carnassial, crown length, 24.8, 24.1, crown width, 13, 11.5; lower carnassial, crown length, 18.2, 17.8; upper canine, alveolar diameter (antero-posterior), 16.6, 14.8. Two adult females, a topotype and one from Encinal, La Salle County, Tex., respectively: Greatest length, 190.7, 190.9; condylobasal length, 172, 171.4; zygomatic breadth, 122.4, 123.2; height of cranium, 66.1, 68.8; interorbital breadth,

34.4, 37.6; postorbital processes, 64.2, 72.5; width of nasals (at anterior tips of frontals), 14.8, 16.1; width of palate (across interpterygoid fossa), 26.5, 27.6; maxillary tooth row, alveolar length (front of canine to back of carnassial), 57.1, 57.5; upper carnassial, crown length, 21.9, 20.7; crown width, 10.2, 10.2; lower carnassial, crown length, 16.3, 15.7; upper canine, alveolar diameter (antero-posterior), 12.5, 12.7.

Remarks.—Intermediate in geographic position, *stanleyana* tends to combine some of the characters of typical *azteca* of the mountains along the backbone of the continent in Chihuahua and southwestern New Mexico, and some of those of *coryi* which formerly inhabited the Gulf coast region from Louisiana to Florida. Among cranial details the nasals, unlike those of *coryi*, are depressed much as in *azteca*. In heavy dentition *stanleyana* agrees closely with *coryi;* in usually grayer coloration a departure from both *azteca* and *coryi* is exhibited.

Specimens examined.—Total number, 75, as follows:
Coahuila: Carmen Mountains (southern end), 1 (skull only).
Tamaulipas: Matamoros, 2.
Texas: Aguilares (16 miles north), Webb County, 1; Aguilares (20 miles south), 1; Allamore, 1; Boquillas, Brewster County, 1; Brownsville, 1 (skull only); Bruni Ranch, Webb County (type locality) 2; Carrizo Springs (20-35 miles south), 2; Catarina, Dimmit County, 3; Catarina (Chupadero Ranch, 30 miles south), Webb County, 7; Comstock, 1 (skull only); Comstock (9 miles south), 1; Cotulla (20-25 miles south), 4; Cotulla (30 miles southeast), 1; Crockett County, 1 (skull only); Davis Mountains (Carr's Ranch), 2 (skull only); Dilley (15 miles east), 5; Eagle Mountains, Hudspeth County, 10 (2 skins without skulls); Eagle Pass, Maverick County, 1 (skull only); Eagle Pass (Indio Ranch), Maverick County, 2; Encinal, La Salle County, 4; Fresno Mountains (Caldwell Ranch, about 75 miles south of Marfa), 1; Galvin, Webb County, 1; Jim Hogg County (without definite locality), 2; Laredo (20 miles east), 1; Laredo (50 miles north), 1; Light Ranch, La Salle County, 2; Martin Ranch, Terrell County, 1; Pearsall (26 miles south), 1; Presidio County, 1; Memphis, Hall County, 1; Sierra Blanca (30 miles south), 1; Sheffield, 1; Soledad Ranch, Webb County, 2; Van Horn (25 miles north), Hudspeth County, 1; Webb County (without definite locality), 2; West Ranch (20 miles south of Catarina), 1; Whitehead Ranch, Maverick County, 1.

FELIS CONCOLOR CORYI Bangs

Florida Puma (Pls. 50, 59, 68)

Felis concolor floridana Cory, Hunting and Fishing in Florida, p. 109, 1896.
    (Not *F. floridana* Desmarest, 1820=*Lynx floridanus* Rafinesque, 1817.)

Felis coryi Bangs, Proc. Biol. Soc. Wash. 13: 15, Jan. 31, 1899. (Renaming of *F. c. floridana* Cory.)

Felis arundivaga Hollister, Proc. Biol. Soc. Wash. 24: 176, June 16, 1911. Type from 12 miles southwest of Vidalia, Concordia Parish, La. No. 137122, skin and skull, ♂ adult, United States National Museum (Biological Surveys collection), collected by B. V. Lilly, June 17, 1905.

Felis concolor coryi Nelson and Goldman, Journ. Mamm., 10(4): 347, Nov. 11, 1929.

Type locality.—"Wilderness back of Sebastian," Fla.

Type specimen.—No. 7742, skin and skull, ♂ old adult, Museum of Comparative Zoology (collection of E. A. and O. Bangs); collected by F. R. Hunter, January 1, 1898.

Distribution.—Present range: isolated parts of southern Florida and perhaps of northeastern Louisiana; formerly doubtless from eastern Texas or western Louisiana and the lower Mississippi River valley east through the Southeastern States in general, intergrading to the north with *couguar*, and to the west and northwest with *stanleyana* and *hippolestes*. Austroriparian Zone.

General characters.—A medium-sized, dark subspecies, with pelage short and rather stiff; skull with broad, flat frontal region; nasals remarkably broad and high arched or expanded upward. Closely allied to *couguar* of Pennsylvania but skull distinguished especially by broader, higher, more inflated nasals and more evenly spreading zygomata (zygomata in *couguar* relatively wider posteriorly, more converging anteriorly). Compared with *stanleyana* of Texas and *hippolestes* of central western Wyoming, the color is darker and the skull differs notably from both in the greater general width and upward expansion of the nasals.

Color.—Top of head, neck, and median dorsal area to base of tail near "tawny," more intense in some specimens than in others, more or less heavily mixed with black, becoming cinnamon-buffy or dull "clay color" on sides of neck, shoulders, along flanks and on outer surfaces of limbs, paling gradually to dark "pinkish-buff" on feet; upper lips near sides of nose, chin and throat nearly pure white; under side of neck "pinkish-buff"; chest, inner sides of limbs and inguinal region dull whitish, the drab basal color showing through; belly more or less distinctly cinnamon-buffy, palest along median line; face in general grayish-brown, the blackish areas at base of vibrissae prominent, but light supraorbital spots rather indistinct; ears usually black externally, but light median spot sometimes faintly indicated, edged with gray, thinly clothed internally with whitish hairs; hairs around pads on feet blackish; tail above near cinnamon, with a narrow, blackish median line present in some specimens and absent in others, becoming dull clay color below to near black tip, the black extending forward 2 or 3 inches on upper side or continuous in some specimens with blackish median line mentioned. In most specimens the head, neck and shoulders are more or less profusely, but irregularly flecked with white.

Skull.—Similar to that of *couguar*, but more elongated; nasals broader, more inflated, higher arched, the upper outline rising to form a distinct convexity about one-third the distance from posterior ends, the lateral margins here usually free and pushed upward, tending to overlap maxillae and frontals; zygomata less widely spreading posteriorly, less strongly converging anteriorly, the sides more nearly parallel; postorbital processes longer; jugal extending farther posteriorly (in two individuals reaching plane of anterior wall of glenoid fossa as in South American forms); auditory bullae variable, but usually larger and bulging more prominently below level of exoccipitals; dentition about as in *couguar*. Similar in general to those of *stanleyana* and *hippolestes* but rostrum less flattened; nasals much more expanded upward, higher arched, especially anteriorly, the antero-external descending processes less widely spreading between outer sides of nares, and the upper outline more strongly convex at a point about one-third the distance from posterior ends; postorbital processes longer; interpterygoid fossa narrower; jugal extending farther posteriorly; auditory bullae usually smaller; dentition similar.

Measurements.—Type of *coryi* (adult male), and an adult female topotype (measured in flesh), respectively: Total length, 2,058, 1,919 mm. *Skull* (type of *coryi*): Greatest length, 208; condylobasal length, 185; zygomatic breadth, 134.9; interorbital breadth, 41.8; postorbital processes, 75.2; width of palate (across interpterygoid fossa), 27.3; maxillary tooth row, alveolar length (front of canine to back of carnassial), 58.8; upper carnassial, crown length, 20.9, width, 11.7. An adult male from Sebastian and one from Alapata Flat, north of Lake Okeechobee, Fla., respectively: Greatest length, 212.8, 206.8; condylobasal length, 188.5, 188.5; zygomatic breadth, 152.2, 136.5; height of cranium, 77.5, 71.4; interorbital constriction, 44.2, 40.8; postorbital processes, 85.8, 74.8; width of nasals (at anterior tips of frontals), 20.4, 20; width of palate (across interpterygoid fossa), 28.2, 26.7; maxillary tooth row, alveolar length (front of canine to back of carnassial), 59.5, 58.5; upper carnassial, crown length, 23.7, 21.7, width, 11.5, 11.6; lower carnassial, crown length, 16.8, 16.1; upper canine, alveolar diameter (antero-posterior), 13.5, 3.1. Two adult females from Sebastian, Fla., respectively: Greatest length, 186.4, 189.4; condylobasal length, 170.4, 171; zygomatic breadth, 126.2, 125; height of cranium, 66.4, 66.5; interorbital breadth, 39.1, 39; postorbital processes, 76, 73.3; width of nasals (at anterior tips of frontals), 20.5, 21; width of palate (across interpterygoid fossa), 26.3, 27.2; maxillary tooth row, alveolar length (front of canine to back of carnassial), 55, 56.2; upper carnassial, crown length, 23.2, 22.5, width, 11.7, 11.6; lower carnassial, crown length, 16, 16; upper canine, alveolar diameter (antero-posterior), 12.4, 12.5.

Remarks.—F. c. coryi is a well-marked subspecies whose former wide range is now restricted to very limited areas in the more inaccessible parts of the Everglade region of southern Florida and possibly cane brakes along the Mississippi River bottoms in Louisiana. Former intergradation with *stanleyana* is suggested by the intermediate characters exhibited by some specimens. In the skull of one from Boerne, Tex., the characters of *stanleyana* predominate, but the trend toward *coryi* seems to be shown by the tendency of the outer borders of the nasals to overlap the anterior processes of the frontals, a character usually distinguishing *coryi*, and in the narrow interpterygoid fossa which is also a feature of the latter. Former intergradation of a form of the *coryi* type, inhabiting the lowlands of the interior basin, with *hippolestes* is suggested by a skull from Catherine, Ellis County, Kans., referred to *hippolestes*, but not typical and especially in width of nasals approaching *coryi*. In dark general color tones *coryi* approaches the geographically distant and not closely allied subspecies, *olympus*, but is usually more distinctly tawny over the median dorsal area. Like other forms from the warmer regions the pelage is short and rather stiff and bristly.

Most of the skins of *coryi* examined have the head, neck, and shoulders irregularly flecked with white, that is, the usual coat is varied by pure white hairs which may appear singly, but are more commonly arranged in tiny patches. Some specimens are more densely speckled than others. A certain amount of white flecking may be seen on pumas from any part of the range, but this character appears to be much more prevalent in the Florida animal for some unexplained reason.

The type of *Felis arundivaga* Hollister (1911: 176) and other specimens from Louisiana have been compared with a larger number of typical *coryi* than was available for study by the describer. The skull of the type of *arundivaga* and of one from Prairie Mer Rouge, La., slightly exceed those from Florida in length, but the canebrake puma does not appear to be satisfactorily separable from the Florida race.

Specimens examined.—Total number, 17, as follows:

Florida: Alapata Flats, north of Lake Okeechobee, 3 (including type of *floridana*, skin only);[1] Chokoloskee, 1;[2] "East Florida," 1 (skull only);[2] Immokalee (3 miles southwest), 1; Marco, 1 (skull only);[3] Miami, 1 (skin only); New Smyrna, 1; Sebastian ("region back of"), 5 (including type).[2]

Louisiana: Prairie Mer Rouge, 2 (skulls only); Vidalia (12 miles south), 1 (type of *arundivaga*).

---

[1]Chicago Nat. Hist. Mus.
[2]Mus. Comp. Zool.
[3]Univ. of Wisconsin.

FELIS CONCOLOR MAYENSIS Nelson and Goldman

Guatemalan Puma (Pls. 50, 59, 68, 77, 83, 89)

Felis concolor mayensis Nelson and Goldman, Journ. Mamm. 10(4): 350, Nov. 11, 1929.

Type locality.—La Libertad, Department of Petén, Guatemala.

Type specimen.—No. 244856, skin and skeleton, ♂ adult, U. S. National Museum (Biological Surveys collection), collected by Harry Malleis, August 22, 1923.

Distribution.—Mainly tropical forested areas from southern Mexico (Vera Cruz) south to Guatemala, doubtless intergrading with *costaricensis* farther south in Honduras.

General characters.—A very small tawny or reddish subspecies, smallest at least of the North American races of the group. Closely allied to *costaricensis* of Costa Rica, but smaller, dorsal area paler, inclining toward "ochraceous-tawny" instead of deep "cinnamon-rufous" or "ferruginous"; skull differing especially in form of nasals and shorter postorbital processes. Also allied to *azteca* of the Sierra Madre of Chihuahua, but decidedly smaller, color richer, more rufescent; skull smaller and lighter in structure, and presenting other differential features, notably the narrower nasals and interpterygoid fossa.

Color.—Top of head, neck and narrow median dorsal area to base of tail varying from between "tawny" and "ochraceous-tawny" to light "cinnamon rufous," richest on rump, slightly darkened by black tips of hairs, becoming "light ochraceous-buff" on sides of neck, shoulders, along flanks and on outer surfaces of limbs, paling gradually to "pinkish-buff" on feet; lips, except conspicuous blackish areas at base of vibrissae, chin and throat nearly pure white; under surface of neck "light ochraceous-buff"; chest, inner sides of limbs and inguinal region dull white; belly varying along sides from dull white to "light ochraceous-buff," becoming more distinctly white along median line; face in general buffy-grayish, mixed with "ochraceous-tawny," the usual light supra-orbital spots indistinct; ears brownish-black externally, thinly clothed internally with whitish hairs; hairs around pads on feet blackish; tail above ochraceous-buffy to near tip in one individual, heavily overlaid with black along median line of distal half in the type, becoming lighter buff below to near black tip, the black limited to extreme end on under side, extending forward about 2 inches on upper side. *Young* (about half grown): Similar to adults, but retaining dark markings on inner sides of limbs, especially a conspicuous black bar across inner side of forearm near elbow.

Skull.—Size very small. Most closely resembling that of *costaricensis*, but smaller; frontal region and rostrum less flattened; nasals with upper outline more convex or expanded at a point distant about one-third their length from posterior ends, the inner margins more strongly deflected at anterior border, forming a deeper median emargination; postorbital processes decidedly shorter; frontal pit small, about as usual in *costaricensis;* dentition similar, but upper sectorial with internal cusp more prominent. Compared with that of *azteca* the skull is decidedly smaller and lighter in structure; nasals much narrower, the inner margins more strongly decurved at anterior border; interpterygoid fossa narrower; postero-external border of palate more deeply excised, the excision reaching or passing posterior plane of upper molars (not normally reaching this plane in *azteca*); dentition similar, but small anterior premolar more nearly filling space between canine and second premolar (anterior premolar in *azteca* with a distinct gap before and behind).

Measurements.—Type: Total length, 1,710 mm.; tail vertebrae, 660; hind foot, 240. An adult female topotype: 1,590; 620; 220. *Skull* (type— an adult male and an adult female, as indicated above, respectively): Greatest length, 183, 160.4; condylobasal length, 163.7, 147.5; zygomatic breadth, 127.7, 107.9; height of cranium, 65.7 56.2; interorbital breadth, 37.7, 31.8; postorbital processes, 72, 62; width of nasals (at anterior tips of frontals), 16.3, 13; width of palate (across interpterygoid fossa), 26.3, 21; maxillary tooth row, crown length (front of canine to back of carnassial), 55.4, 50.5; upper carnassial, 22.3, 20.5, width, 11.1, 9.8; lower carnassial, crown length, 16.9, 15; upper canine, alveolar diameter (antero-posterior), 12.3, 10.3.

Remarks.—F. c. mayensis is distinguished from other North American members of the group by diminutive size. It closely resembles *costaricensis* and combines the rufescent type of coloration and delicate structure of that and some other tropical forms with the short postorbital processes, rather wide interpterygoid fossa and other cranial features characterizing the more northern and plainer-colored *azteca*. Specimens from Catemaco, Veracruz are larger than those from the type locality and point to intergradation with *azteca* farther north. The jugal extends somewhat farther posteriorly than is usual in the more northern forms, and its condition seems to represent a step in the progressive development of this feature from north to south.

*Specimens examined.—*Five, as follows:
Guatemala: La Libertad, Petén, 3 (1 skin only).
Veracruz: Catemaco, 2 (skulls only).

FELIS CONCOLOR COSTARICENSIS Merriam

Central American Puma (Pls. 51, 60, 69, 77, 83, 89)

Felis bangsi costaricensis Merriam, Proc. Wash. Acad. Sci. 3: 596, Dec. 11, 1901.

Felis concolor costaricensis Nelson and Goldman, Journ. Mamm., 10(4): 347, Nov. 11, 1929.

Type locality.—Boquete, Chiriqui, Panama.

Type specimen.—No. 10118, skin and skull, ♀ adult, Museum of Comparative Zoology (Bangs collection); collected by W. W. Brown, Jr., April 22, 1901.

Distribution.—Tropical forested region (mainly rain forest) from eastern Panama west to Costa Rica and probably to Nicaragua; limits of range unknown.

General characters.—Size small; median dorsal area "cinnamon-rufous" or "ferruginous"—one of the most richly colored members of the group. Size about as in *bangsi* of Colombia; color richer, more rufescent or "ferruginous"; skull differing in detail. Closely allied to *mayensis* of Guatemala, but larger; dorsal area darker, "cinnamon-rufous" or "ferruginous" instead of inclining toward "ochraceous-tawny"; skull differing especially in form of nasals and longer postorbital processes.

Color.— Top of head, neck and median dorsal area to base of tail, varying from rich "cinnamon-rufous" and "ferruginous" to dull "tawny" or "cinnamon" on sides of neck, shoulders, along flanks and on outer surfaces of limbs, paling gradually to near "cinnamon-buff" on feet; lips, except conspicuous blackish spots at base of vibrissae, chin and throat nearly pure white; under surface of neck near "cinnamon-buff"; chest, inner sides of limbs and inguinal region dull whitish, the dusky basal color showing through; belly more or less distinctly cinnamon-buffy, palest and in some specimens whitish along median line; face in general buffy-brownish, the whitish supraorbital spots usually distinct; ears black externally, narrowly edged with gray, thinly clothed internally with whitish hairs; hairs around pads on feet usually brownish black, more or less mixed or tinged in some specimens with grayish; tail above near "tawny" rather heavily overlaid with black, becoming "ochraceous-tawny" below to black tip, the black usually limited to extreme end on under side, extending forward 1 to 3 inches on upper side.

Skull.—Size small—very similar to that of *bangsi*, but frontal region somewhat lower, more flattened anteriorly; nasals more flattened anteriorly, with a shallower median groove; postorbital processes longer; jugal variable in posterior extension—in some specimens reaching plane of anterior wall of glenoid fossa, in others ending anterior to it (reaching this plane in *bangsi*); dentition about the same. Similar to that of *mayensis*, but larger; frontal region and rostrum more flattened; nasals straighter (upper outline more convex or abruptly expanded at a point about one-third their length from posterior ends in *mayensis*), the inner margins less strongly deflected at anterior border, leaving a shallower median emargination; postorbital processes decidedly longer; frontal pit usually small as in *mayensis* (without trace in one adult male); dentition similar but upper sectorial with internal cusp less prominent, sometimes absent.

Measurements.—*Type* (female adult): Total length, 1,680 mm.; tail vertebrae, 680; hind foot, 22. *Skull* (an adult male from Pacuare, Costa Rica): Greatest length, 187.3; condylobasal length, 166.4; zygomatic breadth, 134; height of cranium, 65; interorbital breadth, 38; postorbital processes, 73.7; width of nasals (at anterior tips of frontals), 14.3; width of palate (across interpterygoid fossa), 25.5; maxillary tooth row, alveolar length (front of canine to back of carnassial), 54.5; upper carnassial, crown length, 22, width, 9.8; lower carnassial, crown length, 16.5; upper canine, alveolar diameter (antero-posterior), 12.8. Type and an adult female topotype, respectively: Greatest length, 161, 158.9; condylobasal length, 148.4, 145.2; zygomatic breadth, 111.7, 114.3; height of cranium, ——, 58.2; interorbital constriction, 31.7, 31; postorbital processes, 66.2, 71.7; width of nasals (at anterior tips of frontals), ——, 12.4; width of palate (across interpterygoid fossa), 22.1, 24; maxillary tooth row, alveolar length (front of canine to back of carnassial), 49.9, 48.8; upper carnassial, crown length, ——, 18.9; width, ——, 9.8; lower carnassial, crown length, ——, 14.3; upper canine, alveolar diameter (antero-posterior), ——, 10.5.

Remarks.—In its dark cinnamon, rufescent, or ferruginous tones this small subspecies is one of the most richly colored of the group. It occupies the narrow land bridge between the northern and southern continents and forms an important link in the intercontinental chain of forms. In some cranial features, as the posterior extension of the jugal and development of the frontal pit it is somewhat variable and thus annectent between forms in which these characters are more stable. It requires close comparison with *bangsi* of Colombia, with which it apparently has much in common.

Specimens examined.—Total number, 8, as follows:

Costa Rica: Guapiles, 1 (skull only);[1] Pacuare, 1 (skull only); exact locality unknown, 3 (1 skin only).

Panama: Bavano River, 10 miles above mouth of Mamoní River, 1; Boquete, 2.[2]

FELIS CONCOLOR BANGSI Merriam

Colombian Puma

Felis bangsi Merriam, Proc. Wash. Acad. Sci. 3: 595, Dec. 11, 1901.
Felis concolor bangsi Nelson and Goldman, Journ. Mamm. 10 (4): 347, Nov. 11, 1929.

Type locality.—Dibulla, Colombia.

---

[1]Amer. Mus. Nat. Hist.
[2]Including type in collection Mus. Comp. Zool.

Type specimen.—No. 8413, skin and skull, ♂ adult, Bangs collection, Museum of Comparative Zoology; collected by W. W. Brown, Jr., October 8, 1899.

Distribution.—Santa Marta region of northern Colombia; limits of range unknown.

General characters.—A small subspecies, closely allied to *costaricensis;* color duller tawny, less vividly rufescent or rich ferruginous; skull differing in detail. Differing from *concolor* of French Guiana, in duller coloration and well marked cranial characters. Similar, perhaps, to *söderströmi* of Ecuador, but description of latter indicates that it is a darker, longer-haired animal, and differs also in cranial features.

Color.—*Type:* Top of head, neck, median dorsal area and proximal half of upper side of tail rusty-tawny, thinly overlaid with black, richest on lower part of back, rump and part of tail mentioned, this general color shading gradually along sides of neck, shoulders, flanks and under side of tail into dingy "cinnamon-buff"; outer surfaces of limbs paling gradually to lighter "cinnamon-buff" on feet; lips, chin and throat dull white to roots of hairs; under side of neck and general abdominal area dull buffy; chest and inner sides of limbs, including inguinal region, dull whitish, the hairs becoming drab basally; hairs around pads on feet brownish; ears dusky externally, thinly clothed internally with dull whitish hairs; tail above, on distal half, becoming rather abruptly duller, more brownish to tip which is black, the black extending forward less than 2 inches on upper side.

Skull.—Size small—very similar to that of *costaricensis,* but frontal region somewhat higher, less flattened, anteriorly; nasals higher arched anteriorly, with a deeper median groove; postorbital processes shorter and stouter; jugal reaching plane of anterior wall of glenoid fossa (variable in *costaricensis*—in some specimens reaching this plane, in others ending anterior to it); dentition about the same. Compared with that of *concolor* the skull is smaller, less elongated; zygomata comparatively more widely spreading, less convergent anteriorly; nasals higher arched, less depressed anteriorly, less receding from nares; auditory bullae smaller, less inflated; dentition much lighter, the upper sectorial with internal cusp small or absent (large and prominent in *concolor*). Apparently differing from that of *söderströmi* in more constricted nasals, larger upper carnassial, and perhaps in other details.

Measurements.—From original description: "(Female ad. No. 8147 Bangs Coll., from Santa Marta, Colombia, measured in flesh): Total length 1,600 mm.; tail vertebrae 610; hind foot 225; ear 80. Cranial measurements.—An ad. ♂ (the type); and an ad. ♀ (in parentheses) from Santa Marta Mountains, Colombia, both in the Bangs Coll. Basal length, 162 (141); occipito-nasal length 173 (151); zygomatic breadth 128 (115);

occipito-sphenoid length, 60 (50); postpalatal length, 85 (72.5); inter-orbital breadth, 37 (31.5); upper carnassial 22 (20)."

Remarks.—The exact relationship of *bangsi* to *F. c. söderströmi* from northern Ecuador remains to be determined, but the description of the latter seems to be of a darker, longer-haired animal with a distinctive skull.

F. c. bangsi is closely allied to *costaricensis,* but differences in color and cranial characters presented by the scanty material available appear to dis-tinguish it. In specimens of *bangsi* examined the jugal reaches the anterior plane of the glenoid fossa as usual in South American species, but the zygo-mata are more evenly bowed outward as in North American forms, instead of converging anteriorly as in most South American members of the group. In this combination of characters it constitutes one of the links in the chain of intergrading forms.

Specimens examined.—Total number, 2, as follows:
Colombia: Dibulla, 1 (type);[1] Santa Marta Mountains, 1.[1]

FELIS CONCOLOR SODERSTROMI Lönnberg
Ecuadorean Puma

Felis concolor söderströmi Lönnberg, Arkiv. for Zoologi 8 (16): 2, Apr. 28, 1913.

Type locality.—Nono, northwestern slope of Mount Pichincha, Ecuador.

Type specimen.—Young ♂, Natural History Museum, Stockholm, Sweden.

Distribution.—The high Andes of northern Ecuador and probably of southwestern Colombia; limits of range undetermined.

General characters.—A small, well-furred, dark, high-mountain sub-species, apparently similar to *bangsi,* of northern Colombia, but still darker, the skull with peculiarly formed premaxillae and large upper sectorial. Ap-parently differing from *incarum* in smaller size, darker color and cranial details.

Color.—Lönnberg describes the color of the type as follows:

"A very dark Puma of medium size. The upper parts from head to tail are thickly overlaid with shiny black, which on the back is quite dominat-ing over the brownish terra cotta which only shines through. The fur is basally blackish, the outer half brownish terra cotta (Dauthenay: Rep. de Coul. 322, between 3 and 4), and finally provided with long black tips. On the upper neck the black tips are not so long and consequently more of the reddish colour shines through; the same is also the case with the crown of the head where the hairs also are more erect and directed forwards. On the sides of the body and the neck the colour is duller, inclining to dark fawn

[1]Mus. Comp. Zool.

(Rep. de Coul. 307, 1-2), overlaid with the black tips of the hairs. This colour extends over the anterior side of the fore legs and outer side of hind legs and feet. The posterior side of the fore legs is more reddish, similar to brownish terra cotta (322.1, 1.c.) without black tips. The inside of the fore legs is dusky whitish, partly suffused with dull buffish brown, which colour forms two faint cross bars below the elbow. The hairs around the pads of the fore as well as hind feet are black. A large patch (behind and) above the posterior large pad of all feet is greyish white with the dusky basal parts of the hair shining through. The face is dark due to the black tips to the hair. A greyish white spot above either eye. A black moustache from the nose to the upper lip extends half way to the corner of the mouth, but below the nose and this black stripe the upper lip is white. Some of the anterior whiskers are brownish black, the greatest number and the largest, even those emanating from the black moustache-area, are pure white. Posterior side of ears black with a grey spot near the base of the inner margin. Sides of the head greyish with a suffusion of brownish terra cotta (322.1, 1.c.); cheeks whitish with a slight similar suffusion. Chin and throat white. The fore neck is somewhat lighter than the palest shade of dark fawn (307. 1, 1.c.). The chest between the fore legs whitish with a tinge of dark fawn, but further back the lower side of the breast has a colour, which falls between dead leaf (321. 1, 1.c.) and rust red (318. 1, 1.c.). The belly is again lighter, almost whitish with a tinge of rust red colour. The region below anus is buffish. The tail above has the colour of the back, but the end is entirely black for 12-13 cm above and below. Otherwise the lower side of the tail is dull buff."

Skull.—From original description: "Sagittal crest high but short, only extending over the posterior half of the parietals. Frontals flat between the rather strongly pronounced, arcuate temporal ridges. Nasals broad in front, but suddenly narrowed, 'pinched in,' so that the frontal process of the maxillary, above the bulging produced by the root of the canine, is markedly concave. The posterior end of the nasals is bluntly pointed, and there is a considerable pit in the frontals at their junction with the nasals." Apparently similar to that of *bangsi*, but with nasals narrower, more constricted near middle and upper carnassial larger. Differing from that of *incarum* in smaller size, "pinched in" nasals, and probably other features. In photographs of the type and a topotype of *söderströmi* the pointed posterior ends of the premaxillae appear squamosely to overlap the maxillae. This peculiar detail has not been observed elsewhere in the group.

Measurements (skull of type "adult" male from original description).— "Greatest length, 172 mm.; condylo-incisive length, 156; basal length, 143.5; occipito-nasal length, 149; greatest breadth (zygomatic), 117; interorbital width, 31; length of nasals mesially, 38.5; greatest width of nasals in front, 27; width of nasals at the middle of their mesial length, 11; length of upper carnassial, 22.4; from front of canine to back of carnassial, 56; distance between insides of m^1, 59.5; least distance between inside of carnassials, 46; length of bulla, 30."

Remarks.—No specimens that may definitely be regarded as typical of this subspecies have been available for comparison, and its exact relationship to other forms remains to be ascertained. The skin and skull of a young animal from Paramo de Sumapaz (Bogota region), Colombia are, however, tentatively referred to it largely on geographic grounds. The animal was vividly-colored, cinnamon-rufescent, just losing the spots, those on the back indicated by cinnamon markings on the lighter, more ochraceous-buffy background. The specimen appears to be a male, with the permanent teeth replacing the deciduous series. The upper carnassial is large (crown length, 21.3), broad and heavy. The nasals are rather obliquely truncate posteriorly, and the auditory bullae are short and fully inflated. Lönnberg, in the very full original description says: "This Puma is probably most nearly related to *Felis bangsi* Merriam, from which it differs with regard to cranial characters, by its much smaller skull, the basal length in *F. bangsi* being 164, and the zygomatic breadth 128 mm., and all other measurements in proportion, except the carnassial, which is rather larger in this race.

"The type of *Felis concolor söderströmii* . . . is an adult male from Nono, northwestern slope of Pichincha (the mountain, on which Quito is situated). It occurs there up to a height of 12,000 feet according to Consul Söderström's statements, and it is known to kill pigs, mules, donkeys, etc.

"My friend Professor Lagerheim has told me, that it used to prowl around the dwellings of the Indians trying to snatch away their small white dogs of which it appears to be particularly fond. The natives know very well the difference between this furry Puma of the high mountains and the other Puma from lower altitudes, the skin of which latter is of less value.

"Lagerheim informs me, . . . that the Puma of Ecuador usually is not a dangerous animal, and as a rule it does not attack a man. Intoxicated Indians form, however, sometimes an exception. This is of biological interest, because it is evident, that the Puma when seeing the behavior of a tipsy individual believes him to be sick, and it is a general rule, that sick and wounded beings strongly attract carnivorous animals of all kinds."

A young female collected above Cotollac, northwest of Quito at an altitude of 11,000 feet, June 20, 1908, is said to be a little more reddish in general color, the black more confined to the dorsal area than in the type; and there are four dusky "cross-bars" on the inner side of the fore leg, the uppermost at the elbow. Irregular, dusky markings, representing persistent juvenal spots, are apt to be present on the inner sides of the forelimbs of young pumas in general, up to about half-grown, and may remain indistinctly visible in older animals.

The type is described as an adult male with a high, short sagittal crest, extending over only the posterior half of the parietals. The skull measurements show that it is small. The limited extension of the sagittal crest and the small size, which are usual female characters, suggests the possibility that there may be a mistake in regard to the sex of the specimen.

Edward Whymper (1892: 229, 243) refers to the occurrence of pumas, doubtless of this form, at high altitudes in the Andes of Ecuador. Of a camp at 14,762 feet near Mount Cayambe, northeast of Mount Pichincha, he says: "Pumas, indeed, were rather numerous in this neighborhood. A young horse . . . had just been killed by one, and an Indian we passed reported that he had noticed another roving about. Yet we never saw any, although they prowled around us at night, and left their footprints in the snow." And of another camp at 12,779 feet in the same region: . . . "it afforded good protection on one side, of which we were glad, as there were numerous tracks of bears, pumas and other wild beasts about."

Specimens examined.—One, as follows:
Colombia: Paramo de Sumapaz (Bogota region), 1.[1]

FELIS CONCOLOR CAPRICORNENSIS, subsp. nov.
Sao Paulo Puma

Felis concolor Merriam, Proc. Wash. Acad. Sci., Vol. 3, p. 593, Dec. 11, 1901.
Felis concolor concolor Nelson and Goldman, Journ. Mamm., Vol. 10: 346, Nov. 11, 1929.

Type locality.—Piracicaba, about 80 miles northwest of Sao Paulo, Brazil.
Type specimen.—No. 100118, ♂ adult, U. S. National Museum (Biological surveys collection); received from Herman von Ihering, June, 1900.
Geographic distribution.—State of Sao Paulo, southeastern Brazil; limits of range unknown.
General characters.—Similar in size to *acrocodia* of Matto Grosso, but the skull differs especially in broader braincase and frontal region, and more deeply V-shaped nasals. Somewhat similar in general to *pearsoni* of Argentina, and to *puma* of Chile, but smaller; skull less massive and departing widely in detail.
Color.—No specimens showing the colors of the animal from the vicinity of the type locality are at hand.
Skull.—Size medium, but slender; frontal region high and well arched, with scarcely a trace of a median pit near posterior ends of nasals; zygomata rather evenly converging anteriorly, the outer surface continuous with max-

---

[1]Amer. Mus. Nat. Hist.

illae curving gradually inward to rostrum, without a prominent angle or notch at antorbital foramina as in most North American forms when viewed from above; jugal reaching plane of anterior wall of glenoid fossa; postero-external margin of palate excised to posterior plane of upper molars; nasals highly arched anteriorly, rather squarely truncate posteriorly, the inner margins along anterior half depressed, forming a V-shaped median groove deeper than usual in the group; auditory bullae large and fully inflated; dentition especially canines, rather light; upper carnassial with internal cusp weakly developed; obsolescent upper molar comparatively large. Similar to that of *borbensis*, but decidedly broader; rostrum broader; nasals less elevated between anterior processes of frontals, the deep median trough extending farther posteriorly between them; interpterygoid fossa broader; auditory bullae larger; upper carnassials and third upper molars larger. Comparison with *greeni*: Size overall much larger, but frontal region actually as well as relatively narrower, and more highly arched; nasals more decurved along median line anteriorly; auditory bullae much larger; dentition similar but heavier. Comparison with *acrocodia*: Braincase and frontal region broader; nasals more deeply V-shaped along median line; auditory bullae smaller. Compared with those of *pearsoni* and *puma* the skull is much lighter in structure; frontal region narrower; nasals rising higher and steeper over nares with a deeper emargination between them (flattened and depressed in *pearsoni* and *puma*); interpterygoid fossa narrower; jugal usually less extended posteriorly; lachrymal foramen opening more directly outward and upward (opening more directly backward in *pearsoni* and *puma*); auditory bullae more inflated, more broadly attached to exoccipitals posteriorly; dentition lighter, the canines especially more slender.

Measurements.—No body measurements available. *Skull* (an adult, obviously male, from Piracicaba, Sao Paulo, Brazil: Greatest length, 204.2 mm.; condylobasal length, 183.2; zygomatic breadth, 139.2; height of cranium, 73.9; interorbital constriction, 39.9; postorbital processes, 73; width of nasals (at anterior tips of frontals), 17.8; width of palate (across interpterygoid fossa), 28.8; maxillary tooth row, alveolar length (front of canine to back of carnassial), 63; upper carnassial, crown length, 23.5, width, 11.5; lower carnassial, crown length, 17.4; upper canine, alveolar diameter (antero-posterior), 13.9. An adult female, probably from vicinity of Sao Paulo, Brazil: Greatest length, 163.5; condylobasal length, 152; height of cranium, 59.2; interorbital constriction, 31.1; width of nasals (at anterior tips of frontals), 17.4; width of palate (across interpterygoid fossa), 25.6; maxillary tooth row, alveolar length, front of canine to back of carnassial), 52.4; upper carnassial, crown length, 21.9, width, 10.8; lower carnassial, crown length, 17.4; upper canine, alveolar diameter (antero-posterior), 11.

Remarks.—Merriam (1901: 593) gave the type region of *concolor* as probably southeastern Brazil, and he used a skull from Piracicaba, about 80 miles northwest of the city of Sao Paulo as a basis for comparison. This skull obviously that of an adult male, was received along with that of a female from Herman von Ihering, June, 1900. The female, labeled "Brazil," exhibits the same peculiar features and is probably from the same vicinity. Nelson and Goldman (1929: 345) designated the vicinity of Sao Paulo as the type region, and also regarded material from Piracicaba as typical. That this designation was based on an erroneous assumption is shown on pages 202-203, and the change in regional assignment of *concolor* left the Sao Paulo animal without a name.

Specimens examined.—Total number, 2, as follows:
Brazil: Piracicaba, Sao Paulo, 1 (skull only); exact locality unknown, but probably vicinity of Sao Paulo, 1 (skull only).

FELIS CONCOLOR ANTHONYI Nelson and Goldman

Venezuela Puma (Pls. 51, 60, 69)

Felis concolor anthonyi Nelson and Goldman, Journ. Wash. Acad. Sci. 21 (10): 209, May 19, 1931.

Type locality.—Playa del Rio Base, Monte Duida, Territorio de Amazonas, southern Venezuela.

Type specimen.—No. 76935, ♂ adult, American Museum of Natural History, collected by Olalla Brothers, November 22, 1928.

Distribution.—Southern Venezuela; limits of range unknown.

General characters.—A large, short-haired, rusty-reddish subspecies, with a massive skull. Similar in size to typical *concolor* of French Guiana, but type somewhat darker in general tone than specimens referred to that form, and skull differing in important details. Differing from *bangsi*, of Colombia, and *söderströmi*, of Ecuador, in more rufescent coloration and cranial features.

Color.—Type: Upper surface of neck and median dorsal area to base of tail near "ferruginous" or "hazel," moderately mixed with black especially on the rump, becoming light "tawny" on sides of neck, shoulders, along flanks and outer sides of limbs, paling to near "light pinkish-cinnamon" on feet; lips, except near base of vibrissae, chin and throat white; under surface of neck suffused with "light pinkish-cinnamon"; chest, inner sides of limbs, inguinal region, and median line of abdomen dull white; sides of abdomen invaded by irregular light "tawny" spots; top of head "ferruginous" mixed with black; face in general buffy-brownish; a conspicuous black area at base of vibrissae; ears black externally, thinly clothed internally with whitish hairs; hairs around pads on feet blackish; tail above buffy brownish, with a blackish median line, below dull buffy becoming black all around at tip, which is tufted.

Skull.—Size large and structure massive. Similar in general to that of *bangsi*, but much larger; interpterygoid fossa much broader; auditory bullae larger; dentition similar, but heavier. Not very unlike that of *söderströmi*, but larger; ascending branches of premaxillae ending on maxillonasal suture (premaxillary endings slightly deflected outward and incising maxillae in *söderströmi*); jugal reaching farther posteriorly, well into plane of glenoid fossa; auditory bullae larger; dentition similar but heavier. Compared with that of *concolor* the skull is broader; frontal region much broader; nasals more highly arched, less flattened anteriorly; ascending branches of maxillae less compressed, or "pinched in" laterally; interpterygoid fossa much broader; auditory bullae large as in *concolor;* dentition similar, but upper carnassial with internal cusp less prominent.

Measurements.—*Type:* Total length, 1,720 mm.; tail vertebrae, 725; hind foot, 245;. *Skull* (type): Greatest length, 205; condylobasal length, 181.5; zygomatic breadth, 143.6; height of cranium, 70.2; interorbital breadth, 41.2; postorbital processes, 78.4; width of nasals (at anterior tips of frontals), 17.6; width of palate (across interpterygoid fossa), 33.3; maxillary tooth row, alveolar length (front of canine to back of carnassial), 61.1; upper carnassial, crown length, 23.4; width, 12; lower carnassial, 17.7; upper canine, alveolar diameter (antero-posterior), 14.5.

Remarks.—From the Monte Duida region, near the upper Orinoco River, *anthonyi* may range into much of the upper Amazon Valley. The width of the interpterygoid fossa is remarkable and equaled in the known forms of the group only in *pearsoni* and *puma* which are widely different in other respects.

Specimens examined.—One, the type.

FELIS CONCOLOR INCARUM Nelson and Goldman

Inca Puma (Pls. 52, 61, 70)

Felis concolor incarum Nelson and Goldman, Journ. Mamm. 10 (4): 347, Nov. 11, 1929.

Type locality.—Piscocucho, Rio Urubamba, Department of Cuzco, Peru (altitude 8,700 feet).

Type specimen.—No. 194310, skin and skull, ♂ adult, U. S. National Museum, collected by Edmund Heller, July 22, 1915.

Distribution.—High Andes from southern Ecuador to southern Peru; limits of range unknown.

General characters.—A medium-sized, dark-colored, long-furred, high-mountain animal with skull characterized by the combination of a broad frontal region, with posteriorly attenuate nasals, remarkably narrow interpterygoid fossa, small auditory bullae and rather slender canines. Similar in general to *puma* of central Chile, but smaller; color strongly inclining toward dark "tawny" instead of gray, and cranial characters distinctive. Allied to *osgoodi* of

Bolivia, but the richly rufescent coloration of the latter is lacking, and the skull differs notably in detail. Apparently differing from *söderströmi* of Ecuador in larger size, somewhat paler color and in distinctive cranial features.

Color.—Top of head, neck and narrow rather well-defined, median dorsal area to base of tail near "tawny," most intense along posterior part of back and rump, moderately overlaid with black, becoming dull "cinnamon" on sides of neck, shoulders, along flanks and on outer surfaces of limbs, paling gradually to "cinnamon-buff" on feet; lips, except distinct blackish areas at base of vibrissae, chin and throat nearly pure white; under surface of neck "pinkish-buff"; chest and belly pale "cinnamon," becoming whitish along median line; inner sides of limbs and inguinal region dull white, the dark basal color showing through; face in general dark grayish-brown, the whitish supraorbital spots moderately distinct, and areas at anterior angles of eyes extensively blackish; ears blackish externally, thinly clothed internally with light buffy hairs; hairs around pads on feet blackish; tail above dull "tawny" mixed with black, becoming dull "ochraceous-tawny" below to near black tip, the black extending forward about 3 inches on upper side.

Skull.—Similar in general to that of *puma*, but smaller, less massive; sagittal crest higher, more trenchant; rostrum narrower; nasals narrower, more evenly tapering to a nearly acute point posteriorly (broader and obliquely pointed in *puma*); palate and interpterygoid fossa much narrower; auditory bullae smaller; dentition lighter; canines decidedly thinner at alveolus; second upper premolars narrower; upper sectorial with inner cusp moderately prominent, about as in *puma*. In general form the skull aproaches that of *osgoodi*, but is larger and heavier; nasals narrower, and more evenly tapering to a nearly acute point (more blunt or obliquely truncate posteriorly in *osgoodi*); interpterygoid fossa narrower; auditory bullae smaller; dentition similar. Compared with that of *söderströmi*, the description indicates that the skull of *incarum* is much larger, and lacks the "pinched in" nasals ascribed to *söderströmi*.

Measurements.—*Type:* Total length, 1,905 mm.; tail vetebrae, 685. An adult male from La Lejia, a short distance north of Chachapoyas, northern Peru: Total length, 1,805; tail vertebrae, 700; hind foot, 260. *Skull* (type, and an adult male from La Lejia, Peru, already mentioned, respectively): Greatest length, 206, 197; condylobasal length, 190.7, 174; zygomatic breadth, 141.8, 133.4; height of cranium, 71.2, 70; interorbital breadth, 42.8, 49.1 postorbital processes, 79.2, 74.4; width of nasals (at anterior tips of frontals), 13.5, 18.6; width of palate (across interpterygoid fossa), 26.2, 27.9; maxillary tooth row, alveolar length (front of canine to back of carnassial), 62.2, 60.7; upper carnassial, crown length, 24.3, 21.6, width, 12.3, 11.3; lower carnassial, crown length, 18.9, 16.4; upper canine, alveolar diameter (antero-posterior), 14.7, 13.3.

Remarks.—No specimens definitely assignable to *söderströmi*, another high mountain form, described from the Andes of northern Ecuador about 1,000 miles farther north, have been available for comparison with *incarum* and the exact relationship of the two remains to be determined. Lönnberg's description, however, indicates that *söderströmi* is a much smaller, still darker-colored animal with distinctive cranial characters, especially the "pinched in" nasals. The type of *incarum* was examined and referred by Thomas to "*Felis puma*" without comment (Proc. U. S. Nat. Mus. 58: 223, 1921). It should be understood, however, that the author mentioned was not making any extended studies of the group.

A nearly full-grown male from La Lejia a short distance north of Chachapoyas, northern Peru, is similar to the type in color but is smaller and exhibits a departure in cranial details which, if constant, would warrant subspecific separation. Compared with the type of *incarum* the vault of the cranium is higher and more inflated behind the postorbital processes, the rostrum more depressed anteriorly and the zygomata more evenly bowed outward. The nasals are flatter anteriorly, and broader, more abruptly narrowing to a point posteriorly. The dentition is lighter, all of the molariform teeth being decidedly smaller, the crown length of the upper carnassial 21.6. The vestigial upper premolars are suppressed, leaving a diastema exceeding the greatest width of the upper carnassial, a condition observed elsewhere in the group only in extreme examples of *hippolestes* which has normally wide, unoccupied spaces in the tooth rows behind the canines. While this specimen is divergent, it seems best, in view of the wide range of individual variation observed in related forms, to assign it along with others from Peru and southern Ecuador to *incarum*. Furthermore, these specimens may be grading toward *söderströmi* which is imperfectly known. The present subspecies is readily distinguished externally from *osgoodi*, its geographic neighbor to the east, by the duller colors characterizing the Andean animal in that latitude.

Specimens examined.—Five, as follows:

Ecuador: La Toma, Hacienda Durasno, Calamayo Valley ("Purchased on the streets of Loja"), 1 (skin only).[1]

Peru: La Lejia, 1;[1] Piscocucho, Rio Urubamba, 1 (type); exact locality unknown, 2 (1 skin only; 1 skull only).[1]

FELIS CONCOLOR BORBENSIS Nelson and Goldman

Amazon Puma; local name on Rio Negro "Suasurano" (Pls. 52, 61, 70)

Felis concolor borbensis Nelson and Goldman, Journ. Wash. Acad. Sci. 23 (11): 524, Nov. 15, 1933.

Type locality.—Borba, Rio Madeira, Amazonas, Brazil.

---

[1]Amer. Mus. Nat. Hist.

Type specimen.—No. 92298, ♂ adult, skull only, American Museum of Natural History; collected by Olalla Brothers, February 10, 1930.

Distribution.—Middle section of low valley of Amazon River to upper course of Rio Negro; probably widely distributed in low lying parts of Amazon River drainage.

General characters.—A medium-sized, richly rufescent subspecies, closely allied to *capricornensis* of southeastern Brazil, but darker "cinnamon-rufous" or "ferruginous," and cranial details distinctive. Similar in color to *anthonyi* of southern Venezuela, but skull decidedly narrower, less massive. Differing from typical *concolor* of French Guiana in smaller size and important cranial features. Much larger and darker than *greeni* of Rio Grande do Norte, extreme eastern Brazil, and skull characters widely divergent.

Color.—Female from Rasarinho, Rio Madeira, Brazil: Top of head, neck, and narrow, median, dorsal area to base of tail rich "cinnamon-rufous" thinly overlaid with black, passing gradually on sides of neck, shoulders, along flanks and on outer surfaces of limbs, into "cinnamon," becoming "cinnamon-buff" across under surface of neck and on feet; chin, throat, chest, inner sides of limbs, inguinal region and lips, except a black spot near vibrissae, white; belly pale buffy; face in general dark brownish, almost blackish on upper surface of muzzle; ears deep glossy black externally, narrowly edged with gray, thinly clothed internally with whitish hairs; tail above "tawny" on proximal half and "ochraceous-tawny" on distal portion, mixed with black, becoming light ochraceous-buffy below to near black tip. In a specimen from Aurára Igarapé the median dorsal area is darker and nearer "ferruginous."

Skull.—Very similar in general form to that of *capricornensis*, but decidedly narrower; rostrum narrower; nasals rising higher between anterior processes of frontals as viewed in profile from the side, the median trough-like depression deep anteriorly much as in *capricornensis*, but shallowing more rapidly posteriorly; interpterygoid fossa narrower; auditory bullae smaller; upper carnassials smaller. Much narrower, less massive than *anthonyi*; frontal region higher, more evenly arched; nasals less flattened, more inflated and convex between anterior processes of frontals as viewed from the side; rostrum and interpterygoid fossa much narrower; auditory bullae smaller; carnassials and third premolars, above and below, distinctly smaller. Smaller and lighter in structure than typical *concolor*; rostrum less compressed laterally between ascending branches of maxillae; nasals more highly arched, less depressed and V-shaped along median line posteriorly; interpterygoid fossa relatively narrower; auditory bullae relatively smaller; dentition much lighter; upper carnassial with internal cusp less prominent. Contrasted with that of *greeni* the skull exhibits a marked departure in detail, as follows: Size larger; general form more elongated; vault of cranium much higher, more arched; nasals more inflated, less flattened; ascending branches of maxillae narrower; auditory bullae relatively larger, more inflated; dentition relatively heavier; canines relatively much longer.

Measurements.—Two adult females, one from Rosarinho, Rio Madeira, and the other from Tatú, Rio Negro, Brazil, respectively: Total length, 1,500, 1,750 mm.; tail vertebrae, 693, 740; hind foot, 220, 230. *Skull: Type,* adult male: Greatest length, 200; condylobasal length, 176; zygomatic breadth, 135.7; height of cranium, 72; interorbital breadth, 41.7; postorbital processes, 75.8; width of nasals (at anterior tips of frontals), 19.4; width of palate (across interpterygoid fossa), 28.2; maxillary tooth row, alveolar length (front of canine to back of carnassial), 59.2; upper carnassial, crown length, 23.3, width, 11.2; lower carnassial, crown length, 16.8; upper canine, alveolar diameter (antero-posterior), 15. Two adult females, one from Rosarinho, Rio Madeira, and the other from Tatú, Rio Negro, Brazil, respectively: Greatest length, 166, 158.3; condylobasal length, 150.5, 150; zygomatic breadth, 107.2, 113.9; height of cranium, 62.4, 60; interorbital breadth, 29.6, 31.5; postorbital processes, 58.3, 67.5; width of nasals (at anterior tips of frontals), 15.1, 12.3; width of palate (across interpterygoid fossa), 23.4, 24; maxillary tooth row, alveolar length (front of canine to back of carnassial), 50.5, 50.5; upper carnassial, crown length, 20.8, 20.2, width, 9.5, 9.4; lower carnassial, crown length, 14.5, 16; upper canine, alveolar diameter (antero-posterior), 10.3, 9.8.

Remarks.—*F. c. borbensis* will probably prove to be widely distributed in the vast lowland area drained by the Amazon River and its tributaries. Specimens from the region of the type locality appear to be more nearly related to *capricornensis* than to any other known form, but the scanty material available indicates that the cranial details mentioned are quite distinctive. One from Tatú, in the lowlands of the upper part of the Rio Negro, near the mouth of the Rio Uaupes, is not very far distant geographically from *anthonyi,* but agrees closely in the more essential characters with typical *borbensis.* The form, *borbensis,* occupies a somewhat intermediate geographic position and may be expected to intergrade on the north with *anthonyi* and typical *concolor,* on the east with *greeni,* on the south with *capricornensis* and *acrocodia,* and on the west it may possibly pass into *söderströmi,* the dark, high mountain form of northern Ecuador. The local name given by the collector on the Rio Negro as "suasurano" seems to be a variation of "soasoarana" applied by Schomburgk (1840: 325) to the puma of the "open savannahs of the Orinoco."

Specimens examined.—Four, all from Brazil, as follows: Aurára Igarapé, Rio Madeira, 1; Borba, Rio Madeira (type locality), 1; Rosarinho, Rio Madeira, 1; Tatú, Rio Negro, 1.

FELIS CONCOLOR OSGOODI Nelson and Goldman

Bolivian Puma

Felis concolor osgoodi Nelson and Goldman, Journ. Mamm. 10 (4): 348, Nov. 11, 1929.

Type locality.—Buena Vista, Department of Santa Cruz, Bolivia.

Type specimen.—No. 25256, skin and skull, ♂ adult, Chicago Natural History Museum, collected by José Steinbach, June 10, 1924.

Distribution.—Mountains of central Bolivia, doubtless intergarding with *acrocodia* to the eastward, and with *incarum* along the slopes of the Andes to the northwest; limits of range unknown.

General characters.—A medium-sized, short-haired, richly reddish form with a low, flattened skull. Closely allied to *acrocodia* of Matto Grosso, Brazil, but richer rufous, the median dorsal area more distinctly overlaid with black; also distinguished by cranial features. Similar in general to *incarum* of Peru, but much more rufous, pelage shorter, thinner, harsher, and skull differing in detail. Exhibiting a departure from *puma* of Chile in smaller size, shorter pelage, rufescent instead of plain grayish or brownish coloration, and weaker cranial development.

Color.—Top of head, neck and narrow, median dorsal area to base of tail varying from rusty-reddish or rich "cinnamon-rufous" to "hazel," most intense along posterior part of back and rump, moderately overlaid with black, shading through "pinkish-cinnamon" to "cinnamon-buff" on sides of neck, shoulders, along flanks and on outer surfaces of limbs, paling gradually to near "pinkish-buff" on feet; lower part of cheeks, chin and throat nearly pure white; under surface of neck "pinkish-buff"; inner sides of limbs and inguinal region dull white; chest and belly varying from pale "cinnamon-buff" to "pinkish-buff"; face in general "cinnamon-buff" or "clay color" with a light brownish admixture, the light supraorbital spots indistinct; upper lips white near sides of nose; areas at base of vibrissae on sides of muzzle "cinnamon-buff," interrupted by several narrow but distinct, transverse, black lines; ears blackish externally, thinly clothed internally with light buffy hairs; hairs around pads on feet light brownish; tail above light "cinnamon" mixed with black, becoming "cinnamon-buff" below to near black tip, the black extending forward about 2 inches on upper side.

Skull.—Similar to that of *acrocodia*, but lower and flatter; frontal region broader, less highly arched; postorbital processes less decurved; zygomata more evenly spreading, less strongly converging anteriorly, the sides therefore more nearly parallel; auditory bullae smaller, less inflated; dentition about the same. In general form the skull approaches that of *incarum*, but is smaller and lighter; nasals broader, more blunt, or obliquely truncate posteriorly (slender and evenly tapering to point in *incarum*); interpterygoid fossa broader; auditory bullae larger; dentition similar. Differs from that of *puma* in decidedly smaller size, and less massive proportions; rostrum narrower, less flattened; nasals similar in form, but less flattened, the upper outline rising higher about one-third the distance from posterior ends; interpterygoid fossa narrower; auditory bullae more inflated; dentition lighter, the canines especially thinner at alveolus, and vestigial upper molars smaller.

Measurements.—*Type:* Total length, 2,020 mm.; tail vertebrae, 710; hind foot, 280. *Skull:* Greatest length, 200; condylobasal length, 178.7; zygomatic breadth, 133.5; height of cranium, 68; interorbital breadth, 40.7; postorbital processes, 73.7; width of nasals (at anterior tips of frontals), 19.9; width of palate (across interpterygoid fossa), 28.4; maxillary tooth row, alveolar length (front of canine to back of carnassial), 58.3; upper carnassial, crown length, 22.7, width, 11.8; lower carnassial, crown length, 17.3; upper canine, alveolar diameter (antero-posterior), 13.

Remarks.—Intermediate in geographic position, *osgoodi* combines some of the characters of *acrocodia* of Matto Grosso, Brazil, and *incarum*, the Andean animal inhabiting southern Peru. It has the type of rich reddish coloration common to lowland forms of northern and eastern South America along with cranial characters indicating gradation toward the plainer colored Andean subspecies mentioned. Specimens from Puerto Suarez, extreme eastern Bolivia, and from Corumbá and Descalvados, just across the Brazilian boundary, were referred by Nelson and Goldman (1929: 349) to *osgoodi*. Three additional specimens from Descalvados have since been received, and further study of all the material available led to the recognition of another race in the Matto Grosso region.

Specimens examined.—Three, as follows:
Bolivia: Buena Vista, Santa Cruz, 3.[1]

FELIS CONCOLOR ACROCODIA Goldman

Matto Grosso Puma (Pls. 53, 62, 71, 78)

Felis concolor acrocodia Goldman, Journ. Mamm. 24 (2): 230, June 8, 1943.

Type locality.—Descalvados, Matto Grosso, Brazil.

Type specimen.—No. 273256, ♂ adult, skull only, U. S. National Museum (Biological Surveys collection), formerly No. 2390, Colorado Museum of Natural History (skin retained as a mounted specimen in Colorado Museum of Natural History); collected by Frederic W. Miller, November 25, 1925.

Distribution.—Lowlands of the upper part of the Paraguay River Valley, in southwestern Brazil, and eastern Bolivia.

General characters.—Size medium; dorsum nearly clear "tawny" or light "cinnamon-rufous," with little or no blackish admixture; skull slender,

---

[1]One, the type, in Chicago Nat. Hist. Mus.; 2 in Carnegie Mus.

with frontal region narrow, but highly arched behind postorbital processes; jugal reaching transverse plane of anterior walls of glenoid fossae. Similar in size to *capricornensis* of the Sao Paulo region, Brazil, but differs in cranial details, especially the narrowness of the braincase and frontal region, and less deeply V-shaped nasals. Also similar in size to *osgoodi*, of the mountains of central Bolivia, but ground color of upper parts lighter "tawny," and the median dorsal area lacking the overlying black present in the latter race; frontal region narrower, more highly arched, and other cranial details different. Differs from *borbensis* of the Rio Madeira region in lighter, less rich rufescent coloration and cranial characters.

Color.—(Skin No. 273257, U. S. Nat. Mus., from Descalvados, Matto Grosso): Top of head, neck, and median dorsal area to base of tail, light rusty reddish, near "tawny," or light "cinnamon-rufous," becoming "cinnamon-buff" on sides of neck, shoulders, along flanks, and on outer surfaces of limbs, paling gradually to near "pinkish-buff" on feet; lips, except blackish spots near vibrissae, chin, and throat, white; under surface of neck suffused with "pinkish-buff"; chest, inner sides of limbs and inguinal region dull white; belly suffused along sides with "pinkish-buff," becoming whitish along median line; face in general light buffy, with a light brownish admixture, the whitish supraorbital spots distinct; ears brownish or blackish externally, thinly clothed internally with whitish hairs; hairs around pads on feet light brownish; tail above similar to back, but thinly mixed along median line with black, below pinkish-buff to near tip, which is broken off. Another topotype (No. 28334, Chicago Nat. Hist. Mus.) is similar, and the complete tail is dark brown, near "verona brown," for about one and one-half inches at tip.

Skull.—Skull slender; remarkable for narrowness and height of frontal region and narrowness of braincase. Similar in size and general form to that of *capricornensis*, but frontal region narrower, more highly arched behind postorbital processes; braincase narrower; nasals less decurved along inner borders and less deeply and broadly V-shaped to form a median trough anteriorly, more pointed posteriorly; frontal pit at posterior ends of nasals deeper —unusually deep for a South American race; coronoid process of mandible higher; auditory bullae larger, more fully inflated; dentition about the same. About the size of that of *osgoodi*, but frontal region narrower, more highly arched; postorbital processes shorter; dentition about the same. About equal in general size, and in narrowness of braincase to that of *borbensis*, but frontal region more elevated behind postorbital processes; nasals more acutely pointed posteriorly; auditory bullae larger, more inflated; dentition similar.

Measurements.—No body measurements available. *Skull:* Type and a young adult female topotype, respectively: Greatest length, 201.5; 172 mm.; condylobasal length, 175.5, 156.4; zygomatic breadth, 135.5, 115.6; height of cranium, 72.8, 60; interorbital constriction, 37.2, 32.4; postorbital processes, 65.9, 57.9; width of nasals (at anterior tips of frontals), 15.7, 15.1;

width of palate (across interpterygoid fossa), 28.5, 26.5; maxillary tooth row, alveolar length (front of canine to back of carnassial), 57.5, 53.7; upper carnassial, crown length, 22.9, 21.4, width, 11.9, 11.1; lower carnassial, crown length, 17.6, 16.2; upper canine, alveolar diameter (antero-posterior), 14, 10.9.

Remarks.—In the narrowness of the braincase, *acrocodia* suggests relationship to *borbensis* of the Rio Madeira region, and intergradation across low, intervening watersheds seems probable. Toward the west the Matto Grosso animal doubtless passes into *osgoodi,* and toward the east into *capricornensis.* The skins examined are uniformly paler than those from the type locality of *osgoodi,* and the black usually overlying the rufescent, median dorsal area in other tropical races is absent or very inconspicuous, giving them a clearer, brighter general tone.

Specimens examined.—Total number, 8, as follows:
Bolivia: Puerto Suarez, 1 (skull only).[1]
Brazil: Chapada, Matto Grosso, 1;[2] Corumbá, Matto Grosso, 1;[2] Descalvados, Matto Grosso, 5.[3,4,5]

FELIS CONCOLOR GREENI Nelson and Goldman

East Brazilian Puma (Pls. 53, 62, 71)

Felis concolor greeni Nelson and Goldman, Journ. Mamm. 21 (10): 211, May 19, 1931.

Type locality.—Curraes Novos, Rio Grande do Norte, Brazil.

Type specimen.—No. 249896, ♂ adult, skin and skull, U. S. National Museum (Biological Surveys collection), collected by Edward C. Green, November 1930.

Distribution.—Known only from the type locality, but probably has an extensive range in northeastern Brazil.

General characters.—A small, short-haired, richly rusty-reddish subspecies, with small but robust skull and remarkably small teeth. Similar in general to *capricornensis* of Sao Paulo, but much smaller, and cranial characters distinctive. Not very unlike *borbensis* of the Rio Madeira and *osgoodi* of Bolivia in color, but much smaller and skull quite different.

Color.—*Type:* Top of head, neck, and median dorsal area to base of tail "cinnamon-rufous," very thinly mixed with black, the general rufescent tone most intense along lower part of back and rump, becoming light "tawny" on

---

[1]Carnegie Mus.
[2]Amer. Mus. Nat. Hist.
[3]One skin and skull and 2 skins only in Colorado Mus. Nat. Hist.
[4]Skin and skull in Chicago Nat. Hist. Mus.
[5]One skin only in Amer. Mus. Nat. Hist.

sides of neck, shoulders, along flanks and on outer surfaces of limbs, paling gradually to near "light pinkish-cinnamon" on feet; lips, except near base of vibrissae, chin, and throat white; chest, inner sides of limbs, and inguinal region dull whitish; abdomen whitish, the sides with irregular but rather distinct light "tawny" spots; face in general buffy-brownish; ears blackish externally, thinly clothed internally with whitish hairs; hairs around pads on feet brownish-black; tail above "ochraceous-tawny" rather heavily mixed with black along the median line, below ochraceous-buffy, the tip tapering and lacking a distinct black terminal tuft.

Skull.—Skull small, short, rounded and rather heavy. Similar in general to that of *capricornensis*, but much smaller; frontal region actually, as well as relatively, broader and flatter; nasals relatively narrower, more pointed posteriorly, less decurved along median line anteriorly; interpterygoid fossa relatively narrower; auditory bullae relatively much smaller, more flattened, less inflated in front of meatus; jugal extending posteriorly to plane of glenoid fossa about as in *capricornensis;* dentition similar but much lighter, the individual teeth much smaller, except vestigial premolars and molars which are rather large. Compared with that of typical concolor the skull is smaller; frontal region broader; ascending branches of maxillae not compressed or "pinched in" laterally as in *concolor;* interpterygoid fossa narrower; auditory bullae smaller, less inflated anteriorly; dentition much lighter; upper carnassial with internal cusp less developed. Contrasted with that of *borbensis* the skull exhibits a departure in detail, as follows: Size smaller; general form more rounded, less elongated; vault of cranium lower and flatter; nasals less inflated, more flattened; ascending branches of maxillae broader; auditory bullae relatively smaller, less inflated; dentition heavier; canines much shorter. In general form the skull somewhat resembles that of *osgoodi,* but is much smaller and differs in detail, the rostrum being less compressed laterally, the auditory bullae relatively smaller and dentition much lighter.

Measurements.—No body measurements available: *Skull* (type): Greatest length, 189.4 mm.; condylobasal length, 169; zygomatic breadth, 132.5; height of cranium, 64.8; interorbital breadth, 42.5; postorbital processes, 72; width of nasals (at anterior tips of frontals), 16.7; width of palate (across interpterygoid fossa), 26.7; maxillary tooth row, alveolar length (front of canine to back of carnassial), 52.5; upper carnassial, crown length, 20, width, 10.5; lower carnassial, crown length, 15.6; upper canine, alveolar diameter (antero-posterior), 11.5.

Remarks.—*F. c. greeni* from extreme eastern South America requires no very close comparison with any of the other geographic races. In essential characters, however, it agrees so closely with the other subspecies that the use of a trinomial name seems fully warranted. It is readily distinguished by small size and remarkably small teeth. The canines are especially short and weak.

Specimen examined.—One, the type.

FELIS CONCOLOR PUMA Molina

Chilean Puma

Felis puma Molina, Saggio sulla storia Naturale del Chili, 1782, p. 295.

Felis concolor puma Cabrera, Revista Chilena Hist., Nat., Año 15, No. 1, p. 50, Feb. 15, 1911.

Type locality.—Chile. Vicinity of Santiago selected as type locality by Nelson and Goldman (1929, p. 345).

Type specimen.—Not designated.

Distribution.—Central Chile, and probably adjacent parts of Argentina, doubtless integrading with *incarum* to the north, with *araucanus* to the south, and perhaps with *cabrerae* to the east; limits of range unknown.

General characters.—A large, well-furred, dark grayish or brownish form, with massive skull and heavy dentition. Closely allied to *araucanus* of south-central Chile, but apparently grayer, the ears buffy gray without the dark areas which are pronounced in *araucanus*. Similar in general to *incarum* of Peru, but larger, grayer, less tawny, and skull presenting well-marked differential features. Departing rather widely from *osgoodi* of Bolivia and from typical *concolor* of French Guiana in larger size, plain grayish or brownish, instead of rufescent, coloration, and massive cranial features. Relationship to *cabrerae* of northern Argentina not definitely determined.

Color.—Based on the head and neck of a young individual from the vicinity of Santiago, Chile. Face in general and top and sides of head grayish, mixed with brown; upper surface of neck grayish with a light "cinnamon" suffusion, becoming clearer gray on the sides; orbital rings whitish, the eyelashes on upper lids deep black; ears light gray externally, thinly clothed internally with whitish hairs; lips, except dusky spot at base of vibrissae, chin and throat white; under side of neck buffy whitish with a grayish admixture.

Skull.—A young individual, probably male, with teeth of permanent set not yet fully in place. Relatively large and heavy, with broad rostrum, wide interpterygoid fossa, and heavy dentition. Similar in general to that of *incarum*, but larger, more massive; rostrum broader; nasals broader posteriorly, the ends obliquely truncate, instead of tapering to a nearly acute point; palate and interpterygoid fossa much broader; auditory bullae larger; dentition heavier; canines decidedly thicker at alveolus; second upper premolars broader. Differs from that of *araucanus* most notably in heavier dentition.

Measurements.—No external measurements are available. A young male (permanent dentition not quite fully in place) from vicinity of Santiago, Chile: Greatest length, 179.5 mm.; condylobasal length, 164.3; zygomatic breadth, 126.4; height of cranium, 67.5; interorbital constriction, 34; postorbital processes, 69; width of nasals (at anterior tips of frontals), 16.5; width of palate (across interpterygoid fossa), 17.8; maxillary tooth row, alveolar length (front of canine to back of carnassial), 55.5; upper carnassial, crown length,

24, width, 12.5; lower carnassial, crown length, 17.3; upper canine (basal antero-posterior diameter of tooth not fully in place), 14.2.

Remarks.—*F. c. puma* is the little known Andean animal of central Chile, doubtless passing into *araucanus* to the southward and into *cabrerae* to the eastward. In the Andes of northern Chile intergradation with *incarum* may be expected to occur.

Merriam (1901: 598) regarded a young individual from Santiago as representative of *puma*, and Nelson and Goldman (1929: 345) selected the vicinity of that centrally located place as the type region. The Santiago specimen is probably a male. The skull is accompanied by the skin of the head and neck.

Specimen examined.—One only (skull and skin of head and neck) from vicinity of Santiago, Chile.

FELIS CONCOLOR CABRERAE (Pocock)

Argentine Puma

Puma concolor cabrerae Pocock, Ann. Mag. Nat. Hist. 6 (33): 308, September 1940.

Type locality.—La Rioja, Province of La Rioja, northern Argentina (altitude 968 meters).

Type specimen.—Adult male, skull only, No. 74.8.4.2, British Museum; collected by A. Roff.

Distribution.—Known only from the type locality, but may have an extensive range in northern Argentina.

General characters.—From original description: "A race intermediate in many cranial characters between *P. c. puma* and *P. c. pearsoni* on the one hand and *P. c. osgoodi* on the other.

"The skull has the same condylobasal length as the ♀ skulls of *puma* and *pearsoni* . . . but is decidedly shorter than the ♂ skulls of the latter in the British Museum, there being no adult ♂ skull of *puma* wherewith to compare it. It is distinguished principally from the skulls of those races, more particularly from *pearsoni*, in its less robust muzzle, the upper portion of the maxilla being compressed. The nasals also are affected by this compression, their outer edges being more concave than in any of the skulls of the other two races, but they are broad behind and end in a widely obtuse angular point; behind this point there is a longish pit with sloping sides, and defined behind by a strong crescentic edge . . . There is nothing approaching this pit in any of the skulls of *puma* or *pearsoni* . . . The dorsal profile is arched, with the occiput depressed, resembling in these respects the average of the skulls of *pearsoni*, but the postorbital processes are much thinner and the muscular depression in front of the occipital crest is deeper. The teeth are decidedly

smaller than in the ♂ skull of *pearsoni*, about the same size as in a young ♂
•skull of *puma;* and the inner lobe or protocone of pm⁴ is as in *puma,* not as in
pearsoni.

"The mandible differs a little from that of *puma* and *pearsoni* in having
the lower edge straighter, less undulating, and the chin or symphysial region
flatter, less convex . . .

"Although the type of *cabrerae* agrees with the largest adult ♂ skull in
the British Museum of *osgoodi* from Buenavista, Santa Cruz, Bolivia (No.
26.1.12.2), in condylobasal length, in the width of the muzzle at the canines,
in the development of the sagittal crest and the shape of the occipital region,
it is a good deal wider across the zygomata, 147 as against 135 mm., and a
little wider elsewhere, the mastoid widths being 86 and 81 mm., the maxillary
widths above pm⁴ 86 and 80 mm., and the postorbital processes from tip to
tip 78 and 73 mm. Since, however, it is an older skull, these differences may
be, partly at all events, a matter of age. But the postorbital processes are
much thinner, more rod-like, and less angular . . . , and the bullae are much
less inflated. In the skull of *osgoodi* they project in profile view below the
point of the paroccipital process and are 24 mm. wide as against 21, which
results in the narrowed distance between them being only 17 mm. in the skull
of *osgoodi,* whereas it is about the same as the width of the bulla in *cabrerae*
. . . The latter also has bigger nasals, longer in the middle line and decidedly
wider across the middle and posteriorly, and the pit behind them is much
deeper and has a more sharply defined posterior edge . . . . This pit, however,
is variable in its distinctness in the series of *osgoodi* skulls from the type-locality,
and in a ♂ skull from Matto Grosso it is nearly as pronounced as in the type
of *cabrerae.* But in all the skulls of *osgoodi* the bullae are more inflated and
the nasals are relatively considerably shorter, although they vary greatly in
shape, being alike in no two specimens. The two races agree on the average
in the size and structure of the teeth, and also in the shape of the chin and
lower edge of the mandible."

Measurements.—Cranial and dental measurements of type, from original
description: "Total length, 202 mm.; condylobasal length, 183, zygomatic
width, 147; interorbital width, 41; nasal (median length), 47; canine, 13.5;
upper carnassial, 23; lower carnassial, 17."

Remarks.—No specimens of *cabrerae,* which was based on a single skull,
have been examined by me. As in other similar cases the range of individual
variation remains to be determined. The comparisons made by the describer,
and geographic considerations, however, indicate probable validity as a regional
race.

FELIS CONCOLOR PEARSONI Thomas

Patagonian Puma (Pls. 54, 63, 72, 78, 84, 90)

Felis concolor pearsoni Thomas, Ann. Mag. Nat. Hist. (Ser. 7) 8: 188, September 1901.

Felis puma pearsoni Merriam, Proc. Wash. Acad. Sci. 3: 600, Dec. 11, 1901.

Felis concolor pearsoni Cabrera, Revista Chilena. Hist. Nat., Año 15, No. 1, p. 50, Feb. 15, 1911.

Type locality.—Santa Cruz, near mouth of Rio Santa Cruz, and about 70 miles from coast, Patagonia, southern Argentina.

Type specimen.—No. 1.8.12.1, skin only, ♀, British Museum; collected by H. Hesketh Pritchard.

Distribution.—Plains region east of the Andes from near the Strait of Magellan north at least to the Territory of Chubut. Limits of range unknown. Doubtless intergrading with *patagonica* along the Andean chain, and with *cabrerae* in northern Argentina.

General characters.—A very large subspecies with long pelage, pale, generally grayish, but varying to "ochraceous-tawny," coloration, massive skull, and remarkably heavy dentition. Closely allied to *patagonica* of the Andean region to westward; color similar but skull apparently larger, more massive, and differing in detail. Similar to puma of Chile, but paler, the upper parts less heavily mixed with black, and skull more massive, with broader, usually more evenly rounded, nasals. Differing from *capricornensis* of Sao Paulo in decidedly larger size, plainer, generally grayish instead of rufescent, coloration, and in much more massive skull.

Color.—Top of head, neck and narrow, well-defined, median dorsal area varying from grizzled-gray and buffy-gray to "ochraceous-tawny," darkest along posterior part of back and rump, thinly overlaid with black, replaced rather abruptly by grayish, cinnamon-buffy, or rusty-rufous tones on sides of neck, shoulders and flanks, and outer surfaces of limbs, paling to gray or "pinkish-buff" on feet; lips, except usual blackish spots at base of vibrissae, chin and throat nearly pure white; under surface of neck varying from grayish to light "cinnamon-buff"; chest, inner sides of limbs and inguinal region dull white; belly varying from nearly pure white to "light ochraceous-buff" or pale "cinnamon-buff"; face in general brownish-gray, the whitish supraorbital spots distinct; ears blackish externally, edged with gray, the central grayish spot more or less distinct in various widely separated forms extending in some specimens entirely across, and thus separating black areas on base from black areas toward tip, thinly clothed internally with whitish hairs; hairs around pads on feet brownish-black, mixed with gray in some specimens; tail above varying from grayish to cinnamon-buffy, the narrow median line rather heavily overlaid with black, becoming grayish or pale buffy below to near tip which is black or brownish-black, inconspicuous in some specimens, but extending forward about an inch on upper side in others.

Skull.—Very large and massive, with broad, flattened and elongated rostrum, low sagittal crest, wide interpterygoid fossa, and heavy dentition; canines very large; vestigial upper molars comparatively large, equaled only in *puma*. Skull not very unlike that of *patagonica*, but larger, more massive; frontal region broader, more highly arched; nasals broader and more rounded posteriorly; dentition similar. Similar in size and in general form closely resembling that of *puma*, but more massive; nasals broader, flatter anteriorly, usually more evenly rounded posteriorly (narrower and obliquely truncate in *puma*); upper carnassial with internal cusp absent or obsolescent (present and well developed in *puma*). Compared with that of *capricornensis* the skull is much more massive; rostrum broader and flatter; nasals broader and flatter, more receding or sloping backward from nasal opening, slightly upturned near the median line anteriorly, leaving a more or less well defined median depression about one-third the distance from anterior to posterior ends, the median groove much shallower; interpterygoid fossa broader; jugal usually reaching farther posteriorly (in some specimens reaching median plane of glenoid fossa); lachrymal foramen opening more directly backward (opening more directly outward and upward in *capricornensis*); auditory bullae less inflated, less broadly attached to exoccipitals posteriorly; dentition heavier, the canines especially large; obsolescent upper molar comparatively large.

Measurements.—Allen (1905-11: 174-175) gives measurements of two females from Smith's Ranch, near mouth of Rio Coy, about 60 miles south of Santa Cruz, Argentina, one in the red phase and the other in the gray phase, respectively, as follows: Total length, 2,332, 2,285 mm.; head and body, 1,557, 1,470; tail without hairs, 775, 815; hairs at end of tail, 50, 55. Prichard (1902: 250) records the length of a male from near Lake Argentina, Argentina, as 8 feet, 1 inch (= 2,465 mm.), and of a female from near Santa Cruz, Argentina, as 6 feet, 10 inches (= 2,084 mm.). *Skull* (two adult males from Rio Coy, Argentina, respectively): Greatest length, 225, 218.7; condylobasal length, 206.4, 198; zygomatic breadth, 156.4, 156; height of cranium, 79.5, 74.8; interorbital breadth, 46.9, 48; postorbital processes, 84.7, 83; width of nasals (at anterior tips of frontals), 21.2, 23; width of palate (across interpterygoid fossa), 35.5, 32.3; maxillary tooth row, alveolar length (front of canine to back of carnassial), 75, 65.3; upper carnassial, crown length, 26.4, 27.2, width, 13.8, 11.8; lower carnassial, crown length, 21, 20.7; upper canine, alveolar diameter (antero-posterior), 20.7, 16.8. Two old adult females, one from Coy Inlet, and one from Santa Cruz, Argentina, respectively: Greatest length, 201, 188.9; condylobasal length, 183.3, 172.2; zygomatic breadth, 138.5 _____; height of cranium, 71, 64.5; interorbital constriction, 44, 40.3; postorbital processes, 79, 73; width of nasals (at anterior tips of frontals), 18.5, 18.5; width of palate (across inter-pterygoid fossa), 31.4, 29.8; maxillary tooth row, alveolar length (front of canine to back of carnassial), 62.5, 58; upper carnassial, crown length, 24.4, 22.7, width, 11.7, 9.8; lower carnassial, crown length, 18.3, 17.2; upper canine, alveolar diameter (antero-posterior), 14.4, 13.5.

Remarks.—The range of *pearsoni,* east of the Andes, shares with *patagonica* the southern end of the South American mainland. The race presents extreme development as might be expected from its geographic position. In color shades of gray predominate, and contrast strongly with typical *concolor* and other more rufescent tropical allies. Prichard (1902: 251) mentions the "silver-gray variety" of puma as most commonly met with in Patagonia. The skull is more massive, with heavier dentition than in any of the other forms, but is closely approached by those of *patagonica* and *puma.*

In the northern subspecies of the group the jugal overlapping the under side of the squamosal arm of the zygoma ends in advance of the anterior plane of the transverse portion of the zygoma. In the chain of subspecies the jugal tends to extend progressively farther backward, from north to south, reaching its extreme in the present form with the jugal in some examples ending in the plane of the middle of the glenoid fossae. The obsolescent upper molar is irregular in size in the group, but tends to become progressively larger from north to south, reaching its extreme size in *pearsoni* and its near relative *puma.* The heaviest dentition observed in the group is in an old male of *pearsoni* (No. 17437, Amer. Mus. Nat. Hist.), from Rio Coy, Argentina. The zygomata converge anteriorly much as in *capricornensis.* Presumably *pearsoni* may intergrade with the little known subspecies, *cabrerae,* in northern Argentina.

J. A. Allen (1905: 174-178) described what he termed a "red" and a "gray" phase of this animal and illustrated them by two colored plates based on two specimens in the collection of the American Museum of Natural History from the Rio Coy, about 60 miles to the southward of the type locality. These specimens have been examined by me and compared with Allen's description and the plates, which, incidentally, do not portray the true tones. The writer is unable to agree with the emphasis given their differences, or that they represent anything more than individual variation. Both specimens have the upper parts mainly of a grizzled-gray, with a dull rusty-rufous, median dorsal area from crown to base of tail, one of the specimens having a more intense rufous median dorsal area, shading down on the sides to a deeper buffy suffusion due to the buffy color of the underfur. Along the median dorsal area the long overlying hairs have black tips with subapical rusty bands and the underfur is of the same shade of rusty-rufous; this median rufous area, darkened by overlying black tips of hairs, merges into the grayer sides through the subapical bands of black-tipped hairs becoming white and the underfur buffy.   The difference in color between the two specimens is merely a matter of somewhat increased intensity in one of a shade which is present in both. Further evidence that a wide range of individual variation, which cannot properly be termed distinct color phases, exists in *pearsoni* is a letter from J. B. Hatcher, quoted by Allen (l.c., 177) saying that he "frequently saw and examined sets of from six to a dozen skins of these animals killed on the same farm and observed that in each instance there was every shade of color represented from very light brown or gray to tawny. This was true alike of individuals taken on the plains or along the mountains. I believe the color of the pelage due very largely to the season while at the same time depending somewhat on the age and sex of the individual. In no way do I think it of specific importance." His conclusion that the color of the pelage is influenced by the season, and by the age and sex of the animal has been shown by these studies to be for the most part erroneous. The skin of a puma from Chubut (No. 21700, Chicago Nat. Hist. Mus.) referred to *pearsoni*, is extreme in light grayish coloration, there being no trace of the rusty suffusion usually more or less in evidence in specimens in which the gray tone prevails. This skin in general color resembles some gray wolves from the Great Plains region of the United States. The subspecies under review was named for C. Arthur Pearson, of the London Daily Express, and who financed the expedition led by Prichard.

Specimens examined.—Total number, 15, as follows:
Argentina: Arroyo Chalia, Territory of Santa Cruz, 1 (skull only);[1] Cape Fairweather, 1 (skull only);[2] Cañadon Jak, Territory of Santa Cruz, 3;[3] Coy Inlet, 1 (skull only); Rio Chico ("135 miles N. W. of mouth of Rio Gallegos"), 1 (skull only);[2] Rio Coy (about 60 miles south of Santa Cruz), 4 (2 skins only; 2 skulls only);[4] Santa Cruz (type locality), 2 (skulls only); Territory of Chubut, 2 (1 skin only; 1 skull only).[5]

FELIS CONCOLOR PATAGONICA Merriam

South Andean Puma (Pls. 54, 63, 72)

Felis puma patagonica Merriam, Proc. Wash. Acad. Sci. 3: 598, December 1901.

Felis concolor patagonica Nelson and Goldman, Journ. Mamm. 10 (4):346, Nov. 11, 1929.

Type locality.—Lago Pueyrredon (east side), Territorio de Santa Cruz, Argentina.

---

[1]Mus. Vert. Zool.
[2]Kansas Univ. Mus. Nat. Hist.
[3]Colorado Mus. Nat. Hist.
[4]Amer. Mus. Nat. Hist.
[5]One skin only in collection Chicago Nat. Hist. Mus.

Type specimen.—No. 108693, ♂ young adult, skin and skull, U. S. National Museum (Biological Surveys collection); collected by J. B. Hatcher, 1899.

Distribution.—Southern section of Andean mountain region, west of Patagonian plains in southern Chile and western Argentina; limits of range unknown.

General characters.—Size medium; pelage rather long; color grayish; skull of type relatively light in structure. Closely allied to *pearsoni* of the southern Patagonian plains east of the Andes; color about the same, but skull apparently smaller, less massive, and differing in detail. Differs from *araucanus* of south-central Chile, in paler color and heavier dentition.

Color.—About as in pale examples of *pearsoni*.

Skull.—Similar in general to that of *pearsoni*, but apparently less massive; frontal region narrower, less highly arched; nasals narrow and obliquely truncate, instead of broad and evenly rounded posteriorly. Similar to that of *araucanus*, but dentition heavier (crown length of upper carnassial, 24.2, instead of about 22 as in *araucanus*).

Measurements.—No external measurments available. *Skull* (type): Greatest length, 200 mm.; condylobasal length, 179.8; zygomatic breadth, 135; height of cranium, 68.5; interorbital breadth, 35.8; postorbital processes, 65.4; width of nasals (at anterior tips of frontals), 17.2; width of palate (across interpterygoid fossa), 31.4; maxillary tooth row, alveolar length (front of canine to back of carnassial), 62.5; upper caranassial, crown length, 24.2, width, 11.7; lower carnassial, crown length, 18.8; upper canine, alveolar diameter (antero-posterior), 14.5.

Remarks.—*F. c. patagonica* was described from a single specimen, the locality being given as "east base of Andes, Patagonia (lat. 47°30')." The collector, however, stated that the specimen was taken on the east side of Lake Pueyrredon (Allen, 1905: 170). The type closely resembles some of the paler specimens of *pearsoni*, but the skull differs in detail from any of the latter examined. Geographic and ecologic considerations indicate a probable range in the mountainous area along the western side of the extreme southern end of the continent. Among cranial details the form of the nasals is important. The nasals in the type of *patagonica*, a young male, are very similar to those of *puma*, and also closely approach those of a topotype of *pearsoni*, showing the wide range of individual variation. The protocone of the upper carnassial mentioned by Merriam in the original description of the type of *patagonica* is represented by a small cusp. This cusp is small or absent in most specimens of *pearsoni* examined, but well developed in a skull otherwise apparently typical of *pearsoni* from the Territory of Chubut. The development of the protocone in the upper carnassial is variable and of comparatively little diagnostic value throughout the group. Its unreliability as a distinctive character in south Andean pumas has been pointed out by Cabrera (1929, 313-315).

Specimens examined.—Three, as follows:

Argentina: Lago Pueyrredon, Territorio de Santa Cruz, 1. Chile: Rio Nirehuao, Provincia de Llanquihue, 2 (1 skin and skull, 1 skull only).[1]

FELIS CONCOLOR ARAUCANUS Osgood
Chilean Forest Puma

Felis concolor araucanus Osgood, Zool. Ser., Pub. 542, Field Mus. Nat. Hist., vol. 30, p. 77, Dec. 28, 1943.

Type locality.—"Fundo Maitenuhue," Sierra Nahuelbuta, west of Angol, Malleco, Chile.

Type specimen.—No. 50048, ♂ young, skin and skull, Chicago Natural History Museum (formerly Field Museum of Natural History); collected by Dillman S. Bullock, January 3, 1940.

Distribution.—Humid forest of the Valdivian district of south-central Chile, mainly in the provinces of Angol, Valdivia, and Llanquihue.

General characters.—(From original description). "A relatively small, dark, and richly colored puma. Size not greater than *F. c. puma,* considerably less than in *F. c. patagonica;* length of upper carnassial in adult male about 22 mm. Color much darker and more mixed with black than in *puma* or *patagonica;* "red" phase predominant."

Color.—(From original description). "General color of upper parts Ochraceous Tawny heavily mixed with black along middle line, producing a general effect of Cinnamon Brown which becomes somewhat paler laterally; under parts Cinnamon with restricted white areas on the inner sides of the legs and on the chin and throat; upper side of tail like middle of back; tip of tail blackish brown approaching pure black; ears mainly Blackish Brown, grayish basally and on the edges and faintly so in the middle; base of whiskers sharply blackish; sides of face and supraorbital region grayish."

Measurements.—(From original description). "Skulls of adult male and female paratypes, respectively: Greatest length, 193, 174 mm.; condylobasal length, 171, 158; zygomatic width, 140.2, 120.5; interorbital width, 39.7, 37.3; postorbital width, 52.3, 52.1; median nasal length, 45.2, 40.7; length of upper toothrow from front of canine, 67.7, 55.9; length of upper carnassial, 22.2, 21.2."

Remarks.—F. c. *araucanus* appears to be distinguished mainly by its dark

---

[1]Chicago Nat. Hist. Mus.

color which, as pointed out by the describer, is in keeping with the climatic conditions of its habitat, where nearly all mammals are somewhat differentiated from those of other parts of Chila. The exact relationship of this form to *puma* from farther north in the vicinity of Santiago, and to *patagonica* of the Lake Pueyrredon region to the southward and across the boundary in Argentina remains to be determined. The scanty material available, however, indicates that these are grayer animals with larger teeth.

Specimen examined.—One (skin only)[1] from Puerto Montt, Province of Llanquihue, Chile.

---

[1]Chicago Nat. Hist. Mus.

Table 12. Cranial measurements of *adult males* of subspecies of *Felis concolor*
(In U. S. National Museum, unless otherwise indicated[1])

Subspecies and locality	No.	Greatest length	Condylobasal length	Zygomatic breadth	Height of cranium	Interorbital breadth	Postorbital processes	Width of nasals	Width of palate	Maxillary tooth row alveolar length	Upper carnassial crown length	Upper carnassial width	Lower carnassial crown length	Upper canine antero-posterior diameter	Remarks
F. c. concolor:															
No measurements															
F. c. couguar:															
Pennsylvania—															
No measurements															
F. c. missoulensis:															
British Columbia—															
Crow's Nest Pass, Kootenay District	225047	211.8	193.2	153.5	78.4	45.4	83.7	19.7	30.3	61.8	24.0	12.6	17.9	15.2	
Montana—															
Hamilton (12 miles east)	242603	222.5	200.3	162.3	79.3	47.8	85.2	17.2	32.6	65.3	23.0	12.0	19.2	15.4	
Sleeman Creek (S.W. of Missoula)	262116	221.8	203.5	164.3	81.5	45.4	78.7	18.5	28.6	65.7	22.7	12.5	17.7	16.8	Type
Average		218.7	199.0	160.1	79.7	46.2	82.5	18.5	30.5	64.3	23.2	12.4	18.3	15.8	
F. c. hippolestes:															
Colorado—															
Meeker	108681	237.0	210.0	162.5	85.0	46.2	83.2	15.3	30.8	66.9	22.9	12.1	17.5	15.3	
Do.	108622	213.2	197.6	147.9	79.5	45.5	81.0	19.5	30.3	62.8	23.9	12.9	17.5	14.9	
Wyoming—															
Wind River Mountains	57936	227.4	204.4	160.0	81.8	48.5	83.5	17.8	33.3	66.5	23.0	12.7	17.7	16.7	Type
Average		225.8	204.0	156.8	82.1	46.7	82.6	17.5	31.5	65.4	23.3	12.6	17.6	15.6	
F. c. oregonensis:															
Oregon—															
Oak Grove Butte (near Estacada)	227750	211.8	194.6	149.5	72.5	46.9	81.3	19.3	28.8	63.4	25.3	12.3	17.5	15.5	
Washington—															
Lake Chelan	263033	229.4	209.3	160.4	85.5	50.1	82.0	19.7	31.5	66.5	25.7	13.9	18.2	17.1	
Mount Vernon	148882	212.0	196.0	148.4	79.8	42.4	80.0	16.8	27.3	62.3	23.5	12.2	17.2	14.2	
Willard	248733	207.5	192.4	147.8	77.2	46.0	74.5	17.5	29.1	62.6	23.8	12.3	16.7	15.4	
Average		215.2	198.1	151.5	78.8	46.4	79.5	18.3	29.2	63.7	24.6	12.7	17.5	15.6	
F. c. vancouverensis:															
British Columbia—															
Campbell Lake, Vancouver Island	211519	215.0	197.8	146.4	80.0	44.2	79.4	15.3	27.8	62.8	24.4	13.2	18.4	15.2	Type
Do.	211520	209.6	194.4	149.0	80.3	45.2	80.0	15.5	27.8	62.4	24.4	13.3	17.8	15.7	
Campbell River Valley, Vancouver Island	211521	213.7	197.8	145.9	78.0	44.0	78.4	16.4	27.3	63.2	24.2	12.7	18.0	15.8	
Average		212.8	196.7	147.1	79.4	44.5	79.3	15.7	27.6	62.8	24.3	13.1	18.1	15.6	

269

Table 12. Cranial measurements of *adult males* of subspecies of *Felis concolor* (*Continued*)
(In U. S. National Museum, unless otherwise indicated[1])

Subspecies and locality	No.	Greatest length	Condylobasal length	Zygomatic breadth	Height of cranium	Interorbital breadth	Postorbital processes	Width of nasals	Width of palate	Maxillary tooth row alveolar length	Upper carnassial length	Upper carnassial crown width	Lower carnassial crown length	Upper canine antero-posterior diameter	Remarks
F. c. olympus:															
Washington—															
Elwha River	250489	228.2	——	155.8	84.0	51.6	82.5	17.4	32.3	66.4	25.4	12.3	17.7	15.3	
Soleduck River	250487	211.5	——	151.9	77.6	45.2	76.6	16.1	29.7	63.4	24.2	12.4	16.7	15.0	
Average		219.9		152.9	80.8	48.4	79.6	16.8	31.0	64.9	24.8	12.3	17.2	15.2	
F. c. californica:															
California—															
Coyote Creek, Santa Clara County	33428	206.5	186.0	146.7	76.9	40.0	70.5	18.9	28.4	60.8	22.5	11.8	17.5	14.9	Mus. Vert. Zool.
Los Pinos Mountain, San Diego County	37423	211.2	188.0	142.0	73.8	42.6	73.7	18.5	28.4	60.4	21.9	11.2	16.4	12.5	
Lynchburg, Placer County	31252	213.0	188.5	147.5	76.0	45.0	77.0	21.0	30.2	60.3	22.5	11.5	17.8	13.1	
Pack Saddle Creek, near Tulare-Kern County line	34251	214.6	190.0	151.0	80.6	45.0	79.6	20.0	30.1	59.4	23.5	11.9	17.1	13.9	Mus. Vert. Zool.
Riverside County	34991	202.4	183.8	149.4	72.5	41.2	73.7	19.6	30.4	60.0	23.4	11.3	16.7	14.7	do.
San Bernardino Mountains	24534	207.0	185.0	142.5	74.0	42.0	73.8	14.8	28.5	59.8	22.0	11.4	16.9	14.3	do.
Sequoia National Park	33558	213.3	191.4	153.5	79.7	43.1	77.8	19.4	29.0	60.0	24.5	12.8	17.5	14.2	do.
Do.	33559	195.5	180.3	142.5	73.7	40.0	76.0	18.0	29.6	57.0	22.8	11.5	16.5	14.3	do.
Soquel Creek, Santa Cruz County	33451	204.0	192.1	148.7	80.5	43.7	73.5	20.3	28.2	60.7	22.9	11.4	17.2	14.2	do.
Wawona (7½ miles west)	23745	209.7	186.4	154.2	78.9	44.8	78.8	17.4	29.0	60.3	24.0	11.4	16.9	13.2	do.
Average		207.7	187.2	147.8	76.6	42.7	75.4	18.8	29.2	59.9	23.0	11.6	17.1	13.9	
F. c. kaibabensis:															
Arizona—															
Kaibab National Forest	167967	217.3	199.7	142.9	76.8	43.2	79.0	22.1	27.9	61.5	23.1	11.7	16.8	14.0	
Powell Plateau, Grand Canyon National Park	171186	216.8	195.8	141.6	75.2	43.4	75.5	19.4	29.0	62.4	22.5	11.8	17.3	14.9	Type
Nevada—															
Sunnyside	224575	209.5	193.3	144.9	76.3	41.7	74.9	18.0	29.0	58.2	21.7	11.5	16.4	14.0	
Average		214.5	196.3	143.1	75.8	42.8	76.5	19.8	28.6	60.7	22.4	11.7	16.8	14.3	
F. c. browni:															
Arizona—															
Yuma (12 miles south)	125719	205	183.2	139.3	74.0	43.5	......	16.5	......	57.0	20.4	11.2	15.2	14.0	Type
F. c. improcera:															
Baja California—															
No measurements of males															

	Catalog No.														Remarks
F. c. azteca:															
Chihuahua—															
Colonia Garcia	99658	202.9	184.5	146.9	72.4	40.7	73.9	18.3	30.8	60.0	21.6	12.2	15.6	15.0	Type
Do.	117078	214.3	199.6	146.3	76.5	43.8	76.7	23.3	31.0	64.0	23.2	11.4	16.8	14.3	
Do.	117079	213.0	194.0	149.0	77.8	46.6	77.8	18.5	30.7	60.6	23.0	11.9	17.2	14.0	
Do.	99659	202.3	184.0	141.9	72.5	40.3	77.3	17.3	29.5	59.3	21.9	11.8	16.1	13.0	
Do.	10504	205.0	185.4	141.8	70.8	41.6	75.7	17.3	32.2	61.0	23.1	12.4	16.9	13.5	Mus. Comp. Zool.
Average		207.5	189.5	145.6	73.8	42.2	76.3	18.9	30.8	61.0	22.3	11.9	16.5	14.0	
F. c. stanleyana:															
Texas—															
Bruni Ranch (near Bruni)	251419	218.7	198.5	141.9	77.0	42.5	74.8	17.1	29.2	68.4	24.8	13.0	18.2	16.6	Type
Catarina (30 miles south)	265341	212.3	191.0	142.0	72.0	43.0	75.4	20.4	28.9	61.4	22.3	11.6	17.9	14.8	
Cotulla (30 miles southeast)	264178	215.3	194.4	144.8	78.8	40.9	73.4	16.2	31.3	64.8	24.1	11.5	17.8	14.8	
Do.	264180	215.8	197.9	141.8	77.0	43.6	75.3	21.3	26.4	64.3	23.0	12.1	17.9	14.4	
Eagle Pass (Indio Ranch)	262185	220.5	197.3	145.0	82.0	44.6	75.8	19.9	33.0	65.6	23.0	12.0	17.5	15.6	
Laredo (30 miles east)	262700	212.4	188.3	134.4	75.7	41.8	77.3	19.3	29.7	62.5	22.1	9.9	16.2	14.5	
Average		215.5	194.6	141.7	77.1	42.7	75.3	19.0	29.8	64.5	23.2	11.7	17.6	15.1	
F. c. coryi:															
Florida—															
Alapata Flat, north of Lake Okeechobee	14902	206.8	185.5	136.5	71.4	40.8	74.8	20.0	26.7	58.5	21.7	11.6	16.1	13.1	Chicago Nat. Hist. Mus.
Immokalee	265596	212.5	192.3	142.5	76.0	44.5	78.4	23.4	30.7	62.7	24.4	13.1	18.2	15.3	
Sebastian	7742	208.0	185.0	134.9	---	41.8	75.2	---	27.3	58.8	20.9	11.7	---	---	Typo—Mus. Comp. Zool.
Do.	6992	212.8	188.5	152.2	77.5	44.2	85.8	20.4	28.2	59.5	23.7	11.5	16.8	13.5	
Louisiana—															
Prairie Mer Rouge, Morehouse Parish	1158	217.8	192.7	---	77.3	46.1	80.3	21.4	29.6	63.2	23.3	12.4	17.6	15.4	
Vidalia	137122	219.5	195.5	149.4	77.7	43.2	77.3	20.4	29.0	62.5	23.1	12.9	16.9	13.5	Type of "arundinga"
Average		212.9	189.9	143.1	76.0	43.4	78.6	21.1	28.6	60.9	22.9	12.2	17.1	14.2	
F. c. mayensis:															
Guatemala—															
Libertad, Peten	244856	183.0	163.7	127.7	65.7	37.7	72.0	16.3	26.3	55.4	22.3	11.1	16.9	12.3	Type
F. c. costaricensis:															
Costa Rica—															
Pacuare	15967	187.3	166.4	134.0	65.0	38.0	73.7	14.3	25.5	54.5	22.0	9.8	16.5	12.8	
F. c. bangsi:															
Colombia—															
Dibulla	8413	192.0	173.0	---	---	36.9	---	---	24.5	53.2	19.8	---	---	---	Type—Mus. Comp. Zool.
F. c. roderstromi:															
Ecuador—															
Nono, Mount Pichincha	No no.	172.0	---	117.0	---	31.0	---	---	---	---	22.4	---	---	---	Type, young in Stockholm Mus. (original description)
F. c. anthonyi:															
Venezuela—															
Monte Duida	76955	205.0	181.5	143.6	70.2	41.2	78.4	17.6	33.3	61.1	23.4	12.0	17.7	14.5	Type—Amer. Mus. Nat. Hist.
F. c. incarum:															
Peru—															
La Lejia	73221	197.0	174.0	133.4	70.0	49.1	74.4	18.6	27.9	60.7	21.6	11.3	16.4	13.3	Amer. Mus. Nat. His.
Piscocucho	194310	206.0	190.7	141.8	71.2	42.8	79.2	13.5	26.2	62.2	24.3	12.3	18.9	14.7	Type
Average		201.5	182.4	138.6	70.6	46.0	76.8	16.1	27.1	61.5	23.0	11.8	17.7	14.0	

Table 12. Cranial measurements of *adult males* of subspecies of *Felis concolor* (*Continued*)
(In U. S. National Museum, unless otherwise indicated[1])

Subspecies and locality	No.	Greatest length	Condylobasal length	Zygomatic breadth	Height of cranium	Interorbital breadth	Postorbital processes	Width of nasals	Width of palate	Maxillary tooth row alveolar length	Upper carnassial crown length	Upper carnassial crown width	Lower carnassial crown length	Upper canine antero-posterior diameter	Remarks
F. c. missoulensis															
Brazil— Piracicaba, Sao Paulo	100118	204.2	183.2	139.2	73.9	39.9	73.0	17.8	28.8	63.0	23.5	11.5	17.4	13.9	
F. c. borbensis:															
Brazil— Borba	92298	200.0	176.0	135.7	72.0	41.7	75.8	19.4	28.2	59.2	23.3	11.2	16.8	15.0	Type
F. c. osgoodi:															
Bolivia— Santa Cruz	25256	200.0	178.7	133.5	68.0	40.7	73.7	19.9	28.4	58.3	22.7	11.8	17.3	13.0	Type—Chicago Nat. Hist. Mus.
F. c. greeni:															
Brazil— Curras Novos	249896	189.4	169.0	132.5	64.8	42.5	72.0	16.7	26.7	52.5	20.0	10.5	15.6	11.5	
F. c. puma:															
Chile— Santiago	12751	179.5	164.3	126.4	67.5	34	69	16.5	28	55.5	24	12.5	17.3	14.2	Young
F. c. cabrerae:															
Argentina— La Rioja	74.8.4.2.	202.0	183	147	41	------	------	------	------	------	23.0	------	17.0	------	Type (original description)
F. c. pearsoni:															
Argentina— Rio Coy	17437	225.0	206.4	156.4	79.5	46.9	84.7	21.2	35.5	72.0	26.4	13.8	21.0	20.7	Amer. Mus. Nat. His.
Do.	17436	218.7	198.0	156.0	74.8	48.0	83.0	23.0	32.3	65.3	27.2	11.8	20.7	16.8	do.
Average		221.9	202.2	156.2	77.2	47.5	83.9	22.1	33.9	68.7	26.8	12.8	20.9	18.8	
F. c. patagonica:															
Argentina— Lake Pueyrredon (east side)	108693	200	179.8	135	68.5	35.8	65.4	17.2	31.4	62.5	24.2	11.7	18.8	14.5	Type—young adult
Chile— Rio Nireguao Llanquihue	30817	207.8	192.7	142.5	73.3	39.0	66.0	16.6	31.0	63.0	26.0	12.3	19.5	16.8	Chicago Nat. Hist. Mus.

[1]For explanation of measurements see p. 191.

272

Table 13. Cranial measurements of *adult females* of subspecies of *Felis concolor*
(In U. S. National Museum, unless otherwise indicated[1])

Subspecies and locality	No.	Greatest length	Condylobasal length	Zygomatic breadth	Height of cranium	Interorbital breadth	Postorbital processes	Width of nasals	Width of palate	Maxillary tooth row alveolar length	Upper carnassial length	Upper carnassial crown width	Lower carnassial crown length	Upper canine antero-posterior diameter	Remarks
F. c. concolor:															
Surinam															
Venezuela—															
	13006			113.7	63.5	31.2	54.4	13.6	26.4	56.2	22.7	10.6	16.0	12.8	
Caura Valley	137040	175.9	165.3	116.5	60.7	30.8	65.5	9.9	25.8	56.6	22.2	11.9	17.0	12.8	
	Average	175.9	165.3	115.1	62.1	31.0	60.0	11.8	26.1	56.4	22.5	11.3	16.5	12.8	
F. c. couguar:															
New York—															
Adirondack Mountain region	3811	184	168.7	134.5	66.4	35.8	73.2	16.4	27.8	55.8	22.2	10.9	16.7	11.8	
Do.	188639	184	165.0	127.8	62.5	35.9	71.0	14.5	25.8	54.3	20.3	10.7	15.2	10.9	
	Average	184	166.9	131.2	64.5	35.8	72.1	15.5	26.8	55.1	21.3	10.8	16.0	11.4	
F. c. missoulensis:															
Alberta—															
Clearwater River, 50 miles N.W. of Banff	249297	191.0	———	140.7	71.4	39.3	74.0	12.7	30.7	55.1	21.3	10.2	16.1	12.9	
British Columbia—															
Crow's Nest Pass, Kootenay District	225044	190.0	175.0	139.0	70.0	41.6	76.6	15.9	31.0	53.9	20.7	10.7	15.7	11.5	
Montana—															
Adiar Ranch, Glacier National Park	228652	189.4	169.9	135.3	67.3	36.0	67.4	13.4	29.5	59.2	21.6	11.0	16.3	12.8	
	Average	190.1	172.3	138.3	69.6	39.0	72.7	14.0	30.4	55.4	21.2	10.6	16.0	12.4	
F. c. hippolestes:															
Colorado—															
Meeker	108684	203.0	184.4	133.7	70.9	38.0	69.3	15.2	29.2	57.6	20.2	10.6	15.3	11.3	
Do.	108685	199.2	178.9	131.4	68.5	37.7	72.4	16.7	27.0	58.5	21.6	11.4	16.0	12.3	
Do.	108686	196.4	182.1	137.5	71.0	40.3	74.6	16.9	29.8	59.6	22.4	11.3	16.8	12.0	
Do.	108687	193.2	176.4	134.5	68.0	37.7	66.0	14.5	28.0	57.2	22.3	11.3	16.0	12.0	
Do.	108688	191.6	173.2	129.6	67.5	37.4	69.9	14.5	28.8	56.7	21.2	11.6	16.0	11.4	
Do.	108689	196.2	172.5	133.9	69.0	39.7	73.0	16.9	27.3	57.5	21.8	11.5	15.5	12.2	
Do.	108690	191.0	175.0	132.7	70.0	39.9	74.5	17.8	28.2	57.7	21.5	11.8	15.5	12.8	
Do.	108691	187.5	169.0	130.0	66.5	37.0	69.4	15.3	28.7	54.5	20.9	10.6	15.0	10.8	
	Average	194.8	176.4	132.9	68.9	38.5	71.1	16.0	28.4	57.4	21.5	11.3	15.8	11.7	
F. c. oregonensis:															
Oregon—															
Estacada	232458	190.0	174.3	122.2	67.8	39.4	69.4	11.8	28.5	58.0	23.9	12.2	17.2	13.3	
Washington—															
Mount Rainier National Park	245683	192.5	180.0	135.5	69.5	38.8	72.1	14.7	29.7	59.1	23.1	11.2	16.2	13.2	
	Average	191.3	177.2	133.8	68.7	39.1	70.8	14.3	29.1	58.6	23.5	11.7	16.7	13.2	

273

Table 13. Cranial measurements of *adult females* of subspecies of *Felis concolor* (*Continued*)
(In U. S. National Museum, unless otherwise indicated[1])

Subspecies and locality	No.	Greatest length	Condylobasal length	Zygomatic breadth	Height of cranium	Interorbital breadth	Postorbital processes	Width of nasals	Width of palate	Maxillary tooth row alveolar length	Upper carnassial crown length	Upper carnassial crown width	Lower carnassial crown length	Upper canine antero-posterior diameter	Remarks
F. c. vancouverensis:															
British Columbia—															
Vancouver Island	56176	194.5	178.8	136.0	72.0	41.8	80.0	16.9	27.0	56.5	21.8	11.0	15.5	12.8	
Do.	211493	186.9		126.2	68.5	36.8	70.5	12.8	27.0	55.8	22.4	11.3	15.8	12.0	
Do.	211522	187.0	172.8	125.5	71.2	38.5	72.5	15.0	26.7	55.7	22.4	11.7	16.4	13.5	
Average		189.5	175.8	129.3	70.6	39.0	74.3	14.9	26.8	56.0	22.2	11.3	15.9	12.8	
F. c. olympus:															
Washington—															
Lake Cushman	77973	188.8	174.4	126.7	68.5	38.8	71.0	16.8	27.3	57.4	22.4	11.7	16.2	13.5	Type
Olympic Mountains	168176	188.7	175.4	130.5	68.5	39.0	68.2	14.5	21.1	59.1	23.7	11.9	16.7	12.7	
Queets River	250492	195.8	180.7	136.5	69.7	41.5	72.6	15.8	28.9	58.8	23.4	12.0	16.2	13.1	
Average		191.1	176.8	131.2	68.9	39.8	70.6	15.4	25.8	58.4	23.2	11.9	16.3	13.1	
F. c. californica:															
California—															
Dunlap	33556	183.5	170.0	129.6	70.5	40.2	74.7	17.0	27.3	55.0	22.2	10.7	15.2	12.4	Mus. Vert. Zool.
Kern River, 25 miles above Kernville	34180	179.3	161.8	125.5	64.5	37.0	70.0	18.4	28.0	53.9	21.4	9.3	15.2	11.8	do.
Orestimba Creek, Stanislaus County	34302	177.5	162.3	118.9	65.9	34.0	65.9	15.5	25.0	54.5	21.8	11.0	16.0	11.8	do.
San Bernardino Mountains	7145	177.4	162.5	128.3	65.2	36.6	66.7	14.8	28.4	53.2	20.8	10.9	16.0	11.5	do.
San Diego County	37424	179.8	163.9	124.5	67.0	37.3	68.4	15.4	28.8	54.6	21.5	10.2	15.6	12.4	do.
Sespe River, Ventura County	36467	176.5	163.2	128.0	64.5	37.3	70.3	16.9	28.8	55.3	22.5	11.1	15.8	12.2	do.
Wawona	23653	181.6	164.4	122.4	66.3	37.5	69.0	16.8	27.4	54.9	21.0	10.2	15.4	11.9	do.
Average		179.5	164.0	125.3	66.2	37.1	69.3	16.4	27.7	54.5	21.6	10.5	15.6	11.9	
F. c. kaibabensis:															
Arizona—															
Kaibab National Forest	243472	189.6	171.7	127.5	68.2	41.3	75.0	16.2	27.2	58.5	21.5	11.0	15.8	12.5	
Nevada—															
Egan Range	230705	191.5	178.0	126.4	68.0	37.7	71.0	16.0	27.2	56.0	21.2	10.3	15.4	11.8	
Sunnyside	224569	184.5	169.0	120.5	65.0	35.4	62.4	14.0	28.0	56.2	21.0	10.7	15.5	11.3	
Utah—															
Modena	223997	194.2	176.8	131.7	67.3	39.5	68.7	18.0	28.3	58.0	22.8	10.5	16.4	12.5	
Pine Valley Mountains	171131	186.5	171.0	128.8	65.0	37.6	75.2	15.9	27.4	55.4	22.0	11.0	16.4	12.7	
Average		189.3	173.3	127.0	66.7	38.3	70.5	16.0	27.6	56.8	21.7	10.7	15.9	12.2	
F. c. browni:															
Baja California—															
Tres Posos (18 miles south)	203131	173.4	159.0	124.0		37.3	67	15.1	27.5	55.9				12.8	

274

F. c. improcera:

Subspecies / Locality	No.												Type—Mus. Comp. Zool.
F. c. improcera:													
Baja California—Calmalli	12704	183.0	166	123.6	37.5	68.4	17.3	27.5	59.3	20.3	10.6	15.5	11.4
Miraflores	10652	----	----	126.2	39.4	70.7	17.3	27.5	54.8	20.6	10.6	15.5	11.4
Average		183.0	166	124.9	38.5	69.6	17.3	27.5	57.1	20.5	10.6	15.5	11.4
F. c. azteca:													
Chihuahua—Colonia Garcia	117073	174.5	162.3	124.1	36.2	70.7	17.0	27.9	54.3	21.2	10.8	16.3	12.3
Do.	117074	170.5	160.2	117.9	34.1	64.2	15.7	28.3	52.9	20.0	9.9	14.7	10.5
Do.	117075	175.7	165.7	127.2	36.9	71.8	15.4	28.8	54.4	20.3	10.2	15.7	10.7
Do.	117077	176.3	165.0	119.4	34.0	66.8	16.3	28.0	56.0	22.0	10.2	15.5	10.8
Do.	130984	173.5	163.7	120.0	34.8	70.4	18.0	28.3	55.0	20.0	10.5	15.8	11.2
Do.	117080	172.2	157.8	117.7	34.0	65.7	19.3	28.6	55.5	21.5	11.0	15.8	11.5
Pacheco River	99661	179.0	161.8	117.4	34.9	67.8	14.9	27.5	53.2	19.6	11.5	16.2	11.8
Average		174.5	162.3	120.5	35.0	68.2	16.7	28.2	54.5	20.7	10.6	15.6	11.3
F. c. stanleyana:													
Texas—Bruni Ranch (near Bruni)	251418	190.7	172.0	122.4	34.4	64.2	14.8	26.5	57.1	21.9	10.2	16.3	12.5
Catarina	261616	186.4	169.0	126.1	39.8	73.3	18.4	27.8	58.0	21.5	10.7	16.9	13.0
Catarina (30 miles southwest)	262476	182.5	168.7	121.4	35.6	71.2	17.1	27.3	58.1	21.9	10.5	15.7	12.7
Do.	263860	185.5	167.4	124.5	39.0	74.2	18.0	27.3	56.1	21.2	10.6	15.6	12.3
Encinal	261615	190.9	171.4	123.2	37.6	72.5	16.1	27.6	57.5	20.7	10.2	15.7	12.7
Do.	251468	190.8	170.9	123.0	37.5	72.9	16.3	27.5	57.8	20.8	10.2	15.6	12.9
Average		187.8	169.9	123.4	37.3	71.4	16.8	27.3	57.3	21.3	10.4	16.0	12.7
F. c. corpi:													
Florida—Chokoloskee	19855	177.7	160.3	119.9	35.8	70.7	17.3	26.0	53.9	21.9	12.2	16.2	12.4	Mus. Comp. Zool.
Marco	4341	173.2	156.3	119.7	35.5	71.6	16.2	24.5	52.5	21.7	12.2	15.0	11.7	Univ. Wis.
Sebastian	5489	186.4	170.4	126.2	39.1	76.0	20.5	26.5	55.0	23.2	11.7	16.4	12.4	Mus. Comp. Zool.
Do.	5650	189.4	171.0	125.0	39.0	73.3	21.0	27.2	56.2	22.5	11.6	16.0	12.5	do.
Do.	7743	185.9	167.3	123.5	36.2	68.9	18.7	26.5	54.2	22.0	11.2	16.2	11.2	do.
Average		182.5	165.1	122.9	37.1	72.1	18.7	26.1	54.4	22.3	11.8	15.9	12.0
F. c. mayensis:													
Guatemala—Libertad, Peten	244857	160.4	147.5	107.9	31.8	62.0	13.0	21.0	50.5	20.5	9.8	15.0	12.0
F. c. costaricensis:													
Panama—Boquete	10118	161.0	148.4	111.7	31.7	66.2	12.4	22.1	49.9	18.9	9.8	14.3	10.5	Type—Mus. Comp. Zool.
Do.	172990	158.9	145.2	114.3	31.0	71.7	12.4	24.0	48.8	18.9	9.8	14.3	10.5
Average		160.0	146.8	113.0	31.3	64.0	12.4	23.0	49.4	18.9	9.8	14.3	10.5
F. c. bangsi:													
Colombia—Santa Marta Mountains	8147	165.0	151.3	114.9	31.2	64.5	10.8	24.5	52.2	19.6	9.7	14.5	11.4	Mus. Comp. Zool.
F. c. sodersiromi:													
Ecuador—No measurements													

Table 13. Cranial measurements of *adult females* of subspecies of *Felis concolor* (*Continued*)
(In U. S. National Museum, unless otherwise indicated[1])

Subspecies and locality	No.	Greatest length	Condylobasal length	Zygomatic breadth	Height of cranium	Interorbital breadth	Postorbital processes	Width of nasals	Width of palate	Maxillary tooth row alveolar length	Upper carnassial crown length	Upper carnassial crown width	Lower carnassial crown length	Upper canine antero-posterior diameter	Remarks
F. c. anthonyi:															
Brazil—															
No measurements															
F. c. incarum:															
Peru—															
No measurements															
F. c. capricornensis:															
Brazil—															
Vicinity of Sao Paulo	100120	163.5	152.0	------	59.2	31.1	------	17.4	25.6	52.4	21.9	10.8	17.4	11.0	
F. c. borbensis:															
Brazil—															
Rosarinho, Rio Madeira	92205	166.0	150.5	107.2	62.2	29.6	58.3	15.1	23.4	50.5	20.8	9.5	14.5	10.3	Amer. Mus. Nat. Hist.
Tatu, Rio Negro	78554	158.3	150.0	113.9	60.0	31.5	67.5	12.3	24.0	50.5	20.2	9.4	16.0	9.8	do.
Average		162.2	150.3	110.6	61.1	30.6	62.9	13.7	23.7	50.5	20.5	9.4	15.3	10.1	
F. c. osgoodi:															
Bolivia—															
No measurements															
F. c. greeni:															
Brazil—															
No measurements															
F. c. puma:															
Chile—															
No measurements															
F. c. cabrerae:															
Argentina—															
No measurements															
F. c. pearsoni:															
Argentina—															
Coy Inlet	194465	201.0	183.3	138.5	71.0	44.0	79.0	18.5	31.4	62.5	24.4	11.7	18.3	14.4	
Santa Cruz	20918	184.3	171.0	125.2	65.0	46.8	65.0	20.8	28.0	55.5	22.8	11.2	17.3	14.0	
Do.	100117	188.9	172.2	------	64.5	40.3	73.0	18.5	29.8	58.0	22.7	9.8	17.2	13.5	
Average		191.4	175.5	131.9	66.8	43.7	72.3	19.3	29.7	58.7	23.3	10.9	17.6	14.0	

[1]For explanation of measurements see p. 191.

PHOTOGRAPHS OF SKULLS OF PUMAS

[All skulls in U.S. National Museum unless
otherwise indicated; one-fourth natural
size unless otherwise indicated.]

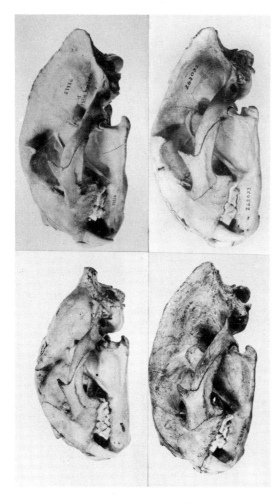

Plate 46. Top: *Felis concolor capricornensis*, sub. sp. nov.; topotype; male adult; Piracicaba, Sao Paulo, Brazil. (No. 100118)

Bottom: *Felis concolor missoulensis* Goldman; type; male adult; Sleeman Creek, 10 miles southwest of Missoula, Mont. (No. 262116) Note large size and posterior ending of jugal well in front of glenoid fossa.

Plate 47. Top: *Felis concolor hippolestes* Merriam; type; male adult; Wind River Mountains, near Cora, Wyo. (No. 57936) Note large size and retreating anterior frontal profile. Bottom: *Felis concolor oregonensis* Rafinesque; male adult; Lake Chelan, Wash. (No. 263033) Note high anterior frontal profile.

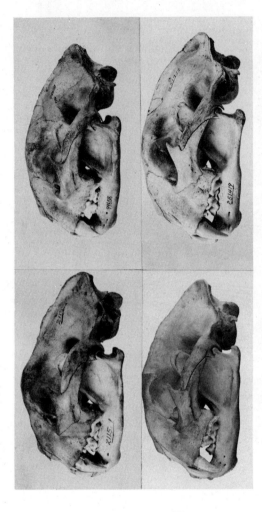

Plate 48. Top: *Felis concolor vancouverensis* Nelson and Goldman; type; male adult; Campbell Lake, Vancouver Island, British Columbia. (No. 211519) Note extreme height of frontal profile.

Bottom: *Felis concolor californica* [May]; male adult; Sequoia National Park, Tulare County, Calif. (No. 33558, Mus. Vert. Zool.) Note medium size and receding frontal profile.

Plate 49. Top: *Felis concolor azteca* Merriam; type; male adult; Colonia Garcia, Chihuahua, Mexico. (No. 99658) Note medium size.

Bottom: *Felis concolor stanleyana* Goldman; type; male adult; Bruni Ranch, near Bruni, Tex. (No. 251419) Note rather large size.

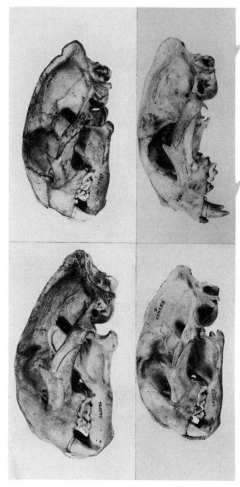

Plate 50. Top: *Felis concolor coryi* Bangs; male adult; Immokalee, Collier County, Fla. (No. 265596) Note high frontal profile anteriorly.
Bottom: *Felis concolor mayensis* Nelson and Goldman; type; male adult; La Libertad, Petén, Guatemala. (No. 244856).
Note very small size.

Plate 51. Top: *Felis concolor costaricensis* Merriam; male adult; Pacuare, Costa Rica. (No. 15967) Note shortness of jugal, ending posteriorly in front of glenoid fossa.
Bottom: *Felis concolor anthonyi* Nelson and Goldman; type; male adult; Mount Duida, Venezuela. (No. 76935, Amer. Mus. Nat. Hist.) Note jugal underlapping squamosal posteriorly to glenoid fossa.

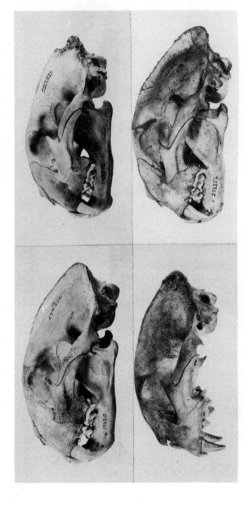

Plate 52. Top: *Felis concolor incarum* Nelson and Goldman; type; male adult; Piscocucho, Department of Cuzco, Peru. (No. 194310)
Bottom: *Felis concolor borbensis* Nelson and Goldman; type; male adult; Borba, Rio Madeira, Amazonas, Brazil. (No. 92298, Amer. Mus. Nat. Hist.)

Plate 53. Top: *Felis concolor greeni* Nelson and Goldman; type; male adult; Curras Novos, Rio Grande do Norte, Brazil. (No. 249896) Note small size and low frontal profile.
Bottom: *Felis concolor acrocodia* Goldman; type; male adult; Descalvados, Matto Grosso, Brazil. (No. 273256). Note high frontal profile.

280

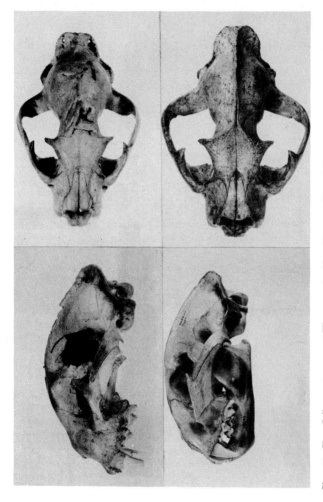

Plate 54. Top: *Felis concolor pearsoni* Thomas; male old; Rio Coy, Territory of Santa Cruz, Argentina. (No. 17437, Amer. Mus. Nat. Hist.)

Bottom: *Felis concolor patagonica* Merriam; type; male young adult; Lake Pueyrredon (east side), Territory of Santa Cruz, Argentina. (No. 108693)

Plate 55. Top: *Felis concolor capricornensis*, subsp. nov.; topotype; male adult; Piracicaba, Sao Paulo, Brazil. (No. 100118) Note posteriorly rounded nasals, and absence of a distinct notch at antorbital foramen.

Bottom: *Felis concolor missoulensis* Goldman; type; male adult; Sleeman Creek, 10 miles southwest of Missoula, Mont. (No. 262116) Note large size, great breadth, and presence of a distinct notch at antorbital foramen.

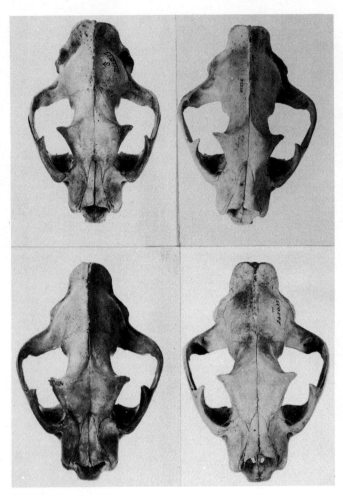

Plate 56. Top: *Felis concolor hippolestes* Merriam; type; male adult; Wind River Mountains, near Cora, Wyo. (No. 57936) Note large size, elongated outlines, and narrow supraoccipital shield.

Bottom: *Felis concolor oregonensis* Rafinesque; male adult; Lake Chelan, Wash. (No. 263033) Note large size, and rather broad supraoccipital shield.

Plate 57. Top: *Felis concolor vancouverensis* Nelson and Goldman; type; male adult; Campbell Lake, Vancouver Island, British Columbia. (No. 211519) Note large size, deep frontal pit and wide supraoccipital shield.

Bottom: *Felis concolor californica* [May]; male adult; Sequoia National Park, Tulare County, Calif. (No. 33558, Mus. Vert. Zool.) Note medium size, and narrow supraoccipital shield.

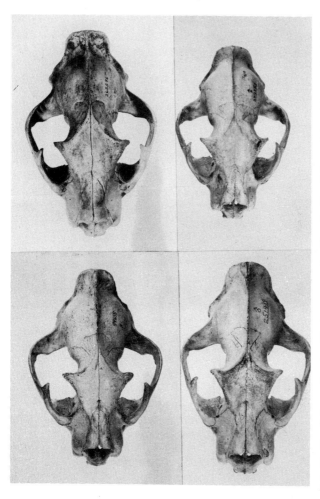

Plate 58. Top: *Felis concolor azteca* Merriam; type; male adult; Colonia Garcia, Chihuahua, Mexico. (No. 99658) Note medium size.
Bottom: *Felis concolor stanleyana* Goldman; type; male adult; Bruni Ranch, near Bruni, Tex. (No. 251419) Note relative narrowness.

Plate 59. Top: *Felis concolor coryi* Bangs; male adult; Immokalee, Collier County, Fla. (No. 265596) Note broad, prominent nasals.
Bottom: *Felis concolor mayensis* Nelson and Goldman; type; male adult: La Libertad, Petén, Guatemala. (No. 244856) Note very small size.

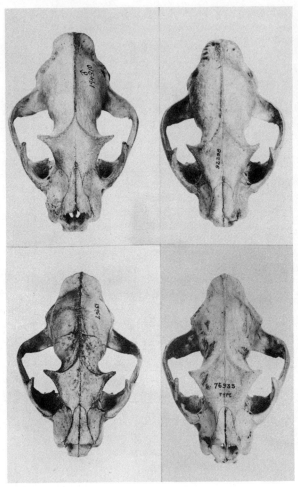

Plate 60. Top: *Felis concolor costaricensis* Merriam; male adult; Pacuare, Costa Rica. (No. 15967) Note small size, and long postorbital processes.
Bottom: *Felis concolor anthonyi* Nelson and Goldman; type; male adult; Mount Duida, Venezuela. (No. 76935, Amer. Mus. Nat. Hist.)

Plate 61. Top: *Felis concolor incarum* Nelson and Goldman; type; male adult; Piscocucho, Department of Cuzco, Peru. (No. 194310) Note posteriorly attenuate nasals.
Bottom: *Felis concolor borbensi* Nelson and Goldman; type; male adult; Borba, Rio Madeira, Amazonas, Brazil. (No. 92298, Amer. Mus. Nat. Hist.) Note deep V-shaped median depression of nasals anteriorly.

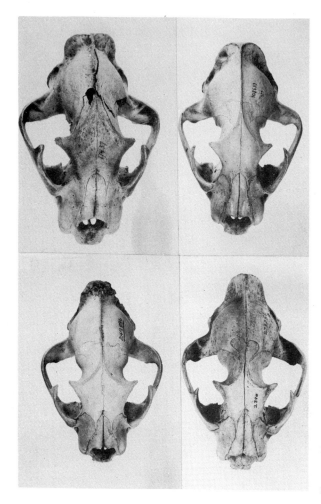

Plate 62. Top: *Felis concolor greeni* Nelson and Goldman; type; male adult; Curraes Novos, Rio Grande do Norte, Brazil. (No. 249896) Note small size. Bottom: *Felis concolor acrocodia* Goldman; type; male adult; Descalvados, Matto Grosso, Brazil. (No. 273256) Note slender proportions.

Plate 63. Top: *Felis concolor pearsoni* Thomas; male old; Rio Coy, Territory of Santa Cruz, Argentina. (No. 17437, Amer. Mus. Nat. Hist.) Note posteriorly rounded nasals. Bottom: *Felis concolor patagonica* Merriam; type; male young adult; Lake Pueyrredon (east side), Territory of Santa Cruz, Argentina. (No. 108693) Note posteriorly narrow nasals.

285

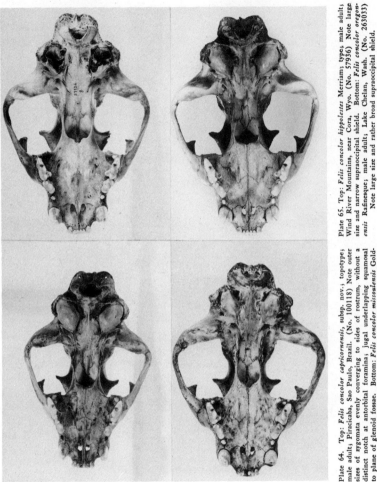

Plate 64. Top: *Felis concolor capricornensis*, subsp. nov.; topotype; male adult; Piracicaba, Sao Paulo, Brazil. (No. 100118) Note outer sizes of zygomata evenly converging to sides of rostrum, without a distinct notch at antorbital foramina; jugal underlapping squamosal to plane of glenoid fossae. Bottom: *Felis concolor missoulensis* Goldman; types; male adult; Sleeman Creek, 10 miles southwest of Missoula, Mont. (No. 262116) Note large size, distinct notch at anterior ends of zygomata, and jugal ending posteriorly in front of plane of glenoid fossae.

Plate 65. Top: *Felis concolor hippolestes* Merriam; type; male adult; Wind River Mountains, near Cora, Wyo. (No. 57936) Note large size and narrow supraoccipital shield. Bottom: *Felis concolor oregonensis* Rafinesque; male adult; Lake Chelan, Wash. (No. 263033) Note large size and rather broad supraoccipital shield.

286

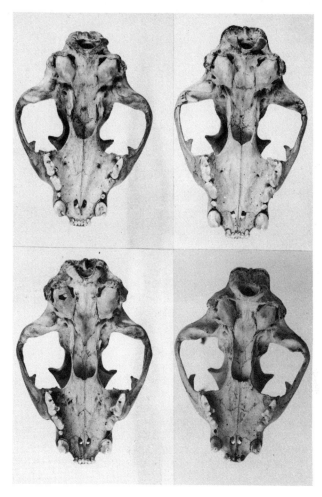

Plate 66. Top: *Felis concolor vancouverensis* Nelson and Goldman; type; male adult; Campbell Lake, Vancouver Island, British Columbia. (No. 211519) Note large size, and wide supraoccipital shield.
Bottom: *Felis concolor californica* [May]; male adult; Sequoia National Park, Tulare County, Calif. (No. 33558, Mus. Vert. Zool.) Note medium size and rather narrow supraoccipital shield.

Plate 67. Top: *Felis concolor azteca* Merriam; type; male adult; Colonia Garcia, Chihuahua, Mexico. (No. 99658) Note medium size.
Bottom: *Felis concolor stanleyana* Goldman; type; male adult; Bruni Ranch, near Bruni, Tex. (No. 251419) Note relative narrowness.

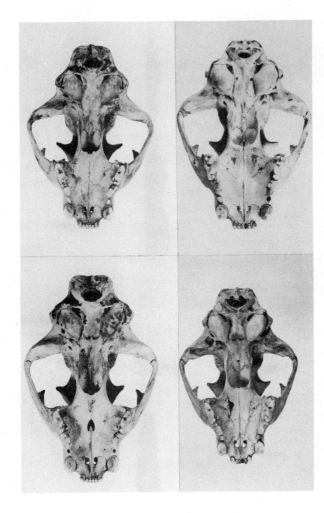

Plate 68. Top: *Felis concolor coryi* Bangs; male adult; Immokalee, Collier County, Fla. (No. 265596) Bottom: *Felis concolor mayensis* Nelson and Goldman; type; male adult; La Libertad, Petén, Guatemala. (No. 244856) Note very small size.

Plate 69. Top: *Felis concolor costaricensis* Merriam; male adult; Pacuare, Costa Rica. (No. 15967) Note small size. Bottom: *Felis concolor anthonyi* Nelson and Goldman; type; male adult; Mount Duida, Venezuela. (No. 76935, Amer. Mus. Nat. Hist.)

288

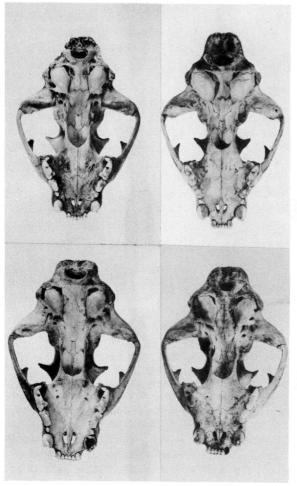

Plate 70. Top: *Felis concolor incarum* Nelson and Goldman; type; male adult; Piscocucho, Department of Cuzco, Peru. (No. 194310)
Bottom: *Felis concolor borbensis* Nelson and Goldman; type; male adult; Borba, Rio Madeira, Amazonas, Brazil. (No. 92298, Amer. Mus. Nat. Hist.)

Plate 71. Top: *Felis concolor greeni* Nelson and Goldman; type; male adult; Curraes Novos, Rio Grande do Norte, Brazil. (No. 249896) Note small size.
Bottom: *Felis concolor acrocodia* Goldman; type; male adult; Descalvados, Matto Grosso, Brazil. (No. 273256) Note slender proportions

289

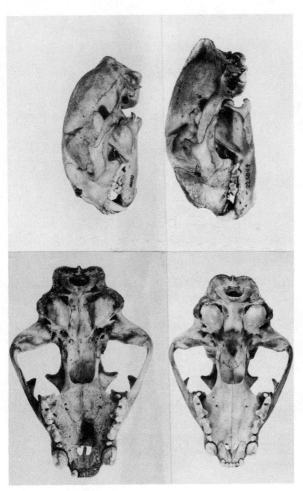

Plate 72. Top: *Felis concolor pearsoni* Thomas; male old; Rio Coy, Territory of Santa Cruz, Argentina. (No. 17437, Amer. Mus. Nat. Hist.) Note large teeth, zygomata gradually converging anteriorly to sides of rostrum, and jugals extending posteriorly to plane of glenoid fossae, compared with North American races.

Bottom: *Felis concolor patagonica* Merriam; type; male young adult; Lake Pueyrredon (east side), Territory of Santa Cruz, Argentina. (No. 108693) Note comparatively slender proportions.

Plate 73. Top: *Felis concolor capricornensis*, subsp. nov.; female adult; probably vicinity of Sao Paulo, Brazil. (No. 100120) Note jugal underlapping squamosal posteriorly to glenoid fossa.

Bottom: *Felis concolor missoulensis* Goldman; female adult; Crowsnest Pass (near Edgewood), Kootenay District, British Columbia. (No. 225044) Note posterior ending of jugal in front of glenoid fossa.

290

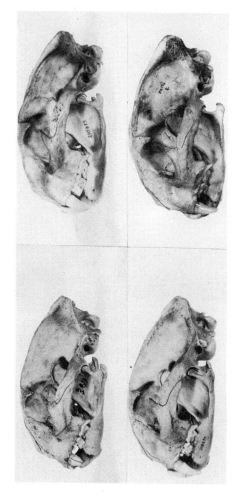

Plate 74. Top: *Felis concolor couguar* Kerr; female adult; Essex County, N. Y. (No. 3811) Bottom: *Felis concolor hippolestes* Merriam; female adult; Meeker, Colo. (No. 108690)

Plate 75. Top: *Felis concolor oregonensis* Rafinesque; female adult; Mount Rainier National Park, Wash. (No. 245683) Note high anterior frontal profile. Bottom: *Felis concolor vancouverensis* Nelson and Goldman; female adult; Vancouver Island, British Columbia. (No. 56176) Note extreme height of frontal region.

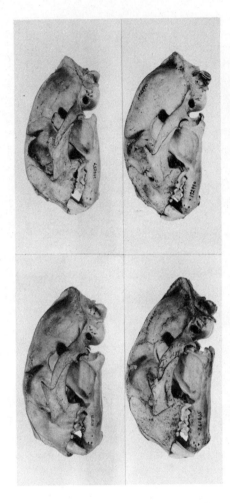

Plate 76. Top: *Felis concolor azteca* Merriam; topotype; female adult; Colonia Garcia, Chihuahua, Mexico. (No. 117073) Note medium size. Bottom: *Felis concolor stanleyana* Goldman; type; female adult; Encinal, Tex. (No. 261615) Note rather large size.

Plate 77. Top: *Felis concolor mayensis* Nelson and Goldman; topotype; female adult; La Libertad, Petén, Guatemala. (No. 244857) Note very small size. Bottom: *Felis concolor costaricensis* Merriam; female adult; Boquete, Panama. (No. 172990) Note small size, and low frontal profile.

292

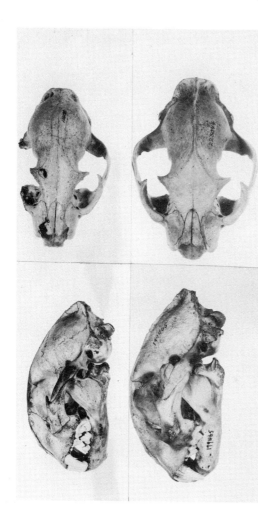

Plate 78. Top: *Felis concolor acrocodia* Goldman; topo-type; female adult; Descalvados, Matto Grosso, Brazil. (No. 28334, Chicago Nat. Hist. Mus.)

Bottom: *Felis concolor pearsoni* Thomas; female adult; Coy Inlet, Territory of Santa Cruz, Argentina. (No. 199465) Note large size, and jugal underlapping squamosal posteriorly to glenoid fossa, in contrast with North American races.

Plate 79. Top: *Felis concolor capricornensis*, subsp. nov.; female adult; probably vicinity of Sao Paulo, Brazil. (No. 100120) Note nasals deeply V-shaped in cross section an-teriorly, and absence of a distinct notch at antorbital foramen. Bottom: *Felis concolor missoulensis* Goldman; female adult; Crowsnest Pass (near Edgewood), Kootenay District, Brit-ish Columbia. (No. 225044). Note large size, great breadth, and excavated lateral border at antorbital foramen, compared with South American races.

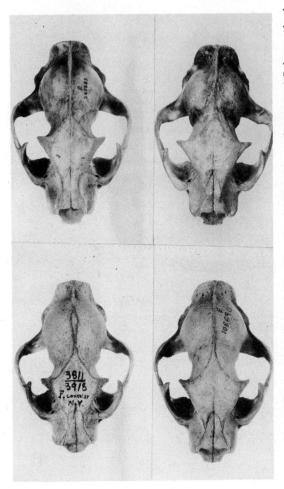

Plate 80. Top: *Felis concolor couguar* Kerr; female adult; Essex County, N. Y. (No. 3811) Relatively short and wide. Bottom: *Felis concolor hippolestes* Merriam; female adult; Meeker, Colo. (No. 108690) Relatively narrow and elongated.

Plate 81. Top: *Felis concolor oregonensis* Rafinesque; female adult; Mount Rainier National Park, Wash. (No. 245683) Note large size and moderately broad supraoccipital shield. Bottom: *Felis concolor vancouverensis* Nelson and Goldman; female adult; Vancouver Island, British Columbia. (No. 56176) Note large size, deep frontal pit and very broad supraoccipital shield.

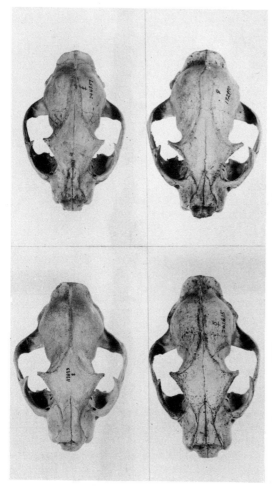

Plate 82. Top: *Felis concolor azteca* Merriam; topotoype; female adult; Colonia Garcia, Chihuahua, Mexico. (No. 117073) Note medium size. Bottom: *Felis concolor stanleyana* Goldman; type; female adult; Encinal, Tex. (No. 261615) Note relative narrowness.

Plate 83. Top: *Felis concolor mayensis* Nelson and Goldman; topotype; female adult; La Libertad, Petén, Guatemala. (No. 244857) Note very small size. Bottom: *Felis concolor costaricensis* Merriam; female adult; Boquete, Panama. (No. 172990) Note small size and long postorbital processes.

295

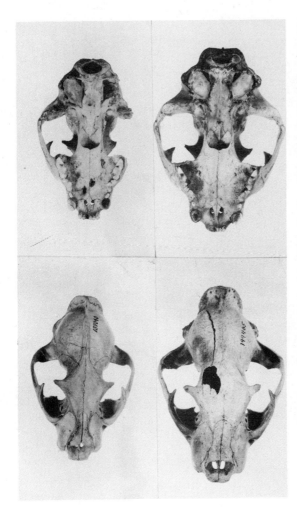

Plate 84 Top: *Felis concolor concolor* Linné; female adult; Caura Valley, Venezuela. (No. 137040) Note laterally compressed ascending branches of maxillae, and narrow nasals. Bottom: *Felis concolor pearsoni* Thomas; female adult; Coy Inlet, Territory of Santa Cruz, Argentina. (No. 199465) Note large size, absence of frontal pit, zygomata gradually converging anteriorly to sides of rostrum, and broad, posteriorly rounded nasals.

Plate 85. Top: *Felis concolor capricornensis*, subsp. nov.; female adult; probably vicinity of Sao Paulo, Brazil. (No. 100120) Note jugal underlapping squamosal to plane of glenoid fossae.
Bottom: *Felis concolor missoulensis* Goldman; female adult; Crows Nest Pass (near Edgewood), Kootenay District, British Columbia. (No. 225044) Note large size, great breadth, and jugal ending posteriorly in front of plane of glenoid fossae.

296

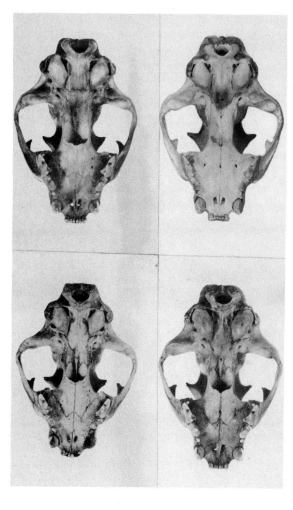

Plate 86. Top: *Felis concolor couguar* Kerr; female adult; Essex County, N. Y. (No. 3811) Relatively short and wide. Bottom: *Felis concolor hippolestes* Merriam; female adult; Meeker, Colo. (No. 108690) Relatively narrow and elongated.

Plate 87. Top: *Felis concolor oregonensis* Rafinesque; female adult; Mount Rainier National Park, Wash. (No. 245683) Note large size and moderately broad supraoccipital shield.

Bottom: *Felis concolor vancouverensis* Nelson and Goldman; female adult; Vancouver Island, British Columbia. (No. 56175) Note large size, and very broad supraoccipital shield.

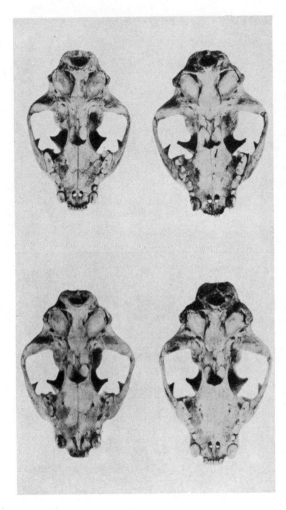

Plate 88. Top: *Felis concolor azteca* Merriam; topotype; female adult; Colonia Garcia, Chihuahua, Mexico. (No. 117073) Note medium size.
Bottom: *Felis concolor stanleyana* Goldman; female adult; Encinal, Tex. (No. 261615) Note relative narrowness and elongation.

Plate 89. Top: *Felis concolor mayensis* Nelson and Goldman; topotype; female adult; La Libertad, Petén, Guatemala. (No. 244857) Note very small size.
Bottom: *Felis concolor costaricensis* Merriam; female adult; Boquete, Panama. (No. 172990). Note small size and long postorbital processes.

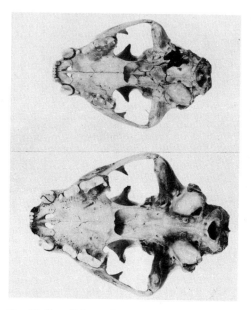

Plate 90, Top: *Felis concolor concolor Linné* female adult; Caura Valley, Venezuela. (No. 137040) Note small size and ending of jugal near anterior plane of glenoid fossae.

Bottom: *Felis concolor pearsoni* Thomas; female adult; Coy Inlet, Territory of Santa Cruz, Argentina. (No. 199465) Note large size, zygomata gradually converging to sides of rostrum, and jugals extending posteriorly well into plane of glenoid fossae.

Plate 91

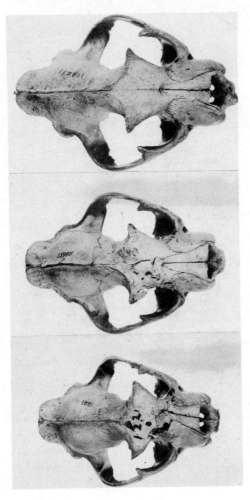

Felis concolor californica [May]; male adult; Monterey, Calif. (No. 1221) Note evidence of injuries.

Felis concolor hippolestes Merriam; male adult; Meeker, Colo. (No. 108-682) Note evidence of frontal injuries.

Felis concolor hippolestes Merriam; male adult; Meeker, Colo. (No. 108681) Note evidence of nasal and premaxillary injuries, and extremely large size (this is the largest of all skulls of Felis concolor examined).

300

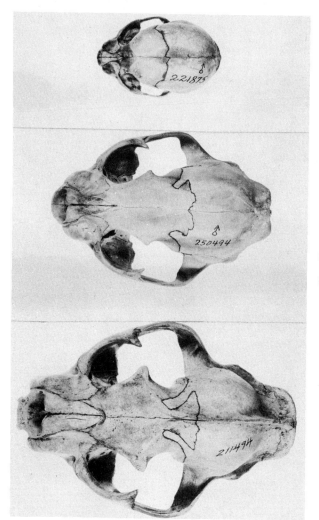

Plate 92
[One-third natural size]

Felis concolor azteca Merriam; male young adult; Clifton, Ariz. (No. 211494) Note full development of bregmatic processes of frontals.

Felis concolor olympus Merriam; male young; Matheny River, Jefferson County, Wash. (No. 250494) Note progressive development of bregmatic processes of frontals.

Felis concolor californica [May]; male very young; Grant's Pass, Oreg. (No. 221-875) Note early condition of bregmatic processes of frontals.

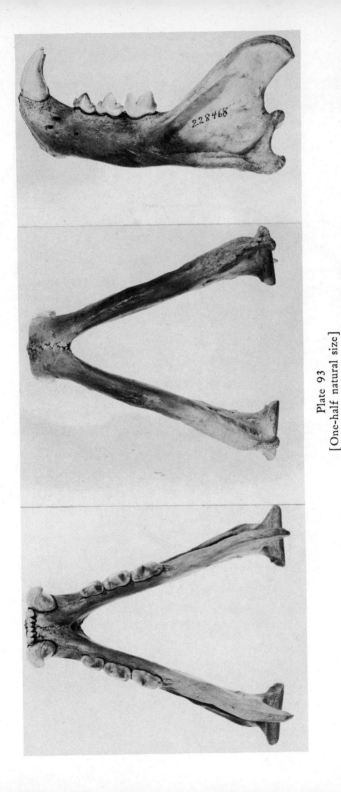

Plate 93

[One-half natural size]

Felis concolor stanleyana Goldman; male adult; Sheffield, Tex. (No. 228468) Note U-shaped space between jaws. (Left, left side; Center, upper, and Right, lower views of ramus.)

XVI

REFERENCES AND SELECTED
BIBLIOGRAPHY

Abert, J. W.
   1845-1846. Journal of J. W. Abert from Bent's fort to St. Louis in 1845.
      U. S. Senate Doc. 8 (377-438): 57; 29th Congr., 1st Sess.
Acosta, José de
   1940. Historia natural y moral de las Indies. Ed. prepared by Edmunds
      O'Gorman, and transcribed from original edition of 1590. Mexico
      638 pp.: 321-322.
Adams, A. Leith
   1873. Field and forest rambles with notes and observations on the natural
      history of eastern Canada. London, 33 pp., illus.; 59. Dist.
      Canada, New Brunswick.
Adams, Charles C.
   1926. The economic and social importance of animals in forestry. Roosevelt
      Wildlife Bull. 3 (4): 505-699; 591-592.
Adams, Samuel Hopkins
   1900. The training of lions, tigers, and other great cats. McClure's Magazine
      15 (5): 387-398; illus. by Charles R. Knight. September.
Aldrich, John Warren, and Benjamin Patterson Bole, Jr.
   1937. The birds and mammals of the western slope of the Azuero Penin-
      sula [Republic of Panama.] Sci. Publ. Cleve. Mus. Nat. Hist. 7:
      160. Cleveland, Ohio, August 31.
Alfaro, Anastasio
   1897. Mamiferos de Costa Rica. La primera exposicion Centroamericana,
      San José, Costa Rica. Museo Nacional, pp. 51: 17.
Allen, Glover M.
   1904. Fauna of New England. Occas. Papers, Bost. Soc. Nat. Hist. 7: 21.

1942.   Extinct and vanishing mammals of the western hemisphere. Spec. Publ. American Committee for Intern. Wildlife Prot. 11 (Dec. 11), pp. xv + 620; illus.: 233-252.

Allen, J. A.
1869.   Catalogue of the mammals of Massachusetts; with a critical revision of the species. Bull. Mus. Comp. Zool. 8: 153. Cambridge, Mass.

1869.   On the mammals of Iowa. Proc. Bost. Soc. Nat. Hist. 13 (Dec. 15): 3-18; 5-6.

1871.   On the mammals and winter birds of east Florida. Bull. Mus. Comp. Zool. 2 (3): 161, 168. Cambridge, Mass.

1871.   The fauna of the prairies. Amer. Nat. 5: 4-9; 5.

1874.   Notes on the mammals of portions of Kansas, Colorado, Wyoming, and Utah. Bull. Essex Inst. 6 (Mar. and Apr.): 53.

1876.   The former range of some New England carnivorous mammals. Amer. Nat. 10: 708-715; 709.

1876.   Geographic variation among North American mammals, especially in respect to size. U. S. Geol. & Geog. Surv. Terr. 2 (4): 321-322. Dept. of Interior, Wash., D. C., July 1.

1894.   On the mammals of Aransas County, Texas, with descriptions of new forms of *Lepus* and *Oryzomys*. Bull. Amer. Mus. Nat. Hist 6 (Art. 6): 165-198; 198. May 31.

1895.   On a collection of mammals from Arizona and Mexico, made by W. W. Price, with field notes by the collector. Bull. Amer. Mus. Nat. Hist. 7 (Art. 6): 192-258; 253-254. June 29.

1896.   On the mammals collected in Bexar County and vicinity, Texas, by H. P. Attwater, with field notes by the collector. Bull. Amer. Mus. Nat. Hist. 8 (Art. 5): 47-80; 80. April 22.

1904.   Report on mammals from the district of Santa Marta, Columbia, collected by Herbert Smith, with field notes by Mr. Smith. Bull. Amer. Mus. Nat. Hist. 20: 407-468; 445.

1905.   Reports of Princeton University expeditions to Patagonia, 1896-1899; J. B. Hatcher, in charge. Ed. by Wm. B. Scott. Zoology 3 (Part 1, Mammalia of southern Patagonia): 1-210; 171-173, 177; pl. i-xxix. Princeton, N. J.

1916. Mammals collected on the Roosevelt Brazilian expedition; with field notes by George E. Miller. Bull. Amer. Mus. Nat. Hist. 35 (Art. 30): 559-610; 579. Aug. 9.

Allen, Paul

1814. History of the expedition under the command of Captains Lewis and Clark to the sources of the Missouri, thence across the Rocky Mountains and down the river Columbia to the Pacific Ocean, performed during the years 1804-5-6. By order of the Government of the United States. 2 vols. Philadelphia. Bradford and Inskeep and A. B. M. H. Inskeep, New York. J. Maxwell, printer. Vol. 2: 99, 178.

Alston, Edward R.

1879-1882. Biologia Centrali-Americana. Mammalia. 220 pp.; 22 pls.: 62-63.

Altsheler, Brent

1936. Natural history index guide. H. M. Wilson Co., Inc., New York. Sec. 2, Zool.—Biol.; Div. 1, Mammals: 120, 131, 135, 136.

Ames, A. E.

1874. Mammalia of Minnesota. Bull. Minn. Acad. Nat. Sci.: 68-71; 69.

Ames, C. H.

1901. Maine panthers again. Forest & Stream 56 (20): 385. May 18.

Anderson, Rudolph Martin

1934. The distribution, abundance, and economic importance of the game and furbearing mammals of western North America. Proc. Fifth Pac. Sci. Congr.: 4055-4075; 4060; 17 maps (1933). Victoria & Vancouver. Univ. of Toronto Press.

1937. Fauna of Canada. Canada Yearbook: 29-52; 42. Dominion Bureau of Statistics, [Ottawa.]

1938. Mammals of the Province of Quebec. Sociéte Provancher d'Hist. Nat. Canada, Ann. Rept. Quebec, Canada: 69. Ottawa.

André Eugène

1904. A naturalist in the Guianas. New York & London, i-xiv; 1-310, illus.; 271, 277.

Anonymous

1830a. Encounter with a panther. Cab. Nat. Hist. 1: 137-140.
1830b. The cougar. Cab. Nat. Hist. 1: 243-245. [Aud. Amer. Ornith. Biog.]

1850. Editorial—Frontier Palladium, Malone, New York. Aug. 1.

1868. Killing of panther, Franklin, Franklin County, N. Y. Malone Palladium, Jan. 2.

1875. A Texas panther hunt. Forest & Stream 4 (2): 19. Feb. 18.

1878.   Adirondack panthers. Forest & Stream 10: 138.

1879a.   The Mexican lion. Forest & Stream 12: 294.
1879b.   A panther hunt. Forest & Stream 12: 157. From Knickerbocker's Magazine, 1855.

1880a.   Big game near Memphis, Tennessee. Chicago Field 13 (1): 11.

1880b.   Does the panther scream? Forest & Stream 15: 307.

1882a.   The American lion. American Field 17: 411.

1882b.   The jaguar or American tiger. Forest & Stream 19 (17): 127. Sept. 14.

1883a.   Mysterious monster (*Felis concolor*). Forest & Stream 20: 48.
1883b.   Habits of the panther. Forest & Stream 20: 344.
1883c.   White mountain lions. American Field 22: 201.

1884a.   Adventures with cougars. American Field 21: 541.
1884b.   A camp-fire symposium on cats. American Field 21: 86.

1884c.   Habits of the panther. Amer. Nat. 18: 1160-1164.

1885.   An encounter with mountain lions. Amer. Field 24 (21): 486. Nov. 21.

1886a.   [A mountain lion killed near San Buenaventura, Calif.] American Field 25: 343.
1886b.   On the hunting of the puma. Longman's Magazine. September.
1886c.   Montana wolves and panthers. Forest & Stream 26: 508.

1887a.   A large California lion killed near Georgetown, Eldorado Co., Calif. American Field 27: 105.
1887b.   After a panther—Banks of Red River. American Field 28: 390.
1887c.   A combat with a puma. American Field 28: 607.

1888.   Forest and Stream 30: 493.

1894.   The panther in Canada. Biological Review of Ontario 1 (3): 49-50. July. Toronto.
————— [= W. B. May.]
1896.   California game "marked down." So. Pac. Co., San Francisco, 64 pp., 58 illus. (half-tones): 21-22.

1911.   Fierceness of the mountain lion. Forest & Stream 77 (27): 941. Dec. 30.

1914. Kills big cougar. Forest & Stream 83 (20): 629. Nov. 14.

1929-1930. Yearbook on Texas conservation of wildlife. Texas Game, Fish & Oyster Comm., Austin, 110 pp., illus.: 24-27.

1931. Animal life 20 (1): 37. Jan. Illus. animal and nature magazine of Canada; official organ of town and Humane Soc. and Ont. Soc. for Prev. Cruelty to Animals, Toronto.

1940. Documentary material on native protection and wildlife preservation in Latin America. Prep. for use of Comm. of Experts in Nature Protection; May 13-16; Vol. 1 (Pt. 1): 161; 128 (Pt. 2): 30. Pan-American Union, Wash., D. C.

1940. Mountain lion, *Felis concolor hippolestes*. Wyo. Wildlife 5 (1): 6, 13. illus. Jan. Cheyenne.

1942. The mountain lion in "Fading Trails." Prep. by Comm. of U. S. Dept. Int. pp. i-xv; 1-279, illus. The Macmillan Co., New York. 109-117.

1943. Outdoor California. Calif. Div. Fish & Game 3 (27): 1. Jan. 4.

1943. Indiana fur value shown in invoice left by Vigo [Francis] of Vincennes three lifetimes ago. Outdoor Indiana 10 (10): 3, 15. November.

————,
1944. These were former Pennsylvanians. Penna. Game News 15 (9): 21. December.

————,
1945. Market report and news letter, January 30. Arizona Cattle Growers' Asso.

1945a. Lion kills antelope. New Mex. Mag. 23 (8): 27. Albuquerque, August.
1945b. Purring puma. Animals 78 (8): 150. August.
Aplin. O. V.
1894. Field notes on the mammals of Uruguay. Pioc. Zool. Soc. London: 297-315; 298. March 3.
Arnold, Bridgewater
1927. A dictionary of fur names. Nat. Assoc. Fur Industry, New York. P. 17.
Arnold, Oren
1935. Wildlife in the southwest. Banks Upshaw & Co., Dallas, Texas: 12-22.
Audubon, John James, and John Bachman
1851. The viviparous quadrupeds of North America. New York. Vol. 1: 256-257; Vol. 2: 305-313.

Aughey, Samuel
  1880. Sketches of the physical geography and geology of Nebraska. Omaha: 119.
Austin, Mary
  1906. The flock. Houghton-Mifflin Co., Cambridge, Mass.: 183-184.
Azara, Felix de
  1802. Apuntamientos para la historia natural de los quadrupedos del Paraguay y Rio De La Plata. Madrid, 2 vols. Vol. 1: 120, 123, 128.
Bach, Ernest
  1919. Destruction of game by predatory animals. Outdoor Life 43 (3): 166. March.
Bach, Roy N.
  1943. The mountain lion (*Felis hippolestes*) in North Dakota. North Dakota Outdoors 6 (2): 14-15; illus. State Game & Fish Dept. Bismarck, August.
Badianus Manuscript
  1940. An Aztec herbal of 1552. Intro., Trans., and Anno. by Emily Walcott Emmart, with foreword by Henry E. Sigerist. (Codex Barberini Latin 241) Vatican Library. Johns Hopkins Press, Baltimore, 341 pp., illus. 118 color plates reproduced. P. 324.
Bailey, Vernon
  1905. Biological survey of Texas. North Amer. Fauna 25: 162-163. Bur. Biol. Surv., U. S. Dept. Agric., Wash., D. C., 222 pp., illus.

  1926. Biological survey of North Dakota. North Amer. Fauna 49: 146. Bur. Biol. Surv., U. S. Dept. Agric., Wash., D. C., 220 pp., illus.

  1928. Animal life of the Carlsbad Cavern. Amer. Soc. Mammal. Monog. 3: 93-94.

  1930. Animal life of the Yellowstone National Park. Charles C. Thomas, Springfield, Illinois, and Baltimore, Maryland, 241 pp., illus.: 129-131.

  1931. Mammals of New Mexico. North Amer. Fauna 53: 290. Bur. Biol. Surv., U. S. Dept. Agric., Wash., D. C., 412 pp., illus.

  1933. Cave life of Kentucky. Amer. Mid. Nat. 14 (5): 47.

  1935. Mammals of the Grand Canyon region. Grand Canyon Nat. Hist. Assoc. Bull. 1: 29-30; 42 pp., illus.

  1936. The mammals and life zones of Oregon. North Amer. Fauna 55: 263. Bur. Biol. Surv., U. S. Dept. Agric., Wash., D. C. June.
———, William B. Bell, and Melvin A. Brannon
  1914. Preliminary report on the mammals of North Dakota. N. D. Agric. Exper. Sta. Circ. 3: 16. Agric. College, N. D., 20 pp.

Baird, Spencer Fullerton
1857. General report of the North American mammals, including descriptions of all known species chiefly contained in The Museum, Smithsonian Inst. J. B. Lippincott & Co., Phila., Pa.: 85-86.

1859. Mammals of the United States and Mexican boundary survey, with notes by the naturalists of the survey. Vol. 2 (Part 2): 5-6; 62 pp.

1859. Mammals of North America. J. B. Lippincott & Co., Phila., Pa.: 83-86; 764 pp. illus. Descriptions of species based chiefly on the collections in the museum of Smiths. Inst., Wash., D. C.

Bakker, M. H.
1918. Roping mountain lions. Outdoor Life 42 (3): 165-168; 7 illus. September.

1921. Experiences of a lion roper. Outdoor Life 43: 171.

Bangs, Outram
1898. The land mammals of peninsula of Florida and the coast region of Georgia. Proc. Bost. Soc. Nat. Hist. 28 (7): 234-235. March, pp. 157-235.

1899. The Florida puma. Proc. Biol. Soc. Wash. 13: 15-17. Jan. 31. New comb.: Felis concolor coryi, p. 15.

1900. List of mammals collected in the Santa Marta region of Colombia by W. W. Brown, Jr., Proc. New Eng. Zool. Club 1: 99. Feb. 23, pp. 87-102.

Barber, Edwin A.
1876. Rock inscriptions of the "Ancient Pueblos" of Colorado, Utah, New Mexico, and Arizona. Amer. Nat. 10: 723. Dec., illus., pp. 716-725.

Barbour, Thomas
1943. Naturalist at large. Pp. i-xii; 1-314; illus., p. 227.

Barker, S. Omar
1944. Mountain memory. New Mexico Mag. 22 (10): 12-13, 29, 31; illus. Albuquerque, October.

Barnes, Claude T.
1922. Mammals of Utah. Bull. Univ. Utah: 107-110. Salt Lake City, Utah, 166 pp.

1927. Utah mammals. Bull. Univ. Utah 17 (12): 68-69. Rev. Ed. June, 183 pp.

Barnes, W. C.
1921. The Bandelier National Monument. Amer. Forestry 27 (333): 562-574; illus. September. Photo. sacred lions of Cochitis of northern N. Mex., p. 570.

Barrere, Pierre
  1741. Eissai sur l'historie naturel France Equinoxiale. Paris, pp. i-xxiv; 1-215.
          Account of the "tigre rouge" (= *F. c. concolor*), p. 166.
Barrett, Robert, and Katherine Barrett
  1931. A Yankee in Patagonia—Edward Chace. Houghton-Mifflin Co., Bos-
          ton and New York; illus. Pp. i-viii; 1-349; p. 81.
Bartlett, A. D.
  1861. Remarks on the breeding of the larger Felidae in captivity. Proc. Zool.
          Soc. London: 140-141; 141.
Bartlett, Charles H.
  1904. Tales of Kankakee Land. Charles Scribner's Sons, New York: 232 pp.,
          illus., 95-97.
Bartram, William
  1928. The travels of William Bartram. Edited by Mark Van Doren; Macy-
          Masius: 34, 63.
Bates, Henry Walter
  1875. Naturalist on the River Amazon. London, John Murray; Boston, Rob-
          erts Bros. Ed. 3: 91-92.
Batty, J. H.
  1874. The Felis Concolor or panther. Amer. Sportsman 4 (4)—New series
          No. 30: 51. Saturday, April 25.
Beebe, William
  1943. Our zoo's former inhabitants. Four mammals and a bird that were
          driven from our grounds long before the Zoological Society took
          possession. Animal Kingdom 46 (5): 111-116; illus. Bull. N. Y.
          Zool. Soc., September-October.
Beechey, F. W.
  1831. Narrative 2: 79.
Belknap, Orin
  1902. Mountain lion and strychnine. Forest and Stream 58 (25): 486. June
          21.
Bell, W. B.
  1920. Hunting down stock killers. Yearbook, U. S. Dept. Agric.: 289-300;
          illus.
Belt, Thomas
  1928. The naturalist in Nicaragua. J. M. Dent & Sons, Ltd., London and
          Toronto; E. P. Dutton & Co., New York. Second Reprint: 306 pp.,
          illus.
Benson, Seth B.
  1935. A biological reconnaissance of Navajo Mountain, Utah. Univ. Calif.
          Pub. Zool. 40 (14): 439-455; 449. Dec. 31.
Beverly, Fred
  1874. The Florida panther. Forest & Stream 3 (19): 290. Dec. 17.
Beverly, Robert
  1705. The history and present state of Virginia. Four parts or books; Book
          4: 73. English version.

1707. Histoire de la Virginie. Thomas Lombrail, Amsterdam, 433 pp.: 417.
Blair, W. Frank
1940. A contribution to the ecology and faunal relationships of the mammals of the Davis Mountain region, southwestern Texas. Misc. Publ. Mus. Zool., Univ. Mich. 46: 25. June 28.
Bole, B. Patterson, Jr., and Philip N. Moulthrop
1942. The Ohio recent mammal collection in the Cleveland Museum of Natural History. Cleve. Mus. Nat. Hist. Sci. Pub. 5 (6): 83-181; 128. Sept.
Boone and Crockett Club
1939. North American big game. Chas. Scribner's Sons, New York and London, 533 pp., illus.: 527. September 12.
Borell, Adrey E., and Monroe D. Bryant
1942. Mammals of the Big Bend area of Texas. Univ. Calif. Pub. Zool. 48 (1): 1-62; 18-19. Berkeley and Los Angeles, Calif., illus.
——————, and Ralph Ellis
1934. Mammals of the Ruby Mountains region of northeastern Nevada. Journ. Mammal. 15 (1): 12-44; 23. February, illus.
Bourke, John G.
1892. On the border with Crook. Chas. Scribner's Sons, New York City. Pp. i-xiii; 1-491; illus.: 39, 40, 111, 116.
Bourne, Benjamin Franklin
1853. The captive in Patagonia, or life among the giants. Gould & Lincoln, Boston, pp. i-xxiv and 1-233; p. 53. Personal narrative, illus.
Bowers, de Mass
1885. A night with a mountain lion. Forest & Stream 25: 46.
Brackett, A. G.
1882. The American lion (Felis concolor). American Field 17: 90.
Brayton, A. W.
1882. Report on the mammalia of Ohio. Geol. Surv. of Ohio 4: 1-185.
Brehaut, Ernest
1912. An encyclopedist of the dark ages, Isidore of Seville. Studies in history, economics, and public law. Edited by faculty of Polit. Sci., Columbia Univ., New York. Longmans, Green & Co., Whole No. 120, Vol. 48 (1): 274 pp.: 225.
Brehm, Alfred C.
1890. Thierleben saugetiere. Vol. 1: 487; illus.
Brimley, C. S.
1939. Mammals of North Carolina. North Carolina Dept. Agric., Div. Entomology: 2.
Brisson, M.
1756. Le regne animal: 2. (Tigre range in Guiana and Brazil.)
British Columbia
1894. Fourth report of Dept. Agric., Prov. British Col., Canada, Victoria. Animal pests: 1126-1131.

1895-1896. Fifth report of Dept. Agric., Prov. British Col., Canada, Victoria. Animal pests: 1167-1177.

1910. Game animals, birds, and fishes of British Columbia. Bureau Prov. Information Bull. 17 (Ed. 6): 27. Victoria.

Brodie, William
1894. The panther in Ontario. Biol. Review of Ont. 1 (2): 27-28.

Brooks, Allan
1930. Early big-game conditions in the Mount Baker District of Washington. Murrelet 11 (3): 65-67; 66. September.

1944. Do predators eradicate disease? Rod and Gun 45 (8): 13, 29; illus. Montreal, Que., Canada. January.

Brooks, Fred E.
1910. Mammals of West Virginia. West Va. State Board of Agric. Report 20: 9-30; 22. Quarter ending December 20, Charleston.

Brown, Arthur Erwin
1904. The zoology of North American big game. Amer. Big Game in its Haunts. The Book of the Boone & Crockett Club, New York. Ed. by Geo. Bird Grinnell: 52-98; 93-94; illus.

Brown, C. Barrington
1876. Canoe and camp life in British Guiana. London, i-x, 1-400; illus.: 334.

Brown, C. Emerson
1925. Longevity of mammals in the Philadelphia Zoological Gardens. Journ. Mammal. 6: 264-267; 265.

1932. My animal friends. Doubleday, Doran & Co., Garden City, N. Y. 262 pp., illus.: 47-49.

1936. Rearing wild animals in captivity and gestation periods. Journ. Mammal. 17 (1): 10-13; 12. February.

Browne, J. Ross, and Alexander S. Taylor
1887. Resources of the Pacific slope, 676 pp.; with a sketch of the settlement and exploration of Lower California, 209 pp.: 171, 172.

Browning, Meshach
1928. Forty-four years of the life of a hunter. Pp. 20, 78, 123, 208, 213, 275, 282.

Bruce, Jay C.
1918. Lioness tracked to lair. Calif. Fish and Game 4 (3): 152-153. July, illus.

1922. The why and how of mountain lion hunting in California. Calif. Fish and Game 8: 108-114.

1925. The problem of mountain lion control in California. Calif. Fish and Game 9: 1-17.

Bryant, H. C.
1917. Mountain lion hunting in California. Calif. Fish and Game 3: 160-
164, illus.
Buffon, Georges Louis Leclerc de
1761. Histoire naturelle 9: 216-230; pls. 19-20. Paris.

1776. Histoire naturelle. General et particuliere. Servant de suite á l'histoire des animaux quadrupides. Supp. Vol. 3: i-xxi, 1-330, 65 pls.:
222-223.
Bull, Charles Livingston
1911. Under the roof of the jungle. A book of animal life in the Guiana
wilds. L. C. Page & Co., Boston, i-xiv; 1-271, illus.: 215-217, 220,
222-239.
Burbridge, Ben
1909. Bear and lion hunting in Mexico. Outdoor Life (Jan.): 17-26; Denver.
Burmeister, Herman
1854. Systematische uebersicht der Thiere Brasiliens, etc. Erster Theil.
Säugethiere, i-x; 1-341: 88-90. Berlin.

1891. Description physique de la republique Argentina 3: 132. 1879.
Burnham, E. I.
1901. A mountain lion hunt. Forest & Stream 37 (3): 45. July 20.
Burt. William Henry
1933. Additional notes on the mammals of southern Arizona. Journ. Mammal.
14 (2): 114-122; 116. May.
Burshnell, David I., Jr.
1938. Drawings by George Gibbs in the far northwest, 1849-1851. Smiths.
Miscl. Coll. 97 (3): 1-28; 18. Publ. No. 3485, Smiths. Inst.,
Wash., D. C. 18 plates.
Butler. Amos W.
1895. A century of changes in the aspects of nature. Proc. Indiana Acad.
Sci. 31-40; 37.
Cabrera. Angel
1911. Catalogo sinonimico de los Felidae Sud Americanos. Revista Chilena de
Hist. Nat. 15 (1): 40-54. February 15.

1929. Datos sobre los pumas de la America Central. Revista de Historia Naturel 33: 312-320.
————, and José Yeppes
1940. Historia natural ediar. Mamiferos Sud-Americanos (Vida, Costumbres y
Descripcion). Compañia Argentina de Editores: 1-370; 168-172;
168-169; illus. Buenos Aires.
Cahalane. Victor H.
1939. Mammals of the Chiricahua Mountains. Cochise County, Arizona.
Journ. Mammal. 20 (4): 418-440; 426-427. November.

1943.   King of the cats and his court. Nat. Geog. Mag. 73 (2): 217-259; 218, 241, 249, 252; illus. Washington, D. C. February.

Calcutt, John
1894.   American panther. Biol. Rev. Ontario 1 (2): 23-26. Toronto, April.

California, State of
1942. . Outdoor California. Div. Fish and Game, Dept. Nat. Res. 3 (1): July 6.

Cameron, Jenks
1929.   The Bureau of Biological Survey; Its history, activities and organization. Service Monograph 54. Brookings Institution, Washington, D. C. Pp. i-x; 1-339.

"Carl"
1886.   Montana wolves and panthers. Forest and Stream 26: 508-509.

Carl, G. Clifford
1944.   The natural history of the Forbidden Plateau area of Vancouver Island, B. C. Rept. Prov. Mus. Nat. Hist. & Anthrop. 1943, Victoria, B. C. Pp. 19-40; p. 39.
—————, and George A. Hardy
1942.   Report on a collecting trip to the Lac la Hache area, British Columbia. Rept. Prov. Mus. Nat. Hist. and Anthrop., Victoria, B. C.: 25-49; 46; illus.

Carpenter, C. R.
1935.   Behavior of red spider monkeys in Panama. Journ. Mammal. 16 (3): 171-180; 171. August.

Carpenter, R. R. M.
1939.   Hunting the puma. North Amer. Big Game, A Book of the Boone & Crockett Club, New York. Chap. 22: 414-420.

Carver, Jonathan
1838.   Carver's travels in Wisconsin—a reprint of "Travels through the interior parts of North America in the years 1766, 1767, and 1768." London, 1781, i-xxxii; 1-376, map and illus. Describes the "Tyger of America," evidently the puma, p. 273, which he saw on an island in the "Chipéway River" (now in Wisconsin).

Cary, Merritt
1911.   A biological survey of Colorado. North American Fauna 33: 163-165; U. S. Dept. Agric., Bur. Biol. Surv., 256 pp., illus.

Catesby, Mark
1743.   The natural history of Carolina, Florida, and the Bahama Islands. London, Vol. 2: xxv.

Chapman, Frank Michler
1927.   Who treads our trails? On an island in the Canal Zone. Nat. Geog. Mag. September: 340-341. Washington, pp. 331-345; illus.

Chase, Stuart
1936.   Rich land; poor land. A study of waste in the natural resources of America. Whittlesey House, New York, London; McGraw-Hill Book Co., Inc. Pp. i-x; 1-361; illus., pp. 178-191.

Chichester, Bertram
   1943.   Cougar trails. Rod and Gun in Canada 45 (3): 12-13, 27; illus. Montreal, Que., Canada, August.
Chittenden, Hiram Martin
   1935.   The American fur trade of the far west. The Press of the Pioneers, New York, 2: 820.
Chubb, S. Harmsted
   1943.   Tools for carpentry. Natural History 52 (4): 168-170; illus.; p. 170. November.
Church, George Earl
   1912.   Aborigines of South America. Chapman & Hull, London, i-xix; 1-314: 267, 294.
Cist, Charles
   1845.   Cincinnati miscellany or antiquities of the west, and pioneer history and general and local statistics, compiled from the Western General Advertiser from October 1, 1844, to April 1, 1845. Vol. 1: 79-80, 219-220. Caleb Clark, Cincinnati, Printer.
Clapp, Henry
   1868.   Notes of a fur hunter. Amer. Nat. 1 (12): 652-666; 652. February.
Clark, James L.
   1939.   The big tom of Beaver Dam, Washington. Natural History 44 (2): 83-93. September, 19 illus.
Clarke, C. H. D.
   1942.   Cougar in Saskatchewan. Canadian Field Nat. 56 (3): 45. March.
Clavigero, D. Francesco Saverio
   1817.   History of Mexico. (English translation from the original Italian.) Vol. 1: 50. Brief mention of the "Miztli" of the Mexicans.
Coape, A. P. F.
   1890.   A puma hunt in New Mexico. Forest and Stream 34: 65.
Colton, H. S.
   1932.   Museum of Northern Arizona Notes 5 (1): 1-4.
Colvin. Verplank
   1879.   Seventh annual report on the progress of the topographical survey of the Adirondack region of New York to the year 1879. Assembly Doc. 87: 159-160. March 7.
Conger, W. B.
   1938.   The real cougar. Nature Mag. 31 (8): 491-492; illus. October.
Cooper, J. G.
   1855.   Report of explorations and surveys to ascertain most practical and economical route for a railroad from the Mississippi to the Pacific Ocean, made under direction of Secretary of War, 1858-1855. Zool. Rept. 12 (Pt. 2) 2: 74.
Coper, Edward D.
   1880a. On the zoological position of Texas. Bull. U. S. Nat. Mus. 17: 9, 47 pp.

   1880b. On the extinct cats of America. Amer. Nat. 14 (12): 834-858. Dec., illus.

Cornish, Charles John
  1907.   Animal artisans and other studies of birds and beasts. Longmans, Green
          & Co., London and New York, Bombay, Calcutta: 199-200; 274
          pp., illus.
Cory, Charles B.
  1896.   Hunting and fishing in Florida, including a key to the water birds
          known to occur in the State. Estes and Lauriat, Boston, Mass.: 41-
          49, 109-110. The Florida panther.
  ─────────
  1912.   The mammals of Illinois and Wisconsin. Field Mus. Nat. Hist. 11:
          153, 280.
Coues, Elliott
  1867.   The quadrupeds of Arizona. Amer. Nat. 1 (6): 281-292; (7): 351-
          363; (8): 393-400; (10): 531-541. Vol. 1 (6): 285-286.
  1874.   Specimen of a cougar [Felis concolor]. American Sportsman. Jan. 24.
  ─────────. and H. C. Yarrow
  1875.   Report upon collection of mammals made in Nevada, Utah, California,
          Colorado, New Mexico, and Arizona, during the years 1871-1874.
          Rept. Geog. & Geol. Exp. & Surv. W. 100th Merid. 5 (Chapter 2):
          40.
  ─────────
  1893.   History of the expedition under the command of Lewis & Clark.
          Francis P. Harper, New York, 4 vols. Vol. 1: 311-312; Vol. 2: 458,
          737, 776; Vol. 3: 864-865.
Cowan, Ian McTaggart
  1939.   The vertebrate fauna of Peace River District of British Columbia.
          Occas. Papers, B. C. Prov. Mus. 1: 76. June 1, 102 pp.
Cox, Ross
  1831.   Adventures on the Columbia River. 2 vols. Vol. 2: 131.
Cragin, Francis W.
  1885.   Notes on some mammals of Kansas, with a few additions to the list of
          species known to inhabit the State. Bull. Washburn College 1 (2):
          42-47; 42. January, Topeka.
Cram, Gardner
  1901.   Panthers in Maine. Forest & Stream 56 (6): 123. Feb. 16.
Crampton, Henry Edward
  1920.   An expedition to Kaieteur and Roraima, British Guiana. Nat. Geog.
          Mag. Sept.: 227-244; 233.
Crane, Jocelyn
  1931.   Mammals of Hampshire County, Massachusetts. Journ. Mammal. 12
          (3): 267-273; 270. August.
Crawford, Robert P.
  1944.   Romantic days on the Missouri. North Dakota Outdoors 6 (9): 10.
          Game & Fish Dept., Bismarck. March.
Cremon, F. C.
  1868.   The Apache race. Overland Monthly 1 (3): 208-209. September.

Crew, F. A. E.
1937.   The sex ratio. Amer. Nat. 71 (737): 529-559. Nov.-Dec.
Crile, George
1941.   Intelligence, power, and personality. McGraw-Hill Book Co., Inc.,
        illus. Ed. by Grace Crile.
Cunningham, Robert Oliver
1871.   Notes on the natural history of the Strait of Magellan and west coast of
        Patagonia, made during voyages of H. M. S. Nassau, in the years
        1866, 1867, 1868, and 1869. Edinburgh, 517 pp., illus.: 106, 109,
        118, 476.
Curtis, Brian
1943.   Twenty-five years ago in California fish and game. Calif. Fish & Game
        29 (4): 204-205. October.
Cutright, Paul Russell
1940.   The great naturalists explore South America. The Macmillan Co.,
        New York. i-xii; 1-340, illus.: 83-90.
Cuvier, Georges (Baron)
1831.   Animal kingdom. H. M' Mustrie edition. Vol. 1: 115.
——————. and Edward Griffith
1827.   The animal kingdom. Vol. 2: 438-439. London.
D., E. T., and H. R. R.
1888.   Habits of the mountain lion. Forest & Stream 30: 289.
Dacy, G. H.
1924.   America's strangest army of hunters. Hunter-Trader-Trapper 48 (5):
        12-14; illus. May.
Dartt, Mary
1879.   On the plains and among the peaks, or how Mrs. Maxwell made her
        natural history collection. Claxton, Remsen, & Heffelfinger, Phila.,
        237 pp., illus.: 218.
Darwin, Charles
1839.   Narrative of surveying voyages of His Majesty's ships "Adventure" and
        "Beagle," between years 1826 and 1836, describing their examina-
        tions of the southern shores of South America and the "Beagle's"
        circumnavigation of the globe. 3 vols. London. Vol. 3: 135, 328.

1874.   The descent of man. Ed. 2: 528; 797 pp., illus.

1882.   Researches into the natural history and geology of the countries visited
        during the voyage of H. M. S. Beagle round the world. New York,
        519 pp.: 183, 269, 270.
Davis, John H., Jr.
1943.   Natural features of southern Florida, especially the vegetation and the
        Everglades. Geol. Bull. 25: 311; illus. Florida Department of Con-
        servation, Tallahassee, pp. 236-237.
Davis, William B.
1939.   The recent mammals of Idaho. (Contr. Mus. Vert. Zool., Univ. Calif.,
        Berkeley, Calif.). Caxton Printers, Ltd., Caldwell, Idaho. 400 pp.,
        illus.: 148-150. April 5.

Davis, William B., and J. L. Robertson, Jr.
 1944. The mammals of Culbertson County, Texas. Jour. Mammal. 25 (3):
        254-273; illus. August: 265.
Dawson, George M.
 1887. Notes and observations on Kwakiool People of northern part of Van-
        couver Island and adjacent coasts, made during the summer of 1885;
        with a vocabulary of about 700 words. Proc. & Trans. Royal Soc. of
        Canada 5 (Sec. II): 63-98.
Dearborn, Ned
 1927. An old record of the mountain lion in New Hampshire. Journ. Mammal.
        8 (4): 311-312. November.

 1932. Food of some predatory animals in Michigan. School of Forestry &
        Cons. Bull. 1: 52, illus. University of Mich., Ann Arbor. p. 50.
De Kay, James E.
 1842. Zoology of New York of the New York fauna. Albany i-xiii; 1-146;
        33 pls.: 47-49.
Dillin, John G.
 1924. The Kentucky rifle. Nat. Rifle Assn. of America, Wash., D. C., 124
        pp., index: 7-10.
Dionne, C. E.
 1902. Les mammiféres de la province de Quebec. Dussault & Proulx, im-
        premeurs, Quebec. 285 pp., illus.: 274-281.
Dixon, Joseph
 1925. Food predilections of predatory and fur-bearing mammals. Journ.
        Mammal. 6 (1): 34-46; 40-41. February, illus.

 1934a. A cougar encountered in the open. Journ. Mammal. 15: 71.

 1934b. A study of the life history and food habits of mule deer in California.
        Calif. Fish & Game 20 (3): 182-282; 272, illus.
Dobie, J. Frank
 1943. Tales of the panther. Sat. Eve. Post 216 (24): 23, 57, 60-61; illus.
        December 11.
Dodge, Henry Irving
 1927. The hour and the man. Forest and Stream 97: 72, 107-108, 156-159,
        182-183.
Dodge, Richard Irving
 1877. The plains of the great west, and their inhabitants. Putnam, New York,
        iv-lv; 1-448, illus.: 217-221.
Doel, John (Rev.)
 1894. The panther in Canada. Biol. Rev. Ont. 1 (2): 18-23; 23. April,
        Toronto.
Donaldson, Thomas
 1887. The George Catlin Indian Gallery in the U. S. National Museum
        (Smiths. Inst.) with memoir and statistics. Wash., D. C., Gov. Print.
        Office, i-vii; 1-939, illus.: 401.

Douglas, Ernest
  1945. The orneriest little pest in Arizona. Read Magazine 17 (1): 61-62.
         January.
Du Pratz, M. Le Page
  1758a. Histoire de la Louisiane. Vol. 2: 91-92.

  1758b. The history of Louisiana. (English translation of French edition, 1758.)
         London, 1774: 263.
"E. G."
  1880. Capt. Bell's panther story. Forest & Stream 15: 110.
East, Ben
  1940. An inch from death. Field & Stream 45: 18-19, 70-71. Sept., 3 illus.
Eastman, Charles Alexander
  1904. Red hunters and the animal peoples. Harper & Bros., New York and
         London, 249 pp.: 3-23, 241-242, 244.
Ebbutt, Percy G.
  1886. Emigrant life in Kansas. Swan Sonnenschein & Co., London, 237 pp.:
         216-217.
Editor
  1887. "A panther 8 feet long, with feet 5 inches across and claws an inch
         long was killed recently in Manatee County, Florida." American
         Field 28: 7.
Elliott, Daniel Giraud
  1883. A monograph of the Felidae. London: 72.

  1901. A synopsis of the mammals of North America, and the adjacent seas.
         Field Columb. Mus., Zool. Ser. Pub. 45 (vol. 11): 293-294. Chi-
         cago, 471 pp., illus.

  1904. The land and sea mammals of Middle America and the West Indies.
         Field Columb. Mus. Zool. Ser. Pub. 95 (vol. 4, Pts. 1 & 2): 454-
         456, Pt. 2. Chicago, 850 pp., illus.
Emmons, Ebenezer
  1840. Report on the quadrupeds of Massachusetts. Cambridge, Mass., 86 pp.:
         36.
Enock, C. Reginald
  1907. The Andes and the Amazon; Life and travel in Peru. Chas. Scribner's
         Sons, New York, i-xii; 1-379, illus.: 150.
Espinosa, Antonio Vazquez de
  1942. Compendium and description of the West Indies. (Transl. by Chas.
         Upson Clark). Smiths. Inst. Miscl. Coll., Vol. 102 (whole vol.)
         Pub. 3646, 337, 376, 550, 555, 614, 663. Sept. 1, 862 pp.
Evans, W. F.
  1922. The super-strength of the mountain lion. Outdoor Life 49: 344-345.
Evermann, B. W., and Amos W. Butler
  1893. Preliminary list of Indiana mammals. Proc. Ind. Acad. Sci.: 120-139;
         138-139.

Fannin, John
    1897.   Panther in British Columbia. Forest & Stream: 184. March 6.

    1898.   Natural history of British Columbia. Victoria: 8.
Faull, J. H.
    1913.   The natural history of the Toronto region, Ontario, Canada. Canad.
            Inst., Toronto, 419 pp.: 41.
Faunce, H. J.
    1944.   Cowardly cougars. Field and Stream 49 (3): 5. July.
Figueira, Juan R.
    1894.   Contribucion al conocimiento de la fauna Uruguaya. Enumeracion de
            mamiferos. Anales del Museo Nac. de Montevideo 2: 187-217;
            207-208. October.
Finley, W. L.
    1925.   Cougar kills a boy. Journ. Mammal. 6 (3): 197-199. August.
Fitzroy, Robert
    1839.   Narrative of the surveying voyages of His Majesty's ships "Adventure"
            and "Beagle," between years 1826 and 1836. Henry Colburn, Lon-
            don, 3 vol. Vol. 3: 107, 135, 313, 327, 357.
Flint, Timothy
    1856.   The first white man of the west, or the life and exploits of Colonel
            Daniel Boone. Cincinnati: 74.
Foote, Leonard E.
    1944.   A history of wild game in Vermont. Vt. Fish & Game Service, State
            Bull. Pittman-Robertson Series 11: 46; illus.
Fountain, Paul
    1902.   The great mountains and forests of South America. London, 306 pp.,
            illus.: 74-79, 85.

    1914.   The river Amazon. London, illus., 321 pp.: 53, 64, 72-74, 76, 190.
Fox, Herbert
    1923.   Diseases in captive wild mammals and birds. J. B. Lippincott & Co.,
            Phila., London, and Chicago. 665 pp., illus.: 156, 171, 390.
Frantzius, A. V.
    1892.   Los mamíferos de Costa Rica. Contribucion al conocimiento de la ex-
            tencion geografica de los mamiferos de America [pp. 60-142]: 91.
            [In Barranteo, Francisco Montero. Geografía de Costa Rica, Comi-
            sión del Gobierno de la República para las Exposiciones Histórico-
            Americana de Madrid y Universınal de Chicago, Barcelona, pp.
            i-vii; 1-350, illus., 1 map.]
Fuller, Devereux
    1832.   Report on the period of gestation of the puma [(Felis concolor)]. Proc.
            Committee Sci. & Corr., Zool. Soc. London, Part 2: 62. April 10.
Funkhouser, William Delbert
    1925.   Wild life in Kentucky. Ky. Geol. Surv., Frankfort, 385 pp., illus.: 33,
            38-40.
G., S. W.
    1875.   Panthers in Vermont. Forest & Stream 5: 300.

Gadow, Hans Friedrich
1908. Through southern Mexico; being an account of the travels of a naturalist. (1902-1904). Chas. Scribner's Sons, New York; Witherby & Co., London; i-xvi; 1-527; illus.: 371-372.
Garcilasso, de la Vega
1869. Royal commentaries of the Yncas. Transl. and ed. with notes and an introduction by Clements R. Markham, London, 2 vols. Vol. 1: 1-359; 232; Vol. 2: 1-553; 30, 116-117, 238, 341, 350, 385, 425, 429, 436, 441.
Garman, H.
1894. A preliminary list of the vertebrate animals of Kentucky. Bull. Essex Inst. 26 (1, 2, 3): 2-3. Jan., Feb. and Mar., 63 pp.
Gay, Claudio
1847. Historia fisica y politica de Chile. Zoologia 1: 494: 65-68.
Gibson, Christopher H. (Sir)
1943. Through Paraguay and southern Matto Grosso. Nat. Geog. Mag. 84 (4): 459-488; illus. October, p. 488.
Gilman, S. C.
1896. The Olympic country. Nat. Geog. Mag. 7 (4): 133-40; 133. April.
Godman, John D.
1826. American natural history. H. C. Carey and I. Lee, Phila. 3 vols., illus. 1: 291-302.
Goldman, Edward Alphonso
1920. Mammals of Panama. Smiths. Miscl. Coll. 69 (5): 1-309; 169.

———— 1932. Management of our deer herds. Trans. 19th Amer. Game Conf.: 49-61; 56-57; New York, Nov. 28, 29, 30.

———— 1935. Requirements for wildlife areas, pp. 1-11, Sec. 1, in "Planning for Wildlife in the United States, Part IX, Suppl. Rept., Land Planning Committee, Nat. Resources Bd., Wash., D. C., 24 pp.: 4.

———— 1936. A new puma from Texas. Proc. Biol. Soc. Wash. 49: 137-138. Aug. 22. New: Felis concolor youngi (= F. c. stanleyana).

———— 1937. The Colorado River as a barrier in mammalian distribution. Journ. Mammal. 18 (4): 427-435; 430-431. Nov.

———— 1938. A substitute name for Felis concolor youngi. Proc. Biol. Soc. Wash. 51: 63. Mar. 18. New comb.: Felis concolor stanleyana.

———— 1939. North American big game. A book of Boone & Crockett Club; Chap. 22: 407-414; 412-413. Chas. Scribner's Sons, New York and London.

———— 1943. Two new races of the puma. Journ. Mammal. 24 (2): 228-231. June 8.

Goode, Monroe H.
  1944.   The real cougar. Field and Stream 49 (4): 26-27, 70-72; illus. August.
Goodwin, George Gilbert
  1932.   New records and some observations on Connecticut mammals. Journ.
          Mammal. 13 (1): 36-40; 39. February.

  _____

  1935.   The mammals of Connecticut. Bull. State Geol. & Nat. Hist. Surv. 53:
          84-86. Hartford, 221 pp., illus.

  _____

  1936.   Big game animals in the northeastern United States. Journ. Mammal.
          17 (1): 48-50. February.

  _____

  1942.   Mammals of Honduras. Bull. Amer. Mus. Nat. Hist. 79 (Art. 2): 107-
          195; 185. New York, May 29.
Graham, Gideon
  1939.   Animal outlaws. Ed. 2. Gid. Graham, Pub., Collinsville, Okla. 1-256,
          illus.
Graham, S. R.
  1918.   The lion of the Rockies. Outdoor Life 41: 91-94, 171-174.
Grant, M. I.
  1884.   How he shot a mountain lion. American Field 22: 462.
Grant, Madison
  1933.   Puma hunting trails on three continents. Boone & Crockett Club: 16-
          18, New York.
Gray, J. E.
  1867.   Notes on the skulls of the cats (Felidae). Proc. Zool. Soc. London: 258-
          277; 265. March 14.

  _____

  1869.   Catalogue of carnivorous, pachydermatous, and edentate mammalia in
          the British Museum. 398 pp. London. Pp. 5-38.
Gray, Prentiss N.
  1932.   [Editor] Records of North American big game. A book of the Boone
          & Crockett Club. Derrydale Press, N. Y. 178 pp., illus.
Greenbie, Sydney
  1929.   Frontiers and the fur trade. New York, February: 208.
Gregg, Josiah
  1905.   Commerce of the prairies or the journal of a Santa Fe trader during
          eight expeditions across the great western prairies and a residence
          of nearly nine years in northern Mexico. Early Western Travels,
          Vols. 19, 20. Ed. by Reuben Gold Thwaites. Arthur H. Clark
          Co. Cleveland, O., p. 327.
Gregory, Tappan
  1936.   Mammals of the Chicago region. Chicago Acad. Sci. 7 (2 and 3):
          21. July, 74 pp., illus.

  _____

  1938.   Lion in the Carmens. Chicago Acad. Sci. Nat. 1: (3) 70-81; (4)
          110-120.

1939.   Eyes in the night. Bobcat and Mountain Lion (Chapter 7): 157-185. Thomas Crowell Co., New York, illus.

Grey, Zane
1908.   Lassoing lions in the Siwash. Everybody's Mag. 18 (6): 776-785; 776. June, illus.

1909.   Roping lions in the Grand Canyon. Field & Stream 13: 739-749, Jan.; 14: 336-342, Aug.

Griffith, Edward
1821.   General and particular descriptions of the vertebrated animals, arranged conformably to the modern discoveries and improvements in zoology. Order Carnivora, London: 74-79.

1827.   In Cuvier's animal kingdom. Vol. 2: 436-440.

Grinnell, George Bird
1904.   The mountain sheep and its range. [American Big Game in its Haunts. A book of Boone & Crockett Club, New York]: 270-348; 289-293.

1926.   Habits of the wolverine. Journ. Mammal. 7 (1): 30-34; 31. February.

Grinnell, Joseph
1914.   An account of the mammals and birds of the lower Colorado Valley with especial reference to the distributional problems presented. Univ. Calif. Publ. Zool. 12 (4): 51-294. March 20.

1933.   Review of the recent mammal fauna of California. Publ. Zoology, Univ. Calif. 40 (2): 71-234; 114-115. Berkeley, September 26.

——————, and Joseph Dixon
1923.   The systematic status of the mountain lion of California. Publ. Zool., Univ. Calif. 21 (11): 325-332. April 7, illus.

——————, Joseph S. Dixon, and Jean M. Linsdale
1937.   Fur-bearing mammals of California; their natural history, systematic status, and relations to man. Contr. Mus. Vert. Zool., Univ. Calif., 2 vols., illus. Vol. 2: 533-589.

——————, and Tracy Irwin Storer
1924.   Animal life in the Yosemite. Contr. Mus. Vert. Zool., Univ. Calif., Berkeley: 95-98.

Grubb, Kenneth G.
1930.   Amazon and Andes. Metheun & Co., London; Lincoln MacVeagh, The Dial Press, New York, 296 pp., illus.: 55.

Guenther, Konrad
1931.   A naturalist in Brazil. Houghton-Mifflin Co., Boston and New York, 400 pp., illus.: 177-178.

Hahn, Walter Louis
1909.   The mammals of Indiana. 33rd Annual Rept. Ind. Dept. Geol. & Nat. Res., Indianapolis, illus.: 417-663; 540-542.

Hakluyt, Richard
  1810. Collection of the early travels and discoveries of the English nation.
         New edition with additions. Vol. 3: 333, 373, 616. London, 623 pp.
Hall, Archibald
  1861. On the mammals and birds of the district of Montreal. Canad. Nat.
         & Geol. & Proc. Nat. Hist. Soc. Montreal, Canada 6: 284-309;
         298-299.
Hall, E. Raymond
  1932. A historical resume of exploration and survey—Mammal types and
         their collectors in the state of Washington. Murrelet 13 (3): 63-91;
         80, 84. September.
Hall, F. S.
  1925. Killing of a boy by mountain lion. Murrelet 6 (2): 33-37, 1 illus.
         Mus. Univ. Wash., Seattle.
Hall, Maurice C.
  1920. The adult taenioid cestodes of dogs and cats, and of related carnivores
         in North America. Proc. U. S. Nat. Mus. 55. 94 pages, illus.
Halliday, W. E. D.
  1940. Nature's wise law of survival. Forest & Outdoors 36 (10): 317-318,
         324, 326, 329. Montreal, October.
Hallock, Charles
  1877. The sportsman's gazetteer and general guide; game animals, birds, and
         fishes of North America; their habits and various methods of
         capture. 688 pp., including a sportsman's directory of principal
         resorts for game and fish in North America, 209 pp., New York:
         9, 153, 167.

  1880. The sportsman's gazetteer and general guide. Forest & Stream Pub. Co.,
         N. Y., Ed. 5, Part 1, 700 pp., Part 2: 1-208; 2-3, 8-10, 26, 37,
         40, 92, 153.
Hamburg, O. D. S.
  1874. Hand to hand with a panther. Forest & Stream 3: 67.
Hamilton, W. J., Jr.
  1937. The value of predatory mammals. N. Y. Zool. Soc. Bull. 40 (2):
         39-45; illus.; March-April.

  1939. American mammals; their lives, habits, and economic relations. Mc-
         Graw-Hill Book Co., Inc., New York and London, 434 pp., illus.:
         42, 139, 169, 278, 303, 335, 336, 341, 347, 368, 369, 405, 412,
         414, 417, 418.

  1941. Notes on some mammals of Lee County, Florida. Amer. Mid. Nat. 25
         (3): 686-691; 688-689. May.
Hariot, Thomas
  1587. A brief and true report of the new found land of Virginia: 33.

Harlan, Richard
   1825.   Fauna Americana; being a description of the mammiferous animals in-
           habiting North America.   Phila.: 94-95.
Harlin, J. E.
   1919.   A cougar trailing incident.   Outdoor Life 43 (6): 356-357.   June.
Harper, Francis
   1920.   Okefenokee Swamp as a reservation.   Nat. Hist. 20: 29-40; 29. January-
           February, illus.

   1926.   Tales of the Okefenokee.   American Speech 1: 407-420; 410-411. May.

   1927.   The mammals of the Okefenokee Swamp region of Georgia.   Proc.
           Bost. Soc. Nat. Hist. 37 (7): 191-396; 317-320; pls. 4-7.

   1945.   Extinct and vanishing mammals of the Old World.   Amer. Comm.
           Intern. Wildlife Prot. Sp. Bull. 12: 21; xx; 850; illus. N. Y. Zoo-
           logical Park.
Hartwig, George Ludwig
   1873.   The tropical world.   London: 1-556; 28, 462-463, illus.
Hausman, Leon Augustus
   1944.   Applied microscopy of hair.   Scientific Monthly 59 (3): 195-202;
           illus., September.
Hegner, Robert
   1935.   Parade of the animal kingdom: 1-675; 614-615; illus.
Heller, Edmund
   1931.   Leopard and puma are best of friends.   Baltimore News, September 16.
Henderson, Archibald
   1920.   The conquest of the old southwest; the romantic story of the early
           pioneers into Virginia, the Carolinas, Tennessee, and Kentucky,
           1740-1790: 1-395; 36; illus.
Henderson, Junius, and Elberta L. Craig
   1932.   Economic mammalogy.   Chas. C. Thomas, Springfield, Ill., and Balti-
           more, Md. i-x; 1-397; 41-43, 56, 67, 97, 103-104, 115, 117, 141,
           161, 178-179, 182-183, 202, 220-221, 232-233, 238.
Hernandez, Francisco
   1651.   Rerum medicarum novae hispaniae Thesaurus.   Tract 1 (Chap. 11): 4.
Herrick, C. L.
   1892.   Mammals of Minnesota.   Bull. Geol. & Nat. Hist. Surv. 7: 68-70.
           Minneapolis.
Hesse, R., W. C. Allee, and K. P. Schmidt
   1937.   Ecological animal geography. i-xiv; 1-597, illus.   John Wiley & Sons,
           New York; Chapman and Hall, Ltd., London.
Hewitt, C. Gordon
   1921.   The conservation of wildlife of Canada.   Chas. Scribner's Sons, N. Y.
           i-xx; 1-344; 195, 198; illus.

Hibbard, Claude W.
1942. Pleistocene mammals from Kansas. State Geol. Surv. Bull. 41 (6): 261-269; 263. August 3, illus.
1943. A check-list of Kansas mammals. Trans. Kans. Acad. Sci. 47: 61-88; p. 71.
Hibben, Frank C.
1937. A preliminary study of the mountain lion (*Felis oregonensis*). Bull. Univ. New Mexico: 1-55. December 15.

1939. The mountain lion and ecology. Ecology 20 (4): 584-586. October.
Hill, S. S.
1860. Travels in Peru and Mexico. Longmans, Green, Longman & Roberts, London, 2 vols. Vol. 1: 43-44; Vol. 2: 140.
Hilton, William
1911. A relation of a discovery made on the coast of Florida, 1644. Charles Scribner's Sons, New York: 47.
Hitchcock, Charles H.
1862. Catalogue of the mammals of Maine. Proc. Portland Soc. Nat. Hist. 1: 65.
Hoffman, W. J.
1877. List of mammals found in the vicinity of Grand River, Dakota Territory. Proc. Bost. Soc. Nat. Hist. 19: 94-102; 95. March 7.
Holder, Charles Frederick
1906. Life in the open; sport with rod, gun, horse, and hound, in southern California. Putnam, New York and London, i-xv; 1-401, illus.: 137-151.
Hollister, Ned
1908. Notes on Wisconsin mammals. Bull. Wisc. Nat. Hist. Soc. 4 (3-4): 141. Oct.

1911. The Louisiana puma. Proc. Biol. Soc. Wash. 24: 175-178. June 16.
Holt, Ernest G.
1932. Swimming cats. Journ. Mammal. 13 (1): 72-73. February.
Holy Bible
———. II Samuel, Ch. xxiii, verse 20.
Hooper, Emmet T.
1941. Mammals of the lava fields and adjoining areas in Valencia County, New Mexico. Miscl. Publ. Mus. Zool. Univ. Mich. 51: 1-47; 22-23, illus.
Hooper, Herschel
1943. Man robs lion. Arizona Wildlife and Sportsman 5 (6): 5. June. Ariz. Game Prot. Assoc. Prescott.
Hornaday, William T.
1922. The minds and manners of wild animals. New York: 1-328; 17, 37, 278, 279, illus.
Horsford, B.
1883. The panther's leap. Forest & Stream 20: 305.

Howell, Alfred Brazier
1944. Speed in animals; their specialization for running and leaping. Univ. Chicago Press, Chicago. Pp. i-xii; 1-270; illus.

Howell, Arthur H.
1921. A biological survey of Alabama. North Amer. Fauna 45: 1-88; 41-42, illus. Bur. Biol. Surv., U. S. Dept. Agric., Wash., D. C.

Hudson, W. H.
1895. Naturalist in La Plata. London: 31-58, 384-386.

Hughes, J. C.
1883. The American panther, *Felis concolor*. Forest & Stream 21 (6): 103. Sept. 6.

Humboldt, Alexander von, and Aime Bonpland
1881. Personal narrative of travels to the equinoctial regions of America during the years 1799-1804. Written in French by Alexander von Humboldt. Trans. and edited by Thomasina Ross. 3 vols. Geo. Bell & Sons, Convent Gardens, London, Vol. 1: 230-232; Vol. 2: 104, 153, 154, 163, 470.

"Humboldt" (Petrolin, California).
1887. A cougar. Forest & Stream 28: 493.

Humphrey, W. E.
1928. Notes on the cougar. Outdoor Life—Outdoor Recreation 61 (4): 102. April.

Hunter, J. S.
1921. The control of the mountain lion in California. Calif. Fish & Game 7: 99-101, illus.

1945. Lion kill in California. Outdoor Calif. 5 (29): 1. Jan. 15.

Hunter, W. Perceval
1837. Selections from the natural history of the quadrupeds of Paraguay and the River La Plata; comprising the most remarkable species of South America. Transl. from the Spanish of Don Felix De Azara, with notes. London, i-xix; 1-288; 19-32.

Huntington, Dwight W.
1904. Our big game. Chas. Scribner's Sons, New York: 1-347; 276, 301-314; illus.

Imlay, George
1793. A topographical description of the western territory of North America. London, Ed. 2: i-xvi; 1-433; [20]: 299; 3 maps.

Im Thurn, Everard F.
1883. Among the Indians of Guiana. London: 1-445; 111; illus.

Ingersoll, Ernest
1906. The life of animals. The Mammals. New York: 1-555; 90-97; illus.

1937. An adventure in etymology, origin and meaning of some animal names. Sci. Monthly 44: 157-165. February.

Ingles, Lloyd G.
    1939. In defense of the lion. American Forests 45 (1): 21-22, illus. Jan.
"J. W. S."
    1884. Experiences with a panther. Forest & Stream 23: 4.
Jackson, C. F.
    1922. Notes on New Hampshire mammals. Journ. Mammal. 3 (1): 13-15;
           13. Feb.
Jackson, Hartley H. T.
    1908. A preliminary list of Wisconsin mammals. Bull. Wisc. Nat. Hist. Soc.
           6 (1-2): 14. April.

    1943. Conserving endangered wildlife species. Trans. Wisc. Acad. Sci., Arts,
           & Letters 35: 61-90, illus., p. 66.
Jardine, Sir William
    1934. Naturalist's Library. Vol. 2, Mamm., Felidae: 266.
Jenkins, Will D.
    1886. Puget Sound cougars. Forest & Stream 27: 104.
Johnson, Maynard S.
    1930. Common injurious mammals of Minnesota. Univ. Minn. Agric. Exper.
           Sta. Bull. 259: 60; 66 pages, illus., St. Paul, January.
Jones, Anna Clark
    1939. Antlers for Jefferson. New Eng. Quart. 12 (2): 333-348; 334. June.
Jones, Gordon W.
    1945. Virginia was once England's wild west. Nature Mag. 38 (6): 317-320.
           June-July.
Jones, Paul V., and Alfred S. Jackson
    1941. Game in early days. Contr. to a wildlife program for Young County,
           Texas, prepared for and in coop. with Young County Land Use
           Planning Committee, and with Soil Conservation Service, U. S.
           Dept. Agric., Texas Game, Fish and Oyster Comm., Agric. & Mech.
           College of Texas, Fish and Wildlife Service, U. S. Dept. Interior:
           1-30; 5-6.
K——, H. J.
    1888. A chase in Missouri. Forest and Stream 30: 493-494.
Kellogg, Remington
    1937. Annotated list of West Virginia mammals. Proc. U. S. Nat. Mus. 84
           (3022): 443-479; 456.

    1939. Annotated list of Tennessee mammals. Proc. U. S. Nat. Mus., Smiths.
           Inst. 86 (3051): 245-303; 268.
Kennedy, Bess
    1942. The lady and the lions. Whittlesey House Pub., McGraw-Hill Book
           Co., New York: 1-221; illus. October.
Kennicott, Robert
    1855. Catalogue of animals observed in Cook County, Illinois. Trans. Ill.
           Agric. Soc. 1: 578-595; 578. Springfield.

Kerr, Robert
  1792. The animal kingdom: 1-644. New: *Felis couguar* (= *F. c. couguar*), p. 151.
Kincaid, Edgar B.
  1931. "The Mexican Pastor." Southwestern Lore 9: 63-64. Texas Folklore Society.
Kingston, William Henry Giles
  1874. The western world. Picturesque sketches of nature and natural history in North and South America. L. Nelson & Sons, London: i-xii; 1-736, illus.: 259, 392-395.
Kirtland, Jared P.
  1838. A catalogue of the mammalia, birds, reptiles, fishes, testacea, and crustacea in Ohio. 2nd Ann. Rept., Geol. Surv. Ohio: 160-200; 176.
"Klamath"
  1884. A bold panther. American Field 21: 451.
Knox, M. V. B.
  1875. Kansas Mammalia, Trans. Kans. Acad. Sci. 4: 18.
Kopman, H. H.
  1921. Wildlife resources of Louisiana. State Dept. Conservation Bull. 10: 29. New Orleans.
Lahille, F.
  1899. Ensayo sobre la distribución geografica de los mamíferos en la republica Argentina. Primera Reunion del Congreso Cientifico Latino Americano, 3: 165-206; 177. Map.
Lanman, Charles
  1856. Adventures in the wilds of the United States and British American provinces with an appendix by Lieut. Campbell Hardy. John Moore, Phila. 2 vols. 1: 352.
Lapham, I. A.
  1853. Systematic catalogue of the animals of Wisconsin. Trans. Wisc. Agric. Soc. 2: 337-340; 339.
Lawrence, Robert H.
  1891. In the great woods of Washington. Forest & Stream 37 (12): 246. Oct. 8.
Lawson, John
  1718. The history of North Carolina. Printed for T. Warner, London: [4]; 1-258; map, p. 117.
Leach, J. P.
  1882. The Felidae. American Field 17: 432.
Leach, John R.
  1941. Letter descriptive of visit from puma in eastern Oregon. Files, Fish and Wildlife Service, U. S. Dept. Interior; March 14, 1941.
Leopold, Aldo
  1936. Game management. Chas. Scribner's Sons, New York and London, i-xxi; 1-481, illus.: 34-36, 55, 77, 86, 233-234, 247-248, 296, 301.

Lesley, Lewis Burt
1929. Uncle Sam's Camels. Journ. May Humphreys Stacey, suppl. by report of Ed. Fitzgerald Beale (1857-1858), Harvard Univ. Press., Cambridge, Mass. 1-298, illus.: 84-85.

Lesson, Rene Primevere
1942. Nouveau tableau règne Animal. Mammiferes. Paris: 50.

Lett, William Pittman
1887. The cougar or panther. Ottawa Nat. 1 (9): 127-132; 127, 129. December.

Lévy, Pablo
1873. Notas geográficas y economicas sobre la república de Nicaragua. Paris, i-xvi; 1-627, with map: 197.

Liais, Emmanuel
1872. Climats geologie, faune et géographie botanique du Brésil. Paris, i-viii; 1-640, map: 459-461.

Ligon, J. Stokley
1927. Wildlife of New Mexico; its conservation and management. 1-212, illus.: 50-52.

Link, Heinrich F.
1794. Beyträge zur naturgeschichte, zweytes stuck. 1-126: 90.

Linné, Carl
1771. Regni animalis; appendix to Mantissa Plantarum: 522.

Linsley, James H. (Rev.)
1842. Catalogue of the mammalia of Connecticut. Amer. Journ. Sci. & Arts 43: 348. New Haven.

Long, Stephen H.
1823. Account of an expedition from Pittsburgh to the Rocky Mountains. Compiled by Edwin James, Botanist and Geologist for the expedition. 2 vols. 1: 369.

Lönnberg, Einar
1913. Mammals from Ecuador and related forms. Arkiv. fur Zoologi, band 8 (16): 1-36; 2; illus. Apr. 28, 1913.

1921. A second contribution to the mammalogy of Ecuador with some remarks on Caenolestes. Arkiv. fur Zoologi 14 (4): 1-104; 9-11; 1 pl. Feb. 23.

Lopez, Carlos M., and Carlos Lopez
1911. Caza Mexicana. i-xix; 1-629; 318-323; illus.

Louisiana, State of
1916. Report of the State Conservation Commission, April 1, 1914, to April 1, 1916. New Orleans, 1-156; 42; illus.

Lowery, George H., Jr.
1936. A preliminary report on the distribution of the mammals of Louisiana. Dept. Zool., Louisiana State Univ., Proc. La. Acad. Sci. 3 (1): 11-39; 23, illus. March.

Lowery, George H., Jr.
    1943.   Check-list of the mammals of Louisiana and adjacent waters. Occas.
            Papers, Mus. Zool., La. State Univ. 13: 234-235. Baton Rouge,
            November 22.

    1944.   Distribution of Louisiana mammals with respect to the physiography of
            the State. Proc. La. Acad. Sci. 8: 63-73; p. 63.
Lowther, J. R.
    1915.   The cougar in British Columbia. Outdoor Life 36: 131-132; illus.
Ludlow, William
    1875.   Report of a reconnaissance of the Black Hills of Dakota, made in the
            summer of 1874. Gov. Print. Office, Wash., D. C., 1-121; 79.

    1876.   Report of a reconnaissance from Carroll, Montana Territory, on the
            Upper Missouri to the Yellowstone National Park and return, made
            in the summer of 1875. Gov. Print. Office, Wash., D. C., 63-72; 63.
Lueth, Francis X.
    1944.   Those we've had. Ill. Conserv. 9 (1): 14-15, illus. Springfield; Spring
            issue.
Lummis, Charles F.
    1920.   The Spanish pioneers. Ed. 8: 1-292; 145-146; illus.
Lyon, Marcus Ward
    1936.   Mammals of Indiana. Amer. Mid. Nat. 17 (1): 1-384; 158-161. Jan.,
            illus.
"M"
    1874.   Hunting the puma or American lion [Felis concolor]. Amer. Sports.
            Mar. 28.
Macnie, J.
    1925.   Work and play in the Argentine. T. W. Laurie, London, i-viii; 1-188;
            illus.: 131.
Maine, State of
    1861.   Sixth annual report of secretary, Maine Board of Agriculture: 123.
            Augusta.
Major, R. H.
    1847.   Select letters of Christopher Columbus, with other original documents
            relating to his four voyages to the new world. Hakluyt Soc.: 1-240;
            193. London.
Mann, Walter G., and S. B. Locke
    1931.   The Kaibab deer; a brief history and recent developments. Mimeo.
            Rept., Forest Service, U. S. Dept. Agric.: 1-67; 24-25. May, 1 map.
Mann, William M.
    1943.   Wild animals in and out of the zoo. Smiths. Sci. Series 6: 302; 374
            pp., illus. Smiths. Inst., Wash., D. C.
Marcgrave, G.
    1648.   Historiae rerum naturalium Brasiliae: 235.

Marcy, Randolph B. (Captain)
  1853. Exploration of the Red River of Louisiana in year 1852, by Randolph
         B. Marcy, Capt. 1st Inf., U. S. Army, assisted by George B. Mc-
         Clellan, Brev. Capt., U. S. Engr. 32nd Congr., 2nd Sess., Sen. Ex.
         Doc. 54: 11. 50-55, 59. Wash., D. C.

  1859. The prairie traveller. A handbook for overland expeditions with maps.
         etc. Harper & Bros., New York; 340 pp., illus., p. 242.
Marge, William B.
  1945. Some extinct wild animals of Tidewater. Md. Tidewater News 2 (1):
         1, 3. June. Solomons, Md.
Markham, Clements R.
  1873. Narratives of the rites and laws of the Yncas. Trans. from original
         Spanish. Hakluyt Soc., London: 1-219; 45.

  1878. The Hawkins' voyages during the reigns of Henry VIII, Queen Eliza-
         beth, and James I. Edited, with an introduction by Markham,
         Clements R. Hakluyt Soc. London: i-li; 1-453; 60.
Marsh, E. G., Jr.
  1943. Does the mountain lion scream? Colo. Conserv. Comments 6 (4): 14.
         Denver, Dec. 15.
Martin, W.
  1833. Notes of the dissection of a puma (*Felis concolor*). Proc. Zool. Soc.
         London, Part I: 120-121. November 12.
Mason, Otis Tufton
  1889. Aboriginal skin-dressing. Rept. U. S. Nat. Mus., year ending June 30,
         1889: 553-589; illus.

  1893. North American bows, arrows, and quivers. Smiths. Inst. Report 962:
         667-668, 675; 631-679, pl. 79, 80. Smiths. Inst., Wash., D. C.
Matthew, W. D.
  1910. The phylogeny of the Felidae. Bull. Amer. Mus. Nat. Hist. 28: 289-
         316; illus. Oct. 19.
Maximilian [Prinz Zu Wied]
  1841. Reise in das innere Nord-America. 2 vols. Vol. 2, p. 357.
Maxwell, Hu
  1898. The history of Randolph County, West Virginia. Morgantown: 1-531;
         216; illus.
[May, W. B.]
  1896. California game "marked down." Southern Pacific R. R. Co. 1-64;
         21-22; illus. San Francisco.
Maynard, C. J.
  1872. Catalogue of the mammals of Florida. Bull. Essex Inst. 4 (9-10): 3.
McDermott, Francis
  1933. The amazing Amazon. Lincoln Williams, London: 1-282; 53-54, 122;
         illus.

McGuire, J. A.
   1916.   The cougar. Outdoor Life 37: 536-544.
McK. J. C., Nica, MacDonald, Henry
   1888.   Mountain lions climb trees. Forest & Stream 30: 308.
McLean, Donald D.
   1917.   The mountain lion, an enemy of the skunk. Calif. Fish and Game 3
            (1): 39. January.
McLennan, J. F.
   1869-1870.   The worship of animals and plants. Fortnightly Review 6 (n.s.)
            Part 1: 407-427; Part 2: 563-582. Vol. 7 (n.s.), Part 2: con-
            cluded; 195-216.
McQueen, A. S., and Hamp. Mizell
   1926.   History of Okefenokee Swamp. Clinton, S. C.: 1-191; 92; 27 pls.
McWhorter, Lucullus Virgil
   1915.   The border settlers of northwestern Virginia, from 1768 to 1795, em-
            bracing the life of James Hughes and other noted scouts of the great
            woods of the Trans-Allegheny, with notes and illustrative anecdotes.
            Hamilton, Ohio, 1-509; 326, 346, 347, 353, 488.
Mead, Charles W.
   1924.   Old civilizations of Inca Land. Amer. Mus. Nat. Hist. Handbook
            Series 11: 1-117; 14, 15, 91; illus.
Mead. J. R.
   1899a. Felis concolor. Trans. 30th & 31st Annual meeting, Kans. Acad. Sci.,
            1897-1898. Ed. by librarian: 16: 278, 279. Topeka. June.

   1899b. Some natural history notes of 1859. Trans. 30th & 31st Annual meet-
            ing, Kans. Acad. Sci. 16: 281. Topeka, June.
Means. Philip Ainsworth
   1931.   Ancient civilizations of the Andes. New York and London: 1-586;
            348; illus.
Mearns, Edgar A.
   1898.   Notes on the mammals of the Catskill Mountains, New York, with gen-
            eral remarks on the fauna and flora of the region. Smiths. Inst.,
            Nat. Mus. Proc. 21 (1147): 341-360.

   1900.   The native mammals of Rhode Island. Circular, Newport Nat. Hist.
            Soc. 1: 1-4; 3. Newport, July 1.
   1907.   Mammals of the Mexican boundary survey. Bull. U. S. Nat. Mus. 56:
            201. Smiths. Inst., Washington, D. C.
Meeker, Ezra
   1907.   The ox team on the old Oregon trail, 1852-1906. Pub. by author,
            New York. 1-248; 198-205; illus.
Merriam, Clinton Hart
   1882.   The vertebrates of the Adirondack region, northeastern New York.
            Trans. Linn. Soc. New York 1: 29-39.

1884.   The mammals of the Adirondack region, northeastern New York. Pub. by author, New York: 9-314; 31. Reprinted from Vols. 1 and 2, Trans. Linn. Soc. New York.

1888.   Remarks on the fauna of the Great Smoky Mountains, with description of a new species of red-backed mouse (*Evotomys carolinensis*). Amer. Journ. Sci., Series 3, Vol. 36 (216): 458-460; 459.

1897.   Descriptions of two new pumas from the northwestern United States. Proc. Biol. Soc. Wash. 11: 219-220. July 15.

1899.   Results of a biological survey of Mt. Shasta, California. North Amer. Fauna 16: 179; 104. Bur. Biol. Surv., U. S. Dept. Agric., illus.

1901.   Preliminary revision of the pumas (*Felis concolor* group). Proc. Wash. Acad. Sci. 3: 577-600; 592, 595, 598. December 11.

1903.   Eight new mammals from the United States. Biol. Soc. Wash. 16: 73-78; 73. May 29.

Merriam, John C., and Chester Stock
1932.   The Felidae of Rancho La Brea. Carnegie Inst. Wash. 1-331; 207, 215, 42 pls. December 16.

Miller, Frederic Walter
1930.   The mammals from southern Matto Grosso, Brazil. Journ. Mammal. 11 (1): 10-22; 15, 16; 2 pls. February.

Miller, Gerrit S., Jr.
1899.   Preliminary list of New York mammals. Bull. N. Y. State Mus. 6 (29): 270-390. Univ. of New York.

Mills, Enos A.
1918.   The mountain lion. Sat. Even. Post 190 (38): 125-126.

1932.   Watched by wild animals. Houghton-Mifflin Co., Boston.

Mills, William C.
1906.   Explorations of the Baum prehistoric village sites. Ohio Archaeological and Historical Quarterly 15 (1): 1-96; 28, 65; illus.

1907-1926. Certain mounds and village sites in Ohio. Columbus, Ohio, 4 vols., illus. Vol. 1 (Part 3): 28, 65; Vol. 2 (Part 3): 149-151.

Milne, J. W.
1894.   The panther in Canada. Biol. Review of Ontario 1 (4): 81-83. Toronto, Oct.

Mitchell, G. E.
1927.   What price cougars? Forest & Stream 97: 227.

Moe, Alfred K.
1904.   Honduras. 58th Congr., 3rd Sess., House of Rep. Doc. 145 (Part 4): 242 pp.; 19, Wash., D. C., illus.

Molina, Christoval de
1873. The fables and rites of the Yncas. Transl. from original Spanish by
Clements R. Markham. Hakluyt Soc., London: 1-219; 45.
Molina, Giovanni Ignazia
1782. Sazzio sulla storia naturale del Chili: 295-300.

1808. The geographical, natural, and civil history of Chili, with notes from
the Spanish and French versions. Transl. from original Italian by
an American gentleman, Mr. Alsop. Middleton, Conn., 2 vols. Vol.
1: 207-211.
Monmouth (pseudonym)
1874. Hunting the California lion. Forest and Stream 3 (17): 257-258.
Dec. 3.
Moorehead, Warren K.
1922. A report on the archaeology of Maine. Andover Press, Andover, Mass.
1-272; 157; illus.
Morley, Jack
1944. A sea going cougar. Outdoorsman 86 (6), Whole No. 511: 25-26; illus.
November-December.
Munro, J. A., and I. McTaggart Cowan
1944. Preliminary report on the birds and mammals of Kootenay National
Park, British Columbia. Canad. Field Nat. 58 (2): 34-51; illus.
March-April: 47-48.
Murie, Adolph
1935. Mammals from Guatemala and British Honduras. Miscl. Papers, Mus.
Zool., Univ. Mich. 26: 1-30; 22; illus. July 15.
Murie, Olaus J.
1917. The cougar at bay. Outing Mag. 60 (5): 605-609; illus. August.
Murphy, John Mortimer
1879. Sporting adventures in the far west. Harper & Bros., New York &
London: 1-469; 106-137.
Murrelet, The
1929. Will the cougar attack man or child? Official Bull. Pacific Northwest
Bird & Mammal Soc., General notes 10 (2): 41-42. May.
Murrill, William A.
1927. American wild cats. Forest and Stream 97: 476-478, 504.
Musgrave, Mark E.
1926. Some habits of mountain lions in Arizona. Journ. Mammal. 7 (4): 282-
285; 285.

1927. The mountain lion is just a "Fraidy Cat." Farm and Fireside 51 (6):
8-9, 61. Crowell Pub. Co., Springfield, O. June.

1938. Ben Lilly—last of the mountain men. Amer. Forests 44 (8): 349-351;
379-380; illus. August.
Nash, C. W.
1908. Manual of vertebrates of Ontario. Dept. Education, Toronto, Sec. 4: 96.

"Ned Buntline"
1880. My first cougar. Forest & Stream 13: 994.
Nelson, Edward W.
1911. A land of drought and desert—Lower California. Two thousand miles on horseback through the most extraordinary cacti forests in the world. Nat. Geog. Mag. 22 (5): 443-474; illus. May.

1916. The larger North American mammals. Nat. Geog. Soc. (Nov.): 385-472; 412; illus., Wash., D. C.

1921. Lower California and its natural resources. Nat. Acad. Sci. 16 (1st Memoir): 1-194; 110, 132. Wash., D. C.

1930. Wild animals of North America. Intimate studies of big and little creatures of the mammal kingdom. Nat. Geog. Soc. : 1-254; 91, 97-98; illus., Wash., D. C.
Nelson. Edward W., and Edward Alphonso Goldman
1929. List of the pumas, with three described as new. Journ. Mammal. 10 (4): 345-350. Nov. 11.

1931. Three new pumas. Journ. Wash. Acad. Sci. 21 (10): 209-212. May 19.

1932. A new mountain lion from Vancouver Island. Proc. Biol. Soc. Wash. 45: 105-108. July 15.

1933a. Revision of the jaguars. Journ. Mammal. 14 (3): 221-240; 221-222, August.

1933b. A new puma from Brazil. Wash. Acad. Sci. 23 (11): 534. Nov. 15.
Nelson, Hazel E.
1945. A cougar in the house. Nature Mag. 38 (3): 146-147, 164, illus. March.
Newberry, J. S.
1859. Explorations and surveys for a railroad route from the Mississippi River to the Pacific Ocean. Route near 35th Parallel explored by Lieut. A. W. Whipple in 1853-54. Report upon the Zoology of the route; report upon the mammals, No. 2: 35-72; 36.
Newhouse, Sewell
1869. The trapper's guide. Ed. 3, by Oneida Community, New York. Oakley, Mason & Co., 21 Murray St., New York.: 58-59.
Nichol, A. A.
1936. Large predatory animals. Arizona and its heritage. Bull. Univ. of Ariz. 7 (3): 1-291; 70-71; illus. Tucson, April 1.
Nicholas, Francis C.
1901. Adventures in tropical America. Forest and Stream 57 (19): 384. Nov. 9.

Nininger, H. H.
  1941. Hunting prehistoric lion tracks in Arizona. Plateau 14 (2): 21-27; 1
    illus. Quart. Pub. Northern Ariz. Soc. of Sci. & Art., Mus. North-
    ern Ariz., Flagstaff.

North, Arthur Walbridge
  1908. The mother of California. Paul Elder & Co., New York and San
    Francisco: 1-169; 38.

  ·1910. Camp and camino in Lower California, with a foreword by Admiral
    Robley D. Evans. Baker & Taylor Co., New York: 1-346; 37, 231,
    271, 277; illus.

Norton, Arthur H.
  1930. Mammals of Portland, Maine and vicinity. Proc. Port. Soc. Nat. Hist.
    4 (Part 1): 49-51.

Nuttall, Thomas
  1821. A journal of travels into the Arkansas territory during the year 1819.
    Phila., Pa.: 1-296; 118, 149; illus.

Oberholser, Harry Church
  1905. Notes on the mammals and summer birds of western North Carolina.
    Biltmore Forestry School, Biltmore, N. C. 1-24; 7. Sept. 30.

Okanogan Independent
  1924. Cougar kills a boy. Okanogan, Washington, Dec. 20.

Oregon Sportsman
  1916. 4: 61.

Oregon, State of
  1893. General and special laws and memorials and adopted by the 17th
    Regular Session, Jan. 9 to Feb. 18. [H. B. 8]: p. 38.

Orr, James E.
  1908. The last panther. Rod & Gun & Motor in Canada 10 (3): 266.
    August.

  1909. Some old reminiscences of Old Ontario. Rod & Gun & Motor Sports
    in Canada 10 (9): 840-842; 840. February.

  1909. Old time stories of Ontario. Rod & Gun & Motor in Canada 11 (3):
    259-261; 260. August.

  1911. Old time stories of old Ontario. Rod & Gun & Motor in Canada 12
    (11): 1439-1446; 1442-1444. April.

Orr, Robert T.
  1937. Notes on the life history of the Roosevelt elk in California. Journ. of
    Mammal. 18 (1): 62-66; 65. February.

Osborn, Henry Fairfield
  1930. The romance of the woolly mammoth. Nat. Hist. 30 (3): 227-241;
    239-241. May-June.

Osgood, Frederick L.
1938.   The mammals of Vermont. Journ. Mammal. 19 (4): 435-441; 438.
         November.
Osgood, Wilfred H.
1912.   Mammals from western Venezuela and eastern Colombia. Field Mus.
         Nat. Hist., Zool. Ser. 10 (5): 6; 33-66; 60. Jan. 10, illus.

1914.   Mammals of an expedition across northern Peru. Field Mus. Nat.
         Hist. Zool. Ser. Pub. 176. 10 (12): 143-185; 175. Apr. 20.

1920.   Attacked by a cougar. Journ. Mammal. 1: 240-241. November 5.

1922.   Death of Charles B. Cory. Journ. Mammal. 3 (2): 119. May.

1943.   The mammals of Chile. Field Mus. Nat. Hist. Zool. Ser. 30 (542):
         75-79. December 28. 268 pp.
Oswald, Felix Leopold
1880.   Summerland sketches, or rambles in the backwoods of Mexico and Cen-
         tral America. (1867) J. B. Lippincott & Co., Phila., Pa.: 1-425;
         78-81, 240, 249, 276, 380, 402; illus.
P. B.
1888.   Mountain lions and deer. Forest & Stream 30: 243.
Paez, Ramon Don
1868.   Travels and adventures in South and Central America. Chas. Scribner's
         Sons, New York. First series. Life in the llanos of Venezuela:
         1-473; 233-237; illus.
Parodi, Adolfo
1930-1931.   Contribucion a la osteologia de los grandes felinos vivientes de
         la Argentina. Physis. Revista de la Sociedad Argentina de Ciencias
         Naturales 10: 75-84; pls. 1-2.
Parratt, Lloyd P.
1942.   Mountain lion observed near Wawona Tunnel. Yosemite Nat. Park
         Notes, 21 (5): 48. Yosemite. May.
Pattie, James O.
1905.   Pattie's personal narrative, 1824-1830. Early western travels, by Reuben
         Gold Thwaites. Arthur H. Clark Co., Cleveland, 18: 88.
Pauw, Cornelius
1771.   Recherches philosophiques sur les Americains. Vol. 3.
Pearson, Oliver P.
1943.   The status of the vicuña in southern Peru, 1940. Journ. Mammal. 24
         (1): 97. Feb.
Pennant, Thomas
1792.   History of quadrupeds. Ed. 3, Vol. 1: 289-290.
"Peregrinus"
1824.   A panther hunt in Pennsylvania. Port Folio, Phila.: 31 (266): 494-
         499. June.

Periolat, C. F.
    1885.   Fur and fur-bearers—No. 4. Amer. Field 24 (17): 391. Oct. 24.
Perry, W. A.
    1890.   [The cougar: 405-427; illus.]. The big game of North America. Ed.
            by G. O. Shields, Chicago and New York: 1-581; 407, 408, 409,
            411-420.
Phelps, C. L.
    1884.   The panther. Forest & Stream 23: 264.
Phillips, John C.
    1912.   A new puma from Lower California. Proc. Biol. Soc. Wash. 25: 85-
            87. May 4, illus.
Philp, James
    1861.   Philp's Washington described. A complete view of the American
            capitol and the Dist. of Col., with many notices, historical, topo-
            graphical, and scientific, of the seat of government. Ed. by Wm. D.
            Haley, New York; Rudd & Carleton, Publ. 1-239; 22.
Pickens, Homer
    1942.   New Mexico safari: Lion hunting. Hunting and Fishing 19 (2): 28-
            29; 59-60; illus. February.
Pierce, James
    1823.   A memoir on the Catskill Mountains, with notices of their topography,
            scenery, mineralogy, zoology, and economic resources. Amer. Journ.
            Sci. & Arts. 6: 93.
Pocock, R. I.
    1917.   The classification of existing Felidae. Ann. Mag. Nat. Hist. Ser. 8,
            Vol. 20: 329-350; 336. November.

    1940.   Description of a new race of puma (*Puma concolor*), with note on an
            abnormal tooth in the genus. Ann. Mag. Nat. Hist. Ser. 11, 6 (33):
            307-313; 308. Sept.
Poole, Charles G.
    1933.   Some facts about predatory animal control. Calif. Fish & Game 19
            (1): 1-9; 8; illus. January.
Porter, J. Hampden
    1903.   Wild beasts. Chas. Scribner's Sons, New York: 1-380; 257-305; illus.
Powell, Addison M.
    1918.   The American panther, or puma. Outdoor Life 42 (4): 243-245,
            illus. Oct.
Powell, J. W.
    1875.   Exploration of the Colorado River of the west and its tributaries, ex-
            plored in 1869, 1870, 1871, 1872. Spec. Publ., Smiths. Inst.:
            i-ix; 1-298; 19; 86 pls., Wash., D. C.
Powell, S. A. (Rev.)
    1885.   Vermont deer and panther. Forest & Stream 25: 306.
Powers, Stephens
    1872.   Afoot and alone. Columbian Book Co., Hartford, Conn.: 299.

Preble, Edward A.
1908. A biological investigation of the Athabaska-Mackenzie region. North
       Amer. Fauna 27: 208-209. Bureau Biol. Surv., U. S. Dept. Agric.,
       Wash., D. C., Oct. 26.

1945. The American cougar. Nature Mag. 38 (3): 137, illus. March.
Prichard, H. Hesketh
1902. Through the heart of Patagonia. New York: 1-346; 30, 44, 45, 62,
       242-244, 250-252; illus.
Prodgers, Cecil Herbert
1922. Adventures in Bolivia, with an introduction by R. B. Cunninghame
       Graham. John Lane, The Bodley Head, Ltd. London: i-xvi; 1-232;
       108-109; illus.
[Putnam, F. W.]
1871. The American panther (Anon.). Amer. Nat. 4 (11): 692.
Quinn, Davis
1930. The antelope's S. O. S. Emergency Conservation Comm., New York
       City: 1-16; 11; 1 map.
"R"
1885. Panthers and deer. Forest & Stream 25: 286.
Rafinesque, C. S.
1817. Extracts from the journal of Mr. Charles Le Raye, relating to some
       new quadrupeds of the Missouri region. Amer. Monthly Mag. 1
       (6): 435-437. October.

1832a. On the North American cougars. Atlantic Journal and Friend of Knowl-
       edge 1 (1): 19, 62-63.

1832b. On the Zapotecus. Atlantic Journal and Friend of Knowledge 1 (2):
       51-56; 52.
Ramsey, J. G. M.
1853. The annuals of Tennessee to the end of the 18th century; Phila.
       i-viii; 1-741; 206; 2 maps.
Rand, A. L.
1944. The southern half of the Alaska highway and its mammals. Nat. Mus.
       Canada Bull. 98 (Biol. Ser. 27): 40. Dept. Mines and Nat. Res.,
       Ottawa. 50 pages, illus.

1945. Mammals of Yukon, Canada. Nat. Mus. Canada Bull. 100 (Biol. Ser.
       29): 38; 93 pp., illus.
Rand, A. L., and Per Host
1942. Results of the Archbold Expeditions. No. 45. Mammal notes from
       Highland County, Florida. Bull. Amer. Mus. Nat. Hist. 80 (Art.
       1): 1-21; 6. August 12.
Randsom, Webster H.
1929. Will the cougar attack man or child? The Murrelet 10 (2): 41-42.
       May.

Ray, John
    1693.   Synopsis methodica animalium quadrupedum et serpentini generis. London: 169.
Rhoads, Samuel N.
    1896.   Contributions to the zoology of Tennessee. Proc. Acad. Nat. Sci. Phila. 48: 175-205; 201.

    1903.   Mammals of Pennsylvania and New Jersey. 266 pp., illus., 130-132, 134.
Rich, J. G.
    1888.   The panther's scream. Forest & Stream 31: 25.
Riley, James Whitcomb
    1913.   What Chris'mas fetched the Wigginses. Complete Works, Biographical Edition, James Whitcomb Riley 4: 172.
Ringbolt, Ralph
    1875.   A panther serenade. Forest and Stream 4 (12): 181. April 29.
Robinson, Wirt, and Marcus Ward Lyon, Jr.
    1901.   An annotated list of mammals collected in the vicinity of La Guaira, Venezuela. Proc. U. S. Nat. Mus. 24 (1246): 135-162; 162. October.
Roenigk, Adolph
    1933.   Pioneer history of Kansas. Pub. by the author, 1-365, and appendix; 24-25.
Roosevelt, Theodore
    1885.   Hunting trips of a ranchman. Review of Reviews (Statesman edition): 32-33.

    1893.   The wilderness hunter. New York: 343.

    1901.   With the cougar hounds. Scribner's Mag. 30 (4), Part 1: 417-435; 434; Oct.; (5) Part 2: 545-564; 556. November.

    1904.   Wilderness reserves. [American Big Game in Its Haunts.] Book of Boone & Crockett Club, New York: 23-51; 26-27, 36; illus.

    1905.   Outdoor pastimes of an American hunter. New York: 1-369; 1-67, 363-369; illus.

    1926.   Through the Brazilian wilderness. National Edition, Roosevelt Works, 20 vols., Chas. Scribner's Sons, New York, Vol. 5: 1-411; 24-27, 66, 69.
    ————, T. S. Van Dyke and D. C. Elliott
    1902.   The deer family. Macmillan Co., N. Y. Pp. i-ix; 1-334; illus.; pp. 2, 44.
Round, W. E.
    1938.   When nature fails. Field and Stream 42 (12): 25, 71-73; 72; illus. April.

Russell, Phillips
1929. Red tiger. Adventures in Yucatan and Mexico. Brentanos, New York:
        1-336; 129, 250, 327; illus. by Leon Underwood.
S., O. D.
1874. Hand to hand with a panther. Forest and Stream 3 (5): 67. Septem-
        ber 10.
Sampson, Alden
1906. Wild animals of Mount Rainier National Park. Bull. Sierra Club 6
        (1): 32-38; 33. San Francisco, January.
Samuels, E. A.
1863. Mammalogy and ornithology of New England. Report, Comm. Agric.:
        265-286; 267-268. Government Printing Office, Washington, D. C.
Sanborn, Colin Campbell
1929. The land mammals of Uruguay. Field Mus. Nat. Hist. Pub. 265,
        Zool. Ser. 17 (4): 147-165; 156. October 24.
Scharff, Robert Francis
1911. Distribution and origin of life in America. London: 1-497; 106-107.
Schmidtmeyer, Peter
1824. Travels in Chile, over the Andes, in years 1820-1821. London: 1-378;
        82-84; illus.
Schoepf, David Johann
1911. Travels in the confederation, 1783-1784. Philadelphia: 107-108.
Schomburgk, Richard
1848a. Versuch einer fauna und flora von British Guiana: 776.

1848b. Travels in British Guiana during years 1840-1844. 2: 68. London.
Schomburgk, Sir Robert H.
1840. Information respecting botanical travellers. Annals Nat. Hist. 4: 325-
        327; 325-326.
Schorger, A. W.
1938. A Wisconsin specimen of cougar. Journ. Mammal. 19 (2): 252. May.

1942. Extinct and endangered mammals and birds of the upper Great Lakes
        region. Trans. Wisc. Acad. Sci., Arts, & Lett. 34: 31-32; 23-44.
Schueren, Arnold C.
1943. Foxy's lion tales. Pub. privately, Chicago, 158 pp., illus.

1945. Utah lion hunt. Field & Stream, 50 (5): 21-23. September.
Schultz, J. W., W. J. MacHaffie, et al
1888. Panthers climb trees. Forest & Stream 30: 350, 411.
Schwartz, John E.
1943. Range conditions and management of the Roosevelt elk on the Olympic
        Peninsula. Forest Service, U. S. Dept. Agric. Mimeo. 1-65; 54, 62;
        illus.

Sclater, Philip Lutley
   1868.   On breeding of mammals in the gardens of the Zoological Society of
           London, during the past twenty years. Proc. Sci. meetings, Zool.
           Soc. London: 623-626; 624.
Scott, Joseph A.
   1807.   A geographical description of the states of Maryland and Delaware: 28.
Scott, William Berryman
   1937.   A history of land mammals in the western Hemisphere. Macmillan Co.,
           New York. Pp. i-xiii; 1-786; illus., pp. 135, 143, 144, 149, 161,
           235, 601-603, 613.
Scott, W. E.
   1939.   Rare and extinct mammals of Wisconsin. Wisc. Cons. Bull. 4 (10)
           21-28; 25. Wisc. Cons. Dept., October.
Seton, Ernest Thompson
   1911.   The Arctic Prairies. Charles Scribner's Sons, N. Y. i-xvi; 1-415, illus.
           56.
   1929.   Lives of game animals. Doubleday, Doran & Co., Garden City, 4 vols.
           Vol. 1 (Part 1), Cats, wolves, and foxes: 1-337; 39, 50, 72-78; illus.
Severtzow, M. N.
   1858.   Notice sur la classification multisériale des carnivores, specialment des
           Félidés, et les etudes de zoologie générale qui s'y rettachent. Rev. et
           Mag. de Zool., Ser. 2 (t. 10): 385-393; 385. September.
Shantz, Homer Leroy
   1937.   The Saguaro forest (Arizona). Nat. Geog. Mag.: 515-532; 529. April.
Sheldon, W. G.
   1932.   Mammals collected or observed in the vicinity of Laurier Pass, British
           Columbia. Journ. Mammal. 13 (3): 196-203; 201; illus.
Shields, G. O.
   1890.   The big game of North America. [The cougar, by W. A. Perry.] Ed.
           by G. O. Shields. Rand-McNally & Co., Chicago: 1-581; 405-427;
           illus.
Shoemaker, Henry W.
   1913.   Stories of Pennsylvania animals. Reprinted from Altoona Tribune: 9-13.

   1914.   The Pennsylvania lion or panther. Altoona Tribune: 1-47; illus.

   1917.   Extinct Pennsylvania animals. Altoona Tribune Pub. Co., Altoona:
           1-134; 1-61; illus.

   1943.   The panther in Pennsylvania. Penna. Game News, Pub. by Penna.
           Game Comm., Harrisburg 13 (11): 7, 28, 32; illus. February.
"Shoshone" (W. M. Wolfe)
   1909.   A big mountain lion. Forest and Stream 72: 532.
Shuffeldt, R. W.
   1921.   The mountain lion, ocelots, lynxes, and their kin. American Forestry
           27 (334): 629-636, 659; illus. October.

Siler, A. L.
    1880. Notes on mammals of southern Utah. Amer. Nat. 14 (9): 673-674.
           Sept.
"Silver Tip"
    1887. Some notes from the Rockies. Forest and Stream 29: 125-126.
Simpich, Frederick
    1938. New Mexico melodrama. Nat. Geog. Mag.: 529-569; 558. May.
Singer, Daniel J.
    1914. Big game fields of America, North and South. Geo. H. Doran Co.,
           New York: 1-368; 253-254; illus.
Skinker, Mary Scott
    1935. Two new species of tapeworms from carnivores and a redescription of
           Taenia laticollis rudolphi, 1819. Proc. U. S. Nat. Mus. 83: 211-
           220; illus.
Skinner, Milton P.
    1927. The predatory and fur-bearing animals of the Yellowstone National
           Park. Roosevelt Wildlife Forest Exp. Sta. Bull. 4 (2): 163-281;
           200-203; illus. June.
Skottsberg, Carl
    1911. The wilds of Patagonia. Edward Arnold, London: i-xix; 1-336; 203;
           illus.
Small, H. Beaumont
    1864. The animals of North America. John Lovell, Montreal: 1-112; 48-50;
           illus.
Smith, Herbert H.
    1879. Brazil, the Amazon, and the coast. Chas. Scribner's Sons, New York:
           i-xv; 1-644; 195-197, 332; illus.
Smith, Captain John
    1884. Captain John Smith's works (1608-1631). Ed. by Edward Arber, Bir-
           mingham: i-cxxxvi; 1-973; cvi; with maps.
Smith, Sam J.
    1918. Do mountain lions scream? Outdoor Life 42 (5): 325-326. November.
Smith, Samuel
    1765. The history of the colony of Nova-Caesaria or New Jersey. James
           Parker, Burlington, N. J., David Hall, Phila.: 1-573; 112, 502-
           503, 540.
Smucker, Isaac
    1876. Centennial history of Licking County, Ohio. Clark & Underwood,
           Newark, O.: 1-80; 45.
Soper, J. Dewey
    1944. Report (typewritten) on wildlife investigations in Grande Prairie-
           Peace River region of northwestern Alberta, Canada. Nat. Parks
           Bureau Lands, Parks, and Forest Branch, Dept. Mines & Resources,
           Winnipeg, Man., 1-189; 173.
Spears, John Randolph
    1895. The gold diggings of Cape Horn. London and New York: 1-316; 190-
           196; illus.

Spencer, Clifford C.
1943. Notes on the life history of Rocky Mountain bighorn sheep in the Tarryall Mountains of Colorado. Journ. Mammal. 24 (1): 1-11; 9; illus. February.
Spencer, Herbert
1870. The origin of animal worship. Fortnightly Review 7 (n.s.): 535-550. London, Jan. 1 to June 1.
Spokane Review
1924. Spokane boy is killed by cougar. Spokane, Wash., Dec. 18.
Standley, Paul Carpenter
1924. The republic of Salvador. Annual Rept., Smiths. Inst. (Pub. No. 2724), year ending 1922: 309-328; 326; 16 pls.
Stanwell-Fletcher, John F. and Theodora C.
1940. Naturalists in the wilds of British Columbia. Sci. Monthly 50 (3): 213. March.

1943. Some accounts of the flora and fauna of the Driftwood Valley region of north-central British Columbia. Occas. Papers, B. C. Prov. Mus. 4: 86. May, 98 pp.
Stearns, R. E. C.
1876. Bears and panthers on the Pacific Coast. Amer. Nat. 10: 177.
Stephens, Frank
1906. California mammals. West Coast Pub. Co., San Diego: 1-351; 208-209; illus.
Stevenson, William Burnet
1829. Historical and descriptive narrative of twenty years' residence in South America. London, 3 vols. 1: 111-114; 2: 80-81.
Stiles, C. W., and Clara Edith Baker
1935. Key-catalogue of parasites for carnivora (cats, dogs, bears, etc.), with their possible public health importance. U. S. Public Health Service, Treasury Dept. Bull. 163: 913-1223; 964, 984.
Stock, Chester
1918. The Pleistocene fauna of Hawver Cave. Bull. Dept. Geology, Univ. of Calif. 10: 461-515; 482; illus.

1929. A census of the Pleistocene mammals of Rancho La Brea, based on the collections of the Los Angeles Museum. Journ. Mammal. 13 (4): 281-289; 286; illus.
Stone, Livingston
1882. The McCloud River panther. Forest & Stream 19: 208.

1883a. The panther of the McCloud River, *Felis concolor*. Forest & Stream 20: 203.
1883b. Habits of the panther in California. Amer. Nat. 17 (11): 1188-1190.
————, and Loren W. Green
1885. Panther on the McCloud River, Calif. Forest & Stream 23: 497.

Stone, Witmer
  1899. The pumas of the western United States. Science (n.s.) 9 (210): 34-
          35. Jan. 6.

  1908. The mammals of New Jersey. Annual Rept., N. J. State Mus. (1907),
          Trenton, 33-110; 109; illus.
  ———, and William Cram
  1902. American animals: 1-318; 290, 291; illus.
Storer, Tracy Irwin
  1923. Rabies in a mountain lion. Calif. Fish and Game 9 (2): 1-4. April.
Strecker, John K.
  1926. The mammals of McLennan County, Texas. Contr. Baylor Univ. Mu-
          seum 9: 1-15. Waco, Texas, Oct. 15. 2nd paper, suppl. notes.
Strickland, W. P.
  1856. Pioneer of the west, or life in the woods. Carlton and Porter, New
          York, and J. P. Magee, Boston: 358-370.
Strong, W. D.
  1926. Indian records of California carnivores. Journ. Mammal. 7: 59-60.
Sturgis, Robert S.
  1939. The Wichita Mountain Wildlife Refuge. Chicago Nat., Chic. Acad.
          Nat. Sci. 2 (1): 9-20; 16.
Suckley, George, and J. G. Cooper
  1860. The natural history of Washington territory and Oregon. New York:
          74, 108.
  ———, and George Gibbs
  1855. Report of explorations and surveys to ascertain most practicable and eco-
          nomical route for a railroad from the Mississippi to the Pacific Ocean,
          made under the direction of Sec. of War, 1853-1855. Vol. 10
          (Part 2), Chap. 3: Mammals, 108.
Surber, Thaddeus
  1932. The mammals of Minnesota. Minn. Dept. Conserv., Div. Fish and
          Game, St. Paul: 1-84; 12; illus.
Svihla, Ruth Dowell
  1931. Mammals of the Uinta Mountain region. Journ. Mammal. 12 (3):
          256-266; 260; illus. August.
Swan, James G.
  1857. The northwest coast or three years' residence in Washington territory.
          Harper & Bros. New York: 1-435; 28, 256.
Swanson, G., T. Surber, and T. S. Roberts
  1945. The mammals of Minnesota. Minn. Dept. Conserv. Tech. Bull. 2: 18,
          73. 108 pp., illus.
Sykes, W. H.
  1833. [On the foetus of a panther, exhibiting all the markings of the adult
          animal.] Proc. Zool. Soc. London 1: 49-50.
Tate, G. H. H.
  1931. Random observations on habits of South American mammals. Journ.
          Mammal. 12 (3): 248-256; 254.

Taylor, Walter P., and William T. Shaw
  1927. Mammals and birds of Mount Rainier National Park. Nat. Park Serv.,
         Dept. Int., Govt. Prt. Office, Wash., D. C.: 1-249; 56-58; 1 illus.

  1929. Provisional list of land mammals of the State of Washington. Occas.
         Papers, Chas. R. Conner Museum, State College, Pullman, Wash-
         ington 2: 1-32; 13. December.
Temminck, Coenraad Jacob
  1827. Monographies de mammalogie, Paris: i-xxxii; 1-268; 134-136.
Tench, C. V.
  1933. Cougar adventures. Rod and Gun in Canada: 15-17, 28. February.
Thomas, Oldfield
  1901. On a new form of puma from Patagonia. Ann. Mag. Nat. Hist. Ser.
         7 (8): 188-189. September.

  1928. The Godman-Thomas Exp. to Peru. Ann. Mag. Nat. Hist., London,
         Series 10 2 (9): 249-265; 259
Thompson, Zadock
  1853. The natural history of Vermont: 37.
Thomson, William
  1896. Great cats I have met; adventures in two hemispheres. Alpha Pub. Co.,
         Boston: 1-179; 1-85.
Thurn, Everard F.
  1883. See Im Thurn.
Thwaites, Reuben Gold
  1905. Early western travels. Vol. 20: 106.
Tinsley, Henry G.
  1920. Western mountain lions. Century Mag. 100 (5): 691-698; illus. Sep-
         tember.
Towne, Charles Wayland, and Edward Norris Wentworth
  1945. Shepherd's empire. Univ. Okla. Press: Norman, Okla. i-xii; 1-364,
         illus. 213-238.
Townsend, C. H. Tyler
  1893. Notes on the occurrence of the puma (*Felis concolor* L.) in southern
         New Mexico. Zoe 3: 309-311. June.
Townsend, Charles H.
  1887. Field notes on the mammals, birds, and reptiles of northern California.
         Proc. U. S. Nat. Mus. 10: 159-241; 189.
Townsend, John K.
  1839. Narrative of a journey across the Rocky Mountains to the Columbia
         River. p. 149.
Tozzer, Alfred M., and Glover M. Allen
  1910. Animal figures in Maya Codices. Papers, Peabody Mus. Amer. Arch.
         & Ethn. 4 (3): 280-372. Harvard Univ., Cambridge, Mass. illus.,
         February. p. 358, pl. 34.

348   THE PUMA, MYSTERIOUS AMERICAN CAT

Trautman, Milton B.
  1939. The numerical status of some mammals throughout historic time in
         vicinity of Buckeye Lake, Ohio. Ohio Journ. Sci. 39 (3): 136.
         May.
True, Frederick W.
  1889. The puma, or American lion: *Felis concolor* of Linnaeus. Rept. U. S.
         Nat. Mus. 1889: 591-608; 596-597; 1 illus.
Tschudi, J. J. von
  1849. Travels in Peru during the years 1838-1842. New York: 1-354; 221,
         294.
Tyrrell, J. B.
  1888. The mammalia of Canada. Read before Canad. Inst. April 7, and publ.
         in advance. Toronto. 28 pp; 8.
United States Government
  1848. Notes of a military reconnaissance from Fort Leavenworth in Missouri
         to San Diego, California, including parts of Arkansas, Del Norte,
         and Gila Rivers. U. S. Topo. Engr. W. H. Emory (Major) in
         charge, made in 1846-1847 with advanced guard of the U. S.
         Army of the West. 30th Congr., 1st Sess., Sen. Ex. Doc. 7 (App. 6):
         405.

  1888. Annual report of the ornithologist. Dept. of Agric., Wash., D. C.: 431.

  1934. Conservation of wildlife. Hearing, House of Rep. Spec. Comm. on
         Conserv. Wildlife, 73rd Congr., 2nd Sess., Wash., D. C.: 320.

  1936. The western range. 74th Congr., 2nd Sess., Senate Ex. Doc. 199:
         1-620; 341-361.

  1939. Wildlife conditions in national parks. Nat. Park Serv., Dept. Int.
         Conserv. Bull. 3: 1-37; 31.
United States Senate
  1944. Wildlife conservation. Report Progress of Wildlife Restoration and
         Management, Pursuant S. Res. 246 (71st Congr.) Continued in S.
         Res. 105 (78th Congr.). A resolution appointing a special com-
         mittee to investigate matters pertaining to replacement and conser-
         vation of wildlife, pp. 111, 80-84; 84. U. S. Gov. Print. Office,
         Wash., D. C.
Van Der Donck, Adriaen
  1656. A description of the New Netherlands. Coll. N. Y. Hist. Soc. Ed. 2
         (1): 167.
Van der Klaauw, C. J.
  1931. On the auditory bulla in some fossil mammals, with a general introduc-
         tion to this region of the skull. Bull. Amer. Mus. Nat. Hist. 42:
         1-352.

Van Doren, Mark
   1928. The travels of William Bartram. Macy-Masius, Publ., Mark Van
          Doren, editor. 63.
Van Hyning, T., and Frank C. Pellett
   1910.   Mammals of Iowa. Extract Proc. Iowa Acad. Sci.: 218.
Van Huizen, Peter J.
   1940. Occurrence of mountain lion on Sacramento Refuge, California. The
          Survey, Bur. Biol. Surv., U. S. Dept. Agric. 21 (6): 155. May 27.
Von Ihering, Hermann
   1911. Os mammiferos do Brazil meriodinal. I. Contribuçao. Revista do Museu
          Paulista 8: 159-163.
Von Poeppig, Eduard Friedrich
   1836. Reise in Chile, Peru, und auf def Amazonenstrome, während der jahre
          1827-1832. Leipzig: 1-464; 332.
Vose, C. L.
   1939. Cougar on the bridge. Forest and Outdoors 5 (5): 140. Montreal,
          Canada. May.
"W. T."
   1884. The American jaguar and panther (cougar). American Field 22: 7.
Waddell, J. M.
   1887. A panther hunt in the canebrake. Forest and Stream 28 (15): 323.
          May 5.
Wade, J. G.
   1929. Mountain lion seen killing a doe. Calif. Fish and Game 15: 73-75.
Wailes, Benjamin Leonard Covington
   1854. Report on the agriculture and geology of Mississippi. E. Barksdale,
          State Printer: 1-371; Chap. 6, Fauna, 315; illus.
Wallace, Alfred Russell
   1876. The geographical distribution of animals. New York: 1: 1-503; 2:
          1-607; 192-194; illus.
Wallihan, Allen Grant
   1901. Camera shots at big game, with introduction by Theodore Roosevelt.
          Doubleday, Page & Co., New York, 1-77; 6-7, 10-11, 19-20, 50-
          74; illus.
————————, and Mrs.
   1894. Hoofs, claws, and antlers of the Rocky Mountains by camera. Frank S.
          Thayer, Denver, Colo., unpaged, illus.
Ward, H. G.
   1828. Mexico in 1827. London, 2 vols. 2: App. B, 549, 552.
Warden, D. B.
   1819. Statistical, political, and historical account of the United States of North
          America, from the period of their first colonization to the present
          day. 3 vols. Edinburgh. 1: 430; 2: 38, 124, 326, 351, 411, 524.
Warren, Edward Royal
   1910. The mammals of Colorado. 1-300; 256-258; illus.

1927.   The beaver; its work and its ways. Monograph 2, Amer. Soc. Mammal., Williams & Wilkins: 1-177; 146-149.

Watkins, John
1804.   Notices of the natural history of the northerly parts of Louisiana in letter to Dr. Barton. Trans. Amer. Philos. Soc. 6 (Part 1): 69-72; 70.

Webber, Charles Wilkins
1875.   Wild scenes and wild hunters; or the romance of sporting. Phila.: 1-610; 403-424; illus.

Webster, E. B.
1920.   The king of the Olympics, the Roosevelt elk and other mammals of the Olympic Mountains. Pub. by author, Port Angeles, Wash.: 1-227; 55-69; illus.

1924.   Cougar attacks man on woodland trail. The Murrelet 5 (2): 12. May.

"Webster Parish"
1883.   My first panther. Forest & Stream 20: 125.

Wells, James William
1886.   Exploring and traveling three thousand miles through Brazil from Rio de Janeiro to Maranhao. J. B. Lippincott, Phila., 2 vols.; illus. Low, Marston, London. 1: 67, 152-153.

Wells, William
1901.   Animals and man. Forest and Stream 57 (2): 24. July 13.

1932.   Cougar! Field and Stream: 16-18, 80. March.

Wetmore, Helen Cody
1899.   Last of the great scouts. Grosset & Dunlap, New York: 1-333; 15-16; illus.

White, George
1849.   Statistics of Georgia. (Fauna and flora, John Bachman.) W. Thorne Williams, Savannah, Ga. 1-624; appendix; 1-77; App. 3.

Whitlow, Wayne B., and E. Raymond Hall
1933.   Mammals of the Pocatello region of southeastern Idaho. Univ. of Calif. Pub. in Zool. 40 (3): 235-275; illus. 250. Sept. 20.

Whitney, Casper W.
1895.   The cougar; hunting in many lands. Book of Boone & Crockett Club. Ed. by Theodore Roosevelt and George Bird Grinnell. Forest & Stream Pub. Co., New York: 253-254.

Whymper, Edward
1892.   Travels amongst the great Andes of the Equator. Chas. Scribner's Sons, New York: i-xxiv; 1-456; 115, 229, 243; 4 maps, 118 illus.

Wilcox, Alvin H.
1907.   A pioneer history of Becker County, Minnesota. Pioneer Press, St. Paul: 73-76.

Wildman, Edward Embree
1933.   Penn's woods, 1682-1932. 1-192; 14; illus.

Wilkes, Charles
 1845. Narrative of U. S. exploring expedition during years 1838-1842.
        Phila. 5 vols. 4: 372.
"Will"
 1885. Deer and panthers. Forest & Stream 25: 343.
Williams, Samuel Cole
 1930. Beginnings of west Tennessee. In the land of the Chickasaws, 1541-
        1841. Watauge Press, Johnson City: i-xii; 1-331; 96, 161, 180.
Wilson, Robert W.
 1942. Preliminary study of the fauna of Rampart Cave, Arizona. Carnegie
        Inst. of Wash. Pub. 530: 169-185; 180-181. Jan. 19.
Wolffsohn, John A.
 1923. Medidas maximas y minimas de algunos mamiferos chilenos colectados
        entre los anos 1896 y 1917. Rev. Chil. Hist. Nat. 27: 159-167.
────────, and Carlos E. Porter
 1908. Catalogo metodico de los mamiferos Chilenos existentes en el Museo de
        Valparaiso en Diciembre de 1905. Rev. Chil. Hist. Nat. 12: 66-85.
Wood, Norman A.
 1914. An annotated checklist of Michigan mammals. Occas. Papers, Univ.
        Mich. Mus. Zool. 4: 8. Ann Arbor, Apr. 1.

 1922. The mammals of Washtenaw County, Michigan. Occas. Papers, Mus.
        Zool., Univ. Mich. 123: 1-23; 13-14. July 10.
Woodbury, A. M., J. W. Thornton, Walter Russell, Donald J. Jolley, and D. T.
        Scoyden
 1929. The cougar. Zion-Bryce Nature Notes 1 (3): 6. Oct. Zion-Bryce
        Canyon National Park, Utah. Nat. Park Service, Dept. Int., Wash.,
        D. C.
Woodhouse, S. W.
 1853. Report on the natural history of country passed over by exploring ex-
        pedition under command of Capt. L. Sitgreaves, U. S. Topo. Engrs.,
        1851. 32nd Congr., 2nd Sess., Sen. Ex. Doc. 59: 37, 47. Wash.,
        D. C.
Wright, George M.
 1934. Cougar surprised at well-stocked larder. Journ. Mammal. 1£: 321.
────────, Joseph S. Dixon, and Ben H. Thompson
 1933. Fauna of the national parks of the United States. A preliminary survey
        of faunal relations in national parks. Contr. of Wildlife Survey,
        U. S. Dept. Int., Wash., D. C. Fauna Series 1: i-vi; 1-157; illus.
        35, 36, 44, 76, 87, 88, 92, 93, 97, 98, 99, 106, 110, 117, 122,
        125, 128, 129, 131, 132, 136, 139. May 1932.
Wright, W. N.
 1906. Lynx and lion. Amer. Mag. 62 (5): 523-529; illus. September.
Yeager, Dorr G.
 1931. Our wilderness neighbors. A. C. McClurg & Co., Chicago: 126-133;
        illus.

Young, Stanley P.
   1927.   Mountain lion eats its kittens. Journ. Mammal. 8 (2): 158-160. May.

   1933.   Hints on mountain lion trapping. Bur. Biol. Surv. Leaflet 94, 1-8, 5
           illus. U. S. Dept. Agric., Wash., D. C.

   1940a. Review, North American big game. Book, Boone & Crockett Club.
           Compiled by Committee on Records of North Amer. Big Game.
           1-533; illus. Journ. Mammal. 21 (1): 96-98.

   1940b. Catniping our big cats. Western Sportsman 4 (6): 4-8; 4 illus. Den-
           ver, Colorado. May.

   1941.   Does the puma (mountain lion) scream? Western Sportsman 6 (6):
           6-9, 24; 11 illus. Denver, Colorado. May.

   1942.   The war on the wolf. Amer. Forests 48 (11): 492-495, 526; illus.
           Nov. 48 (12): 552-555, 572-574; illus. December.

   1943.   Early wildlife Americana. American Forests 49 (8): 387-389, 414;
           3 illus. August.

   1944.   Other working dogs and the wild species. Nat. Geog. Mag. 86 (3):
           363-384; illus. September. Nat. Geog. Soc., Wash., D. C.
   1945.   Mountain lion trapping. Circ. 6, Fish & Wildlife Service, U. S. Dept.
           Interior, Wash., D. C., 7 pp., illus.
   ——————, and Edward Alphonso Goldman
   1944.   The wolves of North America. American Wildlife Inst., Wash., D. C.,
           i-xx; 1-636; illus. 150, 262.
Young, W. D.
   1917.   Does the cougar scream? Outing Mag. 70 (4): 480-482. July.
Zahn, John Augustine
   1910.   Up the Orinoco and down the Magdalene. D. Appleton & Co., New
           York & London: i-xiii; 1-439; 94; illus.

   1911.   Along the Andes and down the Amazon. D. Appleton & Co., New York
           & London: i-xx; 1-542; 412, 416; illus.
Zeigler, Wilbur Gleason
   1883.   The heart of the Alleghanies; or western North Carolina. 386 pp., illus.

INDEX

[New names and principal page references to a species in **boldface**; synonyms in *italic*]

CATALOG OF DOVER BOOKS

Books Explaining Science and Mathematics

WHAT IS SCIENCE?, N. Campbell. The role of experiment and measurement, the function of mathematics, the nature of scientific laws, the difference between laws and theories, the limitations of science, and many similarly provocative topics are treated clearly and without technicalities by an eminent scientist. "Still an excellent introduction to scientific philosophy," H. Margenau in PHYSICS TODAY. "A first-rate primer . . . deserves a wide audience," SCIENTIFIC AMERICAN. 192pp. 5⅜ x 8. S43 Paperbound **$1.25**

THE NATURE OF PHYSICAL THEORY, P. W. Bridgman. A Nobel Laureate's clear, non-technical lectures on difficulties and paradoxes connected with frontier research on the physical sciences. Concerned with such central concepts as thought, logic, mathematics, relativity, probability, wave mechanics, etc. he analyzes the contributions of such men as Newton, Einstein, Bohr, Heisenberg, and many others. "Lucid and entertaining . . . recommended to anyone who wants to get some insight into current philosophies of science," THE NEW PHILOSOPHY. Index. xi + 138pp. 5⅜ x 8. S33 Paperbound **$1.25**

EXPERIMENT AND THEORY IN PHYSICS, Max Born. A Nobel Laureate examines the nature of experiment and theory in theoretical physics and analyzes the advances made by the great physicists of our day: Heisenberg, Einstein, Bohr, Planck, Dirac, and others. The actual process of creation is detailed step-by-step by one who participated. A fine examination of the scientific method at work. 44pp. 5⅜ x 8. S308 Paperbound **75¢**

THE PSYCHOLOGY OF INVENTION IN THE MATHEMATICAL FIELD, J. Hadamard. The reports of such men as Descartes, Pascal, Einstein, Poincaré, and others are considered in this investigation of the method of idea-creation in mathematics and other sciences and the thinking process in general. How do ideas originate? What is the role of the unconscious? What is Poincaré's forgetting hypothesis? are some of the fascinating questions treated. A penetrating analysis of Einstein's thought processes concludes the book. xiii + 145pp. 5⅜ x 8. T107 Paperbound **$1.25**

THE NATURE OF LIGHT AND COLOUR IN THE OPEN AIR, M. Minnaert. Why are shadows sometimes blue, sometimes green, or other colors depending on the light and surroundings? What causes mirages? Why do multiple suns and moons appear in the sky? Professor Minnaert explains these unusual phenomena and hundreds of others in simple, easy-to-understand terms based on optical laws and the properties of light and color. No mathematics is required but artists, scientists, students, and everyone fascinated by these "tricks" of nature will find thousands of useful and amazing pieces of information. Hundreds of observational experiments are suggested which require no special equipment. 200 illustrations; 42 photos. xvi + 362pp. 5⅜ x 8. T196 Paperbound **$1.95**

THE UNIVERSE OF LIGHT, W. Bragg. Sir William Bragg, Nobel Laureate and great modern physicist, is also well known for his powers of clear exposition. Here he analyzes all aspects of light for the layman: lenses, reflection, refraction, the optics of vision, x-rays, the photoelectric effect, etc. He tells you what causes the color of spectra, rainbows, and soap bubbles, how magic mirrors work, and much more. Dozens of simple experiments are described. Preface. Index. 199 line drawings and photographs, including 2 full-page color plates. x + 283pp. 5⅜ x 8. T538 Paperbound **$1.85**

SOAP-BUBBLES: THEIR COLOURS AND THE FORCES THAT MOULD THEM, C. V. Boys. For continuing popularity and validity as scientific primer, few books can match this volume of easily-followed experiments, explanations. Lucid exposition of complexities of liquid films, surface tension and related phenomena, bubbles' reaction to heat, motion, music, magnetic fields. Experiments with capillary attraction, soap bubbles on frames, composite bubbles, liquid cylinders and jets, bubbles other than soap, etc. Wonderful introduction to scientific method, natural laws that have many ramifications in areas of modern physics. Only complete edition in print. New Introduction by S. Z. Lewin, New York University. 83 illustrations; 1 full-page color plate. xii + 190pp. 5⅜ x 8½. T542 Paperbound **95¢**

THE STORY OF X-RAYS FROM RONTGEN TO ISOTOPES, A. R. Bleich, M.D. This book, by a member of the American College of Radiology, gives the scientific explanation of x-rays, their applications in medicine, industry and art, and their danger (and that of atmospheric radiation) to the individual and the species. You learn how radiation therapy is applied against cancer, how x-rays diagnose heart disease and other ailments, how they are used to examine mummies for information on diseases of early societies, and industrial materials for hidden weaknesses. 54 illustrations show x-rays of flowers, bones, stomach, gears with flaws, etc. 1st publication. Index. xix + 186pp. 5⅜ x 8. **T622 Paperbound $1.35**

SPINNING TOPS AND GYROSCOPIC MOTION, John Perry. A classic elementary text of the dynamics of rotation — the behavior and use of rotating bodies such as gyroscopes and tops. In simple, everyday English you are shown how quasi-rigidity is induced in discs of paper, smoke rings, chains, etc., by rapid motions; why a gyrostat falls and why a top rises; precession; how the earth's motion affects climate; and many other phenomena. Appendix on practical use of gyroscopes. 62 figures. 128pp. 5⅜ x 8. **T416 Paperbound $1.00**

SNOW CRYSTALS, W. A. Bentley, M. J. Humphreys. For almost 50 years W. A. Bentley photographed snow flakes in his laboratory in Jericho, Vermont; in 1931 the American Meteorological Society gathered together the best of his work, some 2400 photographs of snow flakes, plus a few ice flowers, windowpane frosts, dew, frozen rain, and other ice formations. Pictures were selected for beauty and scientific value. A very valuable work to anyone in meteorology, cryology; most interesting to layman; extremely useful for artist who wants beautiful, crystalline designs. All copyright free. Unabridged reprint of 1931 edition. 2453 illustrations. 227pp. 8 x 10½. **T287 Paperbound $2.95**

A DOVER SCIENCE SAMPLER, edited by George Barkin. A collection of brief, non-technical passages from 44 Dover Books Explaining Science for the enjoyment of the science-minded browser. Includes work of Bertrand Russell, Poincaré, Laplace, Max Born, Galileo, Newton; material on physics, mathematics, metallurgy, anatomy, astronomy, chemistry, etc. You will be fascinated by Martin Gardner's analysis of the sincere pseudo-scientist, Moritz's account of Newton's absentmindedness, Bernard's examples of human vivisection, etc. Illustrations from the Diderot Pictorial Encyclopedia and De Re Metallica. 64 pages. **FREE**

THE STORY OF ATOMIC THEORY AND ATOMIC ENERGY, J. G. Feinberg. A broader approach to subject of nuclear energy and its cultural implications than any other similar source. Very readable, informal, completely non-technical text. Begins with first atomic theory, 600 B.C. and carries you through the work of Mendelejeff, Röntgen, Madame Curie, to Einstein's equation and the A-bomb. New chapter goes through thermonuclear fission, binding energy, other events up to 1959. Radioactive decay and radiation hazards, future benefits, work of Bohr, moderns, hundreds more topics. "Deserves special mention . . . not only authoritative but thoroughly popular in the best sense of the word," Saturday Review. Formerly, "The Atom Story." Expanded with new chapter. Three appendixes. Index. 34 illustrations. vii + 243pp. 5⅜ x 8. **T625 Paperbound $1.45**

THE STRANGE STORY OF THE QUANTUM, AN ACCOUNT FOR THE GENERAL READER OF THE GROWTH OF IDEAS UNDERLYING OUR PRESENT ATOMIC KNOWLEDGE, B. Hoffmann. Presents lucidly and expertly, with barest amount of mathematics, the problems and theories which led to modern quantum physics. Dr. Hoffmann begins with the closing years of the 19th century, when certain trifling discrepancies were noticed, and with illuminating analogies and examples takes you through the brilliant concepts of Planck, Einstein, Pauli, Broglie, Bohr, Schroedinger, Heisenberg, Dirac, Sommerfeld, Feynman, etc. This edition includes a new, long postscript carrying the story through 1958. "Of the books attempting an account of the history and contents of our modern atomic physics which have come to my attention, this is the best," H. Margenau, Yale University, in "American Journal of Physics." 32 tables and line illustrations. Index. 275pp. 5⅜ x 8. **T518 Paperbound $1.45**

SPACE AND TIME, E. Borel. Written by a versatile mathematician of world renown with his customary lucidity and precision, this introduction to relativity for the layman presents scores of examples, analogies, and illustrations that open up new ways of thinking about space and time. It covers abstract geometry and geographical maps, continuity and topology, the propagation of light, the special theory of relativity, the general theory of relativity, theoretical researches, and much more. Mathematical notes. 2 Indexes. 4 Appendices. 15 figures. xvi + 243pp. 5⅜ x 8. **T592 Paperbound $1.45**

FROM EUCLID TO EDDINGTON: A STUDY OF THE CONCEPTIONS OF THE EXTERNAL WORLD, Sir Edmund Whittaker. A foremost British scientist traces the development of theories of natural philosophy from the western rediscovery of Euclid to Eddington, Einstein, Dirac, etc. The inadequacy of classical physics is contrasted with present day attempts to understand the physical world through relativity, non-Euclidean geometry, space curvature, wave mechanics, etc. 5 major divisions of examination: Space; Time and Movement; the Concepts of Classical Physics; the Concepts of Quantum Mechanics; the Eddington Universe. 212pp. 5⅜ x 8. **T491 Paperbound $1.35**

Nature, Biology

NATURE RECREATION: Group Guidance for the Out-of-doors, William Gould Vinal. Intended for both the uninitiated nature instructor and the education student on the college level, this complete "how-to" program surveys the entire area of nature education for the young. Philosophy of nature recreation; requirements, responsibilities, important information for group leaders; nature games; suggested group projects; conducting meetings and getting discussions started; etc. Scores of immediately applicable teaching aids, plus completely updated sources of information, pamphlets, field guides, recordings, etc. Bibliography. 74 photographs. + 310pp. 5⅜ x 8½. **T1015 Paperbound $1.75**

HOW TO KNOW THE WILD FLOWERS, Mrs. William Starr Dana. Classic nature book that has introduced thousands to wonders of American wild flowers. Color-season principle of organization is easy to use, even by those with no botanical training, and the genial, refreshing discussions of history, folklore, uses of over 1,000 native and escape flowers, foliage plants are informative as well as fun to read. Over 170 full-page plates, collected from several editions, may be colored in to make permanent records of finds. Revised to conform with 1950 edition of Gray's Manual of Botany. xlii + 438pp. 5⅜ x 8½. **T332 Paperbound $1.85**

HOW TO KNOW THE FERNS, F. T. Parsons. Ferns, among our most lovely native plants, are all too little known. This classic of nature lore will enable the layman to identify almost any American fern he may come across. After an introduction on the structure and life of ferns, the 57 most important ferns are fully pictured and described (arranged upon a simple identification key). Index of Latin and English names. 61 illustrations and 42 full-page plates. xiv + 215pp. 5⅜ x 8. **T740 Paperbound $1.25**

MANUAL OF THE TREES OF NORTH AMERICA, Charles Sprague Sargent. Still unsurpassed as most comprehensive, reliable study of North American tree characteristics, precise locations and distribution. By dean of American dendrologists. Every tree native to U.S., Canada, Alaska, 185 genera, 717 species, described in detail—leaves, flowers, fruit, winterbuds, bark, wood, growth habits etc. plus discussion of varieties and local variants, immaturity variations. Over 100 keys, including unusual 11-page analytical key to genera, aid in identification. 783 clear illustrations of flowers, fruit, leaves. An unmatched permanent reference work for all nature lovers. Second enlarged (1926) edition. Synopsis of families. Analytical key to genera. Glossary of technical terms. Index. 783 illustrations, 1 map. Two volumes. Total of 982pp. 5⅜ x 8. **T277 Vol. I Paperbound $2.00**
T278 Vol. II Paperbound $2.00
The set $4.00

TREES OF THE EASTERN AND CENTRAL UNITED STATES AND CANADA, W. M. Harlow. A revised edition of a standard middle-level guide to native trees and important escapes. More than 140 trees are described in detail, and illustrated with more than 600 drawings and photographs. Supplementary keys will enable the careful reader to identify almost any tree he might encounter. xiii + 288pp. 5⅜ x 8. **T395 Paperbound $1.35**

GUIDE TO SOUTHERN TREES, Ellwood S. Harrar and J. George Harrar. All the essential information about trees indigenous to the South, in an extremely handy format. Introductory essay on methods of tree classification and study, nomenclature, chief divisions of Southern trees, etc. Approximately 100 keys and synopses allow for swift, accurate identification of trees. Numerous excellent illustrations, non-technical text make this a useful book for teachers of biology or natural science, nature lovers, amateur naturalists. Revised 1962 edition. Index. Bibliography. Glossary of technical terms. 920 illustrations; 201 full-page plates. ix + 709pp. 4⅝ x 6⅜. **T945 Paperbound $2.25**

FRUIT KEY AND TWIG KEY TO TREES AND SHRUBS, W. M. Harlow. Bound together in one volume for the first time, these handy and accurate keys to fruit and twig identification are the only guides of their sort with photographs (up to 3 times natural size). "Fruit Key": Key to over 120 different deciduous and evergreen fruits. 139 photographs and 11 line drawings. Synoptic summary of fruit types. Bibliography. 2 Indexes (common and scientific names). "Twig Key": Key to over 160 different twigs and buds. 173 photographs. Glossary of technical terms. Bibliography. 2 Indexes (common and scientific names). Two volumes bound as one. Total of xvii + 126pp. 5⅝ x 8⅜. **T511 Paperbound $1.25**

INSECT LIFE AND INSECT NATURAL HISTORY, S. W. Frost. A work emphasizing habits, social life, and ecological relations of insects, rather than more academic aspects of classification and morphology. Prof. Frost's enthusiasm and knowledge are everywhere evident as he discusses insect associations and specialized habits like leaf-rolling, leaf-mining, and case-making, the gall insects, the boring insects, aquatic insects, etc. He examines all sorts of matters not usually covered in general works, such as: insects as human food, insect music and musicians, insect response to electric and radio waves, use of insects in art and literature. The admirably executed purpose of this book, which covers the middle ground between elementary treatment and scholarly monographs, is to excite the reader to observe for himself. Over 700 illustrations. Extensive bibliography. x + 524pp. 5⅜ x 8. **T517 Paperbound $2.45**

CATALOGUE OF DOVER BOOKS

COMMON SPIDERS OF THE UNITED STATES, J. H. Emerton. Here is a nature hobby you can pursue right in your own cellar! Only non-technical, but thorough, reliable guide to spiders for the layman. Over 200 spiders from all parts of the country, arranged by scientific classification, are identified by shape and color, number of eyes, habitat and range, habits, etc. Full text, 501 line drawings and photographs, and valuable introduction explain webs, poisons, threads, capturing and preserving spiders, etc. Index. New synoptic key by S. W. Frost. xxiv + 225pp. 5⅜ x 8.   T223 Paperbound **$1.35**

THE LIFE STORY OF THE FISH: HIS MANNERS AND MORALS, Brian Curtis. A comprehensive, non-technical survey of just about everything worth knowing about fish. Written for the aquarist, the angler, and the layman with an inquisitive mind, the text covers such topics as evolution, external covering and protective coloration, physics and physiology of vision, maintenance of equilibrium, function of the lateral line canal for auditory and temperature senses, nervous system, function of the air bladder, reproductive system and methods—courtship, mating, spawning, care of young—and many more. Also sections on game fish, the problems of conservation and a fascinating chapter on fish curiosities. "Clear, simple language . . . excellent judgment in choice of subjects . . . delightful sense of humor," New York Times. Revised (1949) edition. Index. Bibliography of 72 items. 6 full-page photographic plates. xii + 284pp. 5⅜ x 8.   T929 Paperbound **$1.50**

BATS, Glover Morrill Allen. The most comprehensive study of bats as a life-form by the world's foremost authority. A thorough summary of just about everything known about this fascinating and mysterious flying mammal, including its unique location sense, hibernation and cycles, its habitats and distribution, its wing structure and flying habits, and its relationship to man in the long history of folklore and superstition. Written on a middle-level, the book can be profitably studied by a trained zoologist and thoroughly enjoyed by the layman. "An absorbing text with excellent illustrations. Bats should have more friends and fewer thoughtless detractors as a result of the publication of this volume," William Beebe, Books. Extensive bibliography. 57 photographs and illustrations. x + 368pp. 5⅜ x 8½.
T984 Paperbound **$2.00**

BIRDS AND THEIR ATTRIBUTES, Glover Morrill Allen. A fine general introduction to birds as living organisms, especially valuable because of emphasis on structure, physiology, habits, behavior. Discusses relationship of bird to man, early attempts at scientific ornithology, feathers and coloration, skeletal structure including bills, legs and feet, wings. Also food habits, evolution and present distribution, feeding and nest-building, still unsolved questions of migrations and location sense, many more similar topics. Final chapter on classification, nomenclature. A good popular-level summary for the biologist; a first-rate introduction for the layman. Reprint of 1925 edition. References and index. 51 illustrations. viii + 338pp. 5⅜ x 8½.   T957 Paperbound **$1.85**

LIFE HISTORIES OF NORTH AMERICAN BIRDS, Arthur Cleveland Bent. Bent's monumental series of books on North American birds, prepared and published under auspices of Smithsonian Institute, is the definitive coverage of the subject, the most-used single source of information. Now the entire set is to be made available by Dover in inexpensive editions. This encyclopedic collection of detailed, specific observations utilizes reports of hundreds of contemporary observers, writings of such naturalists as Audubon, Burroughs, William Brewster, as well as author's own extensive investigations. Contains literally everything known about life history of each bird considered: nesting, eggs, plumage, distribution and migration, voice, enemies, courtship, etc. These not over-technical works are musts for ornithologists, conservationists, amateur naturalists, anyone seriously interested in American birds.

BIRDS OF PREY. More than 100 subspecies of hawks, falcons, eagles, buzzards, condors and owls, from the common barn owl to the extinct caracara of Guadaloupe Island. 400 photographs. Two volume set. Index for each volume. Bibliographies of 403, 520 items. 197 full-page plates. Total of 907pp. 5⅜ x 8½.   Vol. I T931 Paperbound **$2.35**
Vol. II T932 Paperbound **$2.35**

WILD FOWL. Ducks, geese, swans, and tree ducks—73 different subspecies. Two volume set. Index for each volume. Bibliographies of 124, 144 items. 106 full-page plates. Total of 685pp. 5⅜ x 8½.   Vol. I T285 Paperbound **$2.35**
Vol. II T286 Paperbound **$2.35**

SHORE BIRDS. 81 varieties (sandpipers, woodcocks, plovers, snipes, phalaropes, curlews, oyster catchers, etc.). More than 200 photographs of eggs, nesting sites, adult and young of important species. Two volume set. Index for each volume. Bibliographies of 261, 188 items. 121 full-page plates. Total of 860pp. 5⅜ x 8½.   Vol. I T933 Paperbound **$2.35**
Vol. II T934 Paperbound **$2.35**

THE LIFE OF PASTEUR, R. Vallery-Radot. 13th edition of this definitive biography, cited in Encyclopaedia Britannica. Authoritative, scholarly, well-documented with contemporary quotes, observations; gives complete picture of Pasteur's personal life; especially thorough presentation of scientific activities with silkworms, fermentation, hydrophobia, inoculation, etc. Introduction by Sir William Osler. Index. 505pp. 5⅜ x 8.   T632 Paperbound **$2.00**

Puzzles, Mathematical Recreations

SYMBOLIC LOGIC and THE GAME OF LOGIC, Lewis Carroll. "Symbolic Logic" is not concerned with modern symbolic logic, but is instead a collection of over 380 problems posed with charm and imagination, using the syllogism, and a fascinating diagrammatic method of drawing conclusions. In "The Game of Logic" Carroll's whimsical imagination devises a logical game played with 2 diagrams and counters (included) to manipulate hundreds of tricky syllogisms. The final section, "Hit or Miss" is a lagniappe of 101 additional puzzles in the delightful Carroll manner. Until this reprint edition, both of these books were rarities costing up to $15 each. Symbolic Logic: Index. xxxi + 199pp. The Game of Logic: 96pp. 2 vols. bound as one. 5⅜ x 8.   **T492 Paperbound $1.50**

PILLOW PROBLEMS and A TANGLED TALE, Lewis Carroll. One of the rarest of all Carroll's works, "Pillow Problems" contains 72 original math puzzles, all typically ingenious. Particularly fascinating are Carroll's answers which remain exactly as he thought them out, reflecting his actual mental process. The problems in "A Tangled Tale" are in story form, originally appearing as a monthly magazine serial. Carroll not only gives the solutions, but uses answers sent in by readers to discuss wrong approaches and misleading paths, and grades them for insight. Both of these books were rarities until this edition, "Pillow Problems" costing up to $25, and "A Tangled Tale" $15. Pillow Problems: Preface and Introduction by Lewis Carroll. xx + 109pp. A Tangled Tale: 6 illustrations. 152pp. Two vols. bound as one. 5⅜ x 8.   **T493 Paperbound $1.50**

AMUSEMENTS IN MATHEMATICS, Henry Ernest Dudeney. The foremost British originator of mathematical puzzles is always intriguing, witty, and paradoxical in this classic, one of the largest collections of mathematical amusements. More than 430 puzzles, problems, and paradoxes. Mazes and games, problems on number manipulation, unicursal and other route problems, puzzles on measuring, weighing, packing, age, kinship, chessboards, joiners', crossing river, plane figure dissection, and many others. Solutions. More than 450 illustrations. vii + 258pp. 5⅜ x 8.   **T473 Paperbound $1.25**

THE CANTERBURY PUZZLES, Henry Dudeney. Chaucer's pilgrims set one another problems in story form. Also Adventures of the Puzzle Club, the Strange Escape of the King's Jester, the Monks of Riddlewell, the Squire's Christmas Puzzle Party, and others. All puzzles are original, based on dissecting plane figures, arithmetic, algebra, elementary calculus and other branches of mathematics, and purely logical ingenuity. "The limit of ingenuity and intricacy," The Observer. Over 110 puzzles. Full Solutions. 150 illustrations. vii + 225pp. 5⅜ x 8.   **T474 Paperbound $1.25**

MATHEMATICAL EXCURSIONS, H. A. Merrill. Even if you hardly remember your high school math, you'll enjoy the 90 stimulating problems contained in this book and you will come to understand a great many mathematical principles with surprisingly little effort. Many useful shortcuts and diversions not generally known are included: division by inspection, Russian peasant multiplication, memory systems for pi, building odd and even magic squares, square roots by geometry, dyadic systems, and many more. Solutions to difficult problems. 50 illustrations. 145pp. 5⅜ x 8.   **T350 Paperbound $1.00**

MAGIC SQUARES AND CUBES, W. S. Andrews. Only book-length treatment in English, a thorough non-technical description and analysis. Here are nasik, overlapping, pandiagonal, serrated squares; magic circles, cubes, spheres, rhombuses. Try your hand at 4-dimensional magical figures! Much unusual folklore and tradition included. High school algebra is sufficient. 754 diagrams and illustrations. viii + 419pp. 5⅜ x 8.   **T658 Paperbound $1.85**

CALIBAN'S PROBLEM BOOK: MATHEMATICAL, INFERENTIAL AND CRYPTOGRAPHIC PUZZLES, H. Phillips (Caliban), S. T. Shovelton, G. S. Marshall. 105 ingenious problems by the greatest living creator of puzzles based on logic and inference. Rigorous, modern, piquant; reflecting their author's unusual personality, these intermediate and advanced puzzles all involve the ability to reason clearly through complex situations; some call for mathematical knowledge, ranging from algebra to number theory. Solutions. xi + 180pp. 5⅜ x 8.   **T736 Paperbound $1.25**

MATHEMATICAL PUZZLES FOR BEGINNERS AND ENTHUSIASTS, G. Mott-Smith. 188 mathematical puzzles based on algebra, dissection of plane figures, permutations, and probability, that will test and improve your powers of inference and interpretation. The Odic Force, The Spider's Cousin, Ellipse Drawing, theory and strategy of card and board games like tit-tat-toe, go moku, salvo, and many others. 100 pages of detailed mathematical explanations. Appendix of primes, square roots, etc. 135 illustrations. 2nd revised edition. 248pp. 5⅜ x 8.   **T198 Paperbound $1.00**

MATHEMAGIC, MAGIC PUZZLES, AND GAMES WITH NUMBERS, R. V. Heath. More than 60 new puzzles and stunts based on the properties of numbers. Easy techniques for multiplying large numbers mentally, revealing hidden numbers magically, finding the date of any day in any year, and dozens more. Over 30 pages devoted to magic squares, triangles, cubes, circles, etc. Edited by J. S. Meyer. 76 illustrations. 128pp. 5⅜ x 8.   **T110 Paperbound $1.00**

CATALOGUE OF DOVER BOOKS

THE BOOK OF MODERN PUZZLES, G. L. Kaufman. A completely new series of puzzles as fascinating as crossword and deduction puzzles but based upon different principles and techniques. Simple 2-minute teasers, word labyrinths, design and pattern puzzles, logic and observation puzzles — over 150 braincrackers. Answers to all problems. 116 illustrations. 192pp. 5⅜ x 8.
T143 Paperbound **$1.00**

NEW WORD PUZZLES, G. L. Kaufman. 100 ENTIRELY NEW puzzles based on words and their combinations that will delight crossword puzzle, Scrabble and Jotto fans. Chess words, based on the moves of the chess king; design-onyms, symmetrical designs made of synonyms; rhymed double-crostics; syllable sentences; addle letter anagrams; alphagrams; linkograms; and many others all brand new. Full solutions. Space to work problems. 196 figures. vi + 122pp. 5⅜ x 8.
T344 Paperbound **$1.00**

MAZES AND LABYRINTHS: A BOOK OF PUZZLES, W. Shepherd. Mazes, formerly associated with mystery and ritual, are still among the most intriguing of intellectual puzzles. This is a novel and different collection of 50 amusements that embody the principle of the maze: mazes in the classical tradition; 3-dimensional, ribbon, and Möbius-strip mazes; hidden messages; spatial arrangements; etc.—almost all built on amusing story situations. 84 illustrations. Essay on maze psychology. Solutions. xv + 122pp. 5⅜ x 8.
T731 Paperbound **$1.00**

MAGIC TRICKS & CARD TRICKS, W. Jonson. Two books bound as one. 52 tricks with cards, 37 tricks with coins, bills, eggs, smoke, ribbons, slates, etc. Details on presentation, misdirection, and routining will help you master such famous tricks as the Changing Card, Card in the Pocket, Four Aces, Coin Through the Hand, Bill in the Egg, Afghan Bands, and over 75 others. If you follow the lucid exposition and key diagrams carefully, you will finish these two books with an astonishing mastery of magic. 106 figures. 224pp. 5⅜ x 8. T909 Paperbound **$1.00**

PANORAMA OF MAGIC, Milbourne Christopher. A profusely illustrated history of stage magic, a unique selection of prints and engravings from the author's private collection of magic memorabilia, the largest of its kind. Apparatus, stage settings and costumes; ingenious ads distributed by the performers and satiric broadsides passed around in the streets ridiculing pompous showmen; programs; decorative souvenirs. The lively text, by one of America's foremost professional magicians, is full of anecdotes about almost legendary wizards: Dede, the Egyptian; Philadelphia, the wonder-worker; Robert-Houdin, "the father of modern magic;" Harry Houdini; scores more. Altogether a pleasure package for anyone interested in magic, stage setting and design, ethnology, psychology, or simply in unusual people. A Dover original. 295 illustrations; 8 in full color. Index. viii + 216pp. 8⅜ x 11¼.
T774 Paperbound **$2.25**

HOUDINI ON MAGIC, Harry Houdini. One of the greatest magicians of modern times explains his most prized secrets. How locks are picked, with illustrated picks and skeleton keys; how a girl is sawed into twins; how to walk through a brick wall — Houdini's explanations of 44 stage tricks with many diagrams. Also included is a fascinating discussion of great magicians of the past and the story of his fight against fraudulent mediums and spiritualists. Edited by W.B. Gibson and M.N. Young. Bibliography. 155 figures, photos. xv + 280pp. 5⅜ x 8.
T384 Paperbound **$1.25**

MATHEMATICS, MAGIC AND MYSTERY, Martin Gardner. Why do card tricks work? How do magicians perform astonishing mathematical feats? How is stage mind-reading possible? This is the first book length study explaining the application of probability, set theory, theory of numbers, topology, etc., to achieve many startling tricks. Non-technical, accurate, detailed! 115 sections discuss tricks with cards, dice, coins, knots, geometrical vanishing illusions, how a Curry square "demonstrates" that the sum of the parts may be greater than the whole, and dozens of others. No sleight of hand necessary! 135 illustrations. xii + 174pp. 5⅜ x 8.
T335 Paperbound **$1.00**

EASY-TO-DO ENTERTAINMENTS AND DIVERSIONS WITH COINS, CARDS, STRING, PAPER AND MATCHES, R. M. Abraham. Over 300 tricks, games and puzzles will provide young readers with absorbing fun. Sections on card games; paper-folding; tricks with coins, matches and pieces of string; games for the agile; toy-making from common household objects; mathematical recreations; and 50 miscellaneous pastimes. Anyone in charge of groups of youngsters, including hard-pressed parents, and in need of suggestions on how to keep children sensibly amused and quietly content will find this book indispensable. Clear, simple text, copious number of delightful line drawings and illustrative diagrams. Originally titled "Winter Nights Entertainments." Introduction by Lord Baden Powell. 329 illustrations. v + 186pp. 5⅜ x 8½.
T921 Paperbound **$1.00**

STRING FIGURES AND HOW TO MAKE THEM, Caroline Furness Jayne. 107 string figures plus variations selected from the best primitive and modern examples developed by Navajo, Apache, pygmies of Africa, Eskimo, in Europe, Australia, China, etc. The most readily understandable, easy-to-follow book in English on perennially popular recreation. Crystal-clear exposition; step-by-step diagrams. Everyone from kindergarten children to adults looking for unusual diversion will be endlessly amused. Index. Bibliography. Introduction by A. C. Haddon. 17 full-page plates. 960 illustrations. xxiii + 401pp. 5⅜ x 8½.
T152 Paperbound **$2.00**

Entertainments, Humor

ODDITIES AND CURIOSITIES OF WORDS AND LITERATURE, C. Bombaugh, edited by M. Gardner.
The largest collection of idiosyncratic prose and poetry techniques in English, a legendary
work in the curious and amusing bypaths of literary recreations and the play technique in
literature—so important in modern works. Contains alphabetic poetry, acrostics, palindromes,
scissors verse, centos, emblematic poetry, famous literary puns, hoaxes, notorious slips of
the press, hilarious mistranslations, and much more. Revised and enlarged with modern
material by Martin Gardner. 368pp. 5⅜ x 8.   T759 Paperbound **$1.50**

A NONSENSE ANTHOLOGY, collected by Carolyn Wells. 245 of the best nonsense verses ever
written, including nonsense puns, absurd arguments, mock epics and sagas, nonsense ballads,
odes, "sick" verses, dog-Latin verses, French nonsense verses, songs. By Edward Lear,
Lewis Carroll, Gelett Burgess, W. S. Gilbert, Hilaire Belloc, Peter Newell, Oliver Herford, etc.,
83 writers in all plus over four score anonymous nonsense verses. A special section of
limericks, plus famous nonsense such as Carroll's "Jabberwocky" and Lear's "The Jumblies"
and much excellent verse virtually impossible to locate elsewhere. For 50 years considered
the best anthology available. Index of first lines specially prepared for this edition.
Introduction by Carolyn Wells. 3 indexes: Title, Author, First lines. xxxiii + 279pp.
                                                             T499 Paperbound **$1.25**

**THE BAD CHILD'S BOOK OF BEASTS, MORE BEASTS FOR WORSE CHILDREN, and A MORAL ALPHA-
BET, H. Belloc.** Hardly an anthology of humorous verse has appeared in the last 50 years
without at least a couple of these famous nonsense verses. But one must see the entire volumes—with all the delightful original illustrations by Sir Basil Blackwood—to appreciate
fully Belloc's charming and witty verses that play so subacidly on the platitudes of life and
morals that beset his day—and ours. A great humor classic. Three books in one. Total of
157pp. 5⅜ x 8.   T749 Paperbound **$1.00**

THE DEVIL'S DICTIONARY, Ambrose Bierce. Sardonic and irreverent barbs puncturing the
pomposities and absurdities of American politics, business, religion, literature, and arts,
by the country's greatest satirist in the classic tradition. Epigrammatic as Shaw, piercing
as Swift, American as Mark Twain, Will Rogers, and Fred Allen, Bierce will always remain
the favorite of a small coterie of enthusiasts, and of writers and speakers whom he supplies
with "some of the most gorgeous witticisms of the English language" (H. L. Mencken).
Over 1000 entries in alphabetical order. 144pp. 5⅜ x 8.   T487 Paperbound **$1.00**

THE PURPLE COW AND OTHER NONSENSE, Gelett Burgess. The best of Burgess's early nonsense,
selected from the first edition of the "Burgess Nonsense Book." Contains many of his most
unusual and truly awe-inspiring pieces: 36 nonsense quatrains, the Poems of Patagonia, Alpha-
bet of Famous Goops, and the other hilarious (and rare) adult nonsense that place him in the
forefront of American humorists. All pieces are accompanied by the original Burgess illustrations. 123 illustrations. xiii + 113pp. 5⅜ x 8.   T772 Paperbound **$1.00**

**MY PIOUS FRIENDS AND DRUNKEN COMPANIONS and MORE PIOUS FRIENDS AND DRUNKEN
COMPANIONS, Frank Shay.** Folksingers, amateur and professional, and everyone who loves
singing: here, available for the first time in 30 years, is this valued collection of 132 ballads,
blues, vaudeville numbers, drinking songs, sea chanties, comedy songs. Songs of pre-Beatnik
Bohemia; songs from all over America, England, France, Australia; the great songs of the
Naughty Nineties and early twentieth-century America. Over a third with music. Woodcuts
by John Held, Jr. convey perfectly the brash insouciance of an era of rollicking unabashed
song. 12 illustrations by John Held, Jr. Two indexes (Titles and First lines and Choruses).
Introductions by the author. Two volumes bound as one. Total of xvi + 235pp. 5⅜ x 8½.
                                                             T946 Paperbound **$1.00**

HOW TO TELL THE BIRDS FROM THE FLOWERS, R. W. Wood. How not to confuse a carrot with
a parrot, a grape with an ape, a puffin with nuffin. Delightful drawings, clever puns, absurd
little poems point out far-fetched resemblances in nature. The author was a leading
physicist. Introduction by Margaret Wood White. 106 illus. 60pp. 5⅜ x 8.
                                                             T523 Paperbound **75¢**

PECK'S BAD BOY AND HIS PA, George W. Peck. The complete edition, containing both
volumes, of one of the most widely read American humor books. The endless ingenious
pranks played by bad boy "Hennery" on his pa and the grocery man, the outraged pomposity
of Pa, the perpetual ridiculing of middle class institutions, are as entertaining today as they
were in 1883. No pale sophistications or subtleties, but rather humor vigorous, raw, earthy,
imaginative, and, as folk humor often is, sadistic. This peculiarly fascinating book is also
valuable to historians and students of American culture as a portrait of an age. 100
original illustrations by True Williams. Introduction by E. F. Bleiler. 347pp. 5⅜ x 8.
                                                             T497 Paperbound **$1.35**

CATALOGUE OF DOVER BOOKS

THE HUMOROUS VERSE OF LEWIS CARROLL. Almost every poem Carroll ever wrote, the largest collection ever published, including much never published elsewhere: 150 parodies, burlesques, riddles, ballads, acrostics, etc., with 130 original illustrations by Tenniel, Carroll, and others. "Addicts will be grateful . . . there is nothing for the faithful to do but sit down and fall to the banquet," N. Y. Times. Index to first lines. xiv + 446pp. 5⅜ x 8.
T654 Paperbound **$1.85**

DIVERSIONS AND DIGRESSIONS OF LEWIS CARROLL. A major new treasure for Carroll fans! Rare privately published humor, fantasy, puzzles, and games by Carroll at his whimsical best, with a new vein of frank satire. Includes many new mathematical amusements and recreations, among them the fragmentary Part III of "Curiosa Mathematica." Contains "The Rectory Umbrella," "The New Belfry," "The Vision of the Three T's," and much more. New 32-page supplement of rare photographs taken by Carroll. x + 375pp. 5⅜ x 8.
T732 Paperbound **$1.65**

THE COMPLETE NONSENSE OF EDWARD LEAR. This is the only complete edition of this master of gentle madness available at a popular price. A BOOK OF NONSENSE, NONSENSE SONGS, MORE NONSENSE SONGS AND STORIES in their entirety with all the old favorites that have delighted children and adults for years. The Dong With A Luminous Nose, The Jumblies, The Owl and the Pussycat, and hundreds of other bits of wonderful nonsense. 214 limericks, 3 sets of Nonsense Botany, 5 Nonsense Alphabets, 546 drawings by Lear himself, and much more. 320pp. 5⅜ x 8.
T167 Paperbound **$1.00**

THE MELANCHOLY LUTE, The Humorous Verse of Franklin P. Adams ("FPA"). The author's own selection of light verse, drawn from thirty years of FPA's column, "The Conning Tower," syndicated all over the English-speaking world. Witty, perceptive, literate, these ninety-six poems range from parodies of other poets, Millay, Longfellow, Edgar Guest, Kipling, Masefield, etc., and free and hilarious translations of Horace and other Latin poets, to satiric comments on fabled American institutions—the New York Subways, preposterous ads, suburbanites, sensational journalism, etc. They reveal with vigor and clarity the humor, integrity and restraint of a wise and gentle American satirist. Introduction by Robert Hutchinson. vi + 122pp. 5⅜ x 8½.
T108 Paperbound **$1.00**

SINGULAR TRAVELS, CAMPAIGNS, AND ADVENTURES OF BARON MUNCHAUSEN, R. E. Raspe, with 90 illustrations by Gustave Doré. The first edition in over 150 years to reestablish the deeds of the Prince of Liars exactly as Raspe first recorded them in 1785—the genuine Baron Munchausen, one of the most popular personalities in English literature. Included also are the best of the many sequels, written by other hands. Introduction on Raspe by J. Carswell. Bibliography of early editions. xliv + 192pp. 5⅜ x 8.
T698 Paperbound **$1.00**

THE WIT AND HUMOR OF OSCAR WILDE, ed. by Alvin Redman. Wilde at his most brilliant, in 1000 epigrams exposing weaknesses and hypocrisies of "civilized" society. Divided into 49 categories—sin, wealth, women, America, etc.—to aid writers, speakers. Includes excerpts from his trials, books, plays, criticism. Formerly "The Epigrams of Oscar Wilde." Introduction by Vyvyan Holland, Wilde's only living son. Introductory essay by editor. 260pp. 5⅜ x 8.
T602 Paperbound **$1.00**

MAX AND MORITZ, Wilhelm Busch. Busch is one of the great humorists of all time, as well as the father of the modern comic strip. This volume, translated by H. A. Klein and other hands, contains the perennial favorite "Max and Moritz" (translated by C. T. Brooks), Plisch and Plum, Das Rabennest, Eispeter, and seven other whimsical, sardonic, jovial, diabolical cartoon and verse stories. Lively English translations parallel the original German. This work has delighted millions, since it first appeared in the 19th century, and is guaranteed to please almost anyone. Edited by H. A. Klein, with an afterword. x + 205pp. 5⅝ x 8½.
T181 Paperbound **$1.00**

HYPOCRITICAL HELENA, Wilhelm Busch. A companion volume to "Max and Moritz," with the title piece (Die Fromme Helena) and 10 other highly amusing cartoon and verse stories, all newly translated by H. A. Klein and M. C. Klein: Adventure on New Year's Eve (Abenteuer in der Neujahrsnacht), Hangover on the Morning after New Year's Eve (Der Katzenjammer am Neujahrsmorgen), etc. English and German in parallel columns. Hours of pleasure, also a fine language aid. x + 205pp. 5⅝ x 8½.
T184 Paperbound **$1.00**

THE BEAR THAT WASN'T, Frank Tashlin. What does it mean? Is it simply delightful wry humor, or a charming story of a bear who wakes up in the midst of a factory, or a satire on Big Business, or an existential cartoon-story of the human condition, or a symbolization of the struggle between conformity and the individual? New York Herald Tribune said of the first edition: ". . . a fable for grownups that will be fun for children. Sit down with the book and get your own bearings." Long an underground favorite with readers of all ages and opinions. v + 51pp. Illustrated. 5⅜ x 8½.
T939 Paperbound **75¢**

RUTHLESS RHYMES FOR HEARTLESS HOMES and MORE RUTHLESS RHYMES FOR HEARTLESS HOMES, Harry Graham ("Col. D. Streamer"). Two volumes of Little Willy and 48 other poetic disasters. A bright, new reprint of oft-quoted, never forgotten, devastating humor by a precursor of today's "sick" joke school. For connoisseurs of wicked, wacky humor and all who delight in the comedy of manners. Original drawings are a perfect complement. 61 illustrations. Index. vi + 69pp. Two vols. bound as one. 5⅜ x 8½.
T930 Paperbound **75¢**

CATALOGUE OF DOVER BOOKS

Say It language phrase books

These handy phrase books (128 to 196 pages each) make grammatical drills unnecessary for an elementary knowledge of a spoken foreign language. Covering most matters of travel and everyday life each volume contains:

Over 1000 phrases and sentences in immediately useful forms — foreign language plus English.

Modern usage designed for Americans. Specific phrases like, "Give me small change," and "Please call a taxi."

Simplified phonetic transcription you will be able to read at sight.

The only completely indexed phrase books on the market.

Covers scores of important situations: — Greetings, restaurants, sightseeing, useful expressions, etc.

These books are prepared by native linguists who are professors at Columbia, N.Y.U., Fordham and other great universities. Use them independently or with any other book or record course. They provide a supplementary living element that most other courses lack. Individual volumes in:

Russian 75¢	Italian 75¢	Spanish 75¢	German 75¢
Hebrew 75¢	Danish 75¢	Japanese 75¢	Swedish 75¢
Dutch 75¢	Esperanto 75¢	Modern Greek 75¢	Portuguese 75¢
Norwegian 75¢	Polish 75¢	French 75¢	Yiddish 75¢
Turkish 75¢		English for German-speaking people 75¢	
English for Italian-speaking people 75¢		English for Spanish-speaking people 75¢	

Large clear type. 128-196 pages each. 3½ x 5¼. Sturdy paper binding.

Listen and Learn language records

LISTEN & LEARN is the only language record course designed especially to meet your travel and everyday needs. It is available in separate sets for FRENCH, SPANISH, GERMAN, JAPANESE, RUSSIAN, MODERN GREEK, PORTUGUESE, ITALIAN and HEBREW, and each set contains three 33⅓ rpm long-playing records—1½ hours of recorded speech by eminent native speakers who are professors at Columbia, New York University, Queens College.

Check the following special features found only in LISTEN & LEARN:

- **Dual-language recording. 812 selected phrases and sentences,** over 3200 words, spoken first in English, then in their foreign language equivalents. A suitable pause follows each foreign phrase, allowing you time to repeat the expression. You learn by unconscious assimilation.

- **128 to 206-page manual** contains everything on the records, plus a simple phonetic pronunciation guide.

- **Indexed for convenience. The only set on the market** that is completely indexed. No more puzzling over where to find the phrase you need. Just look in the rear of the manual.

- **Practical.** No time wasted on material you can find in any grammar. LISTEN & LEARN covers central core material with phrase approach. Ideal for the person with limited learning time.

- **Living, modern expressions,** not found in other courses. Hygienic products, modern equipment, shopping—expressions used every day, like "nylon" and "air-conditioned."

- **Limited objective.** Everything you learn, no matter where you stop, is immediately useful. You have to finish other courses, wade through grammar and vocabulary drill, before they help you.

- **High-fidelity recording.** LISTEN & LEARN records equal in clarity and surface-silence any record on the market costing up to $6.

"Excellent . . . the spoken records . . . impress me as being among the very best on the market," **Prof. Mario Pei,** Dept. of Romance Languages, Columbia University. "Inexpensive and well-done . . . it would make an ideal present," CHICAGO SUNDAY TRIBUNE. "More genuinely helpful than anything of its kind which I have previously encountered," **Sidney Clark,** well-known author of "ALL THE BEST" travel books.

UNCONDITIONAL GUARANTEE. Try LISTEN & LEARN, then return it within 10 days for full refund if you are not satisfied.

Each set contains three twelve-inch 33⅓ records, manual, and album.

SPANISH	the set $5.95	GERMAN	the set $5.95
FRENCH	the set $5.95	ITALIAN	the set $5.95
RUSSIAN	the set $5.95	JAPANESE	the set $5.95
PORTUGUESE	the set $5.95	MODERN GREEK	the set $5.95
MODERN HEBREW	the set $5.95		

Americana

THE EYES OF DISCOVERY, J. Bakeless. A vivid reconstruction of how unspoiled America appeared to the first white men. Authentic and enlightening accounts of Hudson's landing in New York, Coronado's trek through the Southwest; scores of explorers, settlers, trappers, soldiers. America's pristine flora, fauna, and Indians in every region and state in fresh and unusual new aspects. "A fascinating view of what the land was like before the first highway went through," Time. 68 contemporary illustrations, 39 newly added in this edition. Index. Bibliography. x + 500pp. 5⅜ x 8. T761 Paperbound **$2.00**

AUDUBON AND HIS JOURNALS, J. J. Audubon. A collection of fascinating accounts of Europe and America in the early 1800's through Audubon's own eyes. Includes the Missouri River Journals —an eventful trip through America's untouched heartland, the Labrador Journals, the European Journals, the famous "Episodes", and other rare Audubon material, including the descriptive chapters from the original letterpress edition of the "Ornithological Studies", omitted in all later editions. Indispensable for ornithologists, naturalists, and all lovers of Americana and adventure. 70-page biography by Audubon's granddaughter. 38 illustrations. Index. Total of 1106pp. 5⅜ x 8.
T675 Vol I Paperbound **$2.00**
T676 Vol II Paperbound **$2.00**
The set **$4.00**

TRAVELS OF WILLIAM BARTRAM, edited by Mark Van Doren. The first inexpensive illustrated edition of one of the 18th century's most delightful books is an excellent source of first-hand material on American geography, anthropology, and natural history. Many descriptions of early Indian tribes are our only source of information on them prior to the infiltration of the white man. "The mind of a scientist with the soul of a poet," John Livingston Lowes. 13 original illustrations and maps. Edited with an introduction by Mark Van Doren. 448pp. 5⅜ x 8.
T13 Paperbound **$2.00**

GARRETS AND PRETENDERS: A HISTORY OF BOHEMIANISM IN AMERICA, A. Parry. The colorful and fantastic history of American Bohemianism from Poe to Kerouac. This is the only complete record of hoboes, cranks, starving poets, and suicides. Here are Pfaff, Whitman, Crane, Bierce, Pound, and many others. New chapters by the author and by H. T. Moore bring this thorough and well-documented history down to the Beatniks. "An excellent account," N. Y. Times. Scores of cartoons, drawings, and caricatures. Bibliography. Index. xxviii + 421pp. 5⅝ x 8⅜. T708 Paperbound **$1.95**

THE EXPLORATION OF THE COLORADO RIVER AND ITS CANYONS, J. W. Powell. The thrilling first-hand account of the expedition that filled in the last white space on the map of the United States. Rapids, famine, hostile Indians, and mutiny are among the perils encountered as the unknown Colorado Valley reveals its secrets. This is the only uncut version of Major Powell's classic of exploration that has been printed in the last 60 years. Includes later reflections and subsequent expedition. 250 illustrations, new map. 400pp. 5⅝ x 8⅜.
T94 Paperbound **$2.00**

THE JOURNAL OF HENRY D. THOREAU, Edited by Bradford Torrey and Francis H. Allen. Henry Thoreau is not only one of the most important figures in American literature and social thought; his voluminous journals (from which his books emerged as selections and crystallizations) constitute both the longest, most sensitive record of personal internal development and a most penetrating description of a historical moment in American culture. This present set, which was first issued in fourteen volumes, contains Thoreau's entire journals from 1837 to 1862, with the exception of the lost years which were found only recently. We are reissuing it, complete and unabridged, with a new introduction by Walter Harding, Secretary of the Thoreau Society. Fourteen volumes reissued in two volumes. Foreword by Henry Seidel Canby. Total of 1888pp. 8⅜ x 12¼. T312-3 Two volume set, Clothbound **$20.00**

GAMES AND SONGS OF AMERICAN CHILDREN, collected by William Wells Newell. A remarkable collection of 190 games with songs that accompany many of them; cross references to show similarities, differences among them; variations; musical notation for 38 songs. Textual discussions show relations with folk-drama and other aspects of folk tradition. Grouped into categories for ready comparative study: Love-games, histories, playing at work, human life, bird and beast, mythology, guessing-games, etc. New introduction covers relations of songs and dances to timeless heritage of folklore, biographical sketch of Newell, other pertinent data. A good source of inspiration for those in charge of groups of children and a valuable reference for anthropologists, sociologists, psychiatrists. Introduction by Carl Withers. New indexes of first lines, games. 5⅜ x 8½. xii + 242pp. T354 Paperbound **$1.65**

Art, History of Art, Antiques, Graphic Arts, Handcrafts

ART STUDENTS' ANATOMY, E. J. Farris. Outstanding art anatomy that uses chiefly living objects for its illustrations. 71 photos of undraped men, women, children are accompanied by carefully labeled matching sketches to illustrate the skeletal system, articulations and movements, bony landmarks, the muscular system, skin, fasciae, fat, etc. 9 x-ray photos show movement of joints. Undraped models are shown in such actions as serving in tennis, drawing a bow in archery, playing football, dancing, preparing to spring and to dive. Also discussed and illustrated are proportions, age and sex differences, the anatomy of the smile, etc. 8 plates by the great early 18th century anatomic illustrator Siegfried Albinus are also included. Glossary. 158 figures, 7 in color. x + 159pp. 5⅝ x 8⅜. T744 Paperbound **$1.45**

AN ATLAS OF ANATOMY FOR ARTISTS, F Schider. A new 3rd edition of this standard text enlarged by 52 new illustrations of hands, anatomical studies by Cloquet, and expressive life studies of the body by Barcsay. 189 clear, detailed plates offer you precise information of impeccable accuracy. 29 plates show all aspects of the skeleton, with closeups of special areas, while 54 full-page plates, mostly in two colors, give human musculature as seen from four different points of view, with cutaways for important portions of the body. 14 full-page plates provide photographs of hand forms, eyelids, female breasts, and indicate the location of muscles upon models. 59 additional plates show how great artists of the past utilized human anatomy. They reproduce sketches and finished work by such artists as Michelangelo, Leonardo da Vinci, Goya, and 15 others. This is a lifetime reference work which will be one of the most important books in any artist's library. "The standard reference tool," AMERICAN LIBRARY ASSOCIATION. "Excellent," AMERICAN ARTIST. Third enlarged edition. 189 plates, 647 illustrations. xxvi + 192pp. 7⅞ x 10⅝. T241 Clothbound **$6.00**

AN ATLAS OF ANIMAL ANATOMY FOR ARTISTS, W. Ellenberger, H. Baum, H. Dittrich. The largest, richest animal anatomy for artists available in English. 99 detailed anatomical plates of such animals as the horse, dog, cat, lion, deer, seal, kangaroo, flying squirrel, cow, bull, goat, monkey, hare, and bat. Surface features are clearly indicated, while progressive beneath-the-skin pictures show musculature, tendons, and bone structure. Rest and action are exhibited in terms of musculature and skeletal structure and detailed cross-sections are given for heads and important features. The animals chosen are representative of specific families so that a study of these anatomies will provide knowledge of hundreds of related species. "Highly recommended as one of the very few books on the subject worthy of being used as an authoritative guide," DESIGN. "Gives a fundamental knowledge," AMERICAN ARTIST. Second revised, enlarged edition with new plates from Cuvier, Stubbs, etc. 288 illustrations. 153pp. 11⅜ x 9. T82 Clothbound **$6.00**

THE HUMAN FIGURE IN MOTION, Eadweard Muybridge. The largest selection in print of Muybridge's famous high-speed action photos of the human figure in motion. 4789 photographs illustrate 162 different actions: men, women, children—mostly undraped—are shown walking, running, carrying various objects, sitting, lying down, climbing, throwing, arising, and performing over 150 other actions. Some actions are shown in as many as 150 photographs each. All in all there are more than 500 action strips in this enormous volume, series shots taken at shutter speeds as high as 1/6000th of a second! These are not posed shots, but true stopped motion. They show bone and muscle in situations that the human eye is not fast enough to capture. Earlier, smaller editions of these prints have brought $40 and more on the out-of-print market. "A must for artists," ART IN FOCUS. "An unparalleled dictionary of action for all artists," AMERICAN ARTIST. 390 full-page plates, with 4789 photographs. Printed on heavy glossy stock. Reinforced binding with headbands. xxi + 390pp. 7⅞ x 10⅝. T204 Clothbound **$10.00**

ANIMALS IN MOTION, Eadweard Muybridge. This is the largest collection of animal action photos in print. 34 different animals (horses, mules, oxen, goats, camels, pigs, cats, guanacos, lions, gnus, deer, monkeys, eagles—and 21 others) in 132 characteristic actions. The horse alone is shown in more than 40 different actions. All 3919 photographs are taken in series at speeds up to 1/6000th of a second. The secrets of leg motion, spinal patterns, head movements, strains and contortions shown nowhere else are captured. You will see exactly how a lion sets his foot down; how an elephant's knees are like a human's—and how they differ; the position of a kangaroo's legs in mid-leap; how an ostrich's head bobs; details of the flight of birds—and thousands of facets of motion only the fastest cameras can catch. Photographed from domestic animals and animals in the Philadelphia zoo, it contains neither semiposed artificial shots nor distorted telephoto shots taken under adverse conditions. Artists, biologists, decorators, cartoonists, will find this book indispensable for understanding animals in motion. "A really marvelous series of plates," NATURE (London). "The dry plate's most spectacular early use was by Eadweard Muybridge," LIFE. 3919 photographs; 380 full pages of plates. 440pp. Printed on heavy glossy paper. Deluxe binding with headbands. 7⅞ x 10⅝. T203 Clothbound **$10.00**

CATALOGUE OF DOVER BOOKS

THE AUTOBIOGRAPHY OF AN IDEA, Louis Sullivan. The pioneer architect whom Frank Lloyd Wright called "the master" reveals an acute sensitivity to social forces and values in this passionately honest account. He records the crystallization of his opinions and theories, the growth of his organic theory of architecture that still influences American designers and architects, contemporary ideas, etc. This volume contains the first appearance of 34 full-page plates of his finest architecture. Unabridged reissue of 1924 edition. New introduction by R. M. Line. Index. xiv + 335pp. 5⅜ x 8.　　　　　　　　　　T281 Paperbound **$2.00**

THE DRAWINGS OF HEINRICH KLEY. The first uncut republication of both of Kley's devastating sketchbooks, which first appeared in pre-World War I Germany. One of the greatest cartoonists and social satirists of modern times, his exuberant and iconoclastic fantasy and his extraordinary technique place him in the great tradition of Bosch, Breughel, and Goya, while his subject matter has all the immediacy and tension of our century. 200 drawings. viii + 128pp. 7¾ x 10¾.　　　　　　　　　　T24 Paperbound **$1.85**

MORE DRAWINGS BY HEINRICH KLEY. All the sketches from Leut' Und Viecher (1912) and Sammel-Album (1923) not included in the previous Dover edition of Drawings. More of the bizarre, mercilessly iconoclastic sketches that shocked and amused on their original publication. Nothing was too sacred, no one too eminent for satirization by this imaginative, individual and accomplished master cartoonist. A total of 158 illustrations. Iv + 104pp. 7¾ x 10¾.　　　　　　　　　　T41 Paperbound **$1.85**

PINE FURNITURE OF EARLY NEW ENGLAND, R. H. Kettell. A rich understanding of one of America's most original folk arts that collectors of antiques, interior decorators, craftsmen, woodworkers, and everyone interested in American history and art will find fascinating and immensely useful. 413 illustrations of more than 300 chairs, benches, racks, beds, cupboards, mirrors, shelves, tables, and other furniture will show all the simple beauty and character of early New England furniture. 55 detailed drawings carefully analyze outstanding pieces. "With its rich store of illustrations, this book emphasizes the individuality and varied design of early American pine furniture. It should be welcomed," ANTIQUES. 413 illustrations and 55 working drawings. 475. 8 x 10¾.　　　　　　　　　　T145 Clothbound **$10.00**

THE HUMAN FIGURE, J. H. Vanderpoel. Every important artistic element of the human figure is pointed out in minutely detailed word descriptions in this classic text and illustrated as well in 430 pencil and charcoal drawings. Thus the text of this book directs your attention to all the characteristic features and subtle differences of the male and female (adults, children, and aged persons), as though a master artist were telling you what to look for at each stage. 2nd edition, revised and enlarged by George Bridgman. Foreword. 430 illustrations. 143pp. 6⅛ x 9¼.　　　　　　　　　　T432 Paperbound **$1.50**

LETTERING AND ALPHABETS, J. A. Cavanagh. This unabridged reissue of LETTERING offers a full discussion, analysis, illustration of 89 basic hand lettering styles — styles derived from Caslons, Bodonis, Garamonds, Gothic, Black Letter, Oriental, and many others. Upper and lower cases, numerals and common signs pictured. Hundreds of technical hints on make-up, construction, artistic validity, strokes, pens, brushes, white areas, etc. May be reproduced without permission! 89 complete alphabets; 72 lettered specimens. 121pp. 9¾ x 8.　　　T53 Paperbound **$1.25**

STICKS AND STONES, Lewis Mumford. A survey of the forces that have conditioned American architecture and altered its forms. The author discusses the medieval tradition in early New England villages; the Renaissance influence which developed with the rise of the merchant class; the classical influence of Jefferson's time; the "Mechanicsvilles" of Poe's generation; the Brown Decades; the philosophy of the Imperial facade; and finally the modern machine age. "A truly remarkable book," SAT. REV. OF LITERATURE. 2nd revised edition. 21 illustrations. xvii + 228pp. 5⅜ x 8.　　　　　　　　　　T202 Paperbound **$1.60**

THE STANDARD BOOK OF QUILT MAKING AND COLLECTING, Marguerite Ickis. A complete easy-to-follow guide with all the information you need to make beautiful, useful quilts. How to plan, design, cut, sew, appliqué, avoid sewing problems, use rag bag, make borders, tuft, every other aspect. Over 100 traditional quilts shown, including over 40 full-size patterns. At-home hobby for fun, profit. Index. 483 illus. 1 color plate. 287pp. 6¾ x 9½.　　　　　　　　　　T582 Paperbound **$2.00**

THE BOOK OF SIGNS, Rudolf Koch. Formerly $20 to $25 on the out-of-print market, now only $1.00 in this unabridged new edition! 493 symbols from ancient manuscripts, medieval cathedrals, coins, catacombs, pottery, etc. Crosses, monograms of Roman emperors, astrological, chemical, botanical, runes, housemarks, and 7 other categories. Invaluable for handicraft workers, illustrators, scholars, etc., this material may be reproduced without permission. 493 illustrations by Fritz Kredel. 104pp. 6½ x 9¼.　　　T162 Paperbound **$1.00**

PRIMITIVE ART, Franz Boas. This authoritative and exhaustive work by a great American anthropologist covers the entire gamut of primitive art. Pottery, leatherwork, metal work, stone work, wood, basketry, are treated in detail. Theories of primitive art, historical depth in art history, technical virtuosity, unconscious levels of patterning, symbolism, styles, literature, music, dance, etc. A must book for the interested layman, the anthropologist, artist, handicrafter (hundreds of unusual motifs), and the historian. Over 900 illustrations (50 ceramic vessels, 12 totem poles, etc.). 376pp. 5⅜ x 8.　　　T25 Paperbound **$1.95**

Fiction

FLATLAND, E. A. Abbott. A science-fiction classic of life in a 2-dimensional world that is also a first-rate introduction to such aspects of modern science as relativity and hyperspace. Political, moral, satirical, and humorous overtones have made FLATLAND fascinating reading for thousands. 7th edition. New introduction by Banesh Hoffmann. 16 illustrations. 128pp. 5⅜ x 8. **T1 Paperbound $1.00**

THE WONDERFUL WIZARD OF OZ, L. F. Baum. Only edition in print with all the original W. W. Denslow illustrations in full color—as much a part of "The Wizard" as Tenniel's drawings are of "Alice in Wonderland." "The Wizard" is still America's best-loved fairy tale, in which, as the author expresses it, "The wonderment and joy are retained and the heartaches and nightmares left out." Now today's young readers can enjoy every word and wonderful picture of the original book. New introduction by Martin Gardner. A Baum bibliography. 23 full-page color plates. viii + 268pp. 5⅜ x 8. **T691 Paperbound $1.45**

THE MARVELOUS LAND OF OZ, L. F. Baum. This is the equally enchanting sequel to the "Wizard," continuing the adventures of the Scarecrow and the Tin Woodman. The hero this time is a little boy named Tip, and all the delightful Oz magic is still present. This is the Oz book with the Animated Saw-Horse, the Woggle-Bug, and Jack Pumpkinhead. All the original John R. Neill illustrations, 10 in full color. 287 pp. 5⅜ x 8. **T692 Paperbound $1.45**

FIVE GREAT DOG NOVELS, edited by Blanche Cirker. The complete original texts of five classic dog novels that have delighted and thrilled millions of children and adults throughout the world with their stories of loyalty, adventure, and courage. Full texts of Jack London's "The Call of the Wild"; John Brown's "Rab and His Friends"; Alfred Ollivant's "Bob, Son of Battle"; Marshall Saunders's "Beautiful Joe"; and Ouida's "A Dog of Flanders." 21 Illustrations from the original editions. 495pp. 5⅜ x 8. **T777 Paperbound $1.50**

TO THE SUN? and OFF ON A COMET!, Jules Verne. Complete texts of two of the most imaginative flights into fancy in world literature display the high adventure that have kept Verne's novels read for nearly a century. Only unabridged edition of the best translation, by Edward Roth. Large, easily readable type. 50 illustrations selected from first editions. 462pp. 5⅜ x 8. **T634 Paperbound $1.75**

FROM THE EARTH TO THE MOON and ALL AROUND THE MOON, Jules Verne. Complete editions of 2 of Verne's most successful novels, in finest Edward Roth translations, now available after many years out of print. Verne's visions of submarines, airplanes, television, rockets, interplanetary travel; of scientific and not-so-scientific beliefs; of peculiarities of Americans; all delight and engross us today as much as when they first appeared. Large, easily readable type. 42 illus. from first French edition. 476pp. 5⅜ x 8. **T633 Paperbound $1.75**

THE CRUISE OF THE CACHALOT, Frank T. Bullen. Out of the experiences of many years on the high-seas, First Mate Bullen created this novel of adventure aboard an American whaler, shipping out of New Bedford, Mass., when American whaling was at the height of its splendor. Originally published in 1899, the story of the round-the-world cruise of the "Cachalot" in pursuit of the sperm whale has thrilled generations of readers. A maritime classic that will fascinate anyone interested in reading about the sea or looking for a solid old-fashioned yarn, while the vivid recreation of a brief but important chapter of Americana and the British author's often biting commentary on nineteenth-century Yankee mores offer insights into the colorful era of America's coming of age. 8 plates. xiii + 271pp. 5⅜ x 8½. **T774 Paperbound $1.00**

28 SCIENCE FICTION STORIES OF H. G. WELLS. Two full unabridged novels, MEN LIKE GODS and STAR BEGOTTEN, plus 26 short stories by the master science-fiction writer of all time! Stories of space, time, invention, exploration, future adventure—an indispensable part of the library of everyone interested in science and adventure. PARTIAL CONTENTS: Men Like Gods, The Country of the Blind, In the Abyss, The Crystal Egg, The Man Who Could Work Miracles, A Story of the Days to Come, The Valley of Spiders, and 21 more! 928pp. 5⅜ x 8. **T265 Clothbound $3.95**

DAVID HARUM, E. N. Westcott. This novel of one of the most lovable, humorous characters in American literature is a prime example of regional humor. It continues to delight people who like their humor dry, their characters quaint, and their plots ingenuous. First book edition to contain complete novel plus chapter found after author's death. Illustrations from first illustrated edition. 192pp. 5⅜ x 8. **T580 Paperbound $1.15**

GESTA ROMANORUM, trans. by Charles Swan, ed. by Wynnard Hooper. 181 tales of Greeks, Romans, Britons, Biblical characters, comprise one of greatest medieval story collections, source of plots for writers including Shakespeare, Chaucer, Gower, etc. Imaginative tales of wars, incest, thwarted love, magic, fantasy, allegory, humor, tell about kings, prostitutes, philosophers, fair damsels, knights, Noah, pirates, all walks, stations of life. Introduction. Notes. 500pp. 5⅜ x 8. **T535 Paperbound $1.85**

Music

A GENERAL HISTORY OF MUSIC, Charles Burney. A detailed coverage of music from the Greeks up to 1789, with full information on all types of music: sacred and secular, vocal and instrumental, operatic and symphonic. Theory, notation, forms, instruments, innovators, composers, performers, typical and important works, and much more in an easy, entertaining style. Burney covered much of Europe and spoke with hundreds of authorities and composers so that this work is more than a compilation of records . . . it is a living work of careful and first-hand scholarship. Its account of thoroughbass (18th century) Italian music is probably still the best introduction on the subject. A recent NEW YORK TIMES review said, "Surprisingly few of Burney's statements have been invalidated by modern research . . . still of great value." Edited and corrected by Frank Mercer. 35 figures. Indices. 1915pp. 5⅜ x 8. 2 volumes.   T36 The Set, Clothbound **$12.50**

A DICTIONARY OF HYMNOLOGY, John Julian. This exhaustive and scholarly work has become known as an invaluable source of hundreds of thousands of important and often difficult to obtain facts on the history and use of hymns in the western world. Everyone interested in hymns will be fascinated by the accounts of famous hymns and hymn writers and amazed by the amount of practical information he will find. More than 30,000 entries on individual hymns, giving authorship, date and circumstances of composition, publication, textual variations, translations, denominational and ritual usage, etc. Biographies of more than 9,000 hymn writers, and essays on important topics such as Christmas carols and children's hymns, and much other unusual and valuable information. A 200 page double-columned index of first lines — the largest in print. Total of 1786 pages in two reinforced clothbound volumes. 6¼ x 9¼.
The set, T333 Clothbound **$15.00**

MUSIC IN MEDIEVAL BRITAIN, F. Ll. Harrison. The most thorough, up-to-date, and accurate treatment of the subject ever published, beautifully illustrated. Complete account of institutions and choirs; carols, masses, and motets; liturgy and plainsong; and polyphonic music from the Norman Conquest to the Reformation. Discusses the various schools of music and their reciprocal influences; the origin and development of new ritual forms; development and use of instruments; and new evidence on many problems of the period. Reproductions of scores, over 200 excerpts from medieval melodies. Rules of harmony and dissonance; influence of Continental styles; great composers (Dunstable, Cornysh, Fairfax, etc.); and much more. Register and index of more than 400 musicians. Index of titles. General Index. 225-item bibliography. 6 Appendices. xix + 491pp. 5⅝ x 8¾.   T705 Clothbound **$10.00**

THE MUSIC OF SPAIN, Gilbert Chase. Only book in English to give concise, comprehensive account of Iberian music; new Chapter covers music since 1941. Victoria, Albéniz, Cabezón, Pedrell, Turina, hundreds of other composers; popular and folk music; the Gypsies; the guitar; dance, theatre, opera, with only extensive discussion in English of the Zarzuela; virtuosi such as Casals; much more. "Distinguished . . . readable," Saturday Review. 400-item bibliography. Index. 27 photos. 383pp. 5⅜ x 8.   T549 Paperbound **$2.00**

ON STUDYING SINGING, Sergius Kagen. An intelligent method of voice-training, which leads you around pitfalls that waste your time, money, and effort. Exposes rigid, mechanical systems, baseless theories, deleterious exercises. "Logical, clear, convincing . . . dead right," Virgil Thomson, N.Y. Herald Tribune. "I recommend this volume highly," Maggie Teyte, Saturday Review. 119pp. 5⅜ x 8.   T622 Paperbound **$1.25**

Dover publishes books on art, music, philosophy, literature, languages, history, social sciences, psychology, handcrafts, orientalia, puzzles and entertainments, chess, pets and gardens, books explaining science, intermediate and higher mathematics mathematical physics, engineering, biological sciences, earth sciences, classics of science, etc. Write to:

Dept. catrr.
Dover Publications, Inc.
180 Varick Street, N. Y. 14, N. Y.